War-Torn

For over a hundred years, war ravaged the land as the rulers of the kingdoms of Galifar vied for supremacy. Dynasties rose and fell, and new wonders and unspeakable horrors were born as each faction tried to gain the upper hand.

But after a hundred years of fighting, the war is now over, and the people of Eberron pray that it will be the Last War. An uneasy peace struggles to settle over the continent of Khorvaire.

But what of those soldiers, warriors, nobles, spies, healers, clerics, and wizards whose lives were forever changed by decades of war, who may have no homes to which they can return? What does a world without war hold for those who have known nothing but violence? What fate lies for these, the war-torn?

THE
WAR~TORN

THE CRIMSON TALISMAN
ADRIAN COLE

THE ORB OF XORIAT
EDWARD BOLME

LEGACY OF RUIN
JAMES WYATT

EBERRON

THE CRIMSON TALISMAN

THE WAR-TORN • BOOK 1

ADRIAN COLE

THE CRIMSON TALISMAN

THE WAR-TORN TRILOGY • BOOK ONE

Cover art by Wayne Reynolds
Map by Dennis Kauth
First Printing: May 2005
Library of Congress Catalog Card Number: 2004116894

9 8 7 6 5 4 3 2

ISBN-10: 0-7869-3739-4
ISBN-13: 978-0-7869-3739-4
620-88722000-001-EN

U.S., CANADA,
ASIA, PACIFIC, & LATIN AMERICA
Wizards of the Coast, Inc.
P.O. Box 707
Renton, WA 98057-0707
+1-800-324-6496

EUROPEAN HEADQUARTERS
Hasbro UK Ltd
Caswell Way
Newport, Gwent NP9 OYH
GREAT BRITAIN

Visit our web site at www.wizards.com

To Dave Bodmin,

A true creature of the night.

TABLE OF CONTENTS

PART

FLIGHT FROM KARRNATH

ONE

HORROR AT THE GATES

CHAPTER 1

Through the long slit of the castle window, Vaddi peered out at the gathering gloom. For the last two hours the clouds had been piling together, clashing like huge fleets above the towers of Marazanath Hold, the threat of thunder hanging like doom over the castle and all these remote northern crags. Only the snake-tongue flashes of lightning bathed the surrounding terrain in light, jagged as the rocks that knifed down to the sea two hundred feet below. From out of the north, the icy winds gusted, hurled with a terrible energy.

Vaddi could just make out the combers as they shattered themselves on the shore below, like some mad army determined to dash itself to pieces. The first detonation overhead confirmed that the storm had truly arrived, and Vaddi felt the very walls of the Hold shuddering. There had been storms before. Indeed, they were frequent so far in the north of Khorvaire, along this remote sweep of the Karrn Bay, but somehow he felt that this storm presaged something more ominous, as though within its cloaking darkness some other force was stirring.

Hidden from his eyes by sheets of driving rain, the inner courtyard at the stronghold gates far below was barely lit by the sputtering torches set under the eaves around it. The night watch, a dozen sleepy guards, huddled under the walls, occasionally casting a look out over the parapet at the winding road.

❀ ❀ ❀ ❀ ❀ ❀ ❀

"Looks like we've got company!" called one of the rain-soaked watchers to his companions below, pointing at the churning night.

"You're imagining it, Garrond! Only a lunatic would be out in this muck."

"Supplies coming in, by the look of it."

The watcher shielded his eyes from the blasts of wind and rain. He could see the wide cart as it struggled up the slope toward the castle, its wheels digging into the mud, its sheer weight almost bringing it to a halt. Barrels and crates almost overloaded the vehicle, and two sodden figures hunched over it, urging four huge dray horses forward in defiance of the storm.

"They must've started out before this storm broke," said Amalfax, the other watchman on the wall. "Got so far and thought better of turning back! Hah! Better let them in."

"It's gone midnight. You know the rules."

"Hell's teeth, Garrond, give the poor devils a break! They've half killed themselves getting here. Let them in. That's *our* supplies out there!"

Garrond grunted an obscenity and went on muttering about being flogged for improper discharge of duty but nevertheless operated the massive winch that cranked down the drawbridge. It slapped down into the mud across the chasm. The huge cart eased its way onto the bridge, lumbering toward the gates and inner courtyard. As it did so, one of its wheels tilted, thick spokes snapping, and the cart sagged to one side.

Garrond's shouted obscenities became even more colorful. The two men on the cart were waving frantically. Moments later the night watch scrambled out the gates, all of them setting their shoulders to the tilting cart in an effort to get it upright and into the courtyard. A brief stab of light from one of the guard's

3

lanterns revealed a sudden tear in the hide covering of the cart's load. The tear parted, and men squirmed out from beneath it like maggots from a rotten fruit.

Too late Garrond and Amalfax saw steel. The intruders leaped down and rammed their swords into flesh. Four of the night guards were down at a stroke, blood spilling on to the bridge. The cart leaned drunkenly, two huge barrels breaking loose and smashing on to the boards before tumbling into the ravine. A dozen more intruders jumped from the wagon, and within moments the entire night watch was involved in a furious struggle.

Garrond dragged out his own blade. With a scything chop he ripped open the belly of the nearest intruder. His eyes bulged, for no blood spurted over him—only an explosion of dust. The belly of his assailant opened to reveal rotting clothing and crumbling bone. Its skeletal features were lit by its scarlet eyes, fed by some hellish fires. It grinned at the damage to its gut and attacked anew. The others were akin to this horror, their death-white skin gleaming in the rain, their rusted weapons slashing with terrible efficiency at the guards. They fought in a grim silence, their malign eyes fixed on their victims.

They cut down almost all the defenders and moved into the courtyard. On the bridge, his life seeping out of him from a dozen wounds, Garrond could see other shapes down the road—scores of them. The darkness and the storm had disgorged an entire army, a swarm of invaders, and as they approached, Garrond could see that there were men among them—a ragtag legion of vagabonds and bandits, armed with all manner of weapons.

As he felt life ebbing, Garrond looked up to see one tall figure standing over him like something from a nightmare. Garbed in tight black robes, the being leaned over him, its hideous face gleaming in triumph, its sharp fangs vivid in the brief flicker of lightning-light. *Vampire!* Garrond realised. This rabble of an army was led by one of the undead!

It was his last thought as the creature lunged.

❁ ❁ ❁ ❁ ❁ ❁ ❁

Vaddi heard a soft tread behind him. He turned away from the storm to meet the cool gaze of his father, Anzar Kemmal Orien, head of the household and one of the lords of House Orien.

"Not asleep? After the rigours of training, I would have thought even this storm would not have woken you." Anzar smiled.

For all his years, he seemed imbued with an unusual vitality. He wore a shirt of lightweight steel mesh that hung below his waist, and his long arms were muscular from constant practice with the broadsword. In spite of the hour, his eyes were as alert as those of the ravens that made this rugged hold their home.

"It's an evil night, Father. Do you not sense it?"

Anzar studied his son, seeing the young muscles, taut as a spring. Vaddi was barely eighteen, but already the long hours of training had hardened him. No youth from the distant cities would be a match for him, Anzar could see. So different in looks from his three half-brothers, several years his senior, who had years ago become knights in Thrane before returning to serve here. They were the pride of Anzar, but seeing Vaddi, he felt a stab of emotion. In Vaddi's green eyes there seemed to glow a strange fire, an elemental thing. The youth had jet-black hair that framed narrow features—so like Indreen, Anzar's second wife. She had been an elf, so Vaddi would never grow to the full stature of his three half-brothers. But there were other powers within the youth, Anzar well knew.

"Such storms are not unknown," said Anzar, "but they are, after all, merely storms."

Vaddi's eyes returned to gazing out the window, where more lightning rent the skies. He straightened, his lips pursing, brows furrowed in the familiar determination.

Anzar grinned, in spite of the circumstances, but a shadow in his expression made Vaddi stiffen.

"Something is wrong, isn't it, Father?"

"We live in deeply troubled times, my son. Our lands echo

with the dark schemes and treacheries of earthly powers. The Sovereigns know how all of Khorvaire suffers. It is time for you to know certain truths. Your destiny, I believe, lies elsewhere."

Vaddi tried to smile. "I am eager to serve that call, as you know, Father."

Anzar looked grave. "The world is at a crossroads. The Last War may have ended, but what is left in its place? A cauldron, stirred by the hand of chaos. A hand that will pluck you and crush you, if it can."

"Me? Surely I am the least of your sons?"

Anzar came to him and put his hands on the youth's shoulders, pulling him close. "Never think that, Vaddi. You may not have the physical stature of your half-brothers, but you hold an equal place in my heart. Even more so since your mother died."

"You said that I have enemies."

Anzar pulled away. "I have something for you. Something unique. We spoke of destiny. This is yours. You are man enough now to receive it."

Outside the window, the storm raged on, raising its voice as if in response to Anzar's strange words. Vaddi felt a pulse of deep unease, as if this revelation stirred great powers beyond his understanding. From beneath his light mesh shirt Anzar pulled an object on a thin chain. It looked pale and featureless in the shifting firelight, but Vaddi could see that it was a horn the length of a dirk. Anzar held it in both hands, turning it slowly, cautiously.

"This is Erethindel," he said, his voice almost reverent.

In spite of the ordinariness of the horn, Vaddi's own voice dropped to a whisper. "It seems a plain thing."

"It is not what it seems, Vaddi. It is said that the elves made it, with the aid of the dragons. It stores great power, but only one person can use it while he is alive. The elves have hidden it for centuries. Indreen, your mother, was the last to keep it, here, far from those who might seek it. Since her death, it has been locked away, but now it is for you to bear."

Vaddi drew back. "To do what?"

"You must carry the horn. Guard it with your life until it is needed. You will know when that moment comes."

Very slowly, Vaddi took the horn. He felt heat, as though it were alive. Something in his blood stirred, a response to the horn, as if resonating to a chord of music. Quickly he slipped the silver thong over his head and tucked the horn inside his shirt. He glanced at his hand that had touched it, and to his consternation saw that there was a smear of his blood on it.

If Anzar had seen this, he said nothing, but he nodded, pleased. "You are one with the horn, Vaddi. Powers will seek you because of it. Weigh them with caution. And let no one know what you carry. You were born to serve it and it to serve you. Never forget that."

Ironically, for such a portentous thing, the horn felt like no more than a common ornament about Vaddi's neck. Perhaps it was as well. Even to think of being joined with such powers made him uncomfortable.

He was about to say more when a shout from the stairs below the room made both of them turn in alarm. Anzar flung the door open to reveal a blood-spattered soldier, panting with exertion.

"Lord, we are besieged! An army . . . within the walls!"

"An *army?*" snarled Anzar. "What are you blathering about?"

"The walls are breached, lord! Everyone is arming."

Anzar looked at Vaddi then pushed the man before him as they descended the stairs. Vaddi could hear his father shouting for his weapons.

Vaddi ran to the large wardrobe between the everbright lanterns on the far wall and flung open the doors. He donned a steel-mesh shirt and grabbed the long dirk that was always close at hand. He did not understand this. How could an army breach the castle walls? Marazanath was perched on the crags, aloof and dominant. No enemy had ever taken it. Selecting another sword, he fled the room.

Minutes later, Vaddi emerged on battlements above his chambers, ignoring the blasts of wind and the sting of rain. Not far below he could see, to his horror, that the soldier had been right. Not only were there numerous assailants within the castle, but flames were licking up at the boiling skies from several towers. War had indeed come to Marazanath.

The ring of swords and the snarls of combat came to his ears through the storm. Men were cut down and tossed over the walls. House Orien was well fortified here, with several hundred skilled warriors on hand to defend its master, but Vaddi realised that whatever dark force had burst in upon them was no small thing.

He sped down a stairway and came to the edge of the fighting. A wounded soldier, his side leaking blood, held him back. "Not that way, my lord. It's hopeless."

"Who are they?"

"Bandits."

"Bandits are no match for knights!" snapped Vaddi. "How many are there?"

"Someone—" The man grimaced and fell to his knees. He was trembling, and Vaddi could see the blood loss would soon do him in, but the guard gathered his strength and continued. "Someone has pulled them in. By the . . . hundreds. Every last villain skulking in the Icewood! And . . . the undead—"

"*Undead?*" Vaddi could not keep the horror from his voice.

"Scores of them. They are led by a vampire." The man clutched at Vaddi's arm. "The Emerald Claw, master! It . . . must be. Their agents have stirred up this nest of maggots."

"For what reason?"

But the man had spoken his last. Cursing, Vaddi sped on down the stone corridors. He found blood and death at every turn, where soldiers of the House had been gutted or the invaders had been similarly chopped down. There were indeed undead among the fallen, their twitching, rotting parts still clinging to a semblance of grim life.

"Where is my father?" he shouted at a group of warriors who were barring one of the tall doors to an inner chamber.

"Above us! But have a care, lord. They are like hornets, these invaders. Already we have lost many."

Vaddi raced up another stairway and came out on a long wall. He could see through the murk of the night a parallel wall across another deep courtyard. On it was a grisly spectacle. Squeezed together in a knot of resistance, Anzar and two of his sons hacked and slashed at the invaders. The defenders of Marazanath fought with extraordinary energy, laying about them with their longswords, sending countless foes over the wall.

Vaddi raced along the parapet, through the rooms of a tower, and over to where his father fought. Using every last bit of skill he had been taught in the long and arduous hours of training, he cut into the enemy. Ignoring the cuts he took and the blows that buffeted him, Vaddi let nothing prevent him from chopping through to his father's side. But he saw with a stab of pain far deeper than any sword cut that two of his half-brothers, Brohulan and Dannaharn, had already been speared. They had fallen almost at Anzar's feet, their lives spent.

Anzar and the last of his warriors drove back the enemy, hurling them from the battlements. Gaining a brief respite, Vaddi hugged his father. Howls of anger rose from the enemy below as they gathered themselves for what must be a final assault.

"Where is Ferrumas?" Vaddi asked, naming his third half-brother.

His father shook his head, fighting back a wave of emotion as he dragged ragged breaths into his lungs. "He fought on the western battlements, but we saw a huge wedge of the enemy scaling them on all sides. We are undone, Vaddi. Whoever has engineered this assault has caught us unready."

"Agents of the Claw?"

"They are behind this for certain. They mean to kill us all, but you must not fall." He leaned forward. "You must take the charge I gave you and flee. *It is vital.*"

"You think I would abandon you?"

"There are more important things than me, Vaddi. You must not be taken. You have always fulfilled your duty to House Orien and me. Now you have a greater duty to discharge."

From among the press of surviving warriors on the battlements, another figure emerged, slowly easing its way towards them. "Cellester must be your guide now."

Vaddi scowled. He had no love for the cleric, who had attached himself to House Orien when it had first won this hold back from its scavenging tenants even before Vaddi was born. In those days of the War, Marazanath had been the den of all manner of monstrous beasts.

Anzar ignored Vaddi's distrustful look. "He knows these grim lands well—and the rats that infest them. The cleric's knowledge is formidable. Never forget that, Vaddi, nor underestimate the power of his knowledge."

But I don't trust him, Vaddi wanted to say. Overhead, thunder growled, almost in response to his thoughts.

"He does not serve the Host as other clerics do. That is sometimes the way of it." Anzar gritted his teeth, controlling a sudden fury with an effort. His voice dropped, his eyes gazing at some distant incident, a dire memory. "And Cellester has no love of the Order of the Emerald Claw."

Vaddi's frown deepened. He knew of this dark brotherhood, as elusive and secretive as rats in a sewer. The worst tales spoke of the Blood of Vol, said to make men immortal, but slaves to terrible powers best left alone.

"Marazanath will fall this night," said Anzar. "Nothing can stop that now, but there are allies beyond the border in Thrane." Heavy thunder reverberated overhead, rain driving down like hail. "By land you will be cut off, ringed around, the roads held by our enemies."

"Then what do you advise?"

"Nothing will be easy, but you must not be taken. What I have given you this night—" Anzar's eyes flashed to the object hidden within Vaddi's shirt. "Keep it safe. Get to Rookstack, if you can. The fishermen there are redoubtable fighters. I have friends among them."

"But, Father, to flee, to leave you—"

Anzar faced the storm, shaking his head. When he turned back, his pale features seemed to have aged, the strain etched on his face like pain. "Your hour has come, Vaddi. Everything you have learned, all your skills, must be tested in this. You must seek your destiny alone. You will only endanger others if you take them."

Vaddi felt the weight of the storm, like an enraged beast readying to tear him limb from limb.

"You are afraid?"

He drew in a deep breath. "Of course I am. How could I not be?"

"You underestimate your powers, and the Claw will not expect you to flee alone."

They looked at each other for a moment, their sorrow like an open wound. Anzar thought again of Vaddi's mother, who had died when Vaddi was barely two, victim to a sudden wasting sickness that had leeched the life from hundreds of House Orien's fold all those years ago. It had been another legacy of the War.

"You'll not sneak out like a rat in a sewer," said Anzar.

"My dragonmark."

"The Mark of Passage. It defines you, my son, and your gifts. They are latent, even now. You have not been schooled in them, because only you can unlock them. Know this, there is no storm on Eberron, natural or demon-conjured, that you could not ride. The time for you to put that to the test is now, this very night. Out there, in that maelstrom below."

"*Sail* from Marazanath?"

"In such a storm as this, who would suspect such a thing? Not even the creatures who serve the Emerald Claw."

"Father," Vaddi said, shaking his head, "this is insane! I am immodest enough to admit that I am a very good sailor, and it is true that I have bested more than a few awful storms north of here, but no one would go out in *that*." He indicated the furious storm.

"You must. There is a ship waiting."

"Waiting?" Vaddi said, surprised.

"In the western cave. You must get ready at once. Travel as lightly as you can. I have made preparations." Anzar smiled. "There is a ship, a small craft, but one that can weather any sea in the right hands. And one occupant. I said you and Cellester should go alone, but you will not be quite alone."

Vaddi tried to picture the craft, imagining it tossing and bouncing on the swirling whirlpools within the western cave. One crewman? "Who?"

"Who better than Menneath, son of Drudesh? And unless I'm fed false information, your best friend?"

Vaddi blanched at that. Sons of lords were not encouraged to develop close friendships with sons of a lesser class. But Vaddi and Menneath had struck up a deep friendship as soon as they had learned to walk. They could have been brothers.

"I can't bring him into this, Father. You think these murderers will hesitate to kill a fisherman's son?"

"Menneath knows these waters better than the fish! He'd swim through that storm and come ashore laughing. The two of you will be a powerful team, Vaddi. Menneath's father is from a long line of men of the sea. There is a magic in that line, believe me. You may not know it, Menneath may not know it, but he can take care of himself. None better to guide you westward."

Cellester spoke above the gusting storm and the shouts from below. "My apologies, lord, for this intrusion." He was partly in shadow, his frame shaped in a thick cloak, the lower part of his head and shoulders muffled by its folds. Vaddi saw little more than the silhouette of his head, the shaped hair cut short.

"What is it?"

"My lord, the boat . . ." Cellester's eyes were like steel, never wavering.

Anzar nodded. They could hear the massed ranks of the enemy coming up toward the battlements for a renewed assault.

"We must leave, my lord. Soon it will be too late!"

He spoke to Anzar as though Vaddi was not present and the youth felt his anger flaring. Vaddi pulled his father away and whispered in his ear.

"I don't trust him, Father."

Anzar scowled as he deliberated. Vaddi knew what his father was thinking. The truth was that for some reason Vaddi's powers were subdued. As a dragonmarked son of House Orien, he should have been able to wield a degree of magical skills, yet he could barely teleport. The cleric's skills were well tested. He was a match for any veteran knight, and he had been loyal to House Orien—more so than he had been to the Sovereign Host. He seemed to put more faith in men than in the holy sovereigns.

Vaddi could contain his anger no longer. "Father, I need no cleric to hold my hand!"

Anzar looked him over, knowing that he did so for the last time. "I know you don't, my son, but Cellester's guidance could be the difference between success and disaster. Speed is of the essence, Vaddi. Go below to where the boat awaits. With Cellester."

"But—"

"No time! Go! Quickly! They are coming. We cannot hold them for long!"

Something in his father's voice, in his eyes, made Vaddi hesitate. He knew that this was a pivotal moment in his life, but he was being forced away before he could react. Anzar's plea seemed to have drawn out the last of his strength. He drew himself upright, holding high his sword, and yelled to his knights to ready themselves.

From the darkness the enemy came in fresh waves, demonic faces leering, weapons thrusting forward. Within moments the battle began again with renewed fury. There was no time for further words.

Before Vaddi had time to think, Cellester pulled him away and they were racing toward the narrow stairway in the nearest tower. Vaddi looked back over his shoulder. *Father!* But his eyes met only the dispassionate face of the cleric, who motioned him through another doorway and out on to a narrow wall.

"We dare not linger, Lord Vaddi."

Halfway across the battlement, Vaddi turned to see the last stand of his father and his loyal knights. They were clearly limned in the glow of the fires that were eating into the heart of the citadel. Swarms of the enemy attacked them with sword, fang, and claw. Vaddi stood frozen as he saw Anzar face to face with a black-clad creature, tall and bone white. It wielded a blade that seemed to glow with its own hellish light. In a surrounding crescendo of thunder and victory screams, that red blade sank deep into Anzar's flesh. Vaddi's own scream was torn away by the victorious darkness.

Across the chasm, the eyes of the killer met Vaddi's. The swordsman smiled, his gaze a promise of agonies to come, and in that gaze, Vaddi abruptly understood why the creature was here. The rabble army had come for the hold, but this vampire craved only one thing. The horn.

"We must leave!" shouted Cellester, dragging Vaddi away.

❧ ❧ ❧ ❧ ❧ ❧ ❧

Vaddi blinked back a flood of tears, moving almost blindly down into the vitals of the hold. After what seemed an age, he and Cellester came to a tall cave whose curved dome echoed and re-echoed to the pummelling of the wild tide—wave after wave crashing in from the high entrance, swirling waters spilling over the narrow dock. Lamps flickered against the onslaught of the wind as it funnelled into the space, roaring like a pack of demons. Vaddi saw one frail craft, that of Menneath, bobbing up and down like a cork, its lone occupant waving.

Wading through another broken wave, thigh-deep in places, Vaddi and Cellester struggled toward the craft. Menneath was wrestling with the ropes that set the single, curved sail. Its canvas was plain, without the customary unicorn of House Orien emblazoned upon it. Menneath tied off the rope and swung out over the rocking side of the craft, holding out his hand to Vaddi.

"Come aboard!" he yelled above the scream of the winds.

They clawed at Vaddi as he took his friend's hand, seemingly determined to rip him away and plunge him into the churning seas, but then Vaddi was across the gap and into the craft. Menneath clamped an arm around his shoulders and laughed, mocking the wind.

Both of them turned to the cleric. He was judging his moment to cross, his lips moving as if in a silent prayer. Vaddi remembered that Cellester had powers of his own. There was a lull in the screaming of the wind, a flicker of calmness on the waters. The cleric crossed to the boat, sure-footed as a hill goat, but his face showed no emotion as he took his place down in the stern of the craft.

"Can this tub traverse such a storm?" Vaddi yelled.

Menneath's face was a mask of amusement. "Of course! Call this a storm? And don't speak lightly of *Marella*. She's sturdy enough!"

"*Marella?* Sovereigns, you're not in love *again?* You named your craft after *that* skinny creature?"

"Watch what you say! Marella is not in the least bit skinny, you troll! She's a fine girl—"

Vaddi laughed in spite of the pain that was wrenching at his heart. The craft lurched wildly and he was nearly pitched out, his hands grabbing the lines to steady himself.

"Concentrate!" he yelled. "Time enough to think about your beloved Marella later."

Menneath cast off the mooring lines and turned the sail. He was several inches taller than Vaddi, more muscular, with a shock of thick black hair that constantly threatened to blind him as it tumbled across his face. Straining at the ropes as he did now, head flung back, neck muscles corded with effort, he looked more like an elemental than a man. But the fishermen of these northern waters were bred from such stock, and the men of Thrane often swore they had saltwater for blood.

As the craft slipped out across the heaving waters, Vaddi felt the cleric observing him. He turned and saw the man seated in the stern, strangely relaxed. He nodded to Vaddi.

He's using magic, Vaddi thought. Sovereigns know in this storm we'll need it.

Menneath guided the craft into the raging waters. The *Marella* plunged, seemingly straight to her doom, but miraculously shot forward. Around his neck Menneath wore a pendant, a blue stone carved with a sigil. He swore it was a chip from a dragonshard, fallen from the Rings of Siberys that surrounded the world. In the hours that followed, Vaddi could have believed it as the *Marella* ploughed through the raging sea, past the fangs of numerous rocks, underwater reefs, and tall, looming islands.

CHAPTER 2

The storm showed no sign of abating, but Menneath was able to guide the craft with apparent ease to the east, following the line of islands that clustered about the mainland shores. North of them, on the seaward side, other islands rose up like broken fangs, while overhead clouds tore across the skies like shrouds to cover Marazanath.

Vaddi went back to Menneath, who was looking puzzled over something.

"What's wrong?"

"It's *Marella*. She's not responding fully."

He leaned this way and that, but to Vaddi's eye, the craft seemed to obey her master.

"If I try to swing out into the main channel, north of east, she's sluggish."

"Damaged?" Vaddi asked.

"I don't think so. I would have felt it."

Vaddi grimaced. "Will she make it?"

"To Rookstack? I think so." Menneath spoke the name as though it were a curse. "Ever been there?"

"The freebooter's den? No. Why?"

"I wouldn't want to fetch up in that rat-hole. Why are we

going there?"

"My—" a sob tried to seize Vaddi's throat, but he choked it down. "My father said he has contacts there."

"Your father has contacts all over Khorvaire. Why are we going to thrice-cursed Rookstack?"

Vaddi went back to the Cleric. "Why *are* we going to Rook-stack, cleric?"

Cellester looked uneasy. "Thrane would be safest, true, but our enemies will suspect as much. Their eyes will be turned westward for now."

Vaddi was about to respond, but something overhead made him lift his head to the skies. There was a momentary break in the clouds, like a long gash of light reaching back westward along the coast toward Marazanath. In the far distance, rising up to the heavens like a black, contorted pillar, smoke rose, boiling and contorting itself, masking the coastline as it billowed outward, the very breath of chaos. He thought of his father, his half-brothers, all dead now, wiped away in that one night of carnage.

You must not be taken, his father had said. Vaddi felt again the horrific gaze of the vampire lord upon him, the look of pure lust in his eyes, and the pain of Vaddi's loss clashed with the fury of his anger. The break in the clouds closed, and the storm drew a final veil over the smoking pyre that had been Marazanath.

❀ ❀ ❀ ◉ ❀ ❀ ❀

Rookstack was a unique port, its main area hewn out of the living rock of a tall island, like an oversize rabbit warren. Dominating it and the natural curve of harbor, a dozen columns of rock towered up, their bizarre forms eroded by wind and weather, as if some deranged sculptor had been at work on them. Human skulls and bones hung from them—a warning to outsiders that this was no place to linger. Among these leaning towers, clouds of rooks flocked, their croaks and calls echoing from the chiselled rock. The harbor itself, enclosed by two claw-like outcrops of jagged rock, had been chopped out of the base of the central rock by dwarves in centuries gone by, its quayside narrow, its stone constantly buffeted by the waves that churned in from the sea. This was the leeward side of the island, but only the most skilled of sailors could negotiate the entrance to the harbor and ease their craft up to the quayside.

A dozen unkempt onlookers stood on that quay now, eagerly watching Menneath as he guided *Marella* to a berth. They nodded their reluctant approval as the youth deftly eased the small boat in and flung up a rope. One of them caught it and tied it off. His burly companions, hands on sword hilts, waited for the three intruders to alight.

"Who are you and what business have you got here?" said one of them. A scar down one side of his face danced as he spoke.

"Fleeing from the storm," said Cellester before Menneath could reply.

"Aye," nodded the huge seaman who had tied off the craft. "Not been many like it in our time."

The man with the scar pointed to Menneath. "Yon boy's a fisherman. One of Drudesh's whelps, if I know him. Seen him in coastal waters. But you others—you're not sea folk."

Vaddi felt anger stirring within him, but Cellester spoke before he could voice it. "You'll come across more like us in the days that follow. There's fighting in Marazanath. Some local dispute, I guess. More than a few will have to detour round it. We're from southern Karrnath. On Church business. I am a cleric and this is my novice. We'll go back to our lands when chance permits it."

The men glowered at them for a while longer, then grunted. Few questions were asked in Rookstack, but Cellester knew that they would be watched. House Orien had more than once stated its intent to rid these waters of the freebooters, and the pirates were justifiably not quick to give their trust.

"We need to stay but a night," Cellester said. "We can pay our way."

"Glad to hear it!" The huge fellow snorted. "Let 'em pass, Strang. Rookstack's seen far stranger flotsam and jetsam."

Cellester led the two youths along the quayside. Behind them they heard crude mutterings about the Church of the Silver Flame and the vermin that ran it.

"There are a number of inns," Cellester said. "I suggest we get food and rest and then leave at dawn."

Menneath nodded, but his face was pale. "I can't say as I'll be sleeping this night."

Cellester led them up the narrowest of side streets, its rock-hewn buildings leaning over them, almost smothering them. A number of torches already glowed in cressets overhead. The cleric seemed to know what he was about, for he stopped at the gnarled oak door of a small inn and motioned his companions inside.

There were a few men in here, hunched over steaming plates, others sitting back, swigging at their tankards. They eyed the visitors but kept their focus on their meals. Several sleek-coated hounds stirred beneath tables, uttering low growls, but the men stilled them with a quick dig of their nails or tossed morsels to them.

At the bar, the keeper turned from a conversation with two other men. "If your coin is good, I won't ask your names or the nature of your business," he said. "I take it you want food and drink? The ale's good."

"I hear it's the best in Rookstack," said Cellester.

The innkeeper snorted.

Cellester put some coins down on the scarred wooden bar. "Enough?"

"Generous."

"To include a room."

"Now you're insulting my hospitality."

Cellester added two more coins.

"Less of an insult."

"I'd also heard that the innkeepers of Rookstack were the biggest pirates of all. Obviously my informant spoke from experience."

The innkeeper straightened up, inflating his not inconsiderable chest. A look of annoyance crossed his dark features.

Behind Cellester the two youths stiffened. Vaddi felt suddenly naked, surrounded by dangerous strangers. A false move in here would mean a gruesome death. What was Cellester playing at? The freebooters seemed frozen in time for a moment, silence falling as they all eyed the cleric, waiting his next move.

The innkeeper let out his stored breath in a huge guffaw. His immense fist banged down on the bar, making the coins leap into the air. "You've spirit, I'll give ya that! Siddown and I'll bring you something. It won't be pretty, but it'll fill yer belly. And as it happens, I do have a room."

Cellester smiled, though thinly, and ushered the two youths to a table in a corner, where they could set their backs to the wall and watch the door. Already the occupants of the inn had gone back to their own meals, ignoring the strangers.

"You've been here before?" Menneath asked, leaning over the table like a conspirator at the plotting of a murder.

Cellester shook his head. "He'd have taken all our money if I'd let him. If I hadn't stood up to him, we'd have been marked."

Vaddi frowned. "We may be safe enough for the night, but how exactly are we to find our way to Thrane?"

"I'm not so sure we're safe," said Menneath. He clutched the pendant that he wore around his neck, fingers pressing it to his chest.

Vaddi looked at Cellester. "What do you say to that?"

"I warned you we would be watched. Karrnath has become a melting pot of strife, deceit, and treachery—especially these northern shores. We're as safe here as anywhere else, but we remain here at our peril."

They fell into a brooding silence, each lost in his own thoughts, until three huge bowls of thick soup arrived. Floating in the steaming liquid, chunks of cooked meat vied for space with vegetables, and the three visitors ate hungrily. The innkeeper brought them a tankard of foaming ale each, grinning at the youths but not tarrying to gossip.

As they ate, another figure entered the inn. He was dressed in voluminous clothes—three times as many as any normal man would require—and wore a wide-brimmed hat stuffed with dowdy feathers. Over his shoulder he carried a sack big enough to hide a small wardrobe. He paused in the center of the room, struggling for breath, as if the sack indeed weighed heavily. Bony fingers clawed away the preposterous hat to reveal the face of an aging man, multi-lined and craggy and with a matted beard. Numerous rings gleamed on the man's fingers, and from his ears hung pendulous rings that even the most bombastic of privateers would have thought extravagant. He gazed about the room like a bird of prey, and to Vaddi he seemed to be looking either for a perch or a victim. The man's glance took him in for a moment, his hawk-like head bobbed, and he dragged his sack across to a nearby table, where he sat down, wheezing until he had got his breath back.

"Business is slack this day," he said, dropping his hat down on top of the sack and patting it as though it were a pet. He had spoken to no one in particular, but Cellester put down his tankard and eyed the newcomer with evident interest.

"I take it you're a mendicant," said the cleric.

The man's eyes widened. "Indeed I am not, lord! I am Nyam Hordath, reputable trader. In all of Khorvaire, there is none as widely travelled or with access to such varied resources."

He stopped and looked about. Some of the freebooters were looking at him, grinning as if humoring a simpleton. Clearly some of them knew him. He shuffled his chair closer to Cellester's and leaned forward, voice dropping.

"I am no beggar. I give a fair price for everything, and I ask a fair price for the things I sell. You have only to look at the treasures that, by sheer good fortune, I have with me in this very bag. In this very bag! Wait only one moment while I—"

"Hold!" Cellester said. "I am sure you are right."

Vaddi and Menneath exchanged amused glances, trying not to laugh.

"Everyone seeks something, lord," said the trader. "My purpose in life is to provide it."

"I doubt you can help us," Cellester muttered, not amused.

"Surely I can. What is it you desire?"

"That is my business," said the cleric.

"Of course it is, of course. I meant no offense, but I beg you to reconsider. Nothing is too trivial. Clothes, arms, spells, information—"

"Information?"

"Ah, I have tempted you, lord."

Before the trader could say more, the innkeeper loomed over him. "Hordath, I told you last time your credit has run out. If you want food and drink, find another inn. Either put coin in my palm or go and ply your trade elsewhere."

"Run out? My credit run out? You jest! There is nowhere in all Khorvaire where Nyam Hordath cannot rely—"

"Then use it in Karrnath or Thrane, but if you've no coin—and I'll not take that heap of old rags and corpse-hauled trinkets as coin—then go and annoy other travellers."

Nyam's face screwed itself into a mask of utter horror. *"Corpse-hauled!* By the Rings of Siberys, I have never been so insulted—"

"I'm sure you have, many times," growled the innkeeper, whose body movements suggested that he was about to turn his verbal objections into physical ones.

Cellester interposed. "This matter can be easily enough resolved."

Both the trader and the innkeeper favored him with looks of passing amazement.

Cellester held out some coins for the innkeeper. "Will these pay for the trader's fare this night?"

The innkeeper looked taken aback, but he took the coins and pocketed them. "Very well," he said. "None of my business, of course, but I know this trader. I check *his* coins very carefully." So saying, he muscled his way back to the bar.

"I am in your debt," said the trader to Cellester, unable fully to hide his surprise.

"You are. I want information and one other thing."

"Name it."

"I need to know what is happening on the mainland. You are covered in its mud." Cellester indicated the smears of loam that coated Nyam's lower garments. "I take it you crossed to Rookstack today."

The trader nodded.

"You must have seen strange things there. The movements of a rabble army . . . ?"

Nyam leaned very close. "Indeed! Chaos has broken out on the mainland. Every bandit and pirate of sea, land, and sky has banded together. It is the strangest thing, and there is talk that—" he paused, licked his lips and lowered his voice to a whisper— "that the Emerald Claw is behind it. Worse, it is headed for Marazanath."

"I am a cleric: I have no love of the Emerald Claw."

Nyam looked around furtively.

"What of the mainland?" said Cellester. "Is it passable? Is there a way south? Or east to the Mror Holds?"

Nyam shook his head. "By sea, the reavers from the Lhazaar Principalities have grown bolder than ever. They trawl these very waters. The mainland is dangerous, but with care you could find a way south to less hostile regions. The Claw's agents have been concentrating their energies along the coast. A swift run would be your safest bet, but it would be no more than a gamble."

"Less so with your help," Cellester said.

Nyam screwed up his face. "I am sadly limited—"

"The other thing I require is a boat."

Nyam pursed his lips. "In these times?"

Vaddi and Menneath again exchanged glances. There was no more able craft than the *Marella*. What did Cellester have in mind?

"I am sure, master trader, that you have already planned your own exit from Rookstack, given your dubious credit with its inhabitants. We'll share it with you."

"I confess I had planned such an exit, but I find myself short of the necessary stock to barter—"

"You just get the craft," said Cellester. "I want it ready an hour before dawn, whatever the weather. Is that clear?" He put his hand over the gnarled fingers of the trader. "Your life on it." His eyes were like steel.

Vaddi repressed a shudder. That coldness in the cleric was one of the reasons he could not bring himself to trust the man.

Nyam attempted to smile. "Of course, of course. No need for threats, lords. This is my trade. I excel at it, but I will need a deposit. A craft will be available, no questions asked, but where will you take it?"

"Is the airship port at Scaacrag still in use?"

"Open to all who need it—at least it was the last time I was there."

Cellester handed him a fistful of coins. "Then you must get us there. An hour before dawn. Serve us well, trader, and you'll earn more gold than you can carry in that sack of yours."

The innkeeper returned with food and drink, but Nyam was already on his feet. "How could I turn down such a generous proposition?" With a final nod of his bird-like head, he grabbed his bag and slipped into the night.

Cellester pushed the inviting bowl of stew over to the two youths. "Eat up. We may not get fare like this again for a long time."

"So you mean us to board a windgalleon?" said Vaddi. "Bound for where?"

"It may be a way to Thrane." He spoke quietly. "We won't know until we get to Scaacrag. But my guess is we'll be watched. You saw that creature who struck down your father."

Vaddi nodded, again feeling the anger rising within him.

"A vampire who without doubt serves the Emerald Claw. It will not want survivors from Marazanath who can bear witness to its perfidy there. We *will* be hunted. They will not be satisfied with the spoils of their conquest."

Indeed not, thought Vaddi, glad that the talisman given to him by Anzar was hidden well within the folds of his clothes.

They ate in silence. After a while Menneath leaned closer to Vaddi and spoke in a whisper. "The peddler spoke of reavers from the Lhazaar Principalities. I'm sure there are at least two of them in this very room. I've seen their type before. They don't come more bloodthirsty and don't care too much about what they take from whom."

Cellester had heard the softly spoken words. He, too, leaned forward. "All the more reason for us to quit this place."

CHAPTER 3

In all the years he has served my family, I have learned almost nothing about him—what he feels, what he is thinking. Even now, I'm not sure I understand his motives, though I am sure he holds no love for the Emerald Claw."

Vaddi sat on the narrow bed, scowling at the stained wall. He and Menneath had come upstairs to this cramped room, while Cellester had gone out into the port, preparing to organize their flight from Rookstack.

"My father trusted him," Vaddi added, but the words caught in his throat. At last he was able to let the tears flow, tears that he had held back since the moment he had watched the death of his father.

Menneath overcame his embarrassment at seeing his friend so stricken and put an arm around his shoulders. Vaddi shook for long moments, fists clenching. At length he stiffened, his tear-stained eyes filled with anger and a power that startled his companion.

"I don't understand any of this, Menneath, but by the blood in my veins, I will avenge my family. I swear it." He looked, at that moment, slightly crazed, fury burning off him like heat.

"You know that my people and I will stand beside you, although we are few in number."

Vaddi stood up, pacing the room. "You must go back to your own father and your folk, Menneath. As I said, Cellester is a mystery to me, but if this peddler has a ship, then I must take that. You must sail the *Marella* back."

Menneath stood up in protest. "*What?* Abandon you? I can't do that!"

"Listen. However we leave this rat's nest, it must be inconspicuously. The *Marella* is marked. If those were reavers you saw downstairs, who could say they are not in the pay of my enemies? Two craft would stand out like trees on a reef."

Menneath looked pained. "What of the cleric? You say you don't trust him, yet you would put your life in his hands."

"I've been wondering about our coming to Rookstack. My father said he had contacts here, but Cellester knew of this inn. He's been here before, in spite of anything he says. He *meant* us to come here. But why won't he say more? I don't like such mysteries."

"Then how can you rely on him?"

"I seem to have little choice for now. Later . . . well, I'll see."

"Vaddi, don't make me do this—"

Menneath's words were cut short by the soft tread of footsteps on the stair outside. There was a tap on the door and Cellester rejoined them, dropping a bulky sack. He looked haggard in the dim candle-glow.

"We will have to move more quickly than I thought," he said to Menneath. "You were right. You did see reavers from the Lhazaar Principalities. I've seen through their disguises."

"Why are they disguised?" said Menneath. "They are usually more brash and vociferous than other seafarers."

"Quite so. I strongly suspect that they, too, are in the pay of agents of the Claw. The lands here are crawling with spies and turncoats. Kazzerand, a local warlord and bitter rival of your father, has never done much to strengthen the region, save make a show. I suspect that Marazanath's fall suits his own greed. He'll send knights to take it back and make it yet another of his own possessions. In the name of King Kaius, of course."

"My father was abandoned," said Vaddi coldly. "I spit on this warlord."

"I have seen the peddler again," said Cellester. "He has a craft waiting to take us off Rookstack."

"Menneath will go back to his people," said Vaddi, turning to his friend with an emphatic look.

Cellester nodded. "It will help us. We need a diversion."

Vaddi scowled. "I don't want his life endangered."

Menneath snorted. "I can handle myself. And if I must abandon you, let me at least do something useful. What do you want from me, cleric?"

"I am certain that the reavers at least will try to follow us. You must sail your craft back to your village. Draw them off. We'll make our own departure under cover of darkness."

Vaddi looked horrified. "No! It's too dangerous!"

Menneath laughed. "The *Marella* will outstrip any reaver craft in the coastal reefs. I've played slip and hold with pirates along this coast before. None of them have netted me yet. Their craft are too cumbersome. All right for deep water, but in the shallows they'll never catch me."

Vaddi wanted to protest further, but Menneath had clearly allied himself to Cellester in this. The cleric opened the sack he had brought and took out various nondescript garments.

"Vaddi, you and I will need to change into these. Put what we are wearing now into the sack. Come. There is no time to lose. Menneath, you remain as you are."

As Vaddi and Cellester changed their clothes, Menneath held open the sack for them, and in a few moments they had effected the change. Vaddi and Cellester now looked completely neutral, their robes shabby, slightly voluminous. They were able to conceal their weapons beneath them. In the darkness, they could be anyone, and they each had a deep cowl to obscure their features.

Cellester turned again to Menneath. "Sail swiftly and deviously back to your people. It's unlikely that the rabble army will have attacked them. It will only be a matter of time before they tire of the Hold and disperse. Vaddi and I will take advantage of your deception and flee with Nyam Hordath."

Menneath let out a deep sigh. "Sovereigns of the sea! I see the sense in this, Vaddi, but I fear for your safety."

Vaddi put his arms around his friend and hugged him. "Menneath, this is a parting that will cut me deep. Now, of all times."

"It seems that it must be. How else are you to escape?"

Cellester put a finger to his lips and at once they all fell silent. The night closed about them like a fist, but there was an unnatural silence about it.

"What is it?" hissed Vaddi.

"I fear a trap set down below us. More men had come to the inn, which is strange at so late an hour, even for Rookstack. They may not mean to kill us, but no doubt they want to drag us off and present us to whoever hired them. We could fight them, but Lhazaar Principality axemen, fuelled up on rough mead, are something I'd rather avoid."

Cellester went to the narrow window and opened it with the flat of his hand. It protested, old wood tearing and a hinge ripping loose. Cold air rushed in with the night.

"Follow me," said the cleric, and within seconds he had clambered cat-like onto the narrow ledge, squeezed through the opening, and swung upward into the darkness.

Both Vaddi and Menneath were used to scaling the rocky cliffs around Marazanath's coastline, having tested each other's courage in endless wild games since they were six years old. This climb was meat and drink to them. In no time they had swung out and up over the eaves, kneeling on the cracked tiles of the inn's roof. Below them, in the room they had so swiftly quitted, they heard its door bang open. Gruff voices clotted the night air.

Cellester was above them, his dark shadow limned against

the night sky like a huge, winged predator. The storm had at last abated and through a tear in the clouds a string of Eberron's smaller moons gleamed like pearls. The cleric pointed back along the roof to where it joined the sheer face of one of the great stacks of the port. No one spoke, but they knew what was needed. Quickly they went to the cliff and peered down into the streets. Cellester led them on a dizzy race across a number of leaning, crumbling rooftops and then indicated that they would have to go down the cliff face to the street below. It yawned like an open grave.

Behind them they could hear shouts and others clambering up to the roof. Vaddi glanced back and saw the large figures of the Lhazaar reavers and bits of moonlight glinting off drawn blades. The reavers were perfectly at home scaling cliffs, their own homeland being reputedly as rocky and treacherous as any such lands in the north. It did not take the five men long to get on to the roof and give chase to the runaways.

Cellester and the two youths swung down the cliff that dropped into the street, fingers digging into the cold rock, finding nooks and crannies, toes getting a hold in the most minute crevices. Like spiders they climbed down into the street. The reavers, though adept at this, were less agile, and the runaways gained vital minutes in their flight.

Cellester led them unerringly through the narrow side-streets, and after a short run to a quayside that ran off the main harbor. Several small craft were jammed together, bobbing up and down on the restless waves. On one of them they could see a huddled form. Cellester urged the youths across the decks of three craft until they landed in the far one. The shape proved to be Nyam. Once they were aboard, they all flattened themselves, heads below the gunwale. Only Nyam remained upright, watching the quayside.

The reavers emerged from the alley, split up, and ran up and down the cobbled quay, axes gleaming in the sputtering glow of the street torches. One of the figures saw Nyam and hailed him.

"Three fugitives!" snarled the reaver, his voice ringing back off the houses. "Yer must have seen them. Which way?"

"Aye," Nyam hollered back, cupping his mouth. The wind had dropped, but it was still strong. He pointed back toward the main body of the town. "A man and two youths heading into the port."

"If yer lyin', I'll be back for yer head!" called the reaver and ran down the quay.

Watching the receding figures, Nyam slipped the mooring rope he had been holding out of sight and within moments his craft was away from the others, nosing out into the channel that led down to the harbor. Cellester and the youths kept flat to the deck.

When the cleric spoke, his words were almost lost in the wind. "Peddler, ease us into the harbour and alongside their craft. Menneath, when it's safe, I'll give you the word. Sail away from Rookstack with all haste. We'll slide back into the shadows and leave later."

Vaddi was burning to look out to see what was transpiring, but he thought better of it, his heart racing. Beside him, eyes closed in concentration, Menneath was a coiled spring, ready to be unleashed at a moment's notice.

Nyam manoeuvred his craft, which was slightly larger then the *Marella*, into the harbor and along the main quayside. He could see the reavers entering and leaving some of the dives there, calling out angrily to each other, shaking their heads. For the time being they had not noticed the craft as she drifted along the main body of moored ships. But a snarl of fury signified that one of the reavers at least was intent on going back to interrogate the one he had challenged earlier. His frustration blinded him to the fact that the very same being was no more than thirty yards away in the harbor.

Nyam brought his craft to the place where the *Marella* was tied up. She had not been interfered with. Presumably the reavers or their masters had seen no use in it.

"Into your craft," Cellester told Menneath. "Go right

into the bay and make sure they see you."

Menneath nodded. He gave Vaddi's hand a last pumping, their eyes locking for a moment. "Until next time." Menneath grinned and then, sleek as a sea otter, he was over the side of the craft and into the belly of the *Marella*. He untied her and was about to take her out of the harbor when there was an abrupt movement in her stern. A tarpaulin was flung aside as if by a freak wind and a solitary reaver, blade in hand, leaped forward.

"Thinkin' of leavin' us so soon?" he snarled, slicing the air with the vicious weapon.

Menneath almost toppled over but managed to draw his own thin sword. He darted under another swipe of the reaver's weapon.

Vaddi gasped, instinctively drawing out his long dirk. He hardly noticed Cellester's restraining arm as he made for the prow of the peddler's craft. He watched in horror as Menneath ducked and dived in the rocking *Marella*, the huge pirate slashing this way and that at him. It would only be a matter of time before he cut the youth to ribbons.

"Over here!" bawled the reaver, and there was an answering cry along the quay.

"Quickly, make for the open sea," Cellester barked at the peddler.

"No!" cried Vaddi. "Go forward! Go forward, damn you, or I'll swim to him."

Nonplussed, the peddler sent the prow of his craft toward the *Marella*, which now bumped up hard against the quayside. It was fortunate that she did, for at that moment the pirate had been about to hack into Menneath. Instead, the jarring of the boat against the quay sent him tumbling over her side. Menneath jabbed with his sword, drawing a shriek from the reaver, who slid into the dark water of the harbor.

Vaddi leaped from the peddler's craft into the *Marella* and got Menneath to his feet. He ignored the cleric's cry behind him, and both youths turned to face the oncoming reavers. They would never get the *Marella* free of the harbor and away before they were overcome, so they jumped onto the quay and sprinted hard along it. The reavers roared their delight at the chase. For a moment, Gellester and the peddler were forgotten in their craft, unable to do anything about the pursuit.

"Where to?" gasped Menneath as he and Vaddi raced along the quay.

Vaddi looked at the numerous alleyways that led off the harbor. "Try and lose them in there!"

He led them up a constricted passage and then turned left and down another alley that barely permitted one person to shoulder through it. A shape blocked the way ahead, and Vaddi realized it was another of the reavers, though smaller and armed with only a dirk.

Without pausing he thrust his own dirk into the man's chest. To his horror it burst like a mattress, dust and brittle bone spilling out from it as the reaver fell to his knees, skeletal face screaming. Menneath struck the fleshless head from its shoulders, and the two youths were past and beyond to a wider street, but pursuit was close behind.

They reached a small square, the cramped houses leaning over them, blotting out most of the light. Vaddi cursed. They had trapped themselves. A dozen reavers closed in behind them and on two sides, all exits shut off. Vaddi gripped his long dirk and thought of his father and his half-brothers.

One of the reavers eased forward, an axe slung carelessly over his shoulder. "Come, come, young sirs. No need for bloodshed. All we want is to take you to our master for a little talk."

They remained frozen for a moment only. The huge reaver, who was clearly flesh and blood, laughed and took another step forward and was about to say something else when a sword tore through his chest, slick in the half-light with his blood. He toppled forward with a strangled cry. Behind him, dragging his weapon free of the corpse, Gellester waved the youths to him. They obeyed, though they had to parry the cut and thrust of steel as the other reavers tried to close the trap.

Sparks flew as blade and axe clashed. Vaddi felt the sweep of a weapon as it tore through the fabric of his cloak, inches from his flesh. But he won through to the cleric's side. Then he was running once more, down another narrow alley, close on the cleric's heels. Ahead of them he could barely discern the quayside and the waiting form of the peddler, who held a long blade.

There was a cry behind him and Vaddi turned. Menneath had slowed, clutching at his neck. Vaddi pulled up short only to see his friend crumple to his knees. He had an arrow through his neck, its bloodied point protruding out of his throat.

Vaddi screamed but already he knew it was too late. The first of the reavers towered over his friend. As though watching a slow nightmare, Vaddi saw the axe come down. Something tore at his arm, almost jerking him from his feet as Cellester yanked him away toward the quay.

The reaver shouted as he made his killing blow, but as Menneath toppled, he sprawled in the alley, tangling up the reaver's feet. The youth's last act was to thrust up with his blade, deep into the groin of the man who had killed him. The blade tore into flesh and ground on bone. The reaver's howl of triumph turned to a hideous shriek of agony. He crumpled over the dying Menneath, choking the alley as those behind hacked and thrust at them in an attempt to force their way past.

Vaddi saw everything through a red haze of fury, time ripping past him. The next few moments meant nothing to him as Cellester and Nyam Hordath got him into the peddler's craft and set out from the quayside, the sail snapping in the swirling night wind like a live thing. The craft swept across the harbour, and when the pursuing reavers finally burst out on to the quayside, the boat was far out in the bay. Menneath's life had won them that much.

Vaddi sank into the bottom of the craft, his body wracked with sobs, a combination of exhaustion from the flight and overwhelming horror at the death of his friend. That, coupled with the monstrous events at Marazanath, had driven him to a new depth of grief. Shattered, he gave in to it.

Cellester stood silently in the stern of the boat, watching Rookstack as it dwindled behind them. The peddler, too, was silent, though his face was clouded with pity.

● ● ● ◉ ● ● ●

An hour later, with dawn breaking, they appeared to have outdistanced any pursuit, though Cellester felt sure this would be no more than a temporary respite.

Nyam sniffed the wind, as if it could impart vital knowledge to him. "We're heading for the port of Scaacrag on the mainland. You should be able to get an airship there. What about my payment?"

"All in good time."

"How do you intend to pay me? No tricks, cleric. Not that I don't trust a man of your position."

"I serve House Orien. It is a wealthy house and pays its debts. I promised you more gold than you could carry in a sack. You shall have it."

"In Scaacrag?"

"Just get us there."

The peddler screwed up his wrinkled face but turned his attention once more to the rough seas ahead, weaving his craft through its countless islets and reefs.

● ● ● ◉ ● ● ●

For several days they sailed eastward. Sky and sea alike were calmer than they had been, though there seemed to linger a promise of storm in the air. No ship pursued them—or at least none that they could detect. Nyam had brought enough food for them—dried fish and rough bread, washed down with fresh water. There was little conversation. Vaddi brooded on the horrors he had been through, but he fought back the grief, using anger to stem it. Cellester likewise seemed drawn in on himself, coming out of his reverie only to study the horizons and the numerous rocks, islets and cliff-islands that pocked the seas in this remote region. Nyam hummed tunelessly, affecting the air of a simple man, as he had when he had first met the company in the inn, although Vaddi respected the quick wits that had saved them at Rookstack.

Vaddi reflected, too, on the cleric. What did he really know about him? Cellester was something of a renegade, a servant of the Church of the Silver Flame, but a man who had openly voiced his scepticism not only of the authority of gods over the destiny of men but also of the authority of his church. Yet Vaddi saw within the cleric a shadow, the hand of something outside of himself. Vaddi had only intuition to go on, but in these times intuition could not be ignored. Cellester had been a servant of House Orien since before Vaddi's birth, in happier times, when his mother had been alive. The cleric had undoubtedly aided in the growth and esteem of the House and had been responsible for much of the training and refining of its soldiery. Anzar had told Vaddi that it had suited the taciturn cleric to live in the remote area of northeastern Khorvaire at Marazanath, as his rejection of the more devout aspects of the faith of the Silver Flame would have made him a marked man in Thrane, where the knights expected the clerics to demonstrate an active zeal. Since serving Anzar, Cellester had evidently had to become more circumspect.

Vaddi's eyes met those of Cellester as the latter looked up, and for a moment the youth felt himself scrutinized inwardly, as though his mind were being sifted, but the moment passed and Cellester turned away, calling to Nyam.

"How far is Scaacrag?"

"There are freakish winds about this day. I steer a few points south of east, but the wind and the cursed currents drive me a few points *north* of east. That is not my desired course!"

Vaddi grimaced, thinking of Menneath's skills.

Cellester said nothing but joined Nyam, now at the prow of the craft. They were both puzzling over something.

"What is it?" said Vaddi.

"This current reeks of sorcery. Mind you, that's hardly surprising. We're in the Stammerrak, a narrow gut between a dozen or so islands that bore the brunt of some hellish sorcery gone wrong in the days of the Last War. More than a touch of the Mournland about it."

Vaddi shuddered at mention of the blasted lands, where nature itself was said to have turned inside out.

Cellester scowled. "Stammerrak! Are you mad, peddler? You should have diverted us around this."

"Short cut. I've been across it before. Doesn't usually get a hold like this. Not unless it wants something."

"You idiot!" Cellester snapped. "Get back to the tiller. Did it not occur to you that it probably *does* want something? Us, you fool. The agents of the Claw would make good use of this demented power. They would have no qualms about dirtying their hands or souls with it. The damned are damned. Just pray to whatever gods you believe in that we aren't!"

Nyam nodded, going back to the tiller. As he passed Vaddi he grinned. "Fat lot of good that would do. My gods are notably obese and slothful."

Vaddi smiled thinly, but Cellester's grim demeanour sobered him. "Is it serious?"

The cleric nodded. "Probably. It may not be the Claw, but we must assume that it will use every device available to snare you." Again his voice dropped to the merest whisper. "And what you carry."

Vaddi felt a sudden heat in his chest and his fingers probed his shirt, touching the chain of the object that Anzar had given him. "You know of it?" he said softly.

Cellester drew back, his unease apparent. "My fear is that our enemies know of it. It will draw them like moths to a flame."

"The sea has power," Nyam called "We must free ourselves of the current."

Vaddi felt a pulse of energy within the horn. He whispered to it, as if coaxing aid from a spirit, though he had no more than his instinct to go on.

"A strong spell works against us!" the peddler called above

the wind, which had again freshened, like the voice of the current that had taken a hold of the craft. "The Stammerrak won't be thwarted, not one bit!"

Vaddi concentrated, as a strong gust from behind them seemed to break in half, like a wave split by a rock. Nyam was trying to ease the craft away from a course that was veering them more and more to the north. Now the contest between the craft and the elements was in full evidence, as though wind and sea were powered by an invisible host, elementals that sought to drag, push and buffet the craft to the dark islands north of them. Nyam's skill was no mean thing—a fact that Vaddi found intriguing. The man was no ordinary peddler.

The hidden talisman pulsed more hotly, as if it spoke to the soul of the deep oceans, its own puissance able to wrench the prow of the craft away from the sea's grasp.

A grim struggle ensued, the Stammerrak focusing all its supernatural energies into controlling the craft, but its occupants pouring their own efforts into subverting its purpose.

"We're passing the worst!" Nyam shouted above the thunder of the seas and the crashing of breakers on nearby rocks. "If we must be tossed ashore, we make for one of the last isles of the chain."

Gradually the craft edged away from the main islands, ploughing through huge waves toward clearer sea beyond. With a last rush, the craft slid through a narrow rock passage and buried her prow in a wedge of sand on a solitary island beyond.

* * * * * * *

"You know this place?" Cellester asked the peddler.

Nyam nodded uncertainly. "Right at the very rim of the Stammerrak's influence. We can freshen up here overnight. Tomorrow we'll land at Scaacrag. Shall we find a spring? Bound to be one up near the summit of the island."

Beyond the rim of the cliffs, they found a beaten path that indicated some sort of habitation or at least recent use of the island. The sun had fallen low into the skies, daubing the landscape in ominous deep red hues, casting long shadows like claws across its upper reaches. The island was little more than two miles across and devoid of trees, its exposed rock blasted by the cold storms from the north, like the bones of a gigantic skeleton that had been weathered away to dust.

Nyam pointed to the crest of the hill. "Standing stones. This place is sacred to somebody. Ideal haven for the night."

Cellester glared at him as if he had lost his senses. "Haven? What sort of gods do you think would bless this place?"

"My guess would be those worshiped by the freebooters. I have heard of such places. Just as Rookstack has its honor among thieves, so such an island protects the needy traveller."

As they came closer to the ring of standing stones that circled the level area at the island's crown, Vaddi could make out numerous other stones down among the bracken and windblasted gorse. "Those stones have a familiar look to them," he said to Cellester.

The cleric drew in a sharp breath. "Indeed. They are tombs. This is a graveyard."

"Of course!" Nyam beamed. "You're right. So it is as I said, a haven. We have fetched up on the one place where we are safe from conflict. Listen! Even the wind has died. Come into the standing stones. I'll get a fire going." He produced a tinderbox from his voluminous garb.

Vaddi shook his head in wonder, smiling in spite of his unease.

The sun slipped deep into its cloud bed, barely above the horizon; the light dimmed with it.

Cellester grimaced. "Don't put your dirk away. I don't share the peddler's confidence."

They came before the stone circle—fifteen-foot monoliths that ringed the hill, the space between them beaten flat, free of any growth as though tended regularly. Each monolith had been deeply etched with runes from a language long since lost to the world, as though the stones themselves were from another time, a time that pre-dated the War itself by millennia. But there was an abiding calmness about the place, a unique tranquillity that bathed the travellers in a kind of radiance, almost hypnotic in its quality.

"Be on your guard," whispered Cellester, as though his voice would snap the fabric of this enchantment.

Nyam busied himself with a fire. He had found enough dry wood and bracken to light it and spent a few moments outside the stone circle gathering armfuls of shrub-like plants to feed it. Vaddi could see nothing more than a curtain of darkness beyond the stones. Their runes danced and wavered in the fire-glow, and the stones appeared to lean inward. Overhead, the night sky was obscured, neither the moons nor a single star visible.

They ate and drank more of Nyam's frugal fare.

"Who's first watch?" said the peddler. "I suggest someone other than me. I can hardly stay awake, but I only need an hour or two."

"I doubt I'll sleep at all," said Vaddi. "I'll do it."

After a brief inspection of the perimeter of the circle, Cellester nodded and sat at the heart of the circle. Nyam had curled up like a child and was soon snoring, oblivious to the world.

Vaddi paced about like a cat, quietly examining the monoliths, though he could make nothing of their time-lost inscriptions. Even though he was on his feet, he felt his eyes drooping and had to force himself to stay awake.

How long he had been like this—minutes or an hour perhaps—before he heard the sounds from beyond the circle, he could not tell. It was neither wind nor sea that he heard. He went to the edge beside a stone and tried to peer into the pitch night, but it was impenetrable.

There! Soft susurrations. From several directions. Down among the tombs. The low bushes shifted, though they had not been stirred by the wind. Was that a low moan? An animal perhaps? But here, what could it be?

He called to Cellester. The cleric was on his feet instantly, sword catching the firelight, deflecting a brief shaft of it out into the darkness. But in that fleeting beam, a shape gathered itself—hunched, formed from the very dark, as though the earth had breathed out a fetid cloud that coalesced into substance.

CHAPTER 4

Wake the peddler," said Cellester, something like disgust masking his face.

"What comes?" whispered Vaddi, his voice almost lost.

"The inhabitants of the island. Its black gods alone know how many of them there are. I was a fool to agree to stay here. Wake the peddler!"

Vaddi jumped at the command, which had been almost snarled. His mind was filled with images of the tombs they had seen earlier. Countless scores of them. As he reached down to tug at Nyam's robe, another thought occurred to him. Perhaps the peddler had deliberately led them here. How were they to know he would not benefit by presenting them to their enemies?

Nyam came awake slowly, yawning and scratching his beard, but when he saw the look on Vaddi's face, he sprang up lithely, drawing his sword and staring out at the heaving darkness beyond the stones.

Vaddi and Nyam went to Cellester's side. The cleric held aloft his right arm, and white light shone from an amulet he held—too brilliant to look at. In his left hand he held his sword.

"Take a section of the circle!" Cellester called. "Stay within the stones, as you value your life and soul!"

They spread out, Vaddi's heart hammering. He held his dirk before him. He was getting used to its bloody work. Then he saw what it was that closed in on the stone circle and his heart skipped a beat. In the white light that streamed from the cleric's amulet, faces and hunched shapes thrust out of the night beyond. But such faces! Their skin was cracked and flaked, and their hair was matted and dried like weed. Eyes like huge stones gleamed with the light of madness, inner fires stoked by supernatural agencies. The graves had given up their dead, their *undead*, who trudged forward until they came to the very line of the stones.

One of them reached forward with rotting limbs, cerements hanging from them in strips, blazing eyes fixed on Vaddi as a snake fixes its victim. Vaddi made a swift pass with the dirk. It had been honed to a perfect sharpness by the Orien smiths in the hold and it went through both wrists of the creature as if passing through fabric. The rotted hands fell and the creature staggered. Vaddi saw with horror the dark, viscous blood dripping from the stumps, the fluid that fuelled these groping nightmares.

Light from Cellester's amulet scorched all those that it touched and the stench of charred bones filled the night. For a while it kept the horrors at bay, but they gazed in slack-jawed, hungry silence at the trio in the stones like a pack of starving wolves, desperate to feed.

Dredged up from long burial underground on this isle, these were far worse than the undead that had amassed at Marazanath. Something was driving them on. Several scuttled forward, spider-like, only to burst into flames and crumble to ashes as the light from Cellester's amulet engulfed them.

Behind the wall of undead something else was stirring, scarlet light flooding over the hilltop. It merged with the light from the cleric's amulet, red seeping into white. As though draining his strength, the red light forced Cellester to lower his arm. He stumbled back, numbed.

44

Beside the embers of the small fire, in the very center of the stone circle, the three defenders stood back to back. They were completely surrounded, but the undead had, as one, ceased their forward movement. Instead they waited, their manic eyes fixed on their victims, their skeletal fingers flexing and unflexing. In the shadow-light it was impossible to guess how many there were, but Vaddi knew there were scores of them at least. It would be impossible to break through them.

As he glanced at the cleric, seeing the look of deep anguish on Cellester's face, Vaddi felt something warm within his robes. He had almost forgotten the talisman. His fingers closed on it now, felt it *shift* against his breast. But before he could do more, the front ranks of the creatures opened and a solitary figure came through.

Vaddi was shocked by its appearance. Tall, dressed in dark leather, studded with silver, it was not like the other creatures but almost appeared to be a living man. His skin was pure white, as if leeched of blood, and in the scarlet eyes burned an intense vitality. His long white hair was swept back from the forehead down over his shoulders and beyond his belt. In his right hand he held a sword whose blade throbbed with scarlet light. When he smiled, his teeth were yellow, sharp as a rat's.

"Well, such an intriguing combination of sailors," he said, his voice harsh, his accent suggesting he was from the western lands beyond Thrane.

His sword swung slowly back and forth, marking out the three intruders, as if deciding which to impale first. Only then, with a deep shudder of revulsion and fury, Vaddi realised that this was the vampire who had brought down Marazanath and killed his father.

"Who are you to threaten us?" said Cellester.

The eyes of the swordsman flared. "A protector of the dead, and you are a defiler, treading as you do on this island. But since you are here, you are welcome to join my wards."

"We have no business with you," said Cellester.

"Perhaps not," replied the swordsman, running a black-gloved hand along the blade of his weapon. "You are a cleric, I suspect. There is power in the amulet you wield, but it is no dragonshard. No match for the power in this."

He pointed the blade at Cellester, who dropped to his knees, racked by sudden waves of pain.

"And you," said the swordsman, swinging round to face Nyam, releasing Cellester momentarily from his pain. "What are you? A trader?"

"Me, lord? No, I am a simple traveller."

"A grave-robber to boot, no doubt. Come to filch a few trinkets from this isle to barter back in Rookstack and beyond?"

"Not at all, lord!" said Nyam with well-practiced horror. "I have nothing but respect for the dead."

"Oh, I am so glad to hear that," said the swordsman. "You'll have no regrets about joining them."

Cellester had eased himself back to his feet, but he kept still, studying the massed dead as if looking for a weakness in their ranks.

The swordsman turned to Vaddi. He held up his blade so that its red light picked out the youth's features clearly. "And you are . . . ?"

Vaddi felt those scarlet eyes boring into him, as if behind them was a deeper, more malign force. "Danath, son of Sigbard."

The swordsman laughed, cutting Vaddi's words short. "Come, come. Your rough garb is a thin disguise, especially to my eyes! Are you ashamed of your heritage? Have you so soon abandoned your family to their graves? No backward glances to the still-smouldering stones of Marazanath?"

Vaddi felt his anger rising up, his fingers tightening on the dirk. The swordsman glanced at it, but his feral smile widened.

"Ah, but there is spirit in you yet. Speak up! Say your name, your heritage." He leaned forward, as if taunting Vaddi to attack him. "Orien."

"My father was Anzar Kemmal Orien, but it seems that you know that already."

"Indeed. Vaddi d'Orien. Son of Anzar and the elf-bitch, Indreen."

It took all of Vaddi's self-restraint not to react.

"Well, Vaddi d'Orien, I am Caerzaal, formerly of the city of Shadukar. I grew bored with court life and went in search of far more challenging things."

"You drank the Blood of Vol," said Cellester. "You gave up your humanity to become one of these creatures. You have the disease that corrupts all who taste power. And you serve the Claw."

Caerzaal glared at him as if he would run him through with his blade, but his lips parted in the rictus of a grin. "The Claw is my ally while it suits me, cleric. I serve myself first."

"Like all slaves of the Emerald Claw," Cellester said, "you deceive yourself. When the Claw grips, it does not let go. You are not your own man, though you may think it."

"We shall see," said Caerzaal. He turned to Vaddi. "As for the youth who places so little value on himself, well, there are others who would make very good use of him."

"I serve my House," said Vaddi, "none other."

The sword tip swung up under Vaddi's chin. He could feel its coldness, as if it had been forged from a northern iceberg. "That choice is no longer yours."

Caerzaal stood very close to him. Vaddi could smell something animal about him, something not human, but there was power there, an almost frightening depth to it, as though he was but a vessel, a lens for something infinitely more puissant and evil.

Caerzaal's sword point dipped, flicking across Vaddi's chest. As it moved, Caerzaal's smile became a smirk of satisfaction. He paused, the tip of his weapon caught in the folds of the robe that covered Vaddi's gift from his father. Vaddi was still gripping it.

"By the way that you are clutching it, I would say you have something of value in your robe," Caerzaal breathed, almost a whisper.

Vaddi drew out his hand. "My heart," he said, "since you would threaten it."

"Must I cut the robe from you to prove you a liar?"

Vaddi sensed that Caerzaal would as easily kill him as look at him. He had little choice but to draw out the talisman. His fingers found again the slender chain. For the first time since putting it away he touched the object itself. It was warm. As he gripped it, he felt its rough contours and then understood what they were. They were embossed runes. The talisman itself was tapered, like a dagger, though its inside was hollow. A horn, though far longer and narrower than a normal drinking horn. Vaddi's fingers closed around its outer rim and he drew it slowly from his robe.

"A family gift, no more than that," he said.

As he brought the horn into the light, Caerzaal stepped back, wary of a trick, his sword held as if to make a sudden strike. He grinned as he saw the horn. "A pretty thing. Exquisite workmanship, but then, the elves are masters of such craft."

Vaddi could feel the horn's power, as though it were alive, responding to his life. His blood, pulsing through his veins, was suddenly a strong current. He could feel every vein, every artery in his body. The horn was like a part of that network, as if it, too, had its own veins running through it, interwoven with his. He stared at the horn in shocked fascination. It was no longer white. There was a pink tint to it, which deepened. Blood seeped from his fingers, but instead of dripping down the horn, it was absorbed by it, as though by a sponge.

Caerzaal's face clouded with horror and he made to strike, aiming to cut Vaddi's hand off at the wrist. As his blade came down, another met it before it could do its butcher's work and sparks danced in the night. Nyam had been too quick, his blade countering Caerzaal's. The latter drew back, hissing like a serpent, his tongue flicking out in anger.

"Cover that!" Caerzaal snarled. "Before I have you and your companions ripped to pieces!"

Cellester stepped between Vaddi and the enraged Caerzaal.

"I think not," he said coolly. He seemed unmoved by the appearance of the horn. "It is you who should withdraw, before you tamper with powers beyond your control."

Vaddi could feel his blood running into the horn, filling it. It was a strange feeling, a mixture of headiness, as if he had taken very strong wine, and the coming of darkness, for all around him the foul company seemed to be receding, shut out by thickening shadow, like a dissipating dream. He sheathed his dirk and with his free hand forced himself to cover it and thrust it back inside his robe. As soon as he did so, everything came back into focus, but he felt numbed by the experience.

"If you are wise, vampire," said Cellester, "you will let us go on our way."

Caerzaal laughed. "You, cleric, will crawl at my feet before we are done here."

He drew back and barked commands at the undead. They surged forward.

Cellester and Nyam hacked at them. Vaddi unsheathed his dirk and did likewise. They smashed back the oncoming mass, laying about them with energy born of desperation, piling up mangled and broken undead in a heap, but even as they resisted the first onslaught, they knew that they would inevitably be overwhelmed.

"Do not despair!" Cellester shouted to Vaddi. "They want you alive. They will not kill you."

"Scant consolation to *me!*" yelled Nyam. He fought now with both his blade and a length of burning wood he had dragged from the fire, fanning it into flame and setting alight those who came near.

Caerzaal had drawn back, absorbed into the mass of writhing undead, and Cellester's white fire shone anew from his amulet, bathing everything in a garish light. The nearest ranks of undead screamed and drew back, their skin smoking.

The vampire, shunning the light as if it held for him all the burning terrors of daylight, lifted an amulet of his own by the chain about his neck and held it up to ward off the cleric's power. Vaddi gasped as he saw it, for it was the blue stone of Menneath! His friend's small talisman, carved with its distinctive sigil. Caerzaal could only have taken it from Menneath's body.

Madness burst within Vaddi, but before it could hurl him forward in all its fury, light from Cellester's amulet focused on the blue stone and there was a blinding flash and an explosion of light and sound that blasted outward, powerful as a massive wave of water.

Utter confusion followed. The undead fell like brittle sticks, tangled and smashed. Vaddi's head rang with the echoes of the blast. For a moment stars whirled before him. He felt someone grab his arm and swing him away from the chaos.

"Follow, quickly now!" came the commanding voice of the cleric.

As some semblance of vision returned to Vaddi, he found himself stumbling with Cellester and Nyam out of the circle of ancient stones and back down the hillside, through the edge of the cemetery beyond to the way they had climbed.

"To the boat!" Nyam shouted, though it was hardly necessary.

Vaddi did not look back, but he could hear the cries and shrieks of the undead.

"Caerzaal will not give up so easily," said Cellester.

Racing through the scrub and jagged rocks as fast as they dared, they heard the renewed cries of pursuit, but soon the narrow cove and its beach spread out below them, the boat moored where they had left it. As they struggled over the sand to it, a group of shapes tried to head them off, but Cellester swept them aside with a scythe of light from his amulet. Vaddi cut down another two of the undead, his blows fuelled with all the bitterness and anger he felt, as Nyam shoved the craft into the black water.

Moments later they were rowing out into the current, Nyam unfurling the sail with practiced skill. The wind filled it instantly and swept them seaward before any of the pursuing hordes had even reached the beach. Vaddi looked back and saw Caerzaal watching, his eyes blazing with anger. Overhead the clouds parted, revealing the jewelled bands of the Ring of Siberys and a procession of small moons. By their glow, Vaddi studied the sea, but it had grown quiescent at last.

● ● ● ◉ ● ● ●

Dawn found them closing on the shore of the mainland. Vaddi had snatched a brief sleep, troubled by grim dreams, seeing again the deaths of his family and of Menneath.

"Scaacrag ahead," called Nyam, indicating sunlight on the houses of the small town. It was built at the base of a long range of cliffs, with several jetties thrust out into deep water. Behind them a central core of structures rose up the cliffs like huge nests, topped by a huge, temple-like construction. Vaddi took this to be the airship terminus, though there was no sign of aerial activity about it.

"You've earned your money," Cellester said to the peddler.

"Twice over I should say." Nyam grinned.

"You'll be paid."

As the sun rose higher, the craft sailed easily alongside one of the jetties and Nyam tied it off as his passengers climbed the steps.

"Vaddi, you and I will take passage on an airship," said Cellester. "Come, peddler, we'll settle up at the terminus. I'd be glad if we all remain as inconspicuous as possible."

Nyam pulled down his wide hat, which had survived the events of the night. They went into the town, which was already coming to life. Although it was a small port, Vaddi could see that Scaacrag bustled, as the day's trade was already well under way. If the news of Marazanath's fall had reached the ears of people here, it had had little or no impact on their activities.

They came to the black steel girders of the ancient wheelhouse without incident. Vaddi stared up at the structure, built before the War, rusting and somewhat precarious-looking now, almost neglected. But within its frame the lift rose and fell monotonously, taking handfuls of passengers up the face of the cliffs to the terminus high above.

Cellester dropped a few coins into the palm of the gate-keeper, a wizened old man who nodded sleepily, though his eyes raked the three of them. As the huge wheel at the base of the tower turned, the cogs and ratchets of the ancient machinery ground and creaked, the cage rising up. A dozen other passengers had squeezed in, some coughing nervously, others yawning. No one spoke.

At the top, Cellester disembarked, motioning Vaddi and Nyam to follow him along the wide walkway that clung to the side of the cliff, barely beneath its brow. Several offices and shops had been carved out of the stone. The cleric paused near one of them.

"Wait here."

Nyam was looking about him with feigned indifference and Vaddi could sense his nervousness. Surely there was no danger here. The people going about their business were fairly nonde-script, as though few events troubled this backwater of a town.

Cellester spent some time talking to a clerk at the counter. Vaddi saw him pay over more coins and then sign a number of documents. Eventually he rejoined his companions. He handed Nyam a rolled parchment.

"What's this?" grunted the peddler.

"I've arranged for House Orien to make good payment. That's your surety."

"A sheet of paper?"

"You can take it to the clerk immediately if you wish," said Cellester. "He'll pay you in gold—either that or take it anywhere that deals with House Orien. I trust you'll agree it's a generous amount?"

Nyam's face split in a huge grin within the tangles of his beard. "Indeed, indeed. Almost worth the extraordinary dangers that have come so close to ending my humble career."

"So we bid you farewell," said the cleric. "Come, Vaddi. We must board our craft."

Vaddi nodded to the peddler, feeling slight remorse at having to quit his company. Nyam was undoubtedly a dubious character, but there was something about him that he had warmed to. "Our thanks," he said.

Nyam simply bowed, his numerous rings and bracelets gleaming in the sunlight. "Safe journey," he said, then turned and was almost at once swallowed up in the flow of people.

Vaddi followed the cleric along the walkway to another stairway under the huge canopy of the terminus. "Where are we going?"

"The airships here are infrequent, mostly bound for the west. It would suit us best, I think, to go to Thrane. I have contacts there that will offer us some protection. I have bought us passage. I have the seal of House Orien, which will open doors for us. Keep close to me and remain covered. These places teem with spies of one kind or another."

Once they entered the vast dome of the terminal, with its glittering glass shell stretched over a webwork of rusting steel, Vaddi gaped at the far side of the building, which was a flat area, falling away to emptiness beyond. There were three docks built under the dome, each with a narrow boarding area, a mass of wiring and pipework knotted along their floor. Two of the docks were empty, but in the third rested an airship. Vaddi had heard of such things and had seen diagrams of them in Marazanath's library, but this was his introduction to the reality. He marvelled at the construction of the craft.

The ship seemed to be hovering in mid air. A score of wires and tubes hung from its keel, linked to the mechanics of the dock. Long and relatively sleek, she had the lines of a seagoing vessel, though there were no masts. Curved timbers ran along her sides. The deck was narrow and two tiered, but what struck Vaddi most was her means of propulsion. Around the central part of the craft, two arms curved outwards and within these, shimmering like vivid sunlight on a lake, was a brilliant ring of what appeared to be fire. It sizzled, a live thing, humming softly.

"What is that?" Vaddi asked.

"An elemental. The pilot uses it to control the flight. It is bound to him by strong magic. Without such creatures, the ships could not fly."

They made their way to the narrow gangplank that led up to the stern of the airship, where several uniformed airmen of House Lyrandar were checking the documents of those coming aboard. Cellester handed a seal to one of them and Vaddi noticed that it had been embossed with the unicorn of House Orien. The airman glanced through Cellester's papers and nodded approval. In a moment, the cleric and Vaddi were onboard.

"We'll sit in the stern initially," said Cellester. "I want to see as many of the other passengers as I can."

"You expect trouble?"

"Probably not, though it is wise to assume that our enemies are having us watched. An airship is not the best place to begin a skirmish, although it will be a slow journey. This is an old tub. The more modern ones are made from softwood, built for speed."

Vaddi took one of the seats around the rim of the stern. There were cabins under the main deck and a few of the passengers had evidently gone below. Otherwise there were no more than thirty or so of them and a dozen aircrew, seasoned fliers who were armed but relaxed. Apparently no one was expecting trouble on such a routine flight.

❀ ❀ ❀ ❀ ❀ ❀ ❀

The *Cloudclipper*, for thus was their airship named, left the terminus soon afterwards, her upper and lower deck having filled with a flurry of passengers. Once away from the port, she rose through layers of cloud into the brilliant blue skies. Vaddi pulled tight his thick cloak and hood, for the air up here was very cold in spite of the vivid sunshine. Arcing over the heavens, a curve of the Rings of Siberys sparkled like some immense architectural marvel, and beyond them several small, white moons formed a backdrop. The scene fascinated Vaddi, so much so that for a moment he was unaware that Cellester was nudging him.

"Stay here but keep one eye on those around us," said the cleric. "We cannot assume we are not being watched."

"Where are you going?"

"I would see more of the travellers. No doubt most of them are bound for Thrane on business or local politics. If the Claw has agents aboard, I doubt they'll risk conflict in the sky, but it would pay to be vigilant. The danger will certainly come when we disembark."

Vaddi watched the cleric move across the crowded deck. No sooner had Cellester gone than Vaddi's attention was snared by another movement as one of the passengers also left the deck. Clad in a thick cloak, also wearing a hood, this figure's leaving could easily have been a coincidence, but Vaddi felt deeply uneasy. Trusting his intuition, he got up up, hugging himself in the cold air, and followed.

At the end of the deck, narrow steps led down on to the main forward deck, where another crowd had gathered, most of the people there chatting or simply enjoying the spectacular view of the skies. Vaddi stood by a rail and could easily follow Cellester's movements down below. The cloaked figure mirrored those movements. There was no doubt that he was following the cleric.

Vaddi went below, closing in on the figure. Ahead, Cellester had gone to talk to a small group of men—traders by the look of them. The cloaked figure edged closer, unnoticed by the cleric. Vaddi himself was now mere feet away. As the figure stood by the ship's rail, feigning interest in the skyline, Vaddi took his opportunity to move up directly behind him. He slid his dirk from within his own cloak and, masking his movement, gripped the belt of the stranger's cloak with one hand, pulling him close and pressing the tip of the dirk into his back.

"You show an undue amount of interest in my companion," Vaddi breathed, just loud enough for the stranger to hear him.

He felt the man stiffen and tightened his grip.

"Who are you and what is your business?"

"One who would protect you," came the whispered reply.

"Then show yourself, or would you prefer it if I took you to the airmen?"

The hood turned, enough for Vaddi to see the weather-beaten lines of the face within it and the thick, matted beard.

Vaddi gasped. "Nyam!"

"Softly," said the peddler.

"What are you playing at?" Vaddi still held the dirk hard against the peddler's spine.

"You are being watched. I was watching the watchers. Now you've exposed my cover."

"Watched by whom?"

"Agents of the Claw. This ship is crawling with them."

CHAPTER 5

High above the northernmost shores of the vast continent of Xen'drik, where the archipelago of Shargon's Teeth was washed by the tides of the Thunder Sea, a huge soarwing circled, its rider gazing down on the bleak terrain far below. He could discern a dozen rocky islands, some little more than jagged boulders piercing the topmost waves, their stones crumbling into the fury of the sea. The soarwing swooped down to the ragged clouds about the largest of them.

This was Urgal Shahiz, once the haunt of southern wizards and their hell-spawned sea demons, and as the rider plummeted he could see coiled shapes swimming around the curdled waters at its base—guardians of the bleak shores, endlessly watchful, ever hungry. The rider evinced no emotions, no fear, no awe, or any true understanding of pain. His face was expressionless, set in stone.

The central pile of Urgal Shahiz was infested with caves, linked by ledges, slick with the droppings of the soarwings, and it was to one such ledge that this solitary creature flew. Its hooked claws retracted as it landed and it drew in its long, serpentine neck. From between its shoulder blades the rider slipped down from the high perch and along the ledge, heedless of the drop and the winds, as though he was himself composed of them. The soarwing ducked under the rock overhang of the cave and went within.

The figure, wrapped in a black cloak, climbed a natural stairway in the rock almost to its pinnacle before entering a tall fissure there. Inside, where the wind could not reach, the figure descended another stair, one that had been hewn here by masons in times forgotten. Down, ever down, into the very gut of the tower the figure went, silent as a ghost. Light filtered from high above, but in this grim place it was almost an alien thing, an unnatural force in a realm where darkness and graveyard gloom were the true order.

In the heart of the tower, giants long ago had cut a circular chamber. Its walls were jagged, though its floor was polished smooth like marble. Around the rim of this echoing chamber a few cressets had been set, and within them burned the low flames of cold fire lamps sufficient to light the lower part of the chamber. It was empty, save for one object—a large throne-like seat, itself chopped out of the native stone. Its workings spoke of Xen'drik's past, of sorcerer and beast alike, intertwined in a mockery of love or hate, shapes that seemed to twist and turn, alive in the guttering light.

Within the confines of that great seat something coalesced, a knot of shadows. It thickened, shaping itself into a blurred form, night incarnate. Like the being before it, this shape too had features, but they were indistinct, shifting and flickering like the visage of a ghost. Silently the presence studied the figure that seeped like fog into the chamber. He saw the hood slide partially back from the figure's face, revealing a cold, emotionless expression, the eyes haunted, eyes of a being without a soul. This was one of the undead, a creature living outside the natural laws of man, a being who had once been a warrior, a proud knight. In exchange for dark powers that mocked the grave, this creature had forsworn the ways of men, all normal pleasures of the flesh and soul. He bowed before the stone seat of power to which he was forever bound.

"Your servant, Aarnamor, returns, Zuharrin," said the undead warrior, his inhuman eyes not meeting the gaze of the incorporeal entity before it.

The necromancer paused only briefly to savor his power over the lesser creature he had raised from death. "From Khorvaire?"

"Yes, lord. I did as you bade me. I was not seen. My shadow was not detected."

"What of the Orien heir? Indreen's brat?" The essence of Zuharrin pulsed with something akin to eagerness, the pits of his eyes deepening.

"He has left Marazanath, lord. He has taken a shadow path and slips through the traps set for him by the Emerald Claw."

"You are sure of this?" A tremor of annoyance stirred within Zuharrin's mind. The Claw! An invisible spider with a hundred legs, weaving its accursed intrigues across nation after nation. The time would come when he would have to address this infernal secret sect and bring it to heel. "Well?"

"I am, lord. Vaddi d'Orien is protected."

Zuharrin's form thickened like the gathering of a storm. "He has it with him then?"

"His father passed it to the youth as foreseen. Already he has used it to defy the Claw. One of their servants, the vampire Caerzaal, sought to snare him."

"Indeed? That creature will not be easily shrugged off. Caerzaal is dangerous. Watch for him. He is the most ruthless of hunters."

"My brothers keep watch as we speak, lord."

"There will be a time to strike. In a lonely place where the son of Anzar will be most vulnerable. Gather your brothers. Choose the moment wisely. The Claw must not best us in this."

Aarnamor bowed. In a moment the shadows on the throne had gone. The meeting was over. Aarnamor drifted up the steps into the night above, readying for another continent-spanning flight.

Vaddi and Nyam Hordath had returned to the stern of the *Cloudclipper*. They sat together, and both watched the other passengers about them.

"Why are you following us and why should I believe you are here to protect me?" said Vaddi.

Nyam leaned close, scratching his beard. "No point in keeping the truth from you now, I suppose."

"How long have you been watching?"

"I waited at Rookstack. I heard that Marazanath was under attack. Your father knew it was always possible. Over the past few months, he believed an attack likely and began to make preparations, but even he was caught by surprise. Our sources said the attack was still some months away. The Emerald Claw's machinations grow bolder."

Vaddi felt a stab of unease. "You served my father?"

"Since your mother died. She was from a great elf family, the powerful line of Dendris, once said to have served the dragons themselves."

Vaddi kept his thoughts to himself, but he knew that there was dragon blood in the line of Dendris and thus in him.

"There has been much inter-breeding between men and elves. I was married to an elf myself. She, too, was from the line of Dendris and a cousin of your mother."

Still Vaddi did not comment. How much of this could he believe?

"Indreen was worshipped by Anzar and loved by many of the Oriens, but others were suspicious. It's always the same with these Houses! Power mad, the lot of them. They like pure bloodlines. You must have come across such prejudices."

Vaddi nodded.

"The line of Dendris has been the protector of a certain object of power for centuries."

Again Vaddi said nothing, but it was clear what Nyam was referring to. Of course, the peddler had seen it on the island.

Nyam's voice dropped to a whisper that only Vaddi heard. "It is named Erethindel. Since it was made, the line of Dendris has kept it safe, in the hands of a secret sect called the Keepers of the Horn. Indreen was a Keeper."

"And you?"

"I serve the Keepers. My ties with the line of Dendris are strong, even though my family was killed in the Last War." Nyam looked away, seemingly studying the passengers, though Vaddi could sense a shadow within him.

"What is the horn?"

"I believe it is really a horn—a unicorn's. The totem of your House is a unicorn, is it not?"

"Yes." Vaddi resisted the urge to reach inside his shirt to touch it. How was he to believe this peddler, who was perhaps not a peddler?

Nyam seemed to read his mind. "Why should you believe me, eh? Try this, Vaddi. The horn has runes. Have you read them?"

Vaddi frowned, shaking his head.

"They are in the elf-speech of Aerenal and say:

Who holds this horn
Will hope and honor see
Unless his heart
Shall harsh and hardened be.

When you are alone and can read them, you'll know the truth of what I say."

Vaddi wanted to ask him why he had waited until now to reveal himself, but he heard Cellester approaching.

"Say nothing of this to him," Nyam whispered.

Cellester was pushing his way through a group of passengers and when he saw Nyam, his eyes turned suddenly cold. He sat stiffly beside Vaddi, his manner unruffled.

"I changed my mind." Nyam grinned. "My business will take me to Thrane, now that I've a healthy sum of money to support my ventures. You've no objection to my company? I fear you may require it."

Cellester's look grew even colder. "You think so?"

"I think that the Claw has not done with you."

Vaddi saw the cleric tense, as if someone had slipped the point of a dirk under his cloak.

"Their servants are here," Nyam added, "in numbers."

Cellester nodded. "There are worse things ahead of us. We should be heading a point or two south of west, but this craft is slowly edging round to the *south* toward the Talenta Plains. I suspect the pilot is under threat. Several of the Lyrandar airmen are no longer in evidence."

"You think they have . . . disembarked prematurely?"

In spite of Nyam's turn of phrase, Vaddi felt only horror at the implication.

"Why should you help us?" Cellester asked Nyam bluntly.

"I have no choice. I fought with you on the island. Now the Claw will have marked me. They will consider me your ally. If I'm under threat, I'd rather have you and your not inconsiderable skills at my side."

"Just don't expect to be paid again," Cellester said.

"My continued existence would be reward enough."

Vaddi said nothing but wondered why Nyam did not confide in the cleric as he had in himself. Did he not trust him?

"I would feel safer," said Cellester, "if we spent the rest of the journey in the helmsman's tower, with the last of the airmen. If we can secure ourselves in there, we can defend it from attack and help the pilot keep the ship on course. Let us make our way there slowly. And be ready to draw your steel."

One by one, they each wound their way to the small tower under the huge ring of fire that was the elemental powering the ship's flight. Flames crackled in that perfect circle, writhing and twisting, like no other fire that Vaddi had ever seen—a truly living entity. Outside the pilot's area, a number of men stood in a knot, arms folded as if casually passing the time. But as the cleric and then Nyam approached, they tensed, their eyes betraying their true intent.

"This area is restricted♦growled one of them above the roar of the flames. They were very evidently not airmen.

"I would have a few words with the pilot," said Cellester.

The men had formed a barrier across the doorway. Their leader shook his head.

Cellester slipped his sword from its sheath. "Stand aside."

It was the signal for them all to draw arms. Cellester moved in a blur. His swordpoint tore through the throat of the spokesman and cut into the neck of another in one lightning strike. The first went down and began writhing in a growing pool of his own blood. The other shrieked, clutched at his wound, and backed quickly away.

Others pressed Cellester at once, only to find the blade of Nyam blocking their attack. He cut through the wrist of one of them and wounded another before the group could recover themselves. They shouted, and Vaddi heard a rush behind him. He turned. Two more men were charging them from behind. His own weapon plunged into the chest of the first assailant. Vaddi had no compunction about killing these men if they served the Claw. In his mind he still saw the fall of his father and the death of Menneath.

Nyam hacked down another of the men and Cellester kicked open the door to the pilot's room, smashing aside a defender as he did so. There were two others in the room, clearly forcing the Lyrandar pilot to steer the *Cloudclipper* where they willed under threat of steel. They turned to face Cellester as he burst in on them and their swords clashed, sparks flying in the confined space.

Vaddi and Nyam found themselves the subject of an onslaught as a score of swordsmen came at them. Steel sang as they defended themselves. Vaddi ducked under the sword of one assailant and ran home his dirk, but as the man fell, he pulled Vaddi to one side. Nyam tried to step in to defend him, but they had underestimated the opposition. There were far too many. Something cracked up against Vaddi's temple and he felt the darkness rushing up to meet him like a black wave. His last vision was of Cellester being dragged out of the pilot's room, swords at his throat.

* * * ◉ * * *

Intense pain woke Vaddi. He gently fingered his temple and his hand came away bloody. In the dim light he could see a figure slumped beside him.

"How's your head?" came Nyam's voice.

"Bursting. Where . . . ?"

"The cleric fights like a cornered wolf. I took a few out and then they decided that shutting us up below deck was their best bet for a safer voyage. The cleric's in a smaller hole next door—doubtless knocked senseless, too."

"They want us alive," said Vaddi, slowly shaking himself awake.

"Oh, yes. Very much so. You and what you carry. The cleric and me for . . . well, I suspect Caerzaal will have thought up a suitable ending for us."

Vaddi's fingers touched the horn in the darkness, feeling the embossed runes upon it. "It's still here. Why did they not take it?"

"I doubt these hired thugs could. Its power is attuned to your blood. For another to touch it, he would have to wield great power—certainly more than any of this lot possesses."

"The Emerald Claw," Vaddi breathed. "I know so little about it. There were muted tales at Marazanath. As children, we thought they were myths."

Nyam leaned back in the darkness with a snort of disgust. "Yes, the Claw seems insubstantial as mist, but it is very real. It has infiltrated so many places yet is always hard to confront. The religion and philosophy behind its Order is the Blood of Vol. You've witnessed its disgusting powers. Its adherents worship an ancient line of undead, believing it to be the true path to divinity. And they use blood in their rituals to sustain their power and immortality."

"Caerzaal is one such servant?"

"Yes. Blood is power. You carry the Crimson Talisman, which he craves. If its power could be corrupted to serve the Claw, to infuse their undead servants, it would give them unthinkable resources."

"The Claw's agents stirred up the rabble army and the undead warriors and took Marazanath, my family, so that Caerzaal could win the talisman?"

"Never underestimate it, Vaddi. The Keepers have kept it safe for centuries. Its true powers are untried. Our view is that they should remain so."

Vaddi listened to the distant hum of the elemental fire that powered the ship. Could he trust this peddler? How could he know he was not working for his own ends?

"And what of Cellester?" he said at last, lowering his voice. "What do you know of him?"

"A strange one. He, too, has power. He seems like an ally."

"But you don't trust him?"

"My life has taught me to be very cautious."

"My father trusted him. Before I was born, Cellester exchanged his loyalty to his Church for service to House Orien. My father said that Cellester held his Church to be one of falsehoods and treachery, riddled with corruption."

"He served the Church of the Silver Flame, the church militant, did he not?"

Vaddi was surprised that Nyam knew this but did not comment. "Yes. I know little about it, although it is renowned for its hatred of the Claw."

"Indeed. But power corrupts all but the most devout. Even in Thrane, where the Church has its seat of power, there are those who put themselves and their own profit ahead of the Church's cause. The celebrated paladin Kazzerand himself is one such creature. Publicly he is loyal to the Church, but privately he builds his own empire. He was no friend to your father. Don't be surprised if Marazanath becomes his. The rabble army won't hold it for long."

Vaddi was about to press Nyam for more information, but

there was a sudden lurch of the ship, as if it had either hit a freak air current or been struck by some other force. There were distant shouts.

"How long was I unconscious?"

"Two days and nights. It's dawn out there."

"No wonder I'm so hungry. What's happening?"

As if in answer, the door to their chamber rattled and shook. They both got to their feet, conscious of the fact that they had been stripped of their weapons. In a moment the door groaned and then three of its panels snapped in half and the door banged in on its hinges. A figure was limned in the pale wash of dawn. It was the cleric.

Nyam chuckled, reaching for his broad hat, which had been thrown into the room with him.

"Cellester!" said Vaddi.

"No time for explanations. Follow me and find yourselves some fresh blades."

The ship seemed to be wallowing like a sea vessel in heavy waves. Nyam and Vaddi were quick to follow the cleric along the narrow corridor. There was no sign of any guards.

"The ship is under attack," Cellester said. "Our erstwhile captors are all up on deck, fighting for their lives."

"Attack?" Nyam gaped. "From whom?"

"We must be well out over the Talenta Plains," said Cellester, "so my guess is we've run into a war party of halflings."

"Is that good?" said Vaddi.

Nyam grimaced. "Uh, probably not."

They made their way cautiously to the steps up to the first deck.

"They'll raid anything and anyone crossing their lands. All craft are fair game to them. They're their own masters, but they won't have any sympathies with us. Cellester is right. We'll need fresh swords!"

A shout of pain from above presaged the appearance of one of their captors, a burly fellow who came tumbling down the wooden steps, his neck and chest riddled with arrows.

"Those are indeed halflings arrows," said Nyam.

The man crumpled, eyes wide in death, sword clattering beside him.

"I'll take this one." Nyam lifted the blade.

Gellester nodded. "Very well. You can lead us up."

"Wouldn't it be safer down here, until the dust has settled?"

"Not if the ship plummets to earth."

Nyam's grin melted. "Uh, no. The halflings wouldn't know how to fly it if they did take it over. They'll just strip it of anything of value and abandon it."

They went up to the deck to find absolute chaos. A dozen of their captors were dead, riddled with arrows, some with short spears pinning them to the deck. What few other passengers had survived had evidently gone below. Vaddi and Gellester took the nearest fallen swords and turned to look out at the skies around the ship.

Vaddi drew in his breath. There was a swarm of large, bird-like reptiles surrounding the *Cloudclipper*, and riding them, mostly singly but in some cases in twos and threes, were the ferocious halflings of the Talenta Plains. Whooping and yelling with evident delight, they were unleashing wave after wave of arrows into the defenders of the ship, their extraordinary dexterity in both flying and fighting amazing to behold. Vaddi had to duck quickly to avoid being pinned to the deck.

"Glidewings!" said Nyam.

Vaddi was fascinated by the creatures, which had long, toothy beaks and a head crest, with sharp talons that looked capable of dragging a man off his feet. The halflings sat astride them on exotic saddles, wrought with the most exquisite decoration. But Vaddi had no time to take any more in as a score of the halflings had already leaped aboard and were engaged in a ferocious fight with the warriors. Although they were not much bigger than human children, the halflings tore into their opponents with such abandoned enthusiasm that the warriors struggled to keep them at bay. The entire deck seemed to be covered in clashing combatants.

"Are you sure we wouldn't have been better off below?" said Nyam.

But there was no time to discuss it. A group of halflings rushed at them, blades swinging. Vaddi met the first of them. This was so very different to the training ground. He was facing a swift death. He knew that. The halflings who cut at him wasted no time in going for a kill, and Vaddi realized there was not a great deal of finesse to his opponent's method of attack. Vaddi picked his moment, sidestepped, and plunged his own steel into the halfling's gut. It fell, only to be replaced by another.

The battle raged for long minutes, and although the three of them cut down many halflings, covering their backs as they fought, they knew that a prolonged attack would be impossible to stem.

"Can you see what's happening in the pilot's tower?" Cellester shouted during a brief lull.

"Our captors still hold it," called Nyam. "Locked themselves in, I think."

"If the halflings kill the pilot and the crew, we're finished!"

They redoubled their efforts to cut through the halflings, but most who had boarded the craft were more intent on looting than on continuing the fight. Most of the warriors were dead or too badly wounded to fight on. The glidewings still surrounded the craft, but their fliers were no longer raining down arrows.

Cellester led his companions to the pilot's tower. The door had been ripped aside, leaning at an angle across the deck. Three of their original captors were inside with the pilot. They raised their blades, expecting to be attacked.

The leading warrior spat. "One step more, cleric, and the pilot dies."

"Then we all die," said Cellester.

"Yes, we all die."

Nyam pushed forward. "Somehow I don't think your paymaster would take much pleasure from that. We're wanted alive."

"You want to stay alive, you leave the pilot to me."

Nyam was about to say something more, but Cellester pulled him back. "Leave it. We gain nothing by continuing the fight here."

Vaddi called to them both. "The halflings! I think they're going."

Nyam turned and laughed. "Yes, they've done well. Everything that wasn't bolted down will have been filched. Down!"

This last came just in time, for as the halfling raiders leaped back on to their mounts, their companions unleashed yet another hail of arrows, yelling and howling with glee. They circled the ship twice, then as one, swept up into the blue vault, diving downwards toward the plains in a perfect formation.

Vaddi stood at the rail and watched them go, marvelling at their mastery of flight, for all their barbarism. For the first time, he saw the landscape far below, where grass-covered hills stretched in every direction west and northward, but to the east and curving slightly southward the hills turned to desert. To the east, rising into the clouds, a wall of mountains rose up as the ship flew ever closer to it. He sensed a movement beside him.

"The Endworld Mountains," said Nyam. "We've come a long way south and eastward over the plains. That long stretch of sand at their feet is the Blade Desert."

"Where do you think they are taking us?"

Nyam shrugged. "There are some inhospitable regions ahead of us. If we cross the Endworld range, we'll head into Q'barra, land of the lizardfolk. Not a pleasant prospect. To the far south is Valenar, your mother's homeland, but I cannot believe they will take us there."

Vaddi turned as Cellester joined them, looking about him at the body-strewn deck. "I doubt if any of the airmen are left alive, and there are no passengers that I can see. These mercenaries planned to crew the ship themselves. They're pirates, so they're capable of it. Except that the halflings have wreaked havoc among them."

"How many are alive?" said Nyam.

"Barely enough."

"I have no skill in these matters. Have you?"

Cellester shook his head. "The pilot's powers of telepathy must be thinly stretched. To control the elemental will be very hard." He looked up at the fiery ring surrounding the centre of the ship. It burned evenly, for the moment apparently unaffected by the conflict.

"I know one thing," said Nyam, slipping his sword into his belt. "I'll die of starvation before anything else unless I find something to eat. Let's hope the halflings have left us a few crumbs."

He wound his way across the deck and disappeared down below without further ado.

"For a peddler," said Cellester, "he wields a lively blade."

"You trust him?"

"No. Nor must you, Vaddi."

"Who does he serve?"

"I don't know, but I have my suspicions." Cellester looked out over the rolling plains, pulling his cloak tighter against the cold air. "We are far from Thrane, but it may be better if we go elsewhere. Kazzerand will be waxing strong now that Anzar is dead. If he has any part in your being hunted, we'd do better to go south. To Valenar, perhaps."

"My father had no love for Kazzerand. He told me the warlord was a jealous rival."

"He is not a man to be crossed. Once, as a young man in the Church, I met with his disfavor. I suspected Kazzerand of intrigue and would not follow the path of his ambitions. Anzar, too, spurned his demands. I left Thrane and came to your father's Hold, setting aside the Church and all the hypocrisy I had found within it."

Vaddi was surprised by the cleric's admission, which seemed to have a ring of sincerity about it. "What is it that Kazzerand wants?"

"What do they all want? Power. They go to such lengths. It would not surprise me to learn that Kazzerand has had dealings with the Claw itself. You understand its influence, Vaddi?"

"I saw Marazanath fall."

"Yes, but you have the talisman safe?" The cleric's voice had fallen again.

Vaddi nodded. "The vampire lord may desire it, but I saw the dread of it shake him as a dog shakes a rat."

"He craves it. The Emerald Claw would sacrifice armies to win it, as you have seen."

"What of this Caerzaal? You have crossed his path before?"

"Yes, though he did not recognize me. Years ago, in Thrane, when I was younger and more naïve, I saw him. He was already a paladin, steeped in power, a worthy crusader in the name of the Silver Flame. Yet you see in him now how absolutely the Blood of Vol corrupts! He has passed over entirely into the service of the Claw, trading his soul for a kind of immortality."

"You said he will follow us?"

"For certain."

"Is he, then, an agent of Kazzerand?"

"It is possible, though Caerzaal prefers to think of himself as an independent force," said the cleric. "It is a weakness in him. To drink the Blood of Vol is to become the slave of the Claw. You have no other choice."

"Then we should avoid Thrane?"

"For now." He attempted a smile. "But we may have little say in the matter."

Further discussion was at an end, for Nyam had again appeared, now carrying over his shoulder a sack. With a triumphant grin he set it down upon the deck in front of them, opened it, and proceeded to take out some flagons, loaves of bread, cheese, and a number of crusty cakes.

"Not a king's repast, but enough to fill a hungry belly!" He laughed, uncorking a flagon and sniffing at the contents. He grimaced, tossing the flagon over the side of the craft in disgust. "Gone off! Thankfully there is fresh water."

They ate their fill, Vaddi realising just how ravenous he was. The pain in his head began to abate at last.

"So what's the plan?" said Nyam, wiping his lips.

Cellester was looking up at the fire ring of the elemental.

"Something wrong?" said Nyam, sensing the cleric's unease.

"Yes. The elemental. It is restless. See how it shimmers. The patterns are changing."

"Meaning what?" said Vaddi.

"By the Rings of Siberys," Nyam gasped. "It looks as if it's preparing to take flight! It's abandoning us!"

"If it does," said Cellester, "the ship will go down like a stone."

CHAPTER 6

They inched their way over the body-strewn deck to a point where they could watch the pilot's tower without being seen. They could hear the raised voices of the remaining four mercenaries arguing. The ship gave a lurch and there were loud curses.

"Turbulence," said Nyam. "Common, this close to the mountains."

Vaddi looked to his left and frowned. The huge mass of the Endworld range loomed very near now.

"If they are trying to get the pilot to take the ship into the mountains, they are fools," said Cellester. "Without a full crew, it's suicide."

As if to underline his point, the ship lurched again. Vaddi looked up at the ring of fire. It crackled and fizzed in anger. It knows, he thought.

"We'd do better without these unwanted guests," said Nyam.

Cellester frowned. "You want to risk an attack?"

"Use the turbulence. Left to himself, the pilot could steer us down on to the desert."

"Vaddi?"

73

Vaddi nodded, pulling out his sword. They edged still closer. The mercenaries were concentrating on the way ahead, crowded around the pilot. He brought the ship around in a slow bank, but as he did so, another fierce gust of wind struck it like a heavy wave. In the confined space of the pilot's room, the men staggered.

Cellester and Nyam braced against the shudders of the craft and moved forward in silence, Vaddi close at their heels. They waiting for another lurch, and when the men inside stumbled, Vaddi and his companions leaped inside. Vaddi chopped two of them aside and drove his dirk into the belly of a third. One of the men made a stab for the pilot, his knife scoring a deep gash in his side before Cellester could plunge his sword down to finish the mercenary.

The last of them scrambled to his feet and drew a knife before Nyam could get to him. He raised it to kill the pilot. Vaddi made to deflect the blow, but another sudden lurch of the ship thwarted him and his dirk clanged harmlessly against the ship. For a moment it seemed that Vaddi himself would perish as the mercenary swung round on him, blade inches from his neck, but Cellester's sword struck the hand off at the wrist at the same moment that Nyam ran his own weapon through the mercenary's neck.

Vaddi rolled over and up, shaking his head in relief.

Cellester was beside the pilot, whose face was a mask of agony. "Can you get us down?"

The man's side pumped blood where the knife had opened him, possibly fatally.

"We're being drawn into the mountains. Air currents here are dangerous. Like whirlpools. The elemental wants to be free. Too strong for me. My control is weakening. I think they . . . ring was damaged in the attack. I can feel the elemental struggling to break free."

The ship was dropping, parallel with the lower slopes of the massive range. The pilot was trying to turn the prow back out toward the desert, though it was a gradual process. Too steep a turn would flip the whole ship over.

"I can't hold her," he said, sagging back, eyes closing against the pain.

"She's turning," Cellester encouraged him, watching the rocks below coming ever closer. "Just keep to . . ." But the cleric realized that the man's life had leaked out of him. Cellester swung round to look up at the ring of fire.

The elemental, freed of the mental link with the pilot that bound it to its task, flared. For a moment a face shaped itself in the flames and gave an exultant roar, then the being tore free of the encircling metal frame and soared away in a shower of sparks. The *Cloudclipper* was propelled forward like a bolt from a crossbow, bouncing over the airstreams from the mountains.

"The desert—!" cried Nyam.

The words were ripped from him as the ship dropped lower, its prow dipping dangerously. The three men had to scramble back into the central deck and grip its rails for fear of being hurled out into the ether. Above them the metal arms that had banded the elemental pulled loose, snapping with a loud crack. The frame tore backwards behind the ship, lost overboard. Whole sections of the hull rippled and split. The wing-sails to either side of the ship caught the air, but bereft of propulsion they were still falling at an alarming rate.

The prow dipped, pointing itself at a narrow gorge between two towering peaks at the very edge of the mountains. They were close to the ground now but skimming through the air at a dangerous speed.

The ship's lower keel crashed into the tallest trees and shrubs, funnelled along the gorge, bouncing and bucking, more sections ripped from it, catapulting backwards. Deep into the trench the airship went, the hull completely folding. Clouds of dust shrouded her as she ground to a halt, wedged among boulders and felled trees.

Vaddi and Nyam were flung forward, draped over the last of the pulped spars, coughing as the dust clouds enveloped them. Vaddi lurched to his feet, wiping blood from his nose.

"I feel as though every bone is broken," he gasped.

Nyam, also thick with dust, rose beside him.

"Sovereigns, Vaddi, are we alive?" he said.

He had retrieved his feathered hat from the wreckage and began dusting himself down with it. They watched in amazed relief as Cellester emerged from another jumble of wood and debris, shaking himself.

"We'd better get off the wreckage," said Cellester. "It's about to fall apart completely."

They clambered through the mangled carcass of the groaning ship, crossing on to the rocks and scree of the mountain foot, watching the ship as she collapsed under her own broken weight. A few bent fingers of superstructure poked up from the remains as silence fell again on the remote gorge.

Cellester indicated a rough passage through the boulders. "That way is south. We can travel until nightfall and then set up a camp. There should be water."

Nyam reached inside his voluminous robe and tugged out a small sack. "And food. I thought we might need this."

Vaddi chuckled. "You had more presence of mind than I did."

"I've spent my life scavenging," Nyam said. He showed his teeth in a vivid smile. "No point surviving a disaster like that and then starving to death."

"Try and keep under cover or in shadow," said Cellester. "We have a long journey if we're to try for Valenar, but there'll be no allies here. There are worse things than marauding halflings in these mountains."

They followed the broken course of the gorge out into a wider one, trying to avoid any path that would drive them eastward up into the lower mountain slopes or westward into the desert. Zigzagging through endless boulders and sharp rocks, they made slow progress but for the most part were heading southward. It was exhausting work, made even more so by the oppressive atmosphere, for apart from the occasional muttering of a stream as it chopped down from the heights, swallowed up by the rocks, all was silent. There were no birds, no hint of wildlife.

Eventually, sharing some of Nyam's food and a brief drink from a stream, Vaddi commented on this. "Is this place cursed? There's a strangeness to it."

"I've seen regions like this." Nyam sniffed and tossed aside a well-chewed bone. "Results of the War. There are numerous places where warped magic has wrought its evils, spells that have clashed and released energies that have torn out the heart of the land. This is one such place. It is like a canker. I'll wager if you tried to grow something here, it would either die or turn into a sick mutation."

Vaddi shook his head. It was no way to buoy the spirits, though Nyam had spoken honestly enough.

Cellester nodded. "The sooner we cross to healthier regions, the better."

They moved on as quickly as they could, in shadow now as the sun had dipped low towards the western edge of the plains. There would be no more than an hour of daylight left to them.

Cellester stopped again, squinting up at a low ridge to their left. He studied it for a while. "There may not be any life here now, but it seems that was not always the case."

Vaddi craned his neck, but all he could make out was a stone landscape, tiers rising up into the higher foothills. "What can you see?"

"The bones of an ancient city, but it must be so old that it has long since passed from the records of man. I know of no city in this wilderness."

Vaddi turned back to say something to Nyam, but the man had stopped in his tracks, his eyes wide, as though he had seen something his companions had not.

"Nyam, what is it?" Vaddi asked.

"There is one old legend, no more than a fragment," Nyam muttered, almost to himself. "If there is any truth in it, we must leave here with all haste." He could not disguise the sudden look of horror on his face.

Cellester came down to him. "Don't babble in riddles," he snapped. "What legend?"

"A city built by creatures that were here long before man, from the age of demons. A city called Voorkesh."

Cellester's eyes narrowed at the name. He swung round to study the outline he had seen. "Voorkesh does not exist," he said. "It is a legend, and whatever place that is up there, I sense no life in it."

They wasted no time in picking their way back down the incline toward the lower slopes of the valley. An eerie silence clung to the terrain.

"What is this legend?" Vaddi said to Nyam.

Without slackening pace, Nyam told him. "I've heard of Voorkesh from a number of sources. It was raised by demons that sought human form. They tampered with dangerous sorcery, taking human form and creating monsters to serve them and a legion of blood-hungry warriors, eager to raise up their long banished masters. In Voorkesh they were said to sacrifice their victims. Who knows what tunnels sink down from Voorkesh into the very heart of Khyber itself?"

They came to another stream. Beyond it, cresting a low ridge, several shapes were materialising, vague at first, but gradually forming. They were the color of earth, darkened by the night, hunched like men, their faces no more than smudges, but they had mouths and they gave voice now, speaking barely above a whisper.

"Welcome, strangers. You seem at pains to quit our lands, though you have barely arrived. Yonder, in the city, there is sanctuary, refreshment. Will you not rest with us?"

Already the shapes were coalescing into more tangible form until their transformation was complete. A dozen tall beings, dressed in rich robes, emerged from their shadow cocoons and smiled down at them.

Vaddi was too chilled by their presence to speak, but he sensed instinctively that these creatures were vampires.

"Keep still," said Cellester. "They'll not cross the water."

He was proven right in this, for the shapes came down to the far edge of the stream and halted, their eyes glancing down at it hesitantly, then away. But they smiled, and in their faces was a deceptive warmth, the promise of succor.

To Vaddi's horror, Cellester held out his hand. "We are pleased to be your guests. Come, cross the stream and take my hand as a token of our friendship."

The being that had spoken drew back, for to reach out to take the cleric's hand would have meant stretching across the stream. Instead the unblinking eyes regarded Cellester coolly.

"You do not trust us. We understand. The lands are full of danger."

"Step across the water."

"We cannot," sighed the creature. "It is a sorry tale. We are under an ancient enchantment. We are not allowed to leave the boundary of our city. The springs and rivers close us in. Jealous mages of old trapped us here."

"What is the name of your city?" said Cellester.

"Voorkesh."

Cellester had not let his gaze move from the beings across the stream, but he felt Nyam nudge him the ribs. He leaned toward him as the peddler at last found his voice.

"Beyond us, up in the rocks," he whispered. "More things are stirring. Not everything is on the other side of the stream. This is a trap."

Cellester bowed politely to the men. "We thank you, but our mission is urgent. We cannot linger. But on our return, perhaps we will visit Voorkesh."

With that he moved off down the bank, Nyam and Vaddi on his heels. From across the stream there came a hiss, rising shrilly. The vampires were already writhing, shifting, and changing into something not human. But they did not pursue, turning into shadow once more and sinking back into the earth. Cellester urged his companions to hurry.

They rounded a curve in the stream and found themselves at the head of a long, wider valley that fell into deeper darkness below them, where the stream fed a river that cut across part of the valley before plunging over a small fall on its way to the distant plains. Higher up the valley they could see Voorkesh much more clearly. Although night had dropped like a blanket over the mountains and the fields of rock debris, the ruins of the city were lit from below in a hellish green glow.

"We must cross the river," said Cellester, drawing his blade and uncovering his amulet. "Pray that the water will hold them back."

Vaddi pulled out his sword, but his free hand closed around the wrappings of the horn. If it had served to ward off Caerzaal and his undead, surely it would work against whatever haunted this realm.

As one the group came to an abrupt halt. Below them in the valley, daubed in a pale wash from the moons, something flowed across the broken terrain, amorphous shapes thickening into greater substance, drawing on the primal energies that throbbed up from the depths of their nightmare home. They slithered down to the broken valley floor and came upward hungrily, silent but redolent with menace. Huge, bloated shapes, writhing with tentacles, dragged themselves forward beside aerial horrors with great bat-like wings, claws unfurling, long tails whipping from side to side, poison dripping from numerous stings. Like a massive wave, this revolting legion rose up, eager to suck up into its embrace the three exposed figures.

"The river!" shouted Nyam, as they closed with its bank. "How do we cross it?"

The three of them stood a few yards from it, staring in horror at the raging torrent, for it was no stream, but a fast flowing, tumbling fury. Its waters churned in a gorge thirty feet below them, smashing into the rocks that poked up from its deep bed, white foam bursting skywards. It promised a quick death.

Cellester was looking downstream. The monstrous pursuit was gathering itself, a huge oncoming wave ready to engulf them. From its seething mass a single creature hovered forward, one solitary, malefic eye glaring at the fugitives, a mouth the size of a house opening to reveal a tunnel of scythe-like teeth. The cleric directed a bolt of white light into it, and as it splashed over the interior of that nightmare gut, the creature's eye bulged horribly before the whole monstrous shape burst, filling the air with sickly green light.

The wall of horrors paused for only a moment. Twisted limbs and claws groped for their prey, and the wave surged again, about to fall.

"This way!" Vaddi shouted, racing up along the precarious bank of the river. "There's a bridge!"

They raced for the bridge. It was partly down, but there was enough of a span to risk a crossing. Time had wasted the construction, cracked its arch and removed several of its stones. Vaddi dared not look back. He dashed on to the bridge. Beneath him something groaned and he knew that stone had tumbled into the raging white waters below. Even so he went on to the center of the span. There was a gap at the apex of the bridge, but terror spurred him, and he leaped across. More stonework crumbled and he thought he was doomed to plunge into the river, but he shifted his balance and flung himself forward.

On all fours, he turned. The wall of living nightmare flowed to within mere yards of his companions. The fang-filled mouths of abominations were almost closing over them, while in the maelstrom above them, scores of lunatic faces glared down, eager for the kill, but Nyam and Cellester made it to the bridge. Vaddi backed off, encouraging them to leap. They had no choice. Nyam came over and Vaddi caught his wrist, dragging him to safety as more stonework collapsed.

Cellester jumped, rolling forward, managing to hold his arm and the amulet aloft. The bridge was shaking as if in an earthquake as the monstrous tide surged forward, trying to funnel itself on to the narrow span of the bridge. The noise it made, its scores of mouths screaming, was deafening, the air filled with a thunderous cacophony of noise. Cellester waved the others back and they scrambled like crabs to the far side of the span.

The cleric backed slowly along the bridge, using the light from his talisman to keep the creatures at bay. The huge, amorphous mass hanging fifty feet over him paused, unwilling or unable to approach the holy light. Then the bridge went down, the whole of it collapsing, stone by stone. Cellester scrambled back to its far side, barely ahead of the gaping hole. Vaddi and Nyam reached for him and dragged him to safety. Opposite them, numerous creatures ripped from the writhing mass and wheeled out into emptiness before hitting the racing waters. There they exploded in bloody froth. The press of bodies forced more and more of the horrors over the edge of the bank. They slid and slithered, tumbled and plummeted, their screams and shrieks appalling.

"There's a narrow path!" said Vaddi, pointing to the ledge that had been hacked out of the gorge's side. It led up the valley into darkness.

Cellester nodded and the three of them wormed their way along it, while opposite them the shrieking of the monstrous tide showed no sign of diminishing.

❦ ❦ ❦ ❦ ❦ ❦ ❦

Overhead, clouds piled together to shut out light from the moons. All that they had now to guide them was a faint glow from the cleric's amulet. Behind them they heard a cracking of stone and a sudden rumble. The path had collapsed, like the bridge. The only way now was up the narrowing gorge. A massive wall of rock rose at its head, the foaming waters of the river bursting out of it as if from the mouth of an immense stone structure. The path itself was swallowed by another black opening.

As they came to it, they could see scores of carved faces in the stone, twisted and misshapen, a demonic warning.

"This is the only way forward," said Cellester.

The others said nothing, swords gripped tightly, and went into the darkness. There was a foulness about the air, a graveyard stench. The tunnel was narrow, twisting, turning, and confusing. They listened all the while for sounds of pursuit, but the horrors behind them did not seem to have crossed the river and ventured into the tunnel. Vaddi felt particularly uneasy. He was certain that the tunnel was gradually veering to the left, which meant it must be curving around *toward* the city.

After an age, they saw vague, greenish light ahead—an opening back into the open air and night. Cautiously they emerged to find themselves on another ledge with rock-hewn steps leading down to another bridge. It led across to Voorkesh.

Vaddi looked behind them to where the cliff face rose, sheer and glassy, no way up its smooth surface. Something on its ridge swayed and pulsed, some living entity, another foul guardian of this realm.

They saw clearly now the bizarre architecture of the city, its twisted piles. Its towers leaned at angles, linked by bridges that looked more like the frozen webbing of huge spiders. Windows gaped like misshapen, distorted mouths. Sculpted temple blocks suggested remote antiquity, a world before the time of men, where their denizens crawled or hopped but did not walk on two legs. All this was bathed in a green miasma of light that seeped upward from whatever existed below the city.

"At least it seems deserted," said Vaddi.

Nyam, who had said nothing for a long time, shook his head, his terror clear to see. They went down the dizzy stair to the bridge, and now they could hear something in the tunnel they had left, squeezing its bulk through it, snarling with hungry anticipation.

They crossed the bridge and entered the first street of Voorkesh. Every building was like a mausoleum, towering over them, exuding dark waves of malefic power. They could sense that they were being watched and weighed, but still there was no sign of attack, and the grim beings that had forced them to flee here had not followed.

"We dare not leave the city until dawn," said Cellester. "The creatures will have gone back to their lairs by then. We must find somewhere to wait. If we can just survive this place until the sun comes up . . ."

They came to a wide square, beyond which a grotesque structure rose up. Nyam shuddered. "We've been herded here for a reason."

As if in response to his words, a dozen figures appeared on either side of the building, though they seemed substantial. They crossed the square in silence. To Vaddi's horror they looked like the vampires they had encountered outside the city.

"Welcome, travellers," said the first of them—a tall, angular being, pale-faced and with remarkably piercing eyes. "In the temple, there is food and drink. You need have no fear here. The night is not a good time to be beyond the walls of Voorkesh."

The three men kept close to each other, following the figures, knowing that the streets were no longer empty. Other shapes waited there, possibly in significant numbers.

Inside the temple, its main chamber was huge, reeking with age. Colossal statues reared up, depictions of creatures unknown to man, intensely alien, their presence redolent with hostility. They had long, dangling tentacles, lower faces extended into claw-like mandibles. They glowered down at the puny beings that had invaded their chamber with jewelled eyes that flickered with scarlet light, reflected from the heaped braziers around the rim of the vault.

"Refresh yourselves," said the tall creature. He indicated a circular slab of granite, where food and drink had been spread.

"Touch nothing," whispered Cellester.

Limned in the flickering glow of the coals, more figures flowed forward from the ring of statues, silent as ghosts. Clad in long robes from head to foot, hairless and white as bleached bones, they were unmistakably undead. As one, they awaited some signal.

Vaddi could hear movement on the steps behind and below him. Very slowly he slipped his fingers inside his robe, brushing the wrappings of the horn. If they were to fight, he would unleash whatever power he could draw from it, no matter what the risks might be.

From somewhere beyond the ring of undead acolytes, a being came forward into the garish light, the sound of its boots echoing from the polished flagstones. The three men could feel its eyes upon them—a steel, cruel gaze. There would be no mercy here. Ancient evils had been stirred up by their coming.

The glow of the fires threw this creature's face into sharp relief. Each of them gasped. Vaddi drew back, a cold hand closing over his heart, for it was Caerzaal.

The vampire lord made a brief, mocking bow. "We meet once more. Our parting was all too swift." His feral teeth gleamed.

Beside him stood two other tall men, also dressed in black, long swords strapped to either side of them. By their white skin and scarlet eyes, Vaddi guessed that they, too, were vampires.

Vaddi watched, mesmerised by the tall figure as he strode forward. Like a serpent, the man's eyes were fixed on him, malignant and scathing.

Caerzaal came to within a few feet of the three travellers. "So little to say?"

Cellester's sword hovered inches from the vampire lord's chest. "This abduction will serve you ill," he said softly.

Caerzaal smiled, his teeth again gleaming, but in that smile there was only the promise of torment and pain. "I do not think so, cleric. I should have recognised you on the island, you who cast aside your faith in the Church. So many have, but why be opposed to this union? The Emerald Claw would embrace you and your companions."

"We spit upon the Emerald Claw," said Vaddi, the fury rising in him as he saw again this creature striking down his father, but he felt Nyam's fingers closing on his arm, restraining him.

Caerzaal laughed, a chilling, mocking sound. "Do you indeed? Not for much longer, son of Orien. Once you have taken the Blood of Vol, you will reconsider. You will give your power freely to us. You will wonder why it has taken you so long

to capitulate. You will luxuriate in new powers, new lifetimes."
His eyes dropped to Vaddi's chest, to where the horn lay hidden.
"And you will release the real power inherent in the Crimson
Talisman. It will be such a relief to you."

Vaddi considered drawing out the horn, knowing that
Caerzaal, for all his dominance here, was yet afraid of it, but
some inner voice warned him against it.

"You will taste its retribution before it ever bends to the
Claw's will," said Cellester.

Caerzaal turned upon him, eyes flashing with cruelty. "You
think so? You, who are but a *mock* friend to House Orien."

Cellester's swordpoint dipped closer to the vampire, but the
two guards beside Caerzaal moved with frightening speed, their
own blades crossed protectively in front of their master. Caerzaal stood beside them arrogantly, lips drawn back in scorn.

"Oh yes, Cellester, former servant of the Silver Flame.
Beguiled from that service by House Orien, or should I say,
its mistress?"

Vaddi could sense the fury within Cellester at those words,
the cleric's whole body tensing, as though he would fly at his
hated enemy. He would die instantly on the blades of the guards,
Vaddi was sure of that. His life meant nothing to Caerzaal.

"He was a fine servant to your mother, Vaddi d'Orien," the
vampire said, "but I am sure he has neglected to tell you that.
Oh, he served your father well enough and won plaudits for his
efforts. And Anzar's trust. But the cleric's *love* was reserved for
your mother. Why else do you think he hovered about Marazanath?"

Cellester's face had gone white with repressed fury, but he
did not speak.

"My mother was loved by many," said Vaddi, "and honored
by them."

Caerzaal laughed again. "Of course. I am sure you have faith
in this cleric. He has spent a lifetime courting that faith."

Again Vaddi felt the grip of Nyam's fingers.

"We are not here to bicker over such trivial things," Caerzaal said, turning his back on them and walking away. "The powers of Voorkesh are eager to spring the chains that bind them. There is an appointed time. Tonight, with the tenth moon in ascendancy, you will share in these new powers. You shall drink the Blood of Vol." He looked up into the dark vault overhead. "As that sacred light falls across the stone, we will indulge ourselves in a common destiny."

"You underestimate the power of the Crimson Talisman," said Cellester.

Caerzaal turned, lips drawn back in a sneer. "I think not. The boy will fill it with his blood, and we shall drink it. All those here. See! A hundred of them. All to be enriched as the horn fills and fills again. What warriors we shall become! What *gods!*"

"I will destroy you all first!" said Vaddi.

"No," said Caerzaal, shaking his head as though party to some deep secret. "No, you'll do as commanded. The price of refusal will be more than you or your two companions could bear. I promise you."

Without another word or glance, Caerzaal was gone. Before any of them could react, the two vampire guards used their swords to indicate that they should quit the chamber. In silence they were herded across its floor to another arched doorway, through it and up a spiral stair beyond. They climbed in sullen silence, far up inside the heart of the temple, until they came to a narrow corridor and a room leading off from it. They were thrust into this, the thick wooden door bolted behind them. A single lamp lit the circular room, which was completely devoid of furnishings or windows.

Nyam slumped down, back against the curve of the wall. "The tenth moon," he murmured. "Sypheros. Not a good omen. Caerzaal will call upon terrible forces."

Cellester was deep in thought. "It seems the Claw is active everywhere."

Vaddi sat down. "We have the talisman," he said hopefully.

"In this place, it would be dangerous to use it," said Nyam, looking at the cleric, who nodded in resigned agreement.

"What is the tenth moon?" said Vaddi.

Cellester shook his head. "I know very little of the Claw's methods or of its ceremonies, but they use astrological alignments in them and draw on very ancient powers. The tenth moon, Sypheros, has long been tied to the powers of Shadow. If Caerzaal would draw on the powers of Voorkesh, they will be frightful indeed. It may well be that if you try to use the horn or I my amulet their powers will be warped. You heard Caerzaal refer to the horn as the Crimson Talisman. Instead of countering his dark powers, it will enforce them. Your blood, Vaddi, will be tainted. If you use the horn, you will be playing into his hands."

"Read its inscription again," said Nyam.

Vaddi was reluctant to draw out the horn, but he did so cautiously and read the runes that were embossed upon it. He remembered Nyam's translation:

Who holds this horn
Will hope and honor see;
Unless his heart
Shall harsh and hardened be.

"The horn dispenses great power for good or for evil," said Cellester. "Caerzaal's heart is harsh. If he controlled the horn, he would use it to open gateways that have been locked for eons."

"Then do we simply submit to this ritual?" snapped Nyam. "Are we to be like goats of sacrifice?"

"Caerzaal spoke of the price of refusal if I do not obey him," said Vaddi. "What did he mean?"

Cellester shook his head, but Nyam snorted. "He will give you the dubious pleasure of watching the cleric and myself being subjected to the worst of his rituals. Nothing could prepare you for that."

CHAPTER 7

High above the Endworld Mountains the soarwing circled in silence, the beat of its wings no heavier than those of a moth, wrapped as they were in sorcery. Below, among the jagged peaks that poked up from pitch darkness into the light of the Eberron's moons, the massive saurian sensed the comings and goings of many creatures. The eagles that had wheeled here during daylight were in their secluded aeries, heads bowed against the night and the things that shifted in it.

On the back of the soarwing, Aarnamor studied the broken peaks. With a mental command, he brought his reptilian mount around in one last sweep, gliding downward. With uncanny, instinctive skill, the great shape wove its way between peak after peak, barely evading the naked fangs of rock where one touch would have sent the soarwing tumbling to its doom. Aarnamor, like the beast he rode, had sensed life below. For days he had used his supernatural skills to smell out the progress of the three travellers, tracking them to Voorkesh, the dread city that even he was wary of. He could sense the terrors that welled up from those ruins.

The soarwing dropped to the bizarre buildings, gliding to the uppermost tower of a central mausoleum. Weightless as a shadow, talons gripped, wings folded over so that in a moment it had become one with the building, invisible to all but a sorcerer's eye. Aarnamor whispered something to his mount then slipped from it like a ghost. He paused to listen, as if he could hear the very structure breathing beneath him.

Near the apex of the tower, he found a jagged crack in the ancient stonework and slid into it, lowering himself down, his body shifting like mist. All was darkness, profound and impenetrable, but the undead warrior used other senses developed by his master's sorcery, magic as old as these mountains. Every sound that came from within the building, deep down to its foundations, Aarnamor heard, analyzed, and considered. It was not long before he had learned what he needed to know.

He passed lower through dingy, curling passages until he came to a dusty landing. There was a light up ahead cast from cold fire. Evidently the servants of this city used this tower. He could smell their minions in force farther down below him.

Aarnamor moved down the passage like a stirring of air, one with the shadows. Ahead of him the passage opened. There was a room off it outside of which two guards stood, so motionless they might have been statues, but Aarnamor could sense the half-life within them. Like him, they were undead, but he knew them at once for the mindless reanimates of the Emerald Claw. Beings of a far lower order, they did not have his mental power. He stepped before them.

Zombies though they were, the undead reacted quickly enough, swords cutting the air inches from the intruder, but Aarnamor evaded them with lightning ease. His own blade rang against theirs, sparks hissing in the dim light. The first of the guards was about to cry out, but Aarnamor's weapon sliced through his windpipe and the creature's mouth hung slack. There was another clash of blades, but the contest was soon ended. Aarnamor's speed made him a blur. He decapitated the guards, and though their bodies stumbled about aimlessly, fingers groping at the air, they were useless. He waited, listening to the darkness of the spiral stair that led down from this place, but he heard nothing.

At the door to the room, he paused, slid back the bolts, and pushed the door inward very slowly. He sensed that the three men beyond were coiled like springs, about to launch themselves at him.

● ● ● ◉ ● ● ●

Within the room, the three men felt the coming of something inhuman. They heard the clash of blades then utter silence. The bolts slid and the door creaked open slowly. Vaddi drew back, fingers touching the talisman.

"Cellester," came a soft hiss from the shadows in the doorway.

"Who calls?" replied the cleric.

"The guards are disposed of. Put away your weapons." His voice was little more than a rasp, the breath of a corpse, but it was rich in power, almost hypnotic in quality.

Vaddi saw a great, bat-like shadow ease into the doorway, the light gleaming on his long blade. His face was wreathed in darkness, cowled, but the eyes were vivid yellow, like those of a predator. *Undead!* Vaddi knew at once. Was this yet another of Caerzaal's monsters?

"Aarnamor!" Cellester gasped.

"We have little time." The undead indicated that they follow him. "You must leave this cell with all haste."

Vaddi and Nyam exchanged stunned glances. Vaddi's mind raced. He could make no sense of this. Cellester *knew* this creature? All Vaddi's nagging doubts about the cleric returned, but there was no time for deliberation. Cellester urged them forward, clearly seeing an ally in the black-shrouded stranger.

Aarnamor led them down the passage, past the sprawled undead whose bodies still twitched and spasmed. The men paused only to avail themselves of the fallen swords. Beyond the passage was another door, which Aarnamor opened. A passage lay beyond and they traversed it, up more stairs. At the top of these stairs, a thick door barred the way, but Aarnamor unbolted it. Cool air swept down. Beyond was the uppermost circle of the tower.

"Go outside," Aarnamor said. "Hide there until dawn. Only then will it be safe to quit Voorkesh."

"What of you?" said Cellester.

"Already I sense pursuit. Caerzaal's fury rises like a furnace blast. He will know that two of his filthy minions have been cut down, and he will scent me. I will lead him and his rabble through this city and buy you time until dawn. Go! I will bolt the door and set spells to secure it. Later I will come to you."

Vaddi would have demanded more but had no opportunity to speak. They went out into the cold night and Aarnamor was swallowed by the darkness of the stair. The door shut, its bolts slid from within. There was a faint pulse of light beyond and it shuddered, melding into the stonework.

Vaddi turned to his companions who were looking out over the curved parapet to the city. In the skies overhead, the thin veil of cloud shifted, revealing several moons and the jewelled majesty of the Rings of Siberys. Drawn to this, Vaddi watched as one of the moons freed itself of cloud, a strange light bathing it.

"The Shadow moon," whispered Nyam beside him. "There is some vile significance to this, as Caerzaal threatened. He would tap these conjunctions and their powers. Do you feel the horn responding?"

Vaddi felt only dread.

"Do not touch it while this moon lasts," said Nyam. "It will lead Caerzaal to you—and worse, far worse."

Cellester drew his cloak more tightly about him. The others followed suit. Far below, in the canyons of the city, they heard eerie calls, the slithering movement of large creatures. They did their best to blend with the shadows of the parapet, willing themselves to become invisible.

The hours wore on slowly. Although nothing came to test the door that Aarnamor had closed with his sorcery, the city below was feverish with activity. Shrieks and cries rose up from below, mingling with the roars of creatures prowling the deepest avenues, as if they fought one another. There was a terrible frustration in those dreadful sounds. Overhead, the Shadow moon waxed, spreading its terrible light across the stone tower where the three fugitives squatted, pressed to the stone, their cloaks covering them. They felt exposed, certain to be discovered, and although they heard the constant flapping of wings in the skies and ghoulish cries no more than a few feet above them, they were not touched.

Vaddi yearned to question Cellester. The being called Aarnamor had saved them—there was no question of that—but he was undead. No servant of Caerzaal or the Claw, yet it made Vaddi doubly uneasy.

He gave a sudden jerk and realized that he had been on the edge of sleep. Nyam was gently shaking him.

"Dawn," whispered the peddler.

Vaddi felt a flood of relief, knowing that daylight would be fatal to the vampire and his nest of servants.

Cellester rose, watching as the sunrise began to pick out the towers and roofs of the city, inching across it like a pale tide. The threatening darkness withdrew, a malignant force draining deeper into the depths of Voorkesh—at least for a time.

"Are we to go back through the temple?" Nyam asked.

"Too dangerous," said Cellester, studying the outer walls of the tower.

"Then how do you propose we quit this tower?"

"We will climb down," said Cellester calmly.

"We have no rope and—"

"There is a span crossing to another roof. We will keep to the roofs for as long as we can, until we come to the edge of the city. Then we will go into the mountains and eventually back to the Talenta Plains."

Nyam's eyes bulged. "Are you mad?"

"Would you rather wait for another night and risk Caerzaal's fury when he finds you? Stay here if you wish, but Vaddi and I will climb down."

Nyam gaped at Vaddi, who could not help but grin. "Lesser of two evils by far," he said.

Cellester pointed below. "The tower is old and badly weathered. See. There are enough hand and footholds to get us down to that span. We'll be in open daylight the whole time."

Nyam grimaced.

"I'll lead," said the cleric. "You follow, peddler. Vaddi, bring up the rear."

Vaddi nodded. The descent held no terrors for him. The sheer walls of the coastal cliffs that he had grown up climbing had been far more dangerous than this. He was more concerned for Nyam, whose terror was evident.

Like three spiders, they went over the parapet and down the tower's side. Cellester had been right, for the stones were pocked and loose, affording many footholds, though here and there they tore free or crumbled to dust. Nyam slipped at one point, but Cellester held him, swinging him back to the wall, where he clung like a limpet before finding the courage to move down.

❦ ❦ ❦ ❦ ❦ ❦ ❦

For an hour, with the sunlight mercifully strengthening, they picked their way over the roofs, along crumbling stairs and across walls, some of which toppled loudly into the streets below after their passing. They said little to each other, forced to concentrate on the perilous crossing of Voorkesh. All the while they could feel the city's malice, like the hunger of something animate, as though somewhere in that maze its claws would draw them in.

They could see the city's boundary. Shadows fell across the last square to a collapsing wall—the way to freedom. They climbed down a final set of stone steps and paused at the edge of the shadows.

"Can you feel anything?" Nyam asked the cleric, who seemed to be the most attuned to the pulse of the city.

"Something is watching us. Draw your blades. Make for that gap in the wall. Fast."

As one they made a dash across the square, their feet drumming on the stones, the sound echoing around the buildings, like a summons. Behind them they could hear deep croaking noises and something soft and wet slapping the ground in labored pursuit, but then they were through the gap in the wall and out into the rocky terrain beyond without looking back.

They were in a field of massive boulders and jagged scree, fallen from the steeply rising foothills ahead. Over them towered the mountains, the snows of their uppermost crags gleaming in the sunlight. Tired though they were, the three men ran into the rocks almost to the point of exhaustion, pausing at last to gather breath. They looked back in silence, but the terrain was motionless, bleached and dusty. Beyond the edge of mountain rubble, Voorkesh looked no more than a continuation of the desolation.

"We must . . . keep moving," Cellester said through ragged breaths. "By nightfall . . . we have to be . . . far away from here."

They followed him as he led the way into the foothills. They paused only to drink from the icy streams that tumbled down periodically from the higher slopes. Nyam shared out more of the food he had brought with him in the small sack, and they ate as they walked.

By midday they had put a significant distance between themselves and Voorkesh, heading south, parallel to the mountains. Far to their right, partially obscured by a heat haze, they could see the edge of the Blade Desert. Ahead was a narrow gorge, cutting more steeply into the mountains' skirts as its foaming river tumbled below.

"This should be a barrier to any creatures of Voorkesh that pursue us," said Nyam. "I'll feel easier once we cross it."

Cellester nodded. "Then we go south. Our journey to Valenar will be a long one. That desert stretches far to the south."

"Surely you don't mean us to traverse it!" said Nyam.

"No, we will need to keep to its edge."

Nyam was looking up at the mountains. "There is a better way to Valenar. The elves built a watchtower up in the mountains centuries ago. It is named Taeris Mordel, the Eye of the North."

Cellester frowned.

"We have come far together," Cellester said. Vaddi could see the tension in the cleric, his whole manner one of unease. "Vaddi and I have been glad of your aid. On the airship, your swordsmanship was worthy of a knight. But I wonder . . . why are you here?"

Nyam laughed. "Why am I here? You think I *chose* to fall from the sky in that airship? You think I *chose* to stumble into Voorkesh?"

"Why were you *on* the airship?" Cellester snapped. "You had no need. You were paid handsomely for delivering us to Scaacrag."

"I told you. I heard agents of the Claw plotting against you. I could hardly leave you to their evil ministrations."

"You're lying," said Cellester.

Vaddi knew that Nyam had his own reasons for not revealing his real motives to the cleric. Then again, he could not know for certain that Nyam had told him the truth.

"We have fought together—saved each other's lives!" exclaimed the peddler.

"Indeed!" Cellester snorted. "You are no common peddler."

"If I had not perfected a degree of skill with the sword, I would have died long ago. The world is filled with hostility. Trust is a rare commodity."

Vaddi looked at Cellester. "There is much that needs explaining," he said. "I have put myself in your hands, Cellester, as my father wished, yet we were taken from Caerzaal's clutches by that undead . . . *thing*. Aarnamor, you named him. And he named you. How is it you traffic with such creatures?"

Cellester's frown deepened. He was controlling his anger with difficulty, Vaddi could see. "I had hoped not to use him, but our needs were desperate."

"You summoned him," Nyam said bluntly.

Cellester nodded. "In my younger days as a servant of the Church, I fell in with other clerics who were tempted by the darker arts. Ultimately it led to my disillusionment and is why I left and found solace with House Orien in Anzar's service. Aarnamor was a warrior who sought power where he found it. He thought he could control his destiny. We were young and arrogant—and mistaken. Aarnamor's reward was living death. But he swore never to serve the dark agencies. He detests the Claw and all it represents." Cellester turned his anger on Nyam. "For which you should be thankful!"

Nyam shrugged. "I am alive."

Vaddi felt only deeper confusion. Both these men seemed to have his interests at heart, yet both could equally serve their own causes.

"We are agreed on one thing," said Nyam. "Our best course leads to Valenar, and we will need somewhere safe when night falls. If we go the way you suggest, cleric, we remain exposed."

"You want to go up into those mountains and search for a myth?" snapped Cellester. "You call that safe?"

"What does Vaddi say?"

Vaddi shook his head. Both choices seemed poor ones. "Maybe we should give the mountains a try, at least for a few days. If we don't have any luck, we'll head for the desert's edge."

Cellester looked as though he would argue further, but reluctantly he nodded, as if sensing that Vaddi was resolved. "Then let us hurry."

❂ ❂ ❂ ❂ ❂ ❂ ❂

They threaded their way through the field of broken stones and scree, gradually moving up to a place where a number of fallen boulders had spilled into the river. They crossed it and headed south along the edge of the mountains. With afternoon waning, Nyam pointed.

"An old road," he said. "It must be the way to the Eye of the North."

Cellester looked sceptical, studying the ground. It was a path of sorts, but evidently it had not been used for many years.

Vaddi could see that it went into a narrow mountain pass that closed over it like a fist. "You want to go in there?" he asked.

"We need shelter. I'm exhausted."

"Caerzaal's servants will be out in force by night," said Cellester. "We dare not be caught in the open, but there may be other dangers within the pass."

Nyam drew his sword. "I'd prefer a roof over my head."

A sound from behind them made them all turn. Somewhere in the folds of the rocks, on the edge of vision, something was stirring. The very rock wall shimmered, as though coming to life. As they watched, a huge chunk seemed to *melt* and slither down to the edge of the road.

It was enough to decide their next move and they sprinted for the cover of the gorge. Behind them the protoplasmic mass shook and formed itself into a shape some four feet tall and four across, the color of human skin. Vaddi looked back to see that this skin was stretching to reveal scores of eyes and mouths, teeth gleaming. The thing rolled forward like a massive amoeba, spitting gobbets and snarling, forming and re-forming like a living nightmare.

"Another of Voorkesh's horrors!" cried Nyam.

"I think not," said Cellester as they went into the shadows of the narrow defile. "It's a mouther. Let's just pray that it hunts alone."

The monstrous creature rolled with surprising speed after its prey, its scores of eyes wide in anticipation of feeding, its many tongues lashing, a spray of poison spittle flying in all directions. For a moment the narrow mouth of the defile impeded its bulk, but it merely adjusted its shape and came on, shrieking madly, the sound deafening in the confines.

"Can we outrun it?" Vaddi called.

They had come to a slightly wider passage. Far overhead the light was fading quickly and the first of the moons already rode the sky.

Cellester turned to face the mouther as it squeezed itself through the crevice. The cleric pulled back his sleeve and his amulet glowed as he uttered an incantation. Light formed around the amulet and then speared towards the mouther, striking it and exploding in a brilliant yellow wash. Hideous screams rang through the rock corridor from a score of mouths as the shuddering bulk began to shake, the walls of the passage groaning. Rocks and dust showered down from above and the stench of burning flesh hit the three fugitives like a rancid wave.

Gagging, they watched in horror as the mouther bubbled and frothed, its mass running like gelatinous fat. The rocks that fell upon it sank into the flesh, absorbed by it. Slowly the light from Cellester's bolt died. As it did, the mouther settled, again solidifying, but its eyes glazed, flopping forward on dead stalks, and the mouths hung slack, tongues blackened. The last of the rockfall subsided, leaving the way behind them blocked.

"Excellently done." Nyam laughed. "No one will follow us that way!"

Cellester shook his head. "Perhaps, but I would rather not have used power. It will draw our enemy to us." He turned to Vaddi. "Never use the horn, Vaddi. Not here. It served us well on the island, but in this dark region it will act only as a beacon to every horror that dwells here."

They fell silent again, moving on, winding through the defile, which admitted barely enough moon and starlight for them to see the way ahead. It might once have been a path, but numerous falls of rock had made it a treacherous passage now. In the skies, they could hear the occasional beat of wings and a screech as of something hunting, but they were not attacked.

They were far along the road when Cellester finally agreed to a rest, taking the first watch. Vaddi slept fitfully. He jerked to wakefulness as the first spars of sunlight cut through from above. He turned to find that Cellester had not slept, remaining on guard. Behind him, curled up like a discarded bundle of rags, Nyam snored as sonorously as though he were tucked up in an inn.

Vaddi could not help but laugh. "I wish I had his nerve."

Cellester grunted and shook the peddler.

Nyam came awake slowly, rubbing sleep from his eyes. He gazed up at the two figures standing over him. "Now what?" he grumbled. "I've only just got to sleep."

"You've been asleep for hours," said Vaddi.

Nyam sat up reluctantly. He rummaged in his sack and produced half a loaf and a chunk of cheese. They ate in silence then moved on.

Although they had a constant sense of being studied, as if the rock walls had eyes and ears, they heard nothing all day. The path wound tightly onward, rising up into the mountains. Although Cellester seemed uneasy, he was committed to this journey. They spoke little, pausing only to eat and sip from the occasional fresh spring that welled from the naked stone.

Slowly, every limb aching, they made their way up the mountain. Cut between two peaks, their path seemed more suitable for goats than men. Dust or rock falls choked it in places. It seemed long abandoned, but they remained on their guard.

Just as evening fell once more, Nyam found something on the smooth face of the rock wall ahead. Etched into it were runes—clearly the work of elves, though they seemed as old as the rock itself.

"This is indeed the way to Taeris Mordel. There will be a division in the path. Our way rises steeply."

"Let us make haste," said Cellester. "Our enemy has followed us, as I knew he would. We must be utterly silent. This whole region is like a living entity. The sorcery that spawned

Voorkesh has seeped out far into the very earth. Our every breath will be reported back to Caerzaal."

The path divided and they took the fork that became a steeply hewn stairway. It twisted like the burrow of a worm almost perpendicularly at times, until at last they were out on the open mountainside. A fresh breeze gusted. Clouds scudded across the heavens, shutting out the moonlight. Something stirred in them, shapes that flitted to and fro, ever hunting.

"There!" said Nyam, pointing. "Look at the highest point of the range. Taeris Mordel, the Eye of the North."

Vaddi could see across the void to where a tall finger of rock had been sculpted into what must be the promised watchtower. It stood out from the upper crags around it, black and lifeless as bone.

Nyam grinned, evidently much relieved to see it. "The elves carved it from the peak during the height of the Last War, when they fought bitterly against Karrnath."

"There are more runes here," said Vaddi, studying what he had found on another slab of rock. "Elven runes. I can read some of them. They speak of alliances between elves and men."

"Long ago, many elves fled to Aerenal," Nyam said. "In the War they founded a separate home in Valenar. Taeris Mordel was their window on the north and on the cursed lands around Voorkesh."

They spent another hour traversing the path. Rounding a tight bend, they saw below them the path leading to a wide bridge, its sides studded with carvings and statues of giants, heroic figures cast in warrior-like mould, swords and shields clasped, faces fierce, alive almost with the war-cries frozen into the stone.

Nyam pointed to the statues and columns that rose up on the opposite peak. "That is our goal. It is both a temple and watchtower. We should be safe there."

"It is abandoned?" said Cellester.

"The elves may use it from time to time," said Nyam, "but I see no watchfires up there."

As they peered up into the darkness, something flapped by above, its raucous cry making them all duck down. Cellester urged them down the path to the bridge. They scrambled forward, made reckless by their urgency. Smaller night creatures flitted to and fro in the air around them, as though they had disturbed a colony of bats within the rock walls. As they approached the span across the yawning chasm below, Vaddi knew that their enemies were closing fast. Behind them, on the path, they could hear shrill cries and the fall of rocks.

They came to the bridge. It looked solid enough for all its age. Beyond it, Taeris Mordel rose up, its wall like polished marble, its high doors shut, equally as smooth.

Uneasily they began the crossing. As they went over the bridge, Vaddi could see to his right a deep cleft in the mountains that afforded a view over the far Blade Desert, awash now with sudden brilliant moonlight. By day the view from here must be breathtaking. He had little time to appreciate it now, for a murmur of voices behind him made him swing round. At the foot of the path they had just quitted, a rush of movement alerted them. In the glow of the moons a body of undead were coming in pursuit, boots crunching on the stone of the bridge.

Cellester waved his companions forward, but Vaddi felt a stab of despair. How were they to get into the tower? Its tall doors, their huge iron hinges choked with rust, looked as if they had not been opened for a thousand years.

They reached little over the halfway span when the air hummed about them, as if alive with fresh sorcery. Three arrows sliced through the night air and embedded themselves deep in the stone at their feet. Vaddi realized with another surge of horror that they had been fired from the temple above.

Vaddi pulled up sharply. "We are defenseless! That was a warning volley."

The vibrations of the bridge testified to the pursuit. The undead were closing. They drew up in force no more than a dozen yards away, dead faces expressionless but assured of their triumph. From those ranks a familiar, cold voice shouted its challenge.

"Death awaits you that way. No one has ever entered Taeris Mordel and emerged alive."

Vaddi turned to see the tall, haughty figure of Caerzaal striding toward them.

"Return to me. I promise you something far more fulfilling."

PART

IN THE LANDS OF THE ELVES

TWO

CHAPTER 8

Cloaked in the shadows of night high above the gorge, the soarwing tilted to pass between rock pinnacles, its unerring instinct guiding it through the high walls beyond the lone tower of Taeris Mordel. Its undead rider could discern the bridge to the elf watchtower below, limned in the moonlight. In that ethereal glow he could see figures upon it. He urged his mount down, swooping closer to the bridge.

* * * * * * *

Vaddi was the first to realize what was happening. The vampire was no more than a few feet from him, but as Vaddi brandished his dirk in a vain effort to defend himself, he sensed the coming of the huge shadow-shape.

Caerzaal turned, teeth barred in a bestial snarl, to see the huge soarwing gliding down the gorge. The vampire ducked down and called to his servants. They came forward, and an arrow embedded itself in the neck of the nearest, its force catapulting the vampire from the bridge and over its edge. Beside Caerzaal, the next of his servants suffered the same fate.

Caerzaal staggered back a few paces, sword flaring in his hand as the soarwing closed with the bridge. Its rider brought the creature's rush to a halt, hovering briefly over the span before landing on it, its massive form coming between the vampire and the three fugitives. The head of the soarwing dipped down to the bridge and the dark mouth opened. Caerzaal sprang back, his sword cutting through the air, seeming to dance with bloody fire. The soarwing ducked its head to one side. Caerzaal screamed to his guards. As one they moved back across the bridge.

Satisfied that they were in retreat, the rider turned his mount with extraordinary skill until it faced the three fugitives. They had been watching events in amazement, stunned to silence by the appearance of this formidable creature.

Cellester was the first to gather his wits. Pushing his companions behind him, he faced up to the towering reptile and its rider. It was Aarnamor, who leaned forward, only his serpent-like eyes visible in the darkness.

"The boy! Send the boy to me!" he called, his voice like a whisper of distant thunder.

Vaddi drew back. This rider had rescued them at Voorkesh, but again he asked himself, what was it? Who did it serve? He dare not put his trust in such a creature.

Cellester turned to face Vaddi, a look of bemusement on his face, as though he was unsure of himself for once.

"Quickly!" came the rider's hiss. A clawed hand reached out. "Time is short!"

Overhead there came what they took to be a crack of thunder, though the skies had been clear, with no hint of a storm. Cellester, Vaddi and Nyam instinctively dropped to their haunches as if a great hand was about to reach down and sweep them from the span. They turned to look back up at the elf tower. A searing flash of light lit its upper ramparts and for a second something was silhouetted there. From out of the blinding light, a zigzag of white fire tore down at the bridge, sizzling and crackling. It struck Aarnamor in the chest with a detonating crash. Everything was caught in the blinding flare of the explosion. The three fugitives were thrown flat to the ground and felt the bridge shuddering, as though it would tear free of its foundations and collapse into the abyss below, but it held.

No more than a few yards in front of him, Vaddi saw the lightning strike Aarnamor again, seemingly disintegrating him, for after the glow subsided, there was no sign of him. Too dazed to scream, the soarwing reeled back along the bridge until it lost its footing. As it fell, it unfolded its wings, curved in mid-air and flew back up the gorge. It was swallowed by distance in a matter of moments. Behind it, Caerzaal's warriors had regrouped in silence, watching the bridge and the tower beyond.

His head ringing, Vaddi rose to his knees, blinking away tears as he fought to see clearly. Across the bridge, he saw the vampire lord. For the moment Caerzaal and his minions were holding back, wary of another bolt from above.

"To the tower!" said Nyam, spitting dust and shaking a tiny cloud of it from his hair and beard.

Vaddi and Cellester followed him. They reached the end of the bridge and the first steps that led up to the tall door. It had creaked open.

From beyond it, a voice came to them. "Who are you?"

Cellester, trying to see into the shadows, replied, "I am Cellester, a cleric and servant of House Orien. This is Vaddi d'Orien, son of Anzar Kemmal d'Orien and Indreen of the Dendris family."

"The family of Dendris? It is known to me. Pass within."

Cellester led his companions to the steps.

"Who is this other?" snapped the voice, taut as a wire.

Nyam pulled up short. "I am nothing, good sir. A mere peddler. Just a wayfarer in these troubled lands."

"Pass inside. Quickly now. The maggots of the Claw will not be contained for long."

Someone moved out of the shadows beyond the door, almost too quickly for the eye to follow, then lithely climbed the stairs, turned a corner, and was out of sight. Vaddi and his companions followed. They heard the groaning of machinery as behind them the huge set of doors swung into place, closing off the bridge. As they shut with a loud thud, silence fell over the tower, a deep silence, as if the company had suddenly been rendered deaf. But as they paused on the stair, chests heaving, they heard again the voice of their rescuer.

"Come up! Taeris Mordel must be properly secured. The night has not yet finished spewing up its evils."

The stairs were ancient, but not dust-choked, as if they had recently been swept clean. The walls of the tower were similarly polished, as though this place was inhabited and no forgotten ruin. At the top of the stair was an area open to the stars, ringed around by a number of huge statues. On seeing these, Vaddi gasped, for they were all of dragons. Each of the statues had been cut from a single block of polished obsidian. They gleamed in the moonlight, so life-like and real. The eyes were cut from emeralds the size of a human head and appeared to study the intruders. Immense wings folded back behind the statues, their working incredibly intricate and delicate. The masons who had created them must have laboured a lifetime to attain such perfection.

Beyond the circle of dragons was a raised balcony that looked out across the Endworld Mountains, the highest points of which were touched with moonlight. On either side of the balcony two larger dragon statues looked out over that vista, as though studying what it contained. Light from a number of cold fire lamps gently fell upon them and the others in the silent ring.

Vaddi, fascinated, was studying the circular inlay of the floor, which itself was polished like glass, apparently impervious to the weather, for there was no roof to Taeris Mordel. There were numerous symbols here, clearly elven work linked to dragon motifs.

Cellester seemed more concerned by the presence of the beings that had rescued them. He waited while they saw fit to reveal themselves. From beside one of the looming dragon statues, a solitary figure stepped into its light. Slightly taller than a ten-year-old child, dressed in tunic and trousers of typical elven design, it was an elf girl, who looked no older then Vaddi.

She held a bow in her hand and a quiver of arrows was swung over her shoulder. Her dark hair was cut just below her ears, her features narrow, almost human, but with something more than that—prompted by an arrogance, perhaps, a touch of haughtiness. Vaddi studied her, mesmerised.

She moved with the ease and silence of a huntress, her delicate hands at her side. One word out of place here and Vaddi sensed that those slender fingers would have nocked an arrow and let it fly before anyone was even aware of it.

"We owe you our thanks," said Cellester, inclining his head.

"So you are a cleric," she replied tersely. "I am not sure you are welcome. This ground is sacred to my people." She came closer, studying each of them in turn. "I can see elf blood in the boy."

Vaddi felt himself flushing under her stern gaze. *Boy!* Surely he was no younger than she was! But he was unable to frame a retort, instead glad to find himself out of that imperious gaze as the elf turned her attention to the cleric.

Cellester allowed the girl to weigh him for a moment then said, "It was a timely intervention on the bridge."

"The spells that bind the walls of Taeris Mordel repel the undead. But I wonder why they are here in such great numbers."

She came again to Vaddi. He had been looking at her, his mouth slightly open, eyes wide, since she had first shown herself. Nyam nudged him with his foot, but it had no effect.

"You are the son of Indreen," said the girl, as if the fact was of great interest to her. "Vaddi."

As she spoke his name, Vaddi blinked. "Yes, I, uh, I am. You're an elf."

Nyam nudged him again.

Her expression hardened, not quite into contempt. "Very observant of you. I am indeed. I am Zemella of Pylas Maradal. Why does Caerzaal, vampire servant of the Emerald Claw, seek you?"

Vaddi found himself wanting to blurt out the whole story,

hypnotised by her eyes, but Cellester stepped in before he could speak.

"House d'Orien has long sought to root out the agents of the Claw. Anzar thwarted their intrigues once too often. They stirred up a rabble army and Marazanath has fallen. Anzar and his family died."

"Our spy network, as you would know, is very thorough. The Claw's agents are abnormally active in these mountains," Zemella said. "They seem intent on wiping out the whole of Anzar's family. Caerzaal is no menial servant."

"I believe that Kazzerand is also behind this. I suspect that he has formed an alliance with the vampire."

"Oh, yes, we know Kazzerand and his deceits well. Caerzaal has pursued you from Marazanath itself, has he not?"

"So it seems," said Cellester.

Zemella's right hand came up and she placed it on Vaddi's heart, gently probing. She had touched the wrappings of the horn within his robes before he could respond, but she jerked away as if she had been scalded. Vaddi simply gaped at her, but Cellester pushed himself between them.

"We are protected," said the cleric. "Vaddi is the head of his family now. I am taking him to a safer place."

Zemella's eyes had widened. She massaged her fingers softly. "It is true, then. He bears Erethindel. That is why Caerzaal seeks him!"

"It must not fall into the hands of the Claw," said Cellester.

"Nor any evil power."

"You will help us?"

Vaddi continued to watch her, puzzled. Nyam had said that the elves had wanted to be rid of the horn and had given it into the hands of the Keepers. In which case, the elves of Taeris Mordel might be glad to speed it on its way.

"How many of you guard this tower?" Cellester asked her.

She frowned, as though he had said something doltish. "Me. Why should there be more? Others come by arrangement, to exchange information, to plan, and to bring me supplies."

"You are *alone?*" said Vaddi, at last finding his tongue.

She smiled for the first time. "Why should that surprise you? I am trained well in war. I defy any man to loose a better arrow or best me with a blade."

"Or hurl a bolt of lightning," muttered Nyam, though he immediately seemed to regret saying it as she stood again before him.

"That, too, peddler." She looked at him for some moments, amused by something, but then turned back to Vaddi. "We will have to leave soon. Caerzaal will not be content to sit and watch us. Have you eaten?"

Vaddi shook his head. Every time she looked at him, he felt unable to move.

"I'll prepare something," she said. "If you need sleep, you should rest. Where will you make for? This safe place you speak of, where is it?"

"Valenar," said Cellester.

She considered. "Probably the wisest route. Vaddi will have Orien relatives there. The unicorn emblem flies in a few of Valenar's cities. What do you intend to do with the talisman?"

Cellester turned away from her steely gaze. "Secure it among allies."

She nodded thoughtfully. "Those in Valenar will know where to send it." After a moment she turned again to Cellester. "Go to the tower above the gate. Look to see what the undead are about. I have work to do while your companions rest."

Without another word she left them, disappearing among the enormous statues.

"Stay here," said the cleric. "I will do as she suggests."

Nyam stared after him, shaking his head. "If that vampire lord knows that this tower is protected by a single elf warrior, we'll not be left in peace for long."

Vaddi grinned. "She's . . . well, I've never— "

Nyam laughed. "I'd mask your feelings, if I were you, lad."

Vaddi grimaced. "Nothing wrong in admiring—"

"*Admiring* her? I thought she had flung one of her bolts of lightning over you, the way you were looking at her."

"What do you mean? I was surprised, that's all. One warrior holding this place by herself . . ."

"She's a *sorceress*. That much is obvious. She could snap either of us in half if she had a mind to. I know the Valenar. They like nothing better than a battle."

"She has no reason to detain us."

"Don't let your heart rule your head, Vaddi. She may be the most beautiful creature you've ever seen, and I admit, she is very alluring in a masculine sort of way, but—"

"What are you talking about?" snapped Vaddi. *"Masculine?* Just because she's a warrior?"

Nyam laughed. "I am sorry. It has been a long time since I really looked at a woman. And certainly not through the eyes of love."

Vaddi was about to protest, but something in Nyam's expression stilled his anger. "But you have known love?"

"Of course! I told you I had a wife. When I first met her, I daresay I looked at her as you have done on this elf. To me she was more beautiful than anything I had ever seen. It took me a long while to tell her—all the time she was cursing me for a wastrel and a buffoon and saying that she, an elf, would have to be out of her wits to consider me. Yet when I asked her to wed me, she asked me in return why I had dithered about so long in asking her."

"Then she married you?"

"Naturally! They allow you to chase them until you get them exactly where they want you, so beware of this sorceress."

"You said . . . your wife died?" said Vaddi, the words tumbling out before he could think to be more diplomatic.

"The War, lad. She and my two sons. Like so many others, they died defending the small town that was our home, in a battle that was ultimately meaningless and forgotten. Though not by me. Not by me."

"I'm sorry."

"Well, let's not speak of these things. I have many happy

memories. And long years ahead, I hope."

"Tell me something. That creature. It all happened so quickly. What was it? Why did it free us from Caerzaal?"

"The undead warrior rode a soarwing. They are huge saurians, but their brains are small, easily controlled. The undead . . . that I don't know. It will serve a master, sometimes a sorcerer, a magician of higher powers, or a cleric."

"You mean Cellester?"

Nyam shrugged. "The cleric's powers are no small thing."

Vaddi looked around to be sure they were alone, then leaned close to Nyam and whispered, "You think that . . . thing serves Cellester?"

Nyam considered a long moment, then replied, "I have told you discreetly that I am not certain of Cellester's loyalty, yet he has proved himself on this journey to be a worthy ally."

"Had he not been, both of us would be dead or worse, yet on the bridge, I heard the undead call for Cellester to give me up to him."

Nyam indicated Vaddi's robe, where the horn lay hidden. "Others may be seeking what you carry. Watch your step."

Zemella returned and handed them a tray with food and water. She smiled at them—or rather at Vaddi.

"Have you told him?" she asked Nyam softly, watching to see if the cleric had returned.

Vaddi looked askance at the peddler.

"She has been waiting for us," Nyam said with a grin. "She is a Keeper."

"Then why—?"

Nyam shook his head. "Best that our companion does not know."

Zemella's eyes met Vaddi's and he felt a unique glow. "I suspect his motives," she whispered. "Let him prove himself to me before we give him the truth of our mission."

"The safety of the horn you mean?"

"And yours," she said.

❋ ❋ ❋ ⬤ ❋ ❋ ❋

Cellester climbed the stair to the tower above the tall doors. From its parapet he could look below, where the bridge loomed in the pale moonlight. Of Caerzaal and his undead, there were no immediate signs, but the cleric was certain they were near. They would spare no efforts to give siege and they would waste little time in doing so. If the company was to escape, it must move very soon.

Something among the shadows peeled itself from the vertical wall below him and Cellester started back, amulet glowing faintly. But he saw that it was not one of Caerzaal's minions. It was Aarnamor—or what remained of him. The dark form drifted silently up the tower wall to within a few feet of where he stood, his yellow, serpent-eyes fixing Cellester from within the shrouded confines of his nebulous shape.

When he spoke, his words seemed to hang on the wind, as if he were becoming even less substantial, a ghost returning to the bleak domain from which he had been raised.

"The sorceress has unbound me," came his weak voice.

Cellester watched, seeing Aarnamor's darkness pulsing, growing ever more mist-like. "The soarwing," he whispered, careful to keep his voice low. "Where is it?"

"Awaiting my call, though wary of this place. Why did you come this way? If you had gone down to the Plains, I could have taken the boy."

"I could not force him. He is suspicious, and that infernal peddler is up to something."

"My powers are draining. I must go back to Urgal Shahiz. We cannot get you away. Not now."

"And Caerzaal's forces? Where are they?"

"Rising by the hundreds. This tower will not stem them, for all its spells." The voice grew faint, the outline of the being wavering.

"Is there a way from this tower?"

"Only the sorceress can answer that, but you must be wary of her. Above all, remember your oath. Do not fail our lord."

Vaddi and Nyam were eating the frugal meal prepared by Zemella when the cleric returned. She indicated that he should join them.

"What did you see?" she asked.

"Nothing," said Cellester, "but Caerzaal will have surrounded this tower. There is no telling how many of his servants will be with him. Your sorcery will not hold them indefinitely. Is that bridge the only way off this tower?"

"By foot, yes," said Zemella.

"What about below us?"

"There are no tunnels or crevices," she said with a wry smile. "I would not trust them if there were. These mountains are saturated with old magic, poisons akin to what you have seen at Voorkesh. The lizardfolk of Q'barra dwell not far to the east. Taeris Mordel was chosen for its height, its aerial attributes. Tunnels and the dark below are for the undead and their kind."

"So there's no way off," said Nyam, between mouthfuls.

She gave him a withering stare. "I didn't say that."

"Then you'll help us?" said Cellester.

Again she seemed to be weighing the matter very carefully. She paced about the group, her feet silent on the polished floor. She paused at Nyam's back. "Tell me, peddler, why are you with this company? What is your interest in its quest?"

Nyam scowled. "Me? I am just—"

"A common peddler, yes. I am not blind. It is why I ask you again, what is your interest in House Orien? Why risk your life for them?"

"Initially I helped the boy and the cleric evade some trouble at Rookstack and was paid well for it. Since then . . . well, I have found myself caught up in their flight. Safety in numbers, especially in the terrain we have had to cross."

Zemella's blade whispered from its sheath. "Really? You weren't thinking of turning a handsome profit from the barter of a certain object? Or Vaddi d'Orien himself? You must have wealthy contacts in Valenar."

Nyam's face screwed up into an expression of indignation. "How dare you suggest such a thing!" He stood, only to find Zemella's swordpoint inches from his neck.

Vaddi stepped forward and pushed Zemella's sword away, locking eyes with her. It took all his self-control to avoid grinning inanely as he played along with the hastily contrived exchange.

"We have fought side by side," he said. "All three of us. Had we not done so, we'd likely all be dead, or worse."

Zemella sheathed her sword. A faint smile touched her lips and again Vaddi felt himself coloring under her gaze. "Very well, son of Orien."

"Whatever your motives, peddler," said Cellester, "there's no denying the debt we owe to your sword. We'll need it again and soon. Caerzaal's horde will strike before dawn." He turned to Zemella. " If you know how to get us away from here . . ."

"Come this way," Zemella said.

She led them up beyond the balcony. Above it there was a chamber hollowed from the rock, again without a ceiling. A single huge statue had been cut from the rock there, a superb example of a dragon, wings outspread, gemmed eyes gleaming. In the dim light it seemed almost alive. Zemella waved them back while she knelt before it, as if in the presence of a shrine. She began to sing softly, her voice very low. Vaddi felt his heart lurch, as if the words of the elfsong worked a particular magic for him alone. He found himself watching Zemella as though nothing else existed.

It was the touch of Nyam's hand that brought him out of this state of wonder.

"What?" said Vaddi, almost glaring at the peddler.

Nyam was looking skyward. "See what comes!"

Vaddi lifted his gaze and gasped. Huge, feathered wings beat at the night air, and the tower echoed to a terrifying, raucous cry. A creature with the torso and hindquarters of a horse and the forelegs, wings and head of a giant eagle was hovering above them, its massive beak poised to snatch its human prey. It was truly huge, with a wingspan of over twenty feet. Vaddi dropped to all fours.

"A hippogriff," said Nyam.

"Those claws!" cried Vaddi, trying to tug Nyam to safety.

The peddler merely grinned. "It bears a saddle. See. I don't think we are intended to be its next meal." He indicated the beautifully wrought leather saddle on the back of the hovering monster, its intricate design woven through with elven runes.

Zemella stood and turned to them. The hippogriff landed behind her, making barely more than a sound even on the hard stone.

"Ashtari Mereen will bear us," Zemella said, her expression one of wonder as she reached out to touch the head of the hippogriff. "Do not fear her."

"Can it bear all of us?" said Cellester.

Zemella nodded. "She is a queen among her kind. Come, let us waste no more time."

The hippogriff arched its beautifully feathered neck. Zemella gestured for the company to climb into the broad saddle. They did so in awe. Zemella mounted last, settling herself at the base of the long neck. She leaned forward and another gentle song drifted over the night, coaxing the awesome creature up from the tower. With silken ease, it was airborne, the huge weight forgotten as the extraordinary beast, streamlined and superbly aerodynamic, flapped silently into the night sky. It gave one imperial shriek, as if pouring scorn on whatever creatures swarmed in the darkness below.

Vaddi felt the blood rushing through his veins, his whole being suffused with fire, an ecstasy beyond anything he had ever experienced before. He sat directly behind Zemella. His hands rested on her waist, but she did not react.

Behind him, Nyam and Cellester rode in silence, their thoughts masked.

* * * * * * *

Darkness seethed around the crags of Urgal Shahiz, unnatural and riven with flickering bolts of light. Within the central tower, among its broken, time-lost vaults, Zuharrin waited, his mind focusing on the elements, reading the fates of his servants. Above him, fusing itself with the naked rock, the huge soarwing had returned from the distant northeastern lands. Like a small cloud, the withered shape of Aarnamor came into the chamber, his eyes dimming like the last embers of a fire.

"What of Cellester the cleric?" said Zuharrin.

Aarnamor's shape shifted like mist. "He protects the boy. They have Erethindel. At Taeris Mordel I would have taken them both but was cast down by an elf sorceress."

"The ancient watchtower! Was she set to wait for the boy? By whom?" Zuharrin's annoyance almost fanned into anger. Who else interfered in his plans?

"I had no time to learn. I was struck down before I knew she was there. I was barely able to speak to Cellester, but I charged him with remembering his oath."

The darkness that was Zuharrin pulsed, a promise of torment. "He knows well enough the penalty for betrayal. You must go into the world again, Aarnamor. I will restore your power, and I will send others. If the elves attempt to take Erethindel for themselves, it would be as disastrous for me as if it fell into the hands of the Emerald Claw."

Aarnamor, nearing complete dissipation, felt a renewed flood of energy as his master gifted him with power, drawing upon the darker places, conjuring a regeneration in the dismal chamber. Zuharrin began the workings that would evoke yet more servants bound to his service. Over Urgal Shahiz, thunder rolled like the voices of dark gods. Far out across the ocean beyond it, ships heard the forbidding sound, and their crews shuddered, hands clasped to protective talismans, invoking lighter powers.

CHAPTER 9

As the flight swept them far across the southernmost edges of the Endworld Mountains and over the borderlands of northern Valenar, Vaddi and his companions felt themselves lulled almost to sleep by the ease of the journey. None of them spoke for a long time, though with the wind rushing past them, it would have been difficult. Vaddi, still holding tight to Zemella, felt a mixture of emotions stirring within him. It was as though in crossing into Valenar, something deep had awoken in him—a response, he thought, to his mother's elf blood. There was an undercurrent of excitement to it, as if it reacted to the power that rose off the land below. Coupled with this was the power inherent in the unicorn horn, which seemed almost alive, a tiny engine of power, humming to itself, in tune with the lands so far beneath it. The combined energies did not stop there.

Zemella. There is power in her, he thought, suddenly conscious of touching her. He felt . . .

His mind closed out the thoughts, afraid that she would reach around with her own mind and read them. He felt himself flushing, dreading the thought that she would sense this through his touch.

She has power, he thought. A sorceress. My elf blood is responding to hers. Surely it is no more than that.

Again he tore his mind away from contemplating the girl. Nyam had teased him, but was it that obvious that she had struck him dumb with . . . what? Reverence?

He looked across the cloudy expanses to the east. Rising thermals from the hot land of Valenar turned to banks of cloud up here—an endless quilt of milk, an ocean. The sun heated the company and the skies seemed devoid of other life, but Vaddi sensed something to the east, a huge bulk of movement, just below the white surface of cloud, as though a denizen of this tranquil sky-ocean swam there, effortlessly and lazily. Instinctively he knew what it was. The waking powers within him told him.

Dragon!

"Zemella," he said in a whisper, so close to her ear that his lips almost touched her neck.

"I know," she said, turning her head. "It travels on its own secret mission, heading far to the southeast."

"Has it sensed us?"

"Probably. Who knows the minds of those majestic creatures? Their work is their own. To them we are no more than little birds. You see it?"

"No. I . . . just know it's there. I can feel it."

"In your blood."

"Yes! That's it. I can't explain it."

"You don't have to. I understand."

"Then you sense it also?"

She laughed very softly and his heart lurched.

"Do all elves feel this? Affinity for them?"

She shook her head. "No more than men do—or others in Eberron. There has been much blood spilled between dragons and elves in the past. Some revere them, some would war with them anew. Blood is a strange thing. High magic runs through it in some, none at all in others. Perhaps there is dragon blood in you."

Then it is in you, too, he thought. We have that in common. It was an idea that elated him. He studied the eastern clouds, eager to catch a physical glimpse of the hidden creature, but he felt it moving away, its shape masked from him.

He felt something else within himself, a very different kind of power. Something negative. A cold presence, a shadow that cloaked his own, stirring emotions and powers. All his life this shadow had shifted within him, a sluggish parasite. I am an Orien, my father's powers in me. I am dragonmarked, but I cannot yet unlock the powers that should come with this. What is it that holds me back? Why am I thus crippled? Time and time again he had agonized over this but to no avail. Perhaps the elf sorceress would know and could help him, but now was not the time to speak of it.

"Where are we bound for?"

"We will go to my city, Pylas Maradal. Your House has people there. You are related to its main representative, Kalfar Munjati. Do you know him?"

"No."

"He is distantly related to your family through one of your mother's brothers, who also married a human. He will give you sanctuary, though I am sure he will seek a fee. These Valenar Oriens are great ones for haggling!"

"Then perhaps I should let Nyam do the talking for me. It is an art form he is well versed in."

"He is well known in Pylas Maradal. He has rivals there, some of whom would accord him a less than friendly welcome."

"Then he is a trader?"

"Indeed, and a very successful one, for one reason or another! There will be time enough to explain this when we reach the city. We'll be there before nightfall."

"And you, Zemella? What will you do?" He did not want to contemplate the possibility that she would leave them.

"I must report back to my warclan, the Finnarra. They must be told of the movements of Caerzaal and this minions. They will send others to Taeris Mordel to watch the lands there, although now that the horn has eluded him, Caerzaal will quit the mountains. Be warned, Vaddi, you have not seen the last of Caerzaal, I think."

He shuddered at the thought. "What exactly is the horn?" he said as softly as he could.

"When we reach Pylas Maradal, I will tell you more. It is for you only to know. Its safety is paramount. Let no one know you carry it. Not even Kalfar."

"You do not trust him?"

"If I were you, Vaddi d'Orien, I would put your trust in no one."

"I trust you."

He could feel her smile. "An elf sorceress? You should be more careful."

❧ ❧ ❧ ❧ ❧ ❧ ❧

When they finally dropped down through the cloudbanks, the sun was falling in the west, spreading the heavens with a tide of color—reds and golds and deeper shades of violet over the sea far to the east. Below them was a land that differed markedly from the great expanses of the Talenta Plains. It was flattish, rolling steppes broken by fertile plains, well forested, with rivers gleaming in the dusk as they wound down to the inlets and shores of the coast. There were small hamlets visible but few major cities, and on the higher slopes, Vaddi was sure that he could discern numerous ruins from another age. He recalled what little he had heard of the Valenar lands and the beasts that were still said to roam them. The elf warclans were very active, and several had to keep a close watch on the lands of the western border, where the notorious Mournland intruded, but on this flight, those grim areas were mercifully out of sight, obscured by distance and twilight.

Pylas Maradal was far to the south of Valenar, on its southwestern coast, a large city sheltered from the storms of Kraken Bay by a curve of land. As they swept down toward its towers and minarets, Vaddi felt the blast of warm air come up to meet them.

In spite of the hour, it was hot here, a climate altogether different to what he was used to in the north—humid and dusty. The smells from the city were new to him, too, a strange mixture of spice and sea, the deep blues of which washed up close to the harbor spread out like a map below him.

Zemella guided the hippogriff to one of the numerous towers that rose up from the city like a forest, their amazing architecture matched only by the splendour of their carvings and paintwork. Fascinated, Vaddi was almost disappointed not to be able to drink in more of this compelling vista as the hippogriff glided on to the wide, flat top of the tower, sheltered by a dome overhead, itself supported on four splendidly carved colonnades. These were etched around with dragon motifs, the work of artisans who must have spent incalculable hours perfecting their beauty, their homage to it. Around the rim of the flat space, several tall stone statues, also of dragons, gazed motionlessly out over Pylas Maradal from jewelled eyes.

Once the company had dismounted, Zemella led the hippogriff to the lip of the tower and spoke softly in the Valenar tongue. The beast turned to her and bent its head so that she could run her fingers through the thick mane of feathers. Then it spread its huge wings and took to the skies once more, bound for some private aerie. Vaddi watched, mesmerised more by Zemella than by the magic she had used. He heard Nyam cough discreetly at his elbow.

"Now where?" said the peddler, an insouciant grin on his face.

"I have a relation here by the name of Kalfar Munjati," said Vaddi. "We should go to him."

Zemella nodded. "I have to report to my warclan, though I will take you to Kalfar first."

Cellester was frowning. "In Pylas Maradal, there are many factions, but the house of Kalfar is known to me."

"While I would be only too pleased to enjoy the hospitality of the esteemed house," said Nyam, "I would prefer to visit the harbor district. I used to have some friends in this port. Not seen them for years, but I'd wager a cart full of gold that they're still hanging about the docks."

Zemella smiled as if at a private joke.

"Only for the night," added Nyam. "Perhaps I'll wander back to the house of Kalfar after breakfast?"

Cellester's frown deepened. "We have said before that we both owe you our thanks for your part in our getting here safely, peddler, but you owe us nothing. Consider all debts repaid."

"Are you that anxious to be rid of me?" Nyam chuckled.

Cellester shrugged. "No. But I fail to see how Vaddi's path and yours should interweave from now on. Surely your destiny lies with your own kind."

"For my part," said Vaddi, "Nyam is welcome to enjoy our company."

"This is not the place to debate such things," said Zemella. "Come to Kalfar's house. Or not." She turned on her heel and made for the only opening in the tower, a stairwell down into the tower's heart.

"Better do as she says," Nyam grinned at Vaddi, who glared back at him.

Zemella led them around the stairs into the growing gloom of the tower's very roots. A number of Valenar soldiers were gathered in the room at the foot of the stairway, busily cleaning harness and honing their short swords. They eyed the company coolly but did not comment.

"Always ready for a fight," Nyam muttered to Vaddi. "Valenar. Born to battle, believe me. Keep well clear of them."

Vaddi was about to remind him that he had elf blood himself, but Zemella ushered them through a door and out into the street. Even at this time of the evening, the place was heaving with people, all shouting, bustling—busier, it seemed, than at any other time of the day. Vaddi tucked in close behind Zemella, who strode through the press like the prow of a ship cutting through a sea swell. Vaddi wondered if she was using any kind of spell to ease her passage.

"The docks lie that way," she said, after they had gone into the heart of the city, pointing down a narrow alleyway that seemed half-choked with huge jars. They could smell the sea, pungent and redolent of fish. Masts bobbed up and down in the distance.

"I'll be on my way, then," said Nyam, and with no more than a brief pat on the shoulder for Vaddi, he was off down the alley, like a hungry tomcat on the scent of a meal.

Zemella was already pressing on. Some time later, having broken out of the bazaar-lined streets and the cramped stalls, they climbed a wider path that led to a cleaner residential district. There were a number of imposing edifices lining the landward side of the street looking out over the main bay. Zemella brought them to a pair of tall gates set into which was the unmistakable motif of a prancing unicorn. At once, two guards stepped from the shadows, pikes dipping through the rails of the gate.

"Who comes to the House of Kalfar Munjati?" growled one of them.

Zemella stepped forward. "The son of Indreen and distant cousin to your master. Tell him that Zemella of the Finnarra has brought him here, and be quick about it!"

Surprised at her tone, the two guards gaped through the rails at her. They were men themselves, and though they screwed up their faces at sight of the Valenar girl, her manner also instilled in them a degree of fear and respect that Vaddi could almost taste.

"*You* are related to Kalfar?" one of the guards said.

"Not me, you idiot! Here is Vaddi d'Orien"—she pointed at Vaddi—"from Marazanath."

"Never heard of it."

"That comes as no surprise. Now open the gates before I rip them down!"

She held up her fist and to Vaddi's amazement, the guards reacted as if it contained a fireball that she would hurl at them. The gates swung easily open, the two guards bowing.

"Take Vaddi d'Orien and his companion up to the house,"

Zemella ordered the guards. She turned to Vaddi and Cellester as they entered the gateway. "Go to Kalfar. I will return in the morning."

Cellester stepped close to her. "The matter of Vaddi's arrival here in Pylas Maradal must be treated with the greatest discretion," he said softly. "We are grateful to you for your help, but no one other than Kalfar must know he is here."

Her expression was unreadable. "Of course. Until tomorrow."

With no more ado, she turned on her heel and melted into the growing shadows. Vaddi felt something of himself going with her, as though he had in that moment suddenly become incomplete, but he had no time to reflect. Cellester was urging him up the hill after the guard. The other clanged shut the gates behind them.

"Be guarded in what you say," Cellester told him. "Let us hope he will be Orien enough to help you. Valenar thrives on intrigue."

They waited in the wide atrium of the house while the guard spoke to someone within, and at length another servant met them. A tall, laconic man dressed in a white robe that seemed to depict an office of some importance in the Kalfar household, he bowed and ushered them inside. It was a still, warm night, and their host preferred to meet them in one of his many delightful gardens, which was lit by several cold fire lamps and numerous fireflies that had chosen the fragrant shrubbery as their base.

Kalfar sat on a wide dais, himself corpulent, his many colored robes resplendent, even in this light. He wore a vivid green turban and his face was even more be-whiskered than that of Nyam, his eyes twinkling as he beheld his guests. He struggled to his feet, his legs seemingly too short for his body, and set down the glass from which he had been sipping red wine. He opened his arms to Vaddi.

"My boy, my boy! Indreen's son! A thousand delights to have you visit my humblest of abodes!" He embraced Vaddi, squashing the youth to his bosom as though the emotion of it all was too much for him.

"You know of me then?"

Kalfar released Vaddi and studied him as though looking over a valuable object, another jewel for his collection. On his fingers a dozen rings gleamed. "Of course, of course! Here in Pylas Maradal nothing escapes our ears. The elves, you know! Finest network of spies in all of Khorvaire. Some of us appreciate their skills."

Vaddi was suddenly conscious of Cellester behind him. "Please, let me introduce a valuable friend. This is Cellester, a long-time servant of my father, Anzar Kemmal d'Orien."

Kalfar shuffled before Cellester and eyed him keenly.

"I know of you," said Kalfar. "You served Anzar and Indreen with distinction."

"It was my honor," said Cellester.

"Good, good. Now, before we talk, you must eat, eat!" Kalfar clapped his hands and like emerging wraiths, two servants materialized from the shadows. Kalfar rattled off some instructions to them, then waved his guests to some seats. "Well, well. Here you are then. Good, good. So what brings you to this remotest of outposts, this far-flung bastion of civilization?"

Vaddi smiled. "Pylas Maradal may be remote, sir, but it struck me as the most thriving of places. Its excitement, its pulse, hit me like a wave. I am used to far more modest surroundings."

"Yes, yes. The north. Or to be precise, the northeast. Karrnath. I went there, once. A bit too gray for my taste, though I mean no disrespect, Vaddi."

"Of course not. But to answer your question, I have come here out of necessity. My news of Marazanath is not good."

Kalfar's eyes lost their twinkle, and he sat back with a deep sigh. "I know what you are going to say. Word reached us already."

He was interrupted as the servants brought in the first of the food, cold meats and succulent vegetables. Kalfar motioned for his guests to eat and both Vaddi and Cellester helped themselves to the splendid fare. Kalfar watched them, sipping his wine thoughtfully.

Cellester broke the lengthy silence. "You know what has happened at Marazanath?"

Kalfar seemed to be holding down an outburst of deep anger. "I am so sorry, Vaddi," he said, shaking his head. "Your father and your half-brothers, all murdered. I know who is behind it, as I know who is behind so much of the trouble and the rebellions and the evils in the north. Pah, the north? The accursed minions of the Claw are at work *everywhere*. Like rats they infest every part of Khorvaire."

"Cellester and I left Marazanath for fear of being caught up in the Claw's schemes."

"The Claw wants no witnesses to its treachery," Cellester cut in.

"No doubt," said Kalfar, "but that treachery is known here."

"Can you tell us what news you have of Marazanath?" Cellester asked. "We left in secret and in haste. Whatever news you have received will undoubtedly be more recent than any we could give you."

"Yes, yes. Well, as far as I can tell there's nothing but chaos up there. A local warlord named Kazzerand is sending knights in to disperse the brigands who overran Marazanath. The hold will fall under his stewardship, which means his grip on the lands grows stronger."

Cellester looked at Vaddi.

"I see what is written on your face, cleric," said Kalfar, "and what it implies. This Kazzerand is no ally to the Oriens. Not at all."

"You know the history?"

"Who does not? Kazzerand hated your father, Vaddi. As good as exiled him. Left him isolated. It may even be that Kazzerand is in some way in league with agents of the Claw. You did well to get away."

"My future is unclear," said Vaddi, looking into the darkness as though he could see the bleak northern landscape there, "but my family should be avenged."

"Is your intention to return there?" said Kalfar.

"At the moment I am not sure."

"Stand against Kazzerand? You would have a claim, as the surviving member of your family there. But it's risky, risky."

They ate and drank in silence, each deep in thought for a while.

"What of you, good cleric?" said Kalfar. "You will go with him? Be his shield?"

Cellester nodded. "I am so sworn, but we may not have to travel alone."

"Ah, you have allies in this potential venture?" said Kalfar, brightening.

"Possibly. I have not been to Pylas Maradal for some time, but there are men here who might assist us."

"Paladins?" said Kalfar. "You need men of such ilk. I do have my contacts, but alas, the cost of soliciting such men would be prohibitive. Unless you have access to substantial funding?" His eyes gleamed with expectancy.

Vaddi could not help but grin. "I think not, Kalfar."

Cellester shook his head. "Alas, no, but there may be men here who would stand under the unicorn banner and fight for the honor of Anzar and Marazanath. I will go into the city tonight and begin a search for them."

"If it's a fight you want," said Kalfar, eyes still illuminated, "what about the Valenar? Get a warclan together and let them loose! Teeth of dragons, they'd love a scrap. Got any connections there? Wait, didn't Abdas, my steward, say that a Valenar warrior-girl brought you here? In fact, didn't he say it was Zemella?"

"You know her?" said Vaddi.

"Zemella? Yes, of course! From the esteemed Valenar family of Dendris, your mother's family, Vaddi. Zemella, yes, she's a fine girl. Hard bargainer! Very hard. Especially where livestock are concerned. I tell you, I'd rather have her bargaining on my behalf than against me. Mind you, she charges commission at criminal, *criminal* rates."

Vaddi listened to the flood of words with both confusion and a renewed fascination for the Valenar girl.

Cellester was more guarded. "We must consider her then," he said. "In the meantime, I hope you will not be offended if I go into the city."

"Not at all, not at all." Kalfar nodded. "Do you need a guide? But no, I am sure you prefer to handle things in your own way. No doubt you have connections."

Once they had eaten, the servants cleared away the plates and Kalfar sent for Abdas, the tall steward who had brought his guests to him. "Cellester is leaving us for a while," Kalfar told him. "See that he has anything he needs."

Cellester rose and bowed. "You will be safe here," he told Vaddi quietly. "I will come to you again soon. Keep certain things hidden," he whispered.

Vaddi nodded. Moments later he was alone with Kalfar.

"A powerful man," said his host. "One senses such things. He once served the Church of the Silver Flame before he took post at your father's house."

"I take it you know of him, from what you said?"

"It would have been indiscreet of me to say too much. How well do *you* know him, Vaddi?"

Vaddi felt Kalfar's eyes upon him, as though they would draw something out of him. Appearances were deceptive. Kalfar was no fool. For a moment Vaddi was torn between his lingering uncertainties about the cleric and the fact that Kalfar, relation or not, was a complete stranger.

"I daresay that I know less about him than you do."

"I am glad you are honest with me, Vaddi. I will be honest with you. Your father praised the cleric and called him loyal. He would not have it any other way, but there was one thing he did not know. I will tell you this thing, for you are of my blood."

Vaddi felt himself stiffen. Something inside him shifted, but he waited, the night utterly silent around them.

"The cleric loved your mother, Indreen. That is not to say

that he was her lover, not at all. He revered her too much for that. Many men loved and respected her, but Cellester loved her deeply. It was no crime and he did not speak of it to others. But such feelings cannot remain hidden from those who have the gift of seeing within."

"Then that is why Caerzaal taunted him," said Vaddi, a flood of understanding dawning on him.

"Caerzaal?" said Kalfar, as though Vaddi had jabbed him with a hot iron. "Shades of the Dragon! What have you to do with that monster?"

"First finish your tale of Cellester."

"He masked his love for Indreen, and he served your family well. There were those in your father's house who did not trust Cellester, who said that he was like an ill omen, a stain on the court. Some went so far as to hint that there was an affair, but *my* spies tell me that was never so. Your mother and father were devoted. You were born out of their love. Maybe that's why this cleric protects you as he does."

"He could never tell me."

"Of course not! And you must never let him know that you are aware of this."

"Then I have been wrong not to trust him."

Kalfar was frowning. "I am not sure, Vaddi. I am a naturally suspicious man. A trader, a haggler, a hunter of bargains, I did not win this palatial home without resorting—occasionally—to devious means. There are more than a few who do not trust me entirely. And you! You have met me but a moment ago! Do you trust me?"

Vaddi felt himself coloring, but he covered his embarrassment with a laugh.

"Don't answer that!" Kalfar chuckled.

"You have no reason to harm me, I think."

"None at all. We are of one blood. It should be enough, but be careful. There are those you can trust, I promise you. On my blood."

"The Valenar sorceress?"

"Ah, my boy, do I detect a quickening of the pulse? Zemella? She is a rare gem, is she not?"

"Well, yes, she's a fine girl."

Kalfar sat back and guffawed. "A fine girl! One way of putting it. Well, whether your feelings have completely colored your judgement of her or not, I can tell you that she is one you *can* trust. The blood of Dendris runs through her veins and yours. It is said that it is one of the oldest families of the elves and comes with dragon blood. Such things bind deeply, Vaddi, so you can trust Zemella with your life." He leaned forward, suddenly very serious. "Mark that. With your life."

"She was waiting for me at Taeris Mordel."

Kalfar grunted. "Not a chance meeting then. But enough of this, I want to hear about that other creature, Caerzaal."

Vaddi spent some time going over his flight from the north and the meetings with Caerzaal. Kalfar listened enrapt, alternatively gasping and cursing. The vampire lord seemed to be particularly revolting to him, as though he had also once had the misfortune to cross paths with him. Voorkesh seemed to fascinate him, for he had heard of it but assumed that it was the figment of someone's tortured imagination.

"This peddler intrigues me," said Kalfar during a break in Vaddi's narrative. "Nyam Hordath? If he's been active in Pylas Maradal before, I ought to know of him."

"He's gone in search of old cronies."

"And you say he's coming back? Here? To meet you here?"

"So he says. I have grown somewhat fond of him."

"So you trust him?" said Kalfar, brows knitting in a deep frown.

"So far he has done much to help me, and Zemella clearly trusts him."

"But he's a common peddler! Does it not occur to you that he's hitched his wagon to yours in order to capitalize on your fortunes? Nyam Hordath? Why am I not able to recall that name?" He clapped his hands twice and the tall form of Abdas appeared like a mirage. "Abdas, can you think of anyone we have had dealings with, officially or otherwise, by the name of Nyam Hordath? A peddler from the north. No special traffic."

"I will look into the matter, master," said Abdas with a bow, and he left as discreetly as he had arrived.

"Stickler for details," said Kalfar approvingly. "Marvellous brain, marvellous."

"Do you think that Zemella will help me?"

"Call up her warclan? Maybe. She's a restless type, like a lot of these Valenar. Your pardon, Vaddi, present company excepted, but you know what I mean. You like her, then?"

"Well, I don't know her."

"Ask her to help. Tell her you're going north to wreak havoc among the Claw's vermin. The Valenar, especially the Finnarra warclan, love a fight!"

Vaddi grinned. "We were hoping to travel quietly. Would a Valenar warclan be able to slip into Karrnath unnoticed?"

"You'd be surprised! Especially by the Finnarra. Ah, Abdas, that was quick. Very quick. News, I take it?"

The steward came back into the room with no more than a whisper of his robes.

"Indeed, master. Nyam Hordath appears to be the latest alias of, among others, Daal Hashard, Bereth Alendi, Tutos Munnermal . . . need I go on?"

"Tutos Munnermal? Munnermal? I know *that* name."

Vaddi was intrigued. "From where?"

"Abdas will correct me if I am wrong, but three years ago, someone of that very name swindled me out of a whole string of superb clawfoots. A so-called dealer for the Talenta Clans, the halflings. Nasty lot to deal with. Munnermal was the broker."

"He cheated you?"

"The halflings, too. Swapped thoroughbreds for a scrawny bunch from the Blade Desert. And he is coming to meet you tomorrow? This meeting I will enjoy."

CHAPTER 10

Vaddi was provided with a huge bedroom, lavishly decorated and stuffed with gorgeous drapes, carvings, rugs and
all manner of luxury. Clearly Kalfar believed in enjoying life
to the full and spared no expense in ensuring that his home,
guest rooms included, was second to none. As Vaddi sank into
the huge bed, none of the finery mattered. He could think of
only one thing—the Valenar girl. He closed his eyes and felt
again the heady pleasure of the flight from Taeris Mordel, their
closeness, the scent of her hair. He forced himself to focus on
other things.

Kalfar. Apparently a blood relative, so there seemed to be
no reason not to trust him. But Nyam! If things were as Kalfar
said, it was no wonder he would not come here. He said he would
return in the morning, but will he? Perhaps he feels his work
is done.

Vaddi sat on the edge of the bed. "Zemella," he said softly,
repeating the name.

Across the thickly carpeted floor, a huge window opened
on to the warm night, a spangled sky arching over the city.
Bright moonlight flooded in. By its glow, Vaddi saw something
move. A long velvet drape partially obscured a pillar by the

window. Something hid there, some living thing.

Vaddi eased silently from the bed and picked up his sword. He inched forward, poised to strike. A few feet from the window, the bottom of the curtain flicked out like a huge tongue and wrapped itself around his sword arm. In the few seconds it took him to disentangle it, a swordpoint danced before his eyes.

"If you are to survive in Pylas Maradal, Vaddi d'Orien, you'll need quicker wits than that," said a soft voice.

"Zemella? What are you doing here?" he said, immediately feeling stupid for having said it as she stepped out of the shadows.

She sheathed her sword. "I heard you call me."

"Heard me?"

"There are things I must tell you privately. Sit down. Here." She picked up his weapon and handed it to him. He took it, still bemused.

"I don't have long."

They sat together on the bed and he wondered if she could feel his heart thundering inside his chest, but she made no show of it.

"I have spoken to others in the city. It is a constant hive of activity. Traders from all parts of Khorvaire and beyond come here. Since the War, it has been a center of intrigue and treachery, plot and counterplot. It seems everyone is for sale."

"And you?"

"Up to a point, but there are things I value. Is the talisman safe?" She was as taut as a bowstring, every inch a warrior.

Her question took him by surprise, but he reached for his shirt, balled up beside the pillow. The horn was inside it, tightly wrapped in leather.

"No, don't remove it. Better it stays concealed. It is a very dangerous thing."

"Can you tell me more about it?"

"Erethindel, the sacred horn. It is not what it seems. No one is sure who carved its runes. The Valenar believe it is not a horn but a tooth. A dragon's tooth."

Vaddi gaped at her. In the moons' glow she looked like an exquisite statue, her lines perfect. He felt himself trembling, not daring to move.

"It has been disguised as a unicorn's horn, and some time in the past was given to Indreen, your mother, to protect. It houses great power, but this power is impotent on its own. If it is to be released, Erethindel must be wielded by someone of the blood."

"Dragon blood?"

"Yes. Have you used its power?"

Slowly he nodded. He told her about the island of the undead.

"You risked much in this."

"Then there is dragon blood in me?"

"Yes." She seemed cool, almost aloof.

"What does it mean?"

"No one is certain, but Erethindel seems to have been empowered by the dragons of Argonessen either to control elven magic or to combine with it. It is an enigma to us. Perhaps Erethindel is a relic of former times. It is said to be capable of great good or great evil, depending who wields it. For this reason, the elves were reluctant to put it to use, not trusting its powers. It was given to Indreen to keep safe, far from Aerenal and Valenar."

"Then that is why Caerzaal wanted me alive!"

"The vampire lord. Yes, when I realized just how much of a force he had drawn up around Taeris Mordel, I knew the Emerald Claw was desperate."

"What would Caerzaal have done?"

"Bound you to him and the Claw. You would have become one of the undead. As Caerzaal's slave, you would have been forced to use the horn. To give blood, dragon blood, to him and his vile army through the horn. Once you fill the horn with your blood, those who drink from it are empowered."

Vaddi stared at the shirt bundle in horror. "Perhaps it should be destroyed."

"Perhaps. But you cannot remain here in Pylas Maradal. A thousand eyes will be on you. Mostly enemies. Caerzaal would not dare set foot here himself, but the Claw has agents everywhere. I have seen them already."

"Then I must leave with all haste. And you? Will you help me?" *And come with me?* he wanted to add.

"I will go back now. There are friends I must speak to, and I will arrange for us to leave Pylas Maradal secretly."

"What of the others? Cellester and Nyam?"

"We can only wait for so long. If they are not here tomorrow, we'll leave word for them with Kalfar. He can be trusted, but he does *not* need to know that you carry Erethindel! He would not take it from you by force, Vaddi, but he might think it would be safer with him."

"Where should it go?"

"I am not sure, but it must never leave you."

She rose slowly, stretching like a cat. He made to get up, but she put a hand on his shoulder, gently but firmly keeping him down. He reached for her fingers and touched them.

"Sleep now," she said.

"Sleep? I cannot sleep, not knowing you are out there—"

She laughed, bent down, and brushed his lips with hers before he realized what she had done. At once he felt a warm glow, as if she had released a spell to calm him. Slowly, inch by inch, he slipped back into the folds of the cushions. He was asleep before she reached the window.

❀ ❀ ❀ ❀ ❀ ❀ ❀

The sound of thunder woke him, then he realized with a start that it was the thick wooden door to his chamber. Someone was outside, knocking on it. As he got out of bed, he could still taste the swift kiss of the sorceress. She had imparted something with it, a breath of power, perhaps, that had entered his very blood. He could almost hear it singing in his veins. And something else . . . the shadow, the ever-present *block* that constantly held him in check. It was still there, but it had weakened.

"I'm coming!" he called, going to the door. Yes, there could be no doubt of it: he felt lighter of foot, clearer of head. Zemella had brushed him with power. Beyond the door, one of Kalfar's servants stood.

"Lord, Master Kalfar desires your presence as soon as is convenient. We have a visitor, lord. One who is known to you."

Downstairs, Kalfar waited, dressed no less magnificently than the previous evening—this time with a rich, purple turban encrusted with a burst of gemstones, as though he were the overlord of the city. Vaddi's eyes went from the portly figure to the others in the chamber. In its center, flanked by two armed guards, their pikes hovering at his back, was Nyam, eyes blazing, beard bristling with indignation.

As Vaddi approached, the peddler waved his hat about, the feathers flapping in the air. "Vaddi, will you tell this lunatic who I am?"

Vaddi turned to Kalfar. "What has happened?"

Kalfar folded his arms over his broad chest and chewed his lip for a moment. "It seems that this fellow was caught lurking about in the street outside my home."

"Lurking?" Nyam gasped. "*Lurking?* That is outrageous!"

"Lurking, skulking, creeping about . . . it's all the same to me. An honest man would have come to the gates and called for egress."

"Preposterous," insisted Nyam. "I am in a strange city. These are perilous times. I am a cautious man, as any sensible fellow would be."

"Pah! Let us dispense with deceit. Vaddi, this man claims to know you. Is he that same Nyam Hordath who lately fled with you from Karrnath?"

"Indeed, Kalfar," Vaddi replied, trying to sound solemn, though he could not help but smile. "The very same. I am sure he is right about caution. We have both had good reason to go about our business carefully."

"There!" said Nyam. "My identity is confirmed."

Kalfar drew from its sheath a huge, curved scimitar and

tested the sharpness of its blade. "Were I to remove that expansive bird's nest of a beard, what other identity would be confirmed? Are there any clawfoot traders buried beneath that avalanche of hair?"

Nyam sustained his indignation. *"Clawfoot* trader? Do I look like one?"

"Are you a man of honor?" Kalfar snapped. "Well?"

Nyam looked to Vaddi. "I trust that Vaddi will vouch for me on that score."

Vaddi stepped closer to the peddler. "The truth, Nyam. I have trusted you. Have you been to Pylas Maradal before under another name?"

Nyam drew himself up, preparing to unleash a stream of denials, but as his eyes met Vaddi's, he instead released a huge breath, which seemed to reduce him to almost half his size. His hands flapped briefly at his sides.

"Ah, what is the point of deception?"

"You were once known as Tutos Munnermal?" said Vaddi, still unable to remove the smile from his face entirely.

"Possibly," muttered Nyam.

"Speak up, speak up!" growled Kalfar.

"Oh, yes, yes. You have me at a disadvantage. Yes, I once used that name."

"When you swindled me! You were supposed to bring me a string of thoroughbred clawfoots, and you duped me with creatures fit only to be boiled down for soup! I spent six months hunting you."

"I can only offer my deepest apologies. I did it for good reason."

"Good reason? Yes, to fatten your purse. Where did the string end up?"

"It was during the War," said Nyam.

"I know that!" thundered Kalfar. "They were for the halflings!"

"There were others in the north who needed them more. People less fortunate, whose homes were being overrun."

Kalfar was spluttering with rage.

He means his family! thought Vaddi. Their land, his wife, his sons . . .

"I am in your debt," Nyam told Kalfar, bowing his head.

"Yes, indeed. Indeed you are. So how will you pay me?" The huge sword hovered menacingly.

"Kill me if you must, but I doubt that you'll profit much."

"No," said Vaddi. "Kalfar—"

"You are bound to me, Nyam Hordath. A debt of honor. You agree?"

"How could I not?"

"Then you can discharge it. If you are honorable."

"You have only to say—"

"The time of words is over. Time for *deeds*. Now you have a remarkable network. You must have to have evaded me for as long as you did. You seem capable of slipping in and out of every nook and cranny the length and breadth of Khorvaire. I want you to use that skill now. You see this young man? He needs to travel to Thrane, secretly, *deviously*. Who better to shield him and guide him but you? Do this, be his protector at all times, and your debt to me is discharged."

Nyam looked at Kalfar in surprise. "Would Vaddi not be safer in the hands of a real escort, armed men, a warclan even?"

Vaddi was also looking askance at Kalfar.

"I think not. If you can move about so freely, so much the better for Vaddi. Armed warriors, elves or men, would stand out and attract attention from every eye. And as the agents of the Emerald Claw are also eager to get their talons on you, an armed party would be like a beacon to them. So do we have a deal?"

Nyam turned to Vaddi. "Have you decided on a course?"

Vaddi nodded. "My family must be avenged."

"Very well," said Nyam. "I promise to undertake this."

The momentary silence was broken by a discreet cough. It was Abdas and he held a letter. Kalfar nodded and the steward handed the missive to his master.

"This is for Vaddi. An educated hand." Kalfar passed it to Vaddi.

Vaddi opened it, surprised by its message. "It is from Cellester. He has been delayed. He seeks aid for us, but it will be a week before he is able to join me here. He urges me to prevail upon you, Kalfar, to host me until then."

"Does he indeed? You may stay in my house as long as you wish, but I am not so sure that is wise. Your enemies are bound to learn you are here."

"Since you have bought my service," said Nyam, again inflating himself, "I should begin at once. I know a safe house or two in the city."

"Yes," agreed Kalfar. "Move quickly. What of this . . . Cellester? Is he to join you?"

Nyam looked at Vaddi. "It's your decision."

"I am unsure of him," said Vaddi, "but I will not abandon him. Not yet anyway."

"Then when he comes," Nyam said to Kalfar, "tell him to find word of me at the Black Mare's Nest."

"Ha!" Kalfar guffawed. "That poxy rat hole! I should have known. I doubt that there's a rougher, more run-down, shoddy pit on the entire waterfront! It's a brave man who ducks his head under those beams."

"It has its advantages." Nyam grinned. "Shall we go?"

Vaddi embraced Kalfar, who muttered something about not even bothering to stay for breakfast.

"Tell Cellester where we are, and if Zemella should seek me—"

"Of course, my boy." Kalfar grinned enormously. "Of course."

● ● ● ◉ ● ● ●

An hour before dawn, before Vaddi had awakened, Pylas Maradal fell quiet, though not altogether silent, for there were always those who prowled its streets on secret errands or on dubious business. Dark bargains were struck and strange, exotic commodities exchanged hands while the majority of the Valenar slept. Fortunes were won and lost at the turn of a blade.

Weaving cat-like through the alleyways near the docks, the girl blended with the shadows, well used to the mysteries of her city. Many of the remaining night prowlers did not even see her, but those who did pretended not to notice. This was not an hour for conversation.

Zemella was conscious, however, that she had attracted the attention of someone. More than one of them, she sensed. She slipped her sword from its scabbard, ready to use it. It would not have been the first time she had fought her way out of an alley scrap. A smile played on her lips. A little exercise before dawn would not be unwelcome.

The smile dissolved as she saw the three figures slide from the shadows ahead of her. They were no common thieves. Nor were they Valenar. But they were elves—faces painted deathly white, hands equally as pale, swords at the ready. She eschewed any discussion and launched herself at them, her own blade a blur. The air hummed and she could taste the sorcery in it.

Behind her, others closed in, mouthing spells. She wove her own net of magic about her, but these creatures were powerful and the air continued to crackle, drowning out the clash of blades. Ordinarily Zemella would have been more than a match for any skulking band of cutthroats and they would have been dead or maimed in a matter of moments.

Not so this dark brethren. They kept her at bay, front and back, but drew her onward down the alley to a low doorway that opened into darkness. Zemella could *smell* deeper sorcery within. Spells like thick spider webs threatened to engulf her, her blade forced to weave an even tighter protective circle. She wounded two of her opponents, but others stepped into their breach. They said nothing, wide eyes fixed upon her.

She redoubled her efforts, her blade whirling, drawing thin blood on more than one opponent, but the combination of numbers closed in like the coils of a serpent. A sudden bolt of light burst over her shoulder, blinding her. Dazed, her arm went numb and her blade clattered to the cobblestone. At once she felt swords at her throat and a knife held against her midriff.

"Come with us and live," said a sibilant voice through the haze of the spell.

Gripped by their twisted power, she had no alternative.

* * * ⊚ * * *

"Kalfar Munjati is as parsimonious as they come, relative or not!" Nyam snorted between mouthfuls of hot broth and freshly baked bread.

He sat opposite Vaddi in a cramped booth in the notorious dockside inn, the Black Mare's Nest. Although it was still the breakfasting hour, the inn was stuffed with sailors, travellers and others of questionable trade and disposition. The morning pipesmoke curdled overhead among low beams, mingling with the remnants of the previous night's.

Vaddi, eyes streaming, concentrated on his food, which was good, and closed out the reek and the noise around him. "Why do you say that? We could have eaten with him."

"Aye. But he has spared his purse by hiring me. At no cost. Whatever family ties he has with you and whatever obligation he might feel toward you, he has discharged cheaply! Cleverly done."

"He owes me nothing."

"He's an Orien!"

"Only by marriage. He's no heir. So what was all that about clawfoot trading and swindling him?"

Nyam looked sheepish. "It's a long story. I did put one over on the old skinflint, it's true, but it was no more than he deserved."

"Well, I won't hold you to your agreement with him."

Nyam chewed hungrily, watching Vaddi, frowning.

"I can't expect you to tie yourself to me and my cause," said Vaddi.

"You have doubts about returning to the north?"

Vaddi's look hardened. "Those who murdered my family will be brought to account."

"I will do as I promised and stay with you. To protect what you carry."

"Tell me, why did you come to his house? They caught you outside it. You must have known you would be in trouble with Kalfar if he saw you."

Nyam chuckled. "Thought my beard would fool him. But I wanted to give you some news. After I left you last evening, I thought I'd find out what the cleric was about."

"You followed him?" said Vaddi, surprised.

"Up to a point. Then I had some friends of mine keep an eye on him. I would like to believe he is your ally, but his knowledge of that undead . . . thing disturbs me. We have saved each others' lives, yes, but it was in his interest, too."

"I cannot be sure of him either."

"My contacts will be here soon. More food?"

"No, thank you. That's another thing. I have no money."

Nyam patted his robe and it jingled. "That's no problem. I found a little something on that airship."

"You stole it?"

"Dead men don't need coins." Nyam laughed. "I can see I've a lot to teach you if you're to survive, especially in this part of the world. I've deflected half a dozen grasping fingers already. Pickpockets. Pylas Maradal seethes with them."

"So where are we to go now?"

"After we have seen my contacts, I suggest we consider passage on another airship. We can travel as traders. This time we'll take some support so that we'll deter any of Caerzaal's minions from open attack."

"We travel today?"

Nyam grinned. "Why? Is there someone you wish to see first? A certain sorceress, by any chance?"

Vaddi was about to retort but sat back with a laugh. "Yes, all right. You know I like her—"

"*Like* her? Is that what you call it!"

"Nyam!" said Vaddi, flushing and looking around at the press of bodies, expecting to see everyone grinning at him. "Of course I like her. I can't just walk out of here without seeing her."

Nyam leaned forward, his grin for a moment set aside. "You are sure? Safer if we slip away like mist."

"I must see her, Nyam."

Nyam nodded slowly. "I understand."

"Last night she visited me."

"Oh-ho! Did she indeed?"

Vaddi colored. "Only briefly! Just to explain something of the history of—" he tapped his chest. "She spoke of helping me to leave. She was going to try and arrange for something, so I can't just go."

"No."

"She kissed me," he said softly, as if to himself, and in saying it he felt again the magic of that fleeting moment, the strange power that it had awakened in him.

Nyam was scratching his beard. "I see. Passions are aroused . . ."

"No, it was a brief kiss, barely a touch."

"Not a real kiss then?"

"No . . . well, yes! I don't know. It unlocked something—"

Nyam groaned.

"What?"

"Nothing, nothing. Go on."

"I have felt constrained for so long, yet now, something is working loose in me. Like . . . I don't know. Like a thorn in the flesh, set in deep, and then it slowly rises to the surface."

"It's called love, Vaddi."

"No, not that. Well, yes, it is that, but there is more."

"Well, I can see a difference in you. A glow. Must be your elf blood."

Before they could continue their conversation, two burly ruffians elbowed their way to the table and squeezed themselves on to a bench, swapping crude curses with the existing occupants. Just when it seemed there would be a brawl, the former occupants edged up the bench, grumbling about it never being too early for sticking warthogs. Like dogs growling over a bone, all parties settled down to an uneasy truce. Vaddi tried not to gape at the two newcomers and Nyam laughed aloud.

"Allow me to introduce Skaab and Thucknor. Vaddi."

The two pirates, for Vaddi thought they could be nothing but freebooters, given that their rough dress, sea-beaten features and gnarled hands proclaimed it for all to see, grunted their rude greetings to the youth, showing their teeth, such as they were, in brief but ghastly grins.

Vaddi nodded but found it hard to speak.

"What news have you brought me?" said Nyam.

The bigger of the two, Skaab, was a man twice the girth of most, with a striped shirt that had long since given up being buttoned. His enormous gut, singularly hairy, bulged. He leaned forward, though with difficulty. "We 'ad your man followed. The cleric. Last night. 'E was a busy bird, that one."

Someone from the bar leaned over the table and prepared to set down a tray of huge tankards, foam slopping over their rims. Skaab and Thucknor scooped up a tankard each before they had been set down. Nyam produced a coin and gave it to the barman. Vaddi tried not to grimace at the treacle-like ale. Nyam sipped his own.

"Go on, Skaab."

" 'E came down 'ere to the docks."

"Aye," snorted Thucknor, who was marginally less rotund than his mate. "Keeps strange company."

Nyam leaned forward. "Quietly now."

"Y'know Vortermars? Captains a privateer up and down this southern coast, between Darguun and Q'barra."

"Yes, I know him," said Nyam with a deep scowl. He glanced at Vaddi. "As big a roach as ever crawled out from under a barrel."

Both Skaab and Thucknor laughed, an unnerving sound.

"Well, the cleric met with his first mate, Gez Muhallah. Planned a little trip."

"To where?"

Skaab looked around, but no one appeared to be trying to listen to them. "We know Gez. 'E's a tight-lipped monkey, but we 'ad a few ales with 'im. It's no secret that Vortermars makes the Aerenal run when it suits `im."

"What trade does he ply there?" said Nyam.

"Anything that others won't touch," grinned Skaab. "Forbidden stuff, like the rarer woods, drugs, artifacts . . ."

"So the cleric is bound for Aerenal?"

"Aye, with a valuable cargo, if Gez was to be believed."

"Which was?"

"It took us a while to find out," sniffed Thucknor, draining his ale and leaning back, as big a hint as he could give that he was still thirsty.

"You'll have all the ale you can drink for a week, you dogs! Just tell me what you know."

Skaab nodded. "Aye. We went down to the docks where the *Sea Harlot* was anchored up. Vortermars's ship. Nice lines. Trim, fast—"

"Get on with it!" said Nyam.

"The cleric met elves, but they weren't the ordinary types, not like you see all round Pylas Maradal. These were weird. Can't put me finger on it. Painted for one thing. Cold fish. Didn't like the *smell* of them." Skaab sat back, shaking his head as though the thought of these elves disturbed him.

Nyam, too, looked deeply uneasy.

"What is it?" said Vaddi.

"If it is what I think, I am puzzled as to why the cleric should be trafficking with them. It can only mean the worse for us. So what happened?"

Thucknor took up the tale. "The cleric must have done some deal with these elves. We couldn't hear it all, but we saw them agreeing something."

"What was this cargo you spoke of?"

"A girl. Elf girl."

Vaddi looked askance at Nyam, but then something crossed his mind, a grim shadow. He felt himself growing cold. "A girl? What did she look like?"

"Pretty piece," said Skaab. "We saw 'er with the elves at dawn. They were taking 'er onboard the *Sea Harlot*. At swordpoint. And the air was 'umming with sorcery! Spells locking with spells. Six elves, all with power, otherwise she would've been too much to 'andle. She was . . . well, about the same age as the boy 'ere. Short, dark 'air, slim build."

"*Zemella!*" breathed Vaddi, an icy fist gripping his heart.

"Aye, that was her name!" said Thucknor. "I heard the cleric say it."

Vaddi's mouth went dry. He turned a devastated look on Nyam. "Then Cellester is no ally after all. It has all been a deception!"

"Softly, my boy. What happened? The elves sailed with the girl. And the cleric?"

"He went with them. Bound for Aerenal."

"Do you know which port?"

"Shae Thoridor initially. Unload a legitimate cargo. After that, the east coast, maybe. Even Gez Muhallah don't pass on everything."

"The girl was to be delivered to Shae Thoridor?"

"Dunno," said Skaab and Thucknor in unison. "Unlikely. All the under'and stuff goes on elsewhere. You should know that, Nyam."

Nyam sat back with a sigh. "Yes, I know it only too well."

"What now?" said Skaab.

Vaddi looked intently at the peddler. "We must follow," he said. "Wherever they have taken her, we follow. I cannot believe that Cellester means Zemella anything but harm."

"Khyber's shadows! I fear you are right, but *why?* Why has he abducted her?"

"So you'll want passage to Aerenal?" said Skaab.

Nyam glanced at Vaddi. "Can you arrange it, promptly?"

"If you mean to give chase to the *Sea Harlot* and get into a ruckus with 'er, forget it. No one 'ereabouts will mess with Vortermars, especially as 'is ship is now dripping with sorcery. It's faster than a gale with that accursed crew! Best go as a trader. In disguise, if you get me."

"How soon?"

"We can get you on a ship before noon. Earlier if the money's right."

Nyam patted his robes and his coins clinked. He frowned at Vaddi. "The sooner we go, the better. Vaddi?"

Vaddi glared at him. "There's no other course."

"Yes, I thought as much. I fear that kiss is going to prove very expensive."

CHAPTER 11

In Xen'drik, in what had once been a gigantic temple to powers long buried under the weight of aeons, figures gathered, acolytes in a ritual they had been performing for days. They lit the braziers wherein strange and baleful fires glowed, filling the air above them with writhing mists and aerial phantoms, warped and misshapen. The cloaked ones chanted, the rhythm of their incantations ebbing and flowing, swelling the smoke-shapes in the air, giving life to them. Faces flowed out of that crawling fog—tortured faces, faces that contorted in pain, ethereal bodies straining to be corporeal, like prisoners desperate to be free of bonds that had gripped them for centuries. In the wide circle that was the floor of the ruin, cleaned of its debris and weeds, an immense pentacle had been unearthed, its etchings reeking with sorcery, the sigils and designs of its inner heart alien and blasphemous. They pulsed with life, like the veins of some gigantic beast on the edge of wakefulness.

High above this grim scene, a balcony jutted out from the tallest of the temple walls, where monstrous carvings had been cut into its height. The frozen grimaces of demons from beyond time's long-lost edge howled silently over the gathering, as if adding fuel to the exhortations. A solitary shape leaned on the balustrade, looking down at its minions, watching with deep satisfaction their workings. Around the arena, hunched on its walls, black-winged creatures glared down, restrained by whatever sorcery crackled in the air. Soarwings, bred for warriors of the darkest kind, with sharpened claws and beaks like swords, had the appearance of demonic dragons, as though they would challenge even those masters of the skies if unleashed upon them.

Zuharrin smiled, but his eyes were like coals, hot and filled with power-lust, no hint of humanity in them. Steeped in the powers of ritual magic and demonology, the sorcerer had long ago forsworn his human heritage in search of darker paths to immortality and power. Soon he would be ready to perform the ultimate summoning of that power. As night gathers after sunset, so his power would follow from this working. Below him the acolytes continued with the endless preliminaries, preparing this once hallowed sanctuary, deep in the heart of time-ravaged Xen'drik, for the army that was to be born here. Below them, in the fathomless depths of Khyber itself, the great demon lord T'saagash Mal shrieked and howled in its snare, the dragon chains that had bound it there an eternity ago.

Soon! Zuharrin told himself. Aarnamor will bring the youth and that which he carries—the tools that will unlock this well and bring life anew to T'saagash Mal.

Movement behind him made him turn, his tall, bat-like frame blotting out the grey of the day. A grotesque figure approached from the tunnel, its gargoyle-face grinning up at him. Barely over a foot tall, like some misshapen dwarf, it was a homunculus, created by Zuharrin to run messages for him. It scraped its forehead on the stone floor, spreading scaly arms in supplication.

"Word from Valenar?" said Zuharrin.

When the creature spoke, its voice struggled with human tongue. "Yes, lord. The scouts you loosed sent back messages."

"Does Aarnamor have the boy?"

"Not yet, lord. The Orien cur fell under the protection of an elf sorceress, but Aarnamor reports that in Pylas Maradal she was taken. Removed."

"Killed?"

"No, lord. Not yet. She has been shipped to Aerenal. The cleric has seen to it."

"Where is the Orien whelp?" snapped Zuharrin, his voice carrying the threat of pain.

"In Pylas Maradal, where he is among allies. Too dangerous to capture him there, but now he will follow her, lord. He knows she has been abducted, but not that the cleric was responsible. He has set the trap well."

"To Aerenal! That is even more dangerous! If the elves recover the horn, I cannot secure it. Where is Aarnamor?"

"Waiting, lord. When the time is right, he will meet the cleric. There are many elves in Aerenal, lord. Some can be bought. The boy is of no value to them, except to sell to your servants."

"The sorceress is not a threat?"

"No," sniggered the creature. "A place is prepared for her, a bad place, where her magic will be of no avail. The Madwood."

Zuharrin's face shaped itself into a mirthless grin. The Madwood! Yes, that would be perfect. The wild forest, a living nightmare, remote from the world. The cleric had indeed done his work well.

"The boy will be easy meat, once he reaches Shae Thoridor. The Murughel elves, the Stillborn, will simply snare him there. There will be a trap set in the city with the promise of the elf girl as the bait. The Orien youth will not be able to resist it. Then he will be in the cleric's hands once again. There are many places on the outskirts of Shae Thoridor where Aarnamor can meet them in secret. He will bring the boy and that which he carries to you."

Zuharrin nodded. "Then I am content."

The homunculus shuffled away and Zuharrin turned back to the mustering below, watching its movements with renewed relish. Soon. The great rebirth will be soon, and the dragons themselves will shudder, knowing their power is no longer supreme.

● ● ● ◉ ● ● ●

Cellester gripped the prow of the privateer and stared ahead at the heaving seas. They rose and fell in great swells, their tops breaking up into white spume that the wind flung away in tatters. The *Sea Harlot* was in the grip of greater powers, its sleek form like a living thing, magic propelling it at thrice its normal sailing speed through these waters. The cleric's amulet glowed, adding to the powers at work, those of the dark elves and those of the captain, Vortermars. Cellester brooded on the events of the previous night, his face devoid of expression but his mind in turmoil.

"Pity my ship don't always shift this quick, eh?" sniffed a voice at his back.

The cleric turned to meet the broken grin of the captain. He was dressed in plain clothes, proof against the gales and testing weather of these seas, coat belted tight. Twin swords and a long dirk hung from it, a reminder of his dubious trade.

"There is always a heavy price to pay for the use of such spells," said Cellester.

Vortermars indicated the deck and the prisoner stowed below it. "She must be worth it. Special, is she?"

"All you need to know is that she is very dangerous."

Vortermars screwed up his sea-tanned face. "That's no lie! Wouldn't have touched her but for the other elves. Know what you're dealing with, eh? Murughel. Nasty bastards, but it took all their black power to keep her in check."

"You'll be paid well enough."

"I ain't complainin'. Your gold's no different to anyone else's. Don't suppose it'll be the last time I deal with the Stillborn. Since the War ended, Khorvaire's a smoking ruin. Everyone's looking after himself. Dog eat dog, eh?"

Cellester didn't answer, eyes fixed on the horizon where Aerenal would eventually rise up.

"I could be of further service to you," Vortermars went on,

spitting over the rail. "There'll be a hunt for this girl, no? Family, warclan, whatever. Eh?"

"Perhaps."

"Sure as the sea's the sea. Someone will miss her."

Cellester eyed him coldly. "You are certain that I was not implicated in this? It is important that no one knows it was my work."

"Crew's as tight-lipped as they come, but she's a sorceress. They'll follow. If it's just one ship, I could sink it and all its crew for you, elves or no. If it's a fleet, I could lead it a right dance until it was way off the scent, eh?"

Cellester's eyes widened. "No. I don't want that, but there is more I need you to do."

Vortermars scowled. "You *want* to be followed?"

"There'll be a youth, an Orien, possibly in the company of a peddler. They may be protected."

"Peddler, eh? Got a name?"

"Does it matter?"

"I stay alive by knowing who's skulking about in my waters."

"His name is Nyam Hordath."

Vortermars snorted, again spitting into the sea. "Nyam Hordath, eh? Well, well. What's that old fox sniffing around here for?"

Cellester masked his unease. "You know him?"

"There's not a pirate sinkhole on these coasts that don't. Been wheeling and dealing for years. Must have a bigger stash than any of us. So he's with this Orien boy, eh?"

"Probably. The boy may also have help from a relative, Kalfar Munjati."

Vortermars screwed his face up in confusion. "That don't make no sense! Kalfar and Nyam Hordath don't mix. Rival traders. If Nyam Hordath is with this Orien boy, Kalfar won't be helping them."

Cellester masked his relief. "Then it is likely that Vaddi Orien pursues us alone or with minimal support." Even better, he thought.

"Like I said, easy matter for me to dispose of him for you, eh?"

"No. I want him to follow, but if you want to earn more gold, there is a way."

Vortermars chuckled. "Always is."

"Make sure that the youth reaches Aerenal safely. Keep your distance and don't be seen. If anyone else has any ideas about waylaying him, forestall them."

"Just to Aerenal? Shae Thoridor?"

"Yes. Once the boy has landed, I'll deal with him."

Vortermars nodded. "Easy money."

❀ ❀ ❀ ❀ ❀ ❀ ❀

I should have followed my instincts! Zemella said to herself, over and over again. The cleric. I knew there was something about him. Vaddi was not sure of him. I should have made sure he was watched in Pylas Maradal. Furious with herself, she pounded her fist into her palm.

Here, in this cramped cabin fit only for a dog, she was trapped, pinned down by stronger spells. They were the worst kind, Murughel, steeped in the black arts. They'd been little more than a sect of malcontents at first, but over the past few years they had become dangerous and ever more bold.

There was no point trying to batter the door down, either with her fists or with spells of her own. They had combined their powers to pen her in. Somewhere ahead, wherever they were bound for in Aerenal, for it was there they would take her, she knew, they would slip up. Inevitably, they would provide her with some kind of opening, and then, by the dragons, she would teach them to interfere with a warrior of the Finnarra.

She would will deal with this treacherous cleric. She was sure she knew why she had been abducted. The cleric had no wish to see Vaddi and his burden fall into the hands of the Emerald Claw. Nor did he want him to be welcomed into the halls of the Undying Elves, either in Valenar or in Aerenal. The cleric must have known that they did not seek Erethindel.

It was her that Cellester feared! He realized she would become Vaddi's guide—more than that, perhaps. Thus the cleric would lose his hold on Vaddi.

She began to piece it together. Vaddi said he had felt constrained, his power never properly loosened, like a knot inside him. Of course! The cleric has done this, held him in check for his own purposes. Why does he want control of Vaddi? Erethindel. Useless without Vaddi or one of dragon blood. He desires that power for himself or for someone else.

As the ship ploughed swiftly on to the elf homeland, she dug deeper into the mystery, its shrouds dissipating. The undead warrior, Aarnamor, is part of this! He came for Vaddi. If she had not struck him, crippling him on the bridge at Taeris Mordel, he would have taken Vaddi there and then. And the horn! Not for Cellester, but for whoever it is he serves. She tried to focus her mind, but there was nothing to indicate who this could be.

He was taking her out of Vaddi's reach, where she could no longer be of help to him. Then, when Vaddi was helpless in Pylas Maradal, he would go back to him, begin again his deceit and lead him and his burden to his own master. Yet there was more to this. Why was the cleric onboard? She felt his presence, the stirring of the power he exercised in his own defense and in speeding the vessel onward.

He has allied himself to the Murughel, she thought. Does he labor for the ends of their vile cult? Is Erethindel for them? If so, then I am not merely being removed. I am a *lure*. Bait for Vaddi.

She stood, a fresh wave of fury washing over her. They would be in Shae Thoridor in another day. If she were to free herself, it must be there, before they could plunge her into whatever pit they had prepared for her.

* * * ❀ * * *

Not for the first time that day, Vaddi was amazed at Nyam's resourcefulness. He seemed to be able to pull from thin air the clothes, weapons, and provisions they needed for their pursuit of the *Sea Harlot*. The peddler's connections in Pylas Maradal were remarkable and his credit was no less so. More than ever Vaddi was aware that Nyam was not the simple peddler he affected.

"Not that I'm prying into your past, Nyam," said Vaddi, once he had changed into the nondescript but comfortable robes of a trader and strapped to a concealed belt a fresh dirk plus two other short swords, "but you seem well known to these people."

Nyam grinned. "I confess I have had more than a few dealings along this seaboard, some that I'd rather not discuss! I'm just calling in a few favors, and I do have something set aside, as it were, against my needs."

"And the ship?"

"There's an elven trader bound for Shae Thoridor. Just delivered its cargo to the docks. Ostensibly rare woods from Aerenal."

"You mean there was another cargo?"

"I know the captain. He wouldn't miss a chance to earn some real gold. I suspect there was a weighty supply of contraband weapons onboard. The officials in Pylas Maradal try to control such things, but there's a big demand for elf bows with certain forbidden spells woven into their grain. Dramman Wandel would prefer no passengers on the return, but he'll take us."

"Are you sure?"

Again Nyam laughed. "Oh, yes. We go back a long way, and what's more, he'll vouch for us in our new guises as traders."

"And what are we trading in?"

"Rare woods. They have some of the finest in Eberron. We need a valid reason to be in Aerenal, and trading for wood will satisfy the authorities there."

"What do we have?"

"We are negotiating on behalf of a certain Lord Kazzerand."

"We are?"

"Indeed. We have the seal of Kazzerand himself."

Vaddi's eyes bulged as Nyam proffered a disc that seemed to be made of beaten silver. "But where did you get such a thing?"

"There are smiths in a certain quarter of Pylas Maradal who can reproduce anything. For a price, of course, but my credit is good." He slipped the disc away.

Vaddi grinned, but inwardly his mind was in turmoil. There was so much about Nyam that he knew nothing about. True, he'd have been helpless here without him. But what did the peddler really want? Was he working for someone else? Surely not Kazzerand. That seal! Maybe it was genuine and he was in the warlord's employ.

But no, Vaddi thought, I can't believe it of him. And Zemella trusts him.

There was little time to deliberate, for they had to get to the harbor. Nyam led them through the maze of bazaars that were the perpetual flow of the lifeblood of Pylas Maradal. At last they fought their way to a narrow alleyway that led to a wharf where a ship buzzed with activity. As they went down the alley, a group of elf warriors materialized, blocking their retreat on either side.

Nyam's fingers closed over the haft of his sword, but these elves were armed and not to be provoked. Their spokesmen came close, deep green eyes locking with the peddler's.

"Nyam Hordath," he said in a cold, crisp voice. Although not as tall as a man, he exuded power and seemed to overshadow the peddler.

"What business do you have with me?"

"I am Ardal Barragond. You do not know me. These elves are part of the Finnarra. You are sailing on yon trader?"

"What if I am?"

"I know the cargo you seek. On Vortermars's ship." The elf lowered his voice to just above a whisper.

"What about it?" Nyam held Vaddi gently in check, sensing the youth's sudden concern.

"She is of our clan. If she is harmed, there will be much

blood spilt in her name. I would not have her harmed."

"Nor I," said Nyam. "We seek to free her."

"As do I."

"We dare not go in force. This has to be done very carefully. If our enemies suspect we are close, they will outnumber us. Even your warriors would be compromised."

Ardal nodded. "I am sure you are right, but one of us will go with you. Perhaps not by your side, as that would invite suspicion, but it would not be unusual for a Finnarra to travel to Aerenal."

Nyam hesitated, but then nodded. "You know that the Murughel are involved in this?"

"Yes. They have grown in power in Aerenal. They have made alliances that other elves would shudder at."

"Which of you is to go?"

"I myself," said Ardal.

"Then come." Without further ado, Nyam brushed past the Finnarra warriors. Ardal spoke briefly to them and followed the peddler and Vaddi.

● ● ● ◉ ● ● ●

Vaddi was beset by new doubts. What, precisely was the relationship of this elf to Zemella? They were in the same warband, yes, but was there more to it than that? Could Ardal be Zemella's lover? The thought filled him with horror. He had never even considered the possibility that she already had someone, but why should he have been so unreasonable! Of course, it made perfect sense.

But he had no time to torment himself further. Nyam was finalizing the arrangements for them to get aboard the ship. Once they had embarked, Vaddi settled near the prow. The ship cast off from the harbor and Pylas Maradal was soon a distant outline on the receding shore.

Vaddi felt the power of the sea around them, the enormous energies locked beneath the waves. They seemed to speak to him, and again he felt the gradual release of power within himself, that knot that had restricted him for so long untangling. The ship was knifing through the seas at an unnatural speed, urged on by the power the crewmen used. Instinctively he released power of his own, a subconscious working, to add to the flow.

"It feels good, does it not?" said Nyam beside him, his hair streaming out behind him like a flag.

For a while Vaddi had tried to set aside his anxieties for Zemella, wanting to revel in this release. "A darkness within me is lifting, Nyam."

"I wondered at it. Now I understand it. It was the cleric. For years he has controlled you. Think of it. He shaped our journey, but he lost control in the skies over the Talenta Plains. But always he had a purpose. To take you *away* from Thrane."

"Where did he intend to take me? And why?"

"It is all to do with what you carry and your link to it. Cellester intends to deliver you both to someone, and obviously it is not Caerzaal or anyone else connected with the Emerald Claw."

"These elves that have taken Zemella?"

"Possibly, although the word in Pylas Maradal is that their links with the Claw have strengthened. I fear there are other powers at work here."

In his mind's eye, Vaddi saw again the huge soarwing that had hung over him on the bridge at Taeris Mordel. "That creature that helped us at Voorkesh and Taeris Mordel, the one that Cellester called Aarnamor?"

"He serves whoever seeks you and the horn. Cellester would possibly have delivered you both to it there and then had not Zemella intervened."

"But who is behind this?"

Nyam shook his head. "In Pylas Maradal I tried every avenue of enquiry. I have contacts with contacts. Even inside information in House Phiarlan—and there are no better ones than they! But Aarnamor is not known in Valenar, and I am sure that he is not known in Aerenal—at least, not in Shae Thoridor." The peddler scowled, lost in dark thoughts for a moment, watching the rise and fall of the seas as if in their turbulence he would descry an answer.

"Is there any clue to this mystery?"

"For such a power to maintain anonymity, high sorcery must be employed. Whoever or whatever this is, it must be immensely powerful. To have so cloaked itself, it is almost unprecedented. Like the dragons themselves."

"The dragons?"

"No, no, it is not they. They would never employ such base means as the cleric or the undead, and they would not involve themselves in our affairs."

"The horn is the key to this?"

"I am sure of it. You must keep it hidden. Although its powers have been so vital to our survival so far, I am sure it would be highly unwise of you to exercise them again, unless your very life is threatened. Even then, it may not be wise."

"I confess I am afraid of its power."

"I think there is one advantage you have. While you are free and carry it, your enemy, this unseen power, fears it, just as Caerzaal clearly feared it. Otherwise you would have been an easy target, taken any one of a dozen times on our journey. Power and counter-power, Vaddi, but if the enemy controlled you and the horn, what would that do to the balance of power in Eberron?"

Vaddi was frightened by Nyam's words. What else does he know? He turned back to the sea, hiding his misgivings. Zemella. Where are you now? Have they harmed you?

* * * * * * *

Dawn was the faintest hint on the shifting eastern horizon, the cloud underbelly touched with a blood red glow. From the prow of the *Sea Harlot*, the cleric watched the long, low shape of the oncoming ship clip the waves and ease alongside the slowing trader. Sheathed in shadows, like a predator from the deeps, the craft moved in silence, seeming to drip with sorcery and power. A single occupant came aboard, brought to Cellester by the scowling Vortermars. Dark-robed and hooded, this sinister figure bowed.

"You have brought the relic?" it said.

The face within the hood was white, almost painted, the eyes ringed darkly, as though the being had addicted itself to some dangerous narcotic. Bloodshot eyes locked with those of the cleric, but his own expression was impassive.

"I have." Cellester took from within his robe a small leather package, which he undid. Something within it gleamed in the bloody rays of the rising sun, like an omen of unease. "From Xen'drik," he said.

The hand of the dark-robed one reached out, thin and emaciated, like the hand of one of the undead, reminding Cellester for one grim moment of the Emerald Claw, though he knew this creature to be one of the Murughel. The skeletal fingers lifted the small object, which was made of a black metal, set with a bright gemstone at its end, a miniature scepter. In the pallid light, it had the appearance of a human bone.

"Be wary of its latent powers," said the cleric.

"I feel them."

"Though it is small, it was cast by giants in the days when elves were enslaved in Xen'drik. Its true purpose has become lost, but in the ruins of Xen'drik, there are many such objects made by the ancestors so revered by you. When you have done your work, I will provide you with more."

The dark one shuddered, though not with fear. A strange kind of ecstasy seemed to flow through him as he clutched the artefact more tightly. Then he had slipped it inside his own robe. "And the Valenar sorceress?"

Cellester nodded to Vortermars, who promptly left the deck.

"Treat her with extreme care," said Cellester. "She burns with a fierce desire to unleash her own power, which is no small thing."

The hooded one hissed, a derisive sound. "We have powers

enough to bind a dozen such as she." As he spoke, there was a scuffle behind him.

Zemella had been brought to the deck, her hands bound, an escort of Murughel warding off her curses and powers, her spells breaking like waves on an invisible barrier. She favoured the cleric with a withering glare, but he turned away, looking out at the sea.

"This treachery will be your bane, cleric!" she snarled at him as she was manhandled down to more hooded figures waiting in the low craft alongside.

Though Cellester shivered as if a cold wind had blown over him, he was very still. Zemella's last curse was lost as her captors took her aboard their own vessel and stowed her below.

Vortermars came to stand beside him. "Cursed relief to have her disposed of. Can we proceed to Shae Thoridor, eh? Sooner we are away from those black creatures, the better."

As he spoke, the long ship slid away from the *Sea Harlot*, her decks empty, her bleak crew hidden from view.

"Yes, get us to the port with all haste."

Vortermars gave a signal to his unseen pilot and at once his own ship was moving, again picking up unnatural speed. "She must have served you ill. Wouldn't give a dog to the Stillborn. Sooner have nothing to do with them. There's bad and there's evil. They serve evil. The Claw is bad enough, but—"

"I know well enough who they are," snapped Cellester, his gaze still fixed on the seas ahead.

"Then you know what you're about, eh?"

"Just do what you're paid to do."

Vortermars shrugged and left the brooding cleric alone.

❖ ❖ ❖ ◉ ❖ ❖ ❖

In the cramped, cloying darkness of the hold, the hooded one sat silently. The Valenar bitch was secured—although, as promised, it had taken significant power to achieve it. She was abnormally strong, but the cleric had paid well for her capture.

Beyond the hooded one, another figure stirred, as though it were composed of little more than shadow and smoke, but the face that leered from the fetid dark was real enough.

"The cleric made the venture worth your while?"

The Murughel elf nodded. "There will be other relics released to me when this business is over."

"I can promise you *so much more.*"

The hooded one nodded again. "Our alliance is preferred to that with the cleric. It is much welcomed. The secrets of the Claw and those of the Murughel will be a mixture of the most puissant kind."

"The cleric has defied me for the last time. The Orien boy will follow this Valenar bitch, even to the Madwood, and it will be me who snares him there. We will celebrate our success by sharing in the power of the sacred blood."

"The boy is coming, but he has only one companion."

"Yes. The interfering peddler. I will have his head for a goblet before this is over."

There was no trace of a smile on the white face of the hooded Murughel elf. "As you say, Caerzaal."

BLOODSHED IN SHAE THORIDOR
CHAPTER 12

Early evening was cloaking the world in its first shadows as the trader came in sight of the long outline of Aerenal. Aided by the powers of the traders and by Vaddi's own release of supernatural energy, the ship had raced across the sea to the home of the elves. By Nyam's estimate they were less than a day behind the *Sea Harlot*, which he swore could have docked in Shae Thoridor no earlier than dawn that same day. For a time they followed the northwestern coastline before sweeping around a broad headland and down into its lee, on toward the city. From the steep cliffs of the shoreline, Shae Thoridor rose up in tiers, and Vaddi marvelled at its architecture. From the very quays themselves, layer upon layer of carved buildings lifted up to the bright sky, like living things, giant trunks or roots. Shae Thoridor seemed somehow to *grow* from the cliff side, as though it were a natural thing, an enhancement of the crags and stone. The buildings themselves, dotted with windows, galleries, and walkways, had been crafted with intricate skill, each one part of the whole, both retaining individuality and unity. Above all, pulsing through the sap of the wood, its lifeblood, Vaddi felt the power of the elves, the energy that spoke to his own blood of a unique magic.

"Beautiful, is it not?" said Nyam beside him.

Vaddi nodded, lost in the wonders of this place. In the long harbor, numerous Aereni craft bobbed on the sheltered waters, sleek and built for speed, most with their sails furled. Their sailors moved about them busily, and on the quay others were equally as active so that the entire scene unfolded like the workings of a huge hive.

"From what trees were these buildings born?" said Vaddi. "I have never seen their like, nor could I have imagined such perfection."

"Livewood and soarwood mostly," said Nyam. "I could spend a week telling you of their histories, but we will be docking soon."

He looked over his shoulder. Ardal was not far away. The Valenar from Pylas Maradal had neither spoken to nor acknowledged them on the journey, but a brief nod of his head signalled to Nyam that he was going to keep pace with them in this place of dangers.

There was no sign of the *Sea Harlot*, but that was as Nyam had expected. She would have deposited her cargo promptly and Vortermars would have gone elsewhere to berth, across the bay to the smaller towns where a degree of privacy would have been more readily attainable. Nyam and Vaddi were leaving their ship, walking down her gangway to the quayside, when two Aereni warriors placed themselves in their path. With them was an official, a sharp-eyed Aereni who brandished a quill and a parchment as though in lieu of a weapon.

"Names?" he said in a cutting, haughty voice.

Nyam had invented something appropriate for both of them and gave them.

"Business in Shae Thoridor?"

"Traders, worthiness," said Nyam, bowing. "Drawn to this estimable clime by your excellent and incomparable woods."

"On whose behalf? We do not traffic with the flotsam and jetsam of the oceans. Our woods are sacred." He focused his supercilious gaze elsewhere.

"Yes," Nyam spluttered nervously, and Vaddi had to mask his amusement as Nyam dropped into the bumbling character that he was so adept at calling up when circumstances required. "Yes, of course, worthiness. I have this seal." He fumbled with his cloak, surreptitiously showing to the official the counterfeit seal. "I trust you appreciate the level of funding that I am commissioned to tap into for this venture."

The official reached forward a slender hand, brilliant emeralds sparkling from at least three rings, and clasped the seal, pulling it to him with little regard for Nyam's comfort. He gripped it as an eagle grips its prey, studying it for a moment. The official, blinked, scratched something with his quill on the parchment, and both he and the two Aereni warriors stepped aside.

Neither Nyam nor Vaddi looked back as they entered the port. As usual, Nyam knew where to go. Vaddi sensed that Ardal was not far behind them. Now that they were on Aerenal's soil, something else was striving to come alive in Vaddi, a new energy that almost surged. His ties with the elves, his dragon blood, perhaps. On his arm, his dragonmark itched for a moment.

Through his quickening powers, Vaddi was even more conscious of the Aereni about them, knowing that they were studied openly. The Aereni were not hostile to traders, but they had no real love for men or the other races, holding themselves superior and aloof. Men who came here found trading difficult, usually having to concede to demands that they would have rejected in other lands. Aerenal itself rose up behind the city. Far across the inlet beyond stood the shadow-clung shores of Jaelarthal Orioth, the Moonsword Jungle, an immense, living entity, thrumming with energy, secretive and distant, both forbidding and evocative. Its unseen depths called to Vaddi, a promise of strange destinies in that silent but potent calling.

Not far from the quayside, Nyam led them into a huge, low-beamed hall, which combined as both trading house and hostelry. The Aereni of Shae Thoridor controlled the movements of their visitors closely, restricting their movements in the city. Almost without exception, trading was done in this place under the ever-watchful eyes of the officials, duplicates of the cold-eyed being that had met Nyam and Vaddi at the quay. Hanging from the beams were several flags and similar banners, representing the emblems of houses on the mainland of Khorvaire, though most of them were soot-stained and ill kept. The Aereni banners and beautiful carvings were of the most exquisite workmanship, a reminder that in Aerenal, all bowed to the glory of the elves.

"This is not the healthiest of places," Nyam told Vaddi. "Built and run by men, although the Aereni keep a close eye on it, as you can see. To them, it's a sty and you'd never see them lowering themselves to drink or socialize here. They trade with us here, though reluctantly. It is a dump, but the chances are, we'll bump into some useful contacts."

Nyam, true to his word, had credit in this inn, and after a brief discussion with one of the human hosts, led Vaddi to a table that was as discreet as it could be in such a thriving hall. There was nowhere in here that was far from the glance of an Aereni warrior, whether a guard standing stiffly on watch or leaning against one of the fat, graven pillars.

Nyam brought some food and chewed it slowly, but Vaddi was not hungry, thinking only of Zemella and her potential plight.

"What are we waiting for?" he whispered.

"Ardal is our best hope here. He will have contacts among the Aereni. If the object of our search has landed, he will find out. We have to be patient. If the guards see us as anything but wood traders, they won't bother with an interrogation. They'll let the sharks in the bay do that. Eat."

Vaddi scowled and chewed on the bread. "Then tell me, who or what are these Murughel elves that you seem to fear so much?"

Nyam put a finger to his lips. "Never speak that name aloud in here. The name is a spell in itself." He leaned closer. "They are a faction, broken away from the pure strains of the elves."

As he spoke, his eyes never left the movements in the hall, ever watchful. "Although there is elf blood in you, Vaddi, you know very little about their race and their beliefs."

Vaddi nodded.

"For the elves of Aerenal, death is not something to be feared. Rather it is something to be embraced. Here, necromantic energies flow as deeply as the rocks and underground streams. The Aereni have used these powers to preserve life through rite and ritual and to create the undying. You need to understand what this means. The undying elves are hallowed beings, charged with positive energy and are gifted with longevity. They are a more natural being—healthy, born of an enervating life force. What you and I have seen on our journey here is something else, something very dark."

"The undead?" breathed Vaddi.

"Yes. Vampires, zombies, liches, and their ilk. Loathed by the undying, seen—quite rightly—as perversions. Negative energy, feeding on the living as maggots feed on a carcass. The elves despise them even more then we do. They would stop at nothing to destroy them."

"And the . . . others?"

"The status of being undying is not given to all elves. There are some who bitterly resent the withdrawal of this status. A movement has risen among some of the younger, disaffected Aereni, arrogant and proud, who seek necromantic powers for themselves. They accept vampirism and lichdom in lieu of becoming deathless."

"They *voluntarily* accept this?"

"Sadly, yes, and what is worse, I fear the Emerald Claw has formed an alliance with some of them. The Claw has long harbored the desire to control Aerenal. With the aid of these I have spoken of, it could wreak havoc here."

Vaddi pushed aside the remains of his food and sipped thoughtfully at his cup of water. "You think the Claw is behind this, after all? Cellester is working for the Claw?"

"No, I don't believe that, but these others are as devious

as the Claw. They may have other dark designs."

As Nyam was speaking, he swept an arm out and wrapped it around the shoulders of a hunched figure that was passing their table, drawing the being close to him in an unexpected hug.

"Sfarrag! Dear friend!" he boomed into the ear of the small figure. "Whatever brings you here?"

The diminutive but broad-shouldered being, which Vaddi could now see to be a dwarf, struggled indignantly for a few moments, but perceiving himself to be gripped firmly, snorted and banged his well-stacked tray of food down on the table. His thick beard bristled, brown eyes glaring at his captor. "Daal Hashard."

Nyam shook his head. "I don't go by that name any more."

"Well, then, Bereth Al—"

Again Nyam shook his head. "Nor that. But how are you? Sit down, sit down. You are in good company here. This is my friend and apprentice, Lummis Ortis."

Vaddi managed a curt nod.

The dwarf drew up a stool. He was evidently more interested in feeding than arguing and set to with a will, as though this was his first meal in a month.

"Trading?" said Nyam.

The dwarf nodded.

"Don't suppose you came over on the *Sea Harlot*, by any chance?"

The dwarf shook his head, chewed, chewed some more, then took a hearty swig of his ale. At length he spoke. "Been here a week or so. Usual thing. Ore. They've never got enough of the right stuff in Aerenal. Ironroot ore. Best in Khorvaire."

"True enough, my friend. I've dealt in it myself, as you know."

Sfarrag eyed Nyam suspiciously, but his attention was distracted by a chunk of meat in his stew, which he speared expertly.

"Not on the *Sea Harlot*, then? Not seen that worthy craft, have you?"

"Sure. She berthed this very day. Unloaded and then sailed up the inlet." He grinned, huge teeth smeared with gravy. "Vortermars no doubt had private stuff to unload where the officials wouldn't bother him."

"What did he unload here?"

Sfarrag stopped chewing and gazed even more dubiously at Nyam. "Lot of questions. What's it to you?"

Nyam slipped a small purse from his pocket and slid it over the table. The dwarf snatched at it, fast as a cat, slipping open the drawstrings and peering inside. "These fake?" he snapped.

Nyam drew back, face clouded in horror. "You ask me that? When have I ever dealt in fakes?"

Vaddi could not see what was in the bag, but he assumed it must be more loot filched from the airship.

Sfarrag snorted. "Vortermars dropped off a few casks, a trunk or two. No idea what was in 'em. A few of his crew, including his first mate, Gez Muhallah." The dwarf leaned forward, voice dropping. "And there was them elves. Some of them, too, but they had a dark look about 'em. I didn't stop around."

"Any elf women?"

The dwarf scowled even more deeply, guzzling down the last of his food with remarkable speed. "Dunno. Maybe. Best not to stick yer nose in some places." He slipped the purse into his pocket, swigged at his ale and then got to his feet, easing back out of Nyam's reach. "Must get to business. Pleasure to see you again, Daal—or whatever you call yourself now."

In a moment the throng had absorbed him.

"She may be here?" said Vaddi. It was all he could do to keep still.

"I suspect so." Nyam's gaze raked the hall and he sat back, eyes fixing on someone near the long bar. "And I suspect that little worm was put here to watch out for us. He won't be the only one."

"You're expecting trouble?"

"Vortermars is far too cunning to leave his back exposed.

He would want someone like me watched. Ah, as I thought, there is one of his cronies over there. He will play his hand as though this is purely a chance meeting."

"Who is it?"

"Vortermars's first mate. We'll have to speak to him, but it will be dangerous. Keep quiet throughout this."

"And I'm Lummis Ortis?"

"Good a name as any." Nyam bided his time, watching the first mate of the *Sea Harlot* as he himself studied the many occupants of the long hall. Nyam's eyes and his met a few times, but at length the freebooter thrust himself through the crowd and came to the table.

"I know that face," he said.

He was a tall, rangy man, with a drinker's pronounced stomach. His clothes were shabby, once rich, probably filched from a more noble man's wardrobe. His face was burned brown by the sun and sea, one eye pulled down by a scar cut there, doubtless, by the sweep of a cutlass.

"Gez Muhallah!" said Nyam, getting up and pumping the fellow's arm. "Good to see you! This is Lummis Ortis, my companion. Learning the trade."

"You're in good hands, son. This peddler knows every trick in the book, and plenty that aren't."

"Draw up a seat," said Nyam. "How is your esteemed captain?"

"Vortermars?" said Gez Muhallah, sitting, his twin blades rattling as he did so. Vaddi tried not to gawp at them. They looked as though they were frequently in use. "Same as ever. One jump ahead of the game. And yourself?"

"So-so. We're heading south on the dawn tide. Sailing round to Pylas Talaer. Little deal in darkwood." Nyam tapped the side of his nose. "Can't say too much."

Muhallah laughed. "Of course. Not quite above board, eh?"

"You know how it is. I didn't notice the *Sea Harlot* on the quay."

Muhallah grinned. "Gone farther along the coast. We've dropped the official cargo here. And a few passengers."

Nyam had caught the eye of one of the barmen and within moments he had come across, laden with tankards, knowing a good customer when he saw one. Nyam's plentiful coins exchanged hands and Muhallah began downing the ale at a rate that made Vaddi grimace.

"Anything interesting?" said Nyam nonchalantly.

"I shouldn't say anything."

"Come, there's plenty of drink here, Gez. Surely you can swap a few tales with old friends. We've got the whole night to kill."

Vaddi could see the gleam in Muhallah's eye. The man found it impossible to resist a drink. The sagging paunch and partially rotted teeth attested to that.

"Well," the man yawned. "We did have a few weird customers aboard." His voice dropped to a whisper. "These . . . Stillborn they call themselves. Creepy lot."

Nyam nodded. "I've seen them. Undead some of them."

"Something like that. I let Vortermars deal with 'em. I kept well out of it."

"I suppose they have to travel privately, seeing as the regular Aereni don't think a lot of them," said Nyam, pushing another tankard across the table.

"You're right."

"You ferry them regularly?"

"Not if I can help it, but they brought this girl with 'em. Valenar. Reckon they was bent on initiating her into their weird sect." He smirked suggestively.

Nyam could sense Vaddi's fury, knowing that it was taking the youth every effort to control it. He feigned slight interest. "Valenar girl? Reluctant recruit?"

"Can't blame her for squirmin'. Nasty lot."

"How did they get her ashore? The officials are pretty sharp here. Not too keen on bribes, either."

"Depends who you know." Muhallah winked. "They had her in a casket. It wasn't opened. Don't know where they went. Can't say I care."

He swigged at his ale, leaning back. For a while the conversation lagged, the freebooter drinking more ale and getting progressively more sluggish and sullen. Almost an hour passed before he hauled himself up and excused himself.

As soon as he was out of earshot, Vaddi leaned forward. "She's here! Sold to those filthy—!"

"Softly," warned Nyam. "Gez is no fool. A drunkard, aye, but he's as slippery as any eel. I don't relish spending any more time with him, but when he leaves here, we must follow him. He may contact them. It's our one hope of finding Zemella."

"But what if they're already gone? Cellester wanted her out of the way. He's achieved that. She could be anywhere. She could be dead."

"Be patient," Nyam admonished. "I wish I knew where Ardal Barragond was. If they knew who he was and were watching for him, he could be in danger."

"Why don't we get Muhallah outside and force him to take us to them?"

"He may not know where they are, and I don't want to risk getting on the wrong side of Vortermars. Not here. We have to be patient."

It was evident to Nyam that Vaddi's patience was being torn to shreds. The youth kept looking around, drumming his fingers on the table, grunting with frustration at their non-activity.

The night wore on and there was still no sign of Ardal. Although he did not say so, Nyam feared that the Valenar must have run into problems. He was beginning to think that he and Vaddi would have to leave and begin a new line of search.

Gez Muhallah was circulating, gleaning drinks from others here. Nyam kept an eye on him, watching the first mate getting more and more drunk. It was amazing that the man was still able to stand. At long last he began waving his temporary goodbyes to people.

"He's leaving," said Nyam. "We follow. Discreetly! Though in his condition, that should be easy enough. Have a care,

Vaddi. If we tread on his toes, he'll be like a trapped rat. Very dangerous. He knows how to use a sword, drunk or not. I wouldn't like to list the men he's gutted."

Vaddi nodded, plainly relieved to be doing something. They waited until Gez Muhallah left then rose and followed at a distance. Outside the air was blessedly cool, the sounds and smells of the hall snuffed out by a gentle breeze from off the sea, which slightly eased Vaddi's nerves. Patience, patience, he kept telling himself. They followed Gez Muhallah, who was weaving unsteadily through the first of the narrow streets, turning to begin a steep climb that seemed must surely be too much for him, but the first mate was used to such rigors and trudged ever upward into the higher reaches of Shae Thoridor.

As Nyam and Vaddi followed, keeping out of sight, they passed a few Aereni warriors who either glanced coldly at them or ignored them completely. Not all Aereni in the port tolerated men and the other non-elf races, but they were not halted or questioned.

High above the last dwellings of the port, the path became a narrow passage between two walls cut from solid wood, leading to a gateway. The gate, itself cut from the marvellous wood of the elves and carved with the most beautiful elven designs, was not locked. Gez passed within and could be heard coughing and cursing. Nyam led the way to the gate and from its obscuring shadows, looked beyond.

"What is this place?" whispered Vaddi, cautiously craning his neck to see.

"Old place of worship. Not used much, not at night. There are a few of these up here in the heights. Some of the crews hole up here, away from the night watches. My guess is that Muhallah and his cronies will be here, snoring in one of the old buildings."

Vaddi sniffed at the night air, the brilliant light from several moons glossing a wide courtyard beyond. "It's almost derelict," he said, an inner instinct taking over. "Elves have not worshipped here for many years."

"You can tell that?" Nyam asked.

"Yes. There is a taint to it. Decay, decline."

"Then it's ideal for the freebooters. Ah, I see Muhallah. He's heading for the old temple beyond. Let us go around the courtyard and catch a glimpse of what is within. Draw your dirk, Vaddi. Are you ready to use it if you have to?"

"I am ready," said Vaddi, a grim look about him that made the peddler wince.

Then they were off, moving around the perimeter of the courtyard, clinging to the shadows under its perimeter wall where ivy and other tangled growths had run amok over the years. They had reached halfway around this wall when Gez suddenly reappeared from the broken doorway. He came out, framed now in the vivid light, hands on hips, and stood grinning at the shadows around the walls.

"So you did follow me?" he growled. "No need to be shy, Nyam Hordath. And tell the boy to come out where I can see him."

Behind him, another shape moved, a diminutive but broad figure.

"Sfarrag," said Nyam. "I should have known that little rat was mixed up in this business."

The dwarf stood alongside Muhallah, hawking and spitting. In his hands he held a weighty axe.

Nyam and Vaddi eased out from the wall, both holding their blades. "Let's cut to the chase, Muhallah," said Nyam. "Where's the girl?"

The first mate strode forward a few steps. Already it was clear that he and the dwarf were not alone—the shuffling and scraping sounds in the building were evidence of a number of others. As these figures emerged, Vaddi saw to his horror that they were not freebooters but Aereni. But they were no ordinary Aereni.

"Murughel," breathed Nyam.

A dozen or more of these creatures lined up behind Muhallah. They were tall and angular, dressed in gray robes, studded with silver; their faces were painted bright white, gaudy and shocking, a celebration of being undead. Each carried a long sword.

"You're a bigger fool than I took you for if you think we've got the girl." Muhallah laughed. "She's far from here. They took her off the *Sea Harlot* well before we reached Aerenal."

"Is she alive?" said Vaddi, barely suppressing his fury.

"She won't die, but you should forget about her, son. She'll soon serve new masters—whether she likes it or not."

Nyam had to restrain Vaddi, laying a hand on him. In doing so, he could feel the sudden blaze of power within the youth, the killing fury. It almost scorched his fingers.

"Be careful," he whispered, "and whatever you do, do not use the horn. We must fight our way out of this trap."

I must protect him with my life, thought Nyam. Whatever happens here, neither he nor the horn must fall into their hands. I must die before I can let that happen. He looked around, searching for a way to the gate, but more of the Murughel had stepped through it.

Nyam watched as Gez Muhallah came closer, a look of confidence on his face as the trap closed. He held out his left hand, a cutlass in his right. "Come, Vaddi d'Orien. Give me what you carry. Spare yourself unnecessary pain. I might even let the peddler live."

"I will cut that hand from your arm before I part with anything," Vaddi told him coldly. Nyam sensed his eagerness to fight.

"Really?" said the freebooter. He showed no signs of drunkenness now, instead bearing all the signs of a trained predator. "Brave words. My brief is not to slay you, Orien, but simply to take you. The cleric said nothing about leaving you in one piece. I may cut *your* arm from you. Both perhaps."

"The cleric?" said Nyam, feigning ignorance. "What are you talking about?"

Muhallah laughed. "Of course. You thought him to be your friend. How easily you are duped. You're losing your grip, Hordath. Not the wily old fox you once were. It is time you bowed out. I'll hang you up for the gulls at daybreak."

"Back to back," Nyam whispered to Vaddi. "Try and ease our way to the gate."

Muhallah waved the first of the Murughel forward. They attacked in threes, those who fought Nyam seeking his quick death, while those assailing Vaddi more cautious. Nyam could see that it gave the youth an advantage. Control your anger, he wanted to say to him. Channel it into a positive force.

Vaddi attacked with a unique tenacity, his dirk a blur of reflected moonlight. It ripped the throat of an attacker, tearing flesh and bone, almost severing the head in the ferocity of the strike, then he ducked aside and hamstrung the second of the Murughel, who crashed to the dust, mouthing his silent agony like one struck dumb.

"All those years of hard work under Anzar's weapon's master were not wasted, I see!" Nyam laughed.

He was no slouch with the blade himself, and in a dazzling counter-attack, kept back his tormentors, blades ringing in the night, stars of ozone sizzling in a halo about him. He and Vaddi inched their way toward the gate, one eye on Muhallah and the traitorous Sfarrag, who were watching the fight with interest.

"Give it up, peddler!" shouted the pirate.

Nyam edged Vaddi toward the gate, but a number of Murughel blocked the way. One ran a chain around the gate and one of its posts, snapping shut a lock that effectively sealed off the retreat.

Again Vaddi was beset by three opponents. Once more he ripped open the flesh of a Murughel, kicking it aside as he narrowly ducked the slicing blade of another. They did mean to cut his arms off, but Nyam could see they were no match for his speed. Vaddi must be drawing on elf powers—and something else. He had not used the horn, but whatever the powers were within him that Cellester had repressed for so long, they burst now like a damn.

He has become a killing machine! Nyam's mind cried, almost

horrified by the unleashing of those powers. It is a kind of madness that takes him out of himself.

❀ ❀ ❀ ❀ ❀ ❀ ❀

Above them, from a rotting window in the tower, a solitary figure watched. Cellester kept out of sight, but he focused his own powers on the youth, once more seeking to subdue him. He raised his right arm. On his wrist, the amulet glowed, sending a thin beam of green light down to the youth.

❀ ❀ ❀ ❀ ❀ ❀ ❀

Nyam sensed that something supernatural was happening. He saw Vaddi countering this new wave of negative energy, cutting the sword from the hand of another Murughel, whose nerveless fingers dropped with the steel into the churned earth.

"Give it up, Muhallah! Your rabble are getting carved to pieces!" Nyam cried.

He had been keeping his assailants at bay, but he was tiring. An abrupt probe by one of the Murughel scored a hit high up near his shoulder and the peddler gasped, staggering back, almost into Vaddi. The youth swung round and drove his dirk through the mask of the Murughel. The creature screamed and toppled back, hands clawing at his ruined face.

Yes, Nyam thought, this is why Cellester and his master want him and Erethindel. Combined, they will be a weapon of horrendous power.

Nyam recovered, but the wound hurt him sorely. His defense became more desperate. Vaddi did his best to protect him, but they were both forced into the courtyard nearer its center. They were beset on all sides, unable to use the wall to protect themselves. Nyam was weakening, his blood leaking freely from his wound, though his voluminous clothes soaked it up.

Gez Muhallah called a momentary halt, stepping forward. His cutlass was no more than two feet from engaging Vaddi's weapon. "Give it up, boy. You can't win this. Give me the horn and the peddler goes free."

Nyam swung his blade in a desperate arc, but Muhallah simply stepped back, out of reach. Behind him, the dwarf hefted his axe.

Nyam sensed Vaddi, coiled like a spring, about to unleash himself upon the freebooter, but something seemed to be staying the boy's arm. Nyam tasted sorcery in the air, striving to enervate him. Of course! The cleric must be here!

Nyam swung his blade, but this time Muhallah splintered it. One of the Murughel plunged his blade into Nyam's calf, and the peddler tumbled to the ground, his face gray.

"Your call, Orien," said Muhallah, cutlass preparing to sheer Nyam's head from its shoulders.

CHAPTER 13

Vaddi's fingers slipped inside his tunic, inches from the horn. If he didn't act now, Nyam would die. As Vaddi reached for the horn, he felt something trying to grasp it with him—a duplicate, shadow hand, almost superimposed upon his own. From the tower he saw at last the beam of green light, trained on him. _Cellester!_ The cleric was up there, working to foil the use of the horn.

Vaddi locked gazes with Muhallah. Muhallah was smirking at the puzzled look on the youth's face as he waited for his answer, in complete control of the situation.

Something cut the night air like a knife through soft bread. Vaddi saw an arrow rip into one side of Muhallah's neck and out the other, driving the pirate sideways as if an invisible fist had smashed him off his feet. Muhallah lurched to his feet, dropping the cutlass and clawing with both hands at the lodged arrow. Blood gushed from his mouth and nose. He managed two steps, then his eyes bulged and he buckled over. To Vaddi's relief, Muhallah's death served to put new energy into Nyam, who snatched up the cutlass and cut through the lower legs of two of the Murughel and ran to Vaddi.

Vaddi felt the negative cloud dissipate. His own power

surged and he cut down another of the Murughel that lunged at them. Other forces were at work here now, for more arrows rained down on their foes, driving them back. The dwarf had already withdrawn into the buildings, his retreat masked by more of the Murughel, who had closed ranks to protect him.

The locked gate burst in a cloud of splintered wood, torn from its posts. From beyond came a group of new figures. Dressed in flowing robes, their heads covered in ghastly masks fashioned in the shape of skulls, they unleashed a hail of arrows as they came. The Murughel fell back, the light armor beneath their cloaks no barrier to the shafts. Some took arrows in the eyes and neck. They toppled in silence, but most raced to meet this new attack, swords before them.

In the courtyard, a ferocious battle ensued as the skull-masked warriors drew their own swords. Steel rang and sparks zipped through the night air. The incoming warriors were clearly outnumbered, but it was the Murughel who suffered, their skill no match for the power and tenacity of the new-comers. The latter carried strange blades that flickered in the moonlight with an eerie glow, a green tint of light like subdued fire. As these blades cut through the air and bit into Murughel flesh, they sizzled, casting a web of spells and sorcery about the conflict.

Vaddi's attention turned to the tower, but the beam of light had gone. He dared not leave Nyam, who had sank down again, head bowed in ill-suppressed agony.

The furious conflict was brought to an end after no more than a few minutes. Eschewing the use of their bows at such close quarters, the skull-masked warriors were merciless in their use of their glowing weapons, driving the Murughel back to the walls or the tower, then running them through. There must have been three times as many of the Stillborn, but they were unable to make their advantage count. They fought in an uncanny silence, like solid phantoms, but the skull-masked warriors tore into them without a pause, hounds determined on the merciless destruction of cornered rodents. There would be no quarter here.

One Murughel made a final stab at Vaddi, but he ducked the blade and plunged his dirk into the exposed neck, tearing it open, letting his victim sag down before him, dust spewing out in place of blood, ripped flesh like rags. The body toppled, and Vaddi looked up to see a familiar face near at hand, the only one that was not masked.

"Ardal!" he gasped, for it was indeed the elf from Valenar.

The elf bowed, withdrawing his blade from the gut of a fallen Murughel. Seeing that the fray was over, he slid it back into its scabbard. "You are not injured, Vaddi d'Orien?"

Vaddi stepped aside. "No, but my friend is badly wounded." He bent down and lifted Nyam's head. "Nyam! How is it?"

The peddler's face was ashen, his eyes squeezed almost shut with the pain. "Not good, Vaddi. Missed my vital organs, but it caught my shoulder. Hurts like fury. I can't move my arm."

Ardal barked something to the warriors who were drawing up behind him, and one of them disappeared into the night, swift and silent as a ghost. Ardal turned back to Vaddi.

"A healer will be here soon."

"You followed us?" said Vaddi.

"I suspected they would set a trap for you and the peddler."

"Who are these warriors?"

Ardal's grim expression softened slightly. "They are members of the Deathguard, an elite force, protectors of the Undying Council's laws in Aerenal. There is no body of elves more devoted to the killing of those who defile the dead. When I told them that there were Murughel at work here in Shae Thoridor, they were quick to investigate. It seems we arrived barely in time."

Vaddi indicated the tower. "There was a cleric among these creatures. You must find him. Zemella's life depends upon it."

"The Deathguard are already searching for him. He has used a cloaking spell to hide himself, but they have powers of their own."

Another figure stepped forward. He was the healer and he wore no mask, his long, patrician face marking him as an Aereni. He bent down to Nyam without a word. The peddler winced as the healer touched his wound then cut into his robes to expose clotting blood.

"Your companion will recover," said Ardal, taking Vaddi away from the healer as he began his work. "Vaddi, this is Fallarond, captain of the Deathguard."

The elf bowed slightly. Although he was no taller than Vaddi and had the lithe frame of his race, his bearing and manner spoke of considerable power. Vaddi had already seen the unique strength and speed of his fighting ability. Now that he stood before one of the newcomers, Vaddi saw that Fallarond was not wearing a skull-mask after all. His aquiline head had been tattooed to resemble a skull. His long, golden hair swept back from his forehead. His eyes, even by the light of the moons, were a deep green, piercing as if they could look into a man's soul.

"An honor to meet you, Vaddi d'Orien," he said in a surprisingly deep but musical voice.

"Fallarond is of the Dendris family," said Ardal. "He knew your mother."

"Zemella—" Vaddi said suddenly, turning to the shadows as though expecting to see some clue to her whereabouts.

"We'll find her," said Fallarond. "On my life."

"She, too, is related to the Dendris family," said Ardal. "Vaddi, this is a personal matter to all of us."

And you? Vaddi wanted to ask him. What is your relationship to her? Are you her lover, her betrothed? What has passed between you? But he could not bring himself to frame the words.

Fallarond called out to his warriors. "Gather the fallen!" He turned back to Vaddi. "We are not far from the city limits. We will go up into the forest to a private place and collect timber and brushwood. We'll celebrate this killing tonight with a pyre."

Vaddi followed and watched while the Deathguard worked. In no time they had collected the tangled remains of their enemies together, some of them still twitching, and moved off into the forest beyond the ruins. Well away from the city, the Deathguard heaped up a huge bonfire. The dead Murughel were dragged before it and each of them beheaded before being tossed on to the pyre like so many rag dolls. The grisly severed heads were put to one side in a pile.

While the Murughel corpses burned, filling the night air with a particularly noxious stench, Vaddi turned back to see how the healer was faring with Nyam. The elf had sat the peddler down on a fallen trunk, fingers still dabbing at the wound over which he had placed leaves smeared with a thick paste. Nyam grimaced as Vaddi approached him.

"Close one," he said through gritted teeth. "Thought we'd had it, Vaddi. You timed it a bit fine, Ardal. I thought you were supposed to be looking out for us."

Ardal shook his head and grinned. "Be content, peddler. You're alive." He turned to the healer. "How badly is he hurt?"

"Not as badly as he imagines. He will be stiff for a day or two. After that, as good as new. He is well preserved for a human. The shoulder bone was cracked, but I've repaired it. As with the calf, it will soon be strong again. The peddler is far younger than he might have you believe."

Nyam scowled. "You think so? Just because I look after myself and remain fit, you think me young? Preposterous!"

"Then you'll have energy enough for the pursuit," said Vaddi.

* * * ◉ * * *

Back at the ruins, the Deathguard had dragged aside a last body. It was Gez Muhallah, his face fixed in a rictus of death, eyes gazing lifelessly at the moons overhead. The arrow that had ended his life still pierced his neck. One of the Deathguard rammed a long spear into the ground, splintering slabs with the force of the blow. He and another of the warriors tied the body of Gez Muhallah upright to the spear, its head lolling forward onto the chest.

From the shadows came another of the company. The elf was draped from head to foot in a dark green cloak, head cowled, only the eyes visible. He carried a tall staff that appeared to be cut from bone, though what bone it was, Vaddi could not tell. He watched, not daring to move, as the unnerving figure stood before the dead pirate and began to chant, eyes raised to the moons that now daubed the skies overhead in garish light. Vaddi and Nyam stood back, puzzled and slightly alarmed by these proceedings. Beside them, Ardal and Fallarond also watched. The air crackled with ancient magic.

"This sea rat knew where Zemella was taken," said Fallarond, "so he will impart that knowledge to us—even if we have to rip it from him."

Vaddi felt the hackles on the back of his neck rising as the necromancer produced a small chalice. Yellow light gleamed briefly on its contents as the sorcerer smeared them over the cheeks and chest of the dead pirate. Using his forefinger, he made sigils with the substance, which Vaddi guessed was blood from those who had fallen in the fight.

The necromancer stood back, set down the chalice, and renewed his chant. The other Deathguard gathered in a semicircle behind their leader, silent as menhirs. Light from the moons glistened on the blood.

Gez Muhallah's head *moved*. It swung gently to and fro as if on a broken neck, but then it lifted to the night skies, those bulging eyes still wide, though in them now there seemed to glow a fresh light, sickly and haunted.

"You are Gez Muhallah, first mate of the *Sea Harlot?*" said the necromancer. He lifted his hand and the dead pirate jerked like a puppet, eyes widening even more, as though he looked upon some impossibly horrible sight.

"I am he," came the voice of the dead man, spittle running down over his chin.

Vaddi drew back, appalled, but Nyam gripped his arm.

The necromancer turned to Ardal, nodding to him. "His resistance is drained. Interrogate him. He is bound by my sorcery to answer you."

Ardal went as close to the dead pirate as he dared, himself disturbed by this dreadful working.

"When you left Pylas Maradal, you had a Valenar girl onboard. Is that so?"

The pirate writhed but could not fight the necromancer's will. "We did. A Valenar girl, yes." Blood had begun to seep freshly from the arrow wounds on either side of his neck.

"What happened to her?"

"We were met at sea by more of the Murughel. North of Aerenal, they took her on their craft."

"Bound for where?"

The mad eyes swung round and picked out Vaddi in the shadows. A frightful laugh burst from the drooling, bloodied lips of the pirate. "She is bound for Dolurrh!"

"As are you," Ardal said. *"Where is the girl?"*

"They . . . took . . . her. To the east of Aerenal. To the . . . Madwood."

Ardal's face clouded as if he had been stabbed. "You lie!"

"I give you the truth! There are more Murughel there, serving the cleric. She is alive, to be kept there."

"For what purpose?" said Ardal, though it came out almost as a snarl.

But the head was beginning to sag, the artificial life that had been instilled in it fading quickly, like a guttering candle about to go out. Ardal reached forward in his fury and forced the head up again, but the eyes had closed. Only a ragged last gasp of breath escaped the bruised lips.

Vaddi turned to Nyam and spoke quietly. "What is this Madwood?"

Nyam shuddered, clutching at his wounded shoulder as if it troubled him anew. "It is the nearest thing to Xoriat in this world that you can imagine. I have seen some of the horrors of the Mournland, but the Madwood is in some ways more terrible. If they have indeed taken Zemella there, they must have either skirted its borders or gained some deep supernatural power to shield them."

Ardal, finished with the bizarre interrogation, turned back to the necromancer and nodded. The latter indicated a place at the edge of the courtyard where a pit had been prepared. Two of the Deathguard pulled up the spear and the broken body and carried it to this pit. They tossed it in and the necromancer sprinkled the blood from the chalice over the corpse. Gez Muhallah's body collapsed in on itself within seconds, bursting and popping, the haggard face the last image to dissolve. The Deathguard buried it quickly and the necromancer made a final incantation over the place.

"There was another involved in this," said Fallarond. "A dwarf. I will have the city scoured for him."

"A waste of time!" Nyam snorted. "Sfarrag is a treacherous wart, it is true, but he will know little of Cellester's plans. I'm sure he has played his part. Vortermars, too. A link in the chain, no more. It is the cleric we must find."

"Nevertheless, Shae Thoridor will be searched. In the meantime, come. We must return to the city and plan."

Vaddi was watching Ardal's face. He could see on the elf's bleak features a look of deep sadness, mixed with horror at the fate of Zemella. Surely it was a look of anguish for the fate of a loved one.

❖ ❖ ❖ ❖ ❖ ❖ ❖

The Deathguard base to which they were taken was cut from a single massive tree bole. A high tower, its outer walls were carved in the exquisite workings of the Aereni, where dragons interlaced with other monstrous creatures. Its interior was far more austere, a barracks for the Deathguard of the city, its contents spare and economical, as though these warriors were always on a war footing, prepared to ride out to battle at a moment's notice. Deep inside the secure hold, Vaddi and Nyam were taken to quarters that at least afforded them the comfort of a hot bath. They luxuriated in the steaming waters, while Ardal waited for them in vaguely amused silence.

Afterwards, alone with the Valenar, Vaddi checked Nyam's wounds, amazed at the results of the healer's work. Both shoulder and calf now seemed to be no more than nasty bruises, though the peddler winced and grimaced as though every bone and muscle in his body ached.

"How soon can we set out?" Vaddi asked Ardal.

"We leave before dawn. Fallarond has business to attend to first in the city."

"There's no time!" Vaddi snapped. "Every moment that Zemella is in their hands, she is in mortal danger. What business is more important than following her?"

From the opening doorway, Fallarond himself answered. "Softly, young one," he said, coming forward. Try as he might, Vaddi still found the elf's ghoulish skull-face unsettling. "If I am to leave the city with a company of the Deathguard, my superiors need to sanction it. I have seen them and they have agreed, provided I am satisfied your cause is a worthy one."

"What do you mean? I seek Zemella's rescue—"

"Why?" said Fallarond, his voice hardening. "What is she to you?"

Vaddi's mouth hung open as he groped for an answer.

"She is a Valenar," said Ardal. "This is a matter of honor for us. And pride. I have said it is a family affair. You are related to the Dendris family, but not to Zemella, so why have you and the peddler come here, alone, to face odds that you could never have hoped to overcome?"

Nyam came to his rescue. "You speak of honor. You think that men and half-elves have no understanding of honor? Zemella saved us from the Claw. She protected us and led us to safety in Pylas Maradal. And she would have put her life at risk again to lead us out of Valenar. She has more than *earned* our loyalty."

Fallarond came closer, his face showing no sign of having

been touched by Nyam's outburst. "That is a fair answer, but tell me something else. You are a well-travelled peddler, I think. You know something of Aerenal, as much as any man from the outside. You know of its powers and grave dangers, especially to your race."

"And . . . ?"

"And you came here with Vaddi d'Orien, alone, with no real hope of success. Why have you tied yourself to him?"

Vaddi would have protested, but Nyam eased him aside, meeting the cool challenge of Fallarond's gaze. "He has saved my life more times than I can remember, and I have taken an oath to protect him. In Pylas Maradal. I take my oaths seriously."

"And what is your interest in that which he carries?" said Ardal, his voice barely above a whisper.

Nyam glared at him. "You know?"

Ardal nodded. "Zemella warned me. I know she was a Keeper. She was watching for its coming. It was sent away from Aerenal many years ago. The Undying Court proclaimed it too dangerous to remain here."

"It is what our enemies want," said Vaddi. "That . . . and me."

Again Ardal nodded, indicating Vaddi's robed arm. "You are marked. I saw it when you were bathing. There is power in you, dormant though it may be."

Fallarond frowned. *Marked?* In what way?"

"Show him, Vaddi," Ardal said. Beside him, Nyam nodded.

Vaddi removed his robe and rolled up the loose sleeve of his shirt to reveal the dragonmark. Its beautifully intricate web of interlocking lines was clear to see, a birthmark that looked to be a natural part of him. There was power in those crafted lines, though for now it slept.

Fallarond's eyes widened for a moment. "Where is the horn?"

Vaddi tapped his chest. "It stays with me."

"If we venture into the Madwood, we will face horrors that you can scarcely imagine. Whatever awaits us there will do its uttermost to take that from you. They are the worst kinds of evil in all of Eberron. If they take the horn—"

"Not while I hold it," said Vaddi.

"Perhaps you should leave it here."

"I think not," said Ardal. "Zemella said that it should not be separated from Vaddi. If it is and we all perish in the Madwood, it will be diminished, no more than a token power for some new force."

"This is a dangerous game," said the Deathguard, shaking his head with deep unease.

"Are we going in pursuit of Zemella?" said Vaddi.

Fallarond nodded. "So be it. I can take a score of my best Deathguard. You will come with us, Ardal Barragond?"

Ardal looked directly at Vaddi, almost as if throwing down a challenge to him. "I will. I have a responsibility to Zemella."

Vaddi felt his heart lurch at the words. *Then he is her lover! He has read my thoughts and I can see his anger behind his eyes. It is for her he goes, not for any fealty to me.*

"Get some rest," said Fallarond. "The best steeds will be ready before dawn."

"We go overland?" said Ardal.

"Even with the fastest ship we have, it would take far too long to sail around the northern lands and south to the coast of the Madwood. We ride across the steppes of the Tairnadal. I have sent word to them already."

Ardal frowned. "The Tairnadal have not always been cooperative. Are you sure of their compliance? I would not want to fall foul of one of their warclans."

"We can trust them. After all, it is their steeds that we will be riding. Now rest, all of you. It will be a hard ride."

When he had gone, Ardal also prepared to depart for the remainder of the night. "We are seeking word of Zemella and those who abducted her."

"Pardon what may seem a naïve question," said Nyam, "but where, precisely, are we to enter the Madwood? As I understand it, the place is vast! Every foot of it crawls with danger."

"We will ask it," replied Ardal. "Do as Fallarond suggests. Rest." He grinned and left them to their thoughts.

"Ask it?" Nyam grunted. "*Ask* it? What is he talking about? We are to converse with a forest? A lunatic one at that?"

❋ ❋ ❋ ❋ ❋ ❋ ❋

High above Shae Thoridor, on the uppermost crags of the escarpment that overlooked the night-shrouded harbors and quays, a huge shadow shifted among the trees. Great wings lifted and sank back as the soarwing eased itself into its hiding place. It would have been invisible to any but the keenest observer. Nearby, perched on a rock outcrop like an extension of it, Aarnamor studied the gnarled trees below.

Something was coming. Bushes shivered with more than the stirring of the breeze. Stones were loosened, slipping downhill with no more than the sound a mouse makes, but Aarnamor noticed everything.

From the steep slopes below, a cloaked figure hauled himself up the last of the vertical incline. His face was pale, features haggard with effort. The eyes were dulled with near-exhaustion.

Aarnamor watched as the cleric gazed up through a fog of pain to see his shape up on the crags, forcing himself to go on until he had come to within a few yards of the undead warrior. Cellester sagged, gripping a wiry gorse branch as he perched himself on a narrow ledge.

"You are late," said Aarnamor.

Cellester's mouth was dry. He licked his lips in an attempt to find his own voice, his chest still heaving.

"You are alone," Aarnamor added. "The boy is not with you."

Cellester shook his head. "The trap was well set," he said through gritted teeth. "I did all that could be expected of me."

"Well?"

"There was a counter trap. The boy has allies here."

"Allies?"

"The Deathguard. The Murughel were no match for them."

Aarnamor turned his attention to the city below and the forests above it. He could discern a thin haze of smoke where the forest met a stand of old ruins. He sniffed the hot air rising off the cliffs and sensed the scorched stench of flesh.

"Yes, I understand. In a sacred Aereni grove. The Stillborn have been thrown upon a pyre."

"I could do nothing. I sought to bring the boy under my influence, but here, in this accursed Aereni domain, I am no match for him."

"Then you should have taken him in Valenar," said Aarnamor.

"Half the city would have risen against me. No. Coming here was the best strategy."

"Where is he now?"

"With the Deathguard, I imagine."

"And the girl?"

Cellester paused for breath, wiping sweat from his face. "Other Murughel took her, far out at sea. The trap I set in the ruins had Vaddi believe she was here in Shae Thoridor. I did not need her. I thought it would be safer to have her removed elsewhere, as insurance. The Murughel will have taken her to the Madwood."

"Why there?"

"She will be out of the clutches of the Deathguard and other Aereni who might seek her. She can still be the bait in the trap for Vaddi d'Orien. "

"Does the boy know?"

"I don't know." Cellester sagged down on the ledge. Nor do I care, he thought. I have had enough of this wretched affair. Let me sleep here and not wake. It is over.

But Aarnamor's voice grated along his nerves like raw steel.

"Once he knows—and the elves *will* know—Vaddi d'Orien will continue the pursuit. If he and the peddler travel to the Madwood, especially if they go alone, they will be easy prey."

"I suspect that they will have Aereni with them, possibly even the Deathguard. The Valenar elf raised enough of them to spring my trap."

"Then another trap must be set."

"I cannot go farther. Not now. I need rest."

Aarnamor rose up like the threat of a storm. "You will rest when you deserve it. If you earn the wrath of Zuharrin, you will never know rest again. Stand! Prepare yourself."

Reluctantly Cellester did as bidden.

THE EDGE OF MADNESS
CHAPTER 14

Within the tower of Fallarond, the air worked like a spell on the exhausted travellers. Vaddi, at first unable to sleep, was finally caught in this web, his mind soothed, his fears for Zemella and desperation to be on the move again pushed back like a slow tide until his head fell forward and he slept. A distant sound, like the ebb and flow of soft waves up and down a beach, worked on him like a soporific, holding him until the dark hours just prior to dawn. Then, drifting away from the tranquillity, he was wide awake in the chamber. Nearby Nyam was snoring.

Vaddi grinned at the recumbent figure and nudging him with his boot. "Wake up, Nyam."

While the peddler tossed and turned, struggling to resist full awakening, the door to the chamber opened. By the cold fire lamp beside it, Vaddi made out the figure of Ardal as he entered, closely followed by Fallarond. Both wore their light armor, twin swords strapped to their belts.

"Are you ready to ride?" said Ardal.

Nyam grunted something unintelligible, but Vaddi spoke for both of them. "We are."

"We eat on the road," said Fallarond, no less brusque than usual.

Vaddi went to the raised basin by the wall and tossed cold water over his face. Nyam was less eager to wash but did so with another grunt.

Ardal held out a scabbard of light leather from which the haft of a weapon protruded. "A gift for you," he said. "Draw the blade."

Vaddi did so, aware of the keen eye of Fallarond. It was an elven sword, made not from metal but from bronzewood, the prized wood of Aerenal. As Vaddi wrapped his fingers around the haft and turned the blade in the air, he saw it glow in the dawn light, its length decorated with the most intricate runes. They were of the same script as that of Erethindel, and as the blade passed through the air, it left a brief line of runes behind it, slowly winking out like embers.

"It is beautiful," Vaddi said, feeling that somehow a part of him that had been missing for years had been recovered.

"It is both beautiful and terrible," said Fallarond. "It pleases me to see that the blade might have been made for you. If you did not have elf blood, it would be no more than base wood in your hands."

"Can you read the runes?" said Ardal.

"A little, though some are strange to me."

"Do not speak them aloud. We cannot read them all. They are more than elf runes. Some are draconic. When you use the blade, the runes will empower you, but there is danger in them."

Ardal turned to Nyam, who had been watching with interest. "We have no blade for you, Nyam Hordath, but while you ride and fight with us, you are under our protection."

Nyam grinned, patting the haft of his own weapon. "I'll put my trust in what I have, thank you. Cold steel has served me well enough."

Fallarond motioned to the door. "Then let us go."

Moments later they were out in the morning air, crossing a narrow courtyard to where the Deathguard was already mounted. In the light of day Vaddi saw that they, too, had faces either painted or tattooed to resemble grisly skulls, and more than a few of them bore scars along their faces and hands.

Other steeds had been prepared, and in silence Vaddi and the others mounted. Vaddi stroked the mane of the huge stallion that had been chosen for him, and he felt the vital energy flowing through the creature's muscles and flanks.

The gates of the courtyard swung open, and the company, twenty strong, rode out into the mists of daybreak, hooves drumming on the streets as they made their swift way along the upper passages of the Shae Thoridor, bound for its edge and the sloping hills that curved away eastward to the new dawn. Aside from their swords, each of the Deathguard had a bow slung over his back, accompanied by a quiver full of arrows, their iridescent green feathers picking up the sunlight. Strapped to the flanks of their steeds were their shields, each embossed with the skull mask emblem of their station. Vaddi and Nyam had also been provided with shields, though these had the plain markings and sigils of the city painted upon them. Although there was no time on the rapid journey to study them, Vaddi could see that they were also made of wood, but of a type so hard that they must be almost impenetrable—bronzewood most likely, though they might've been densewood.

Once they were up on the higher slopes of the hills, the warriors tossed small loaves to and fro. It was like a game to them played at fantastic speed. They caught the loaves and tore pieces from them with their teeth, laughing musically as they chewed. Vaddi was thrown a half loaf and caught it instinctively, biting into its delicious flavour, savoring its heat. It needed no butter, for it almost melted in his mouth as he swallowed. He could feel his whole being reacting to it, as though he had been given a drug. But this was no drug, it was wholesome power—the clean, invigorating magic of the Aereni.

Beside him, hair streaming behind him, face enrapt by the thrill of the ride, Nyam was also tossed bread. He almost fumbled it but caught it and stuffed a thick chunk in his mouth, eyes streaming. He tried to shout his appreciation, but the words were lost in the chewing.

Once the bread had been eaten, the Aereni passed to each other a number of waterskins, and again Vaddi and Nyam partook. It was icy water, the purest they had yet tasted, but its effect was more potent than any wine.

"Wonderful! I am reborn!" Nyam cried to the wind, and the Deathguard around him smiled.

"How sad to be a man," Ardal called to him, "to spend your life asleep except for moments such as these." But he was smiling as he said it.

Nyam responded, but his words were lost in a spray of crumbs.

Vaddi was aware that their stallions rode at an unnatural rate, infused with powers that he could not begin to guess at. This was, after all, Aerenal, a land of magic so ancient and powerful that it surpassed almost all supernatural powers known in Khorvaire. What last vestiges of torpor had been forced into his veins by the tampering of Cellester were shredded in this almost ethereal ride, and he knew for the first time the awakening of his true nature. He *felt* the earth beneath him, the power of this ancient land, as if it not only spoke to him but claimed him. It was as though his very flesh had been molded from it. As he thought of Zemella and those who had stolen her, his anger arose afresh, fed by darker emotions, no less powerful than his new zest for life. The sword at his belt pulsed with energies that hungered for satisfaction.

An hour flew by, then two, but they seemed no more than the fleeting passage of seconds, as if the company had slipped out of time altogether and sped down some separate stream. The land around them was a blur, a rushing, whirling flicker of colors. From time to time Nyam looked across at Vaddi, his face crinkled up in wonder and sheer joy, like an adolescent revelling in unbridled freedom.

When the company at last stopped, taking cover in a small copse that overlooked a deep inlet far below them, Fallarond bid them all dismount.

"So soon?" said Nyam.

"It is mid-morning." Vaddi indicated the sun.

Ardal joined them. "Fallarond sent watchers ahead of us last night. Their hawks will meet us here shortly."

"How long before we reach the forest?" Vaddi asked.

Ardal pointed down the hillside. The inlet wound further eastward, its far shore very dark, as though the sunlight made little impact on its thick, endless forest. "That is the Jaelarthal Orioth, the Moonsword Jungle. We ride far through it until we reach the river Naalbarak, which is called the River of Whispering Evil, being a deeply cursed place. On its eastern shores, the Madwood begins. Naalbarak is one way into it, though it is a terrible, living thing and would test our sanity to its limit. It is a consolation that our enemies also risk much by entering the Madwood."

"They come!" called one of the Deathguard.

Vaddi, Nyam, and Ardal turned to see two winged shapes plummeting from the skies, dropping like stones out of the sun. They were hawks, companions of the watchers who had gone on ahead the previous night. Fallarond stretched out his arm and both hawks alighted, talons gripping the arm, heads bowing to the Deathguard. Fallarond cocked his head, listening, reminiscent of a huge predatory bird himself. Then he handed the hawks to one of his warriors, who fed them with the meat of a fat lizard they had just killed.

Fallarond joined Vaddi and the others. "There is news. Thumeridor has been watching the far coast and the birds come from him. Zemella has been seen. She is alive, though a prisoner."

"In the Madwood?" said Ardal.

"I fear so, but we are not so far behind. The Murughel who took her from Vortermars's ship sailed around the east of Aerenal no more than half a day ahead of the ship that brought Vaddi and Nyam to Shae Thoridor. The Murughel landed in Valen Bay, at its southern tip. This was at dawn yesterday. There is a path there into the jungle. If we ride throughout the day and tonight, we can be there by dawn tomorrow."

"They'll have two days start on us," said Ardal, "but if they have entered the Madwood, they will have to return the same way, will they not?"

Fallarond nodded. "It is likely. To move from the path is suicide."

"How many?" said Vaddi.

"From the ship, no more than a dozen, but they were met at Valen Bay by a number of ships. Altogether there are at least a hundred of the Murughel gathered. They mean to hold what they have."

Ardal scowled. "A hundred?"

"The hawks have seen other ships beyond the bay, sheltered by the islands beyond it in the east. They may not be Murughel, but I smell the reek of some dark alliance."

Vaddi felt himself turning cold in spite of the strength of the sun. "Could it be agents of the Emerald Claw?"

"There is nowhere safe from their machinations. We know they lust after the necromantic powers of Aerenal," said Fallarond. "The Murughel drink the Blood of Vol."

Nyam tugged at his beard. "It's a trap, of course. Zemella is the bait. You'll need an army to spring it."

Fallarond spoke coldly. "The Undying will not sanction the release of any more of the Deathguard than you see here."

"But Zemella is an elf!" said Vaddi. "One of their own kind—"

"This is not Valenar," said Fallarond. "The Undying Court would act, in time, but it does not know that Erethindel has returned to Aerenal. Better it does not know or else it may consider taking it from you. Thus your role as Keeper would be over, and the Court would see this pursuit of Zemella as unimportant in itself, a mere family dispute. Ties with Valenar are not strong. Some of us wish it were otherwise."

"Elf pride, elf arrogance," muttered Nyam.

"A small unit may be better," said Fallarond, ignoring the comment. "A campaign of stealth, a wearing down."

"There is something that puzzles me," said Vaddi. "Why has

the cleric delivered Zemella to the Claw, his enemy? You say the Murughel took her from Vortermars's ship. All Cellester wanted was to have her taken away, bait for me, but suppose he had no knowledge that agents of the Claw had forged an alliance with the same Murughel."

"Then," said Nyam, "it is not the cleric we are dealing with here but the Claw, which can only mean Caerzaal. Those ships must be his."

"Where *is* this cleric?" said Ardal.

"My watchers have not found him," said Fallarond. "He left the place where we fought the Murughel last night, but he has covered his trail."

"If the Murughel have betrayed *him*," said Vaddi, "then he is cut off, for all his powers."

"I wouldn't say that," warned Nyam. "His master will not want to give up the hunt so readily. His undead warriors are abroad. We know that." He told Ardal and Fallarond of Aarnamor and his part in Cellester's intrigues.

"We must act swiftly," said Fallarond. "We will go east and cross the highlands between the headwaters of the Naalbarak. Soon after that, the fringes of the Madwood will be below us."

"What do you propose?" said Ardal, as the whole company remounted.

"We skirt the jungle. Somewhere, midway between the Naalbarak and Valen Bay, we must find a way in. Carve our own, if we have to."

❧ ❧ ❧ ❧ ❧ ❧ ❧

The wild ride began anew and the miles flew past. The afternoon sun was lowering in the west behind them as they crested a final ridge that fell away to a deep declivity in the landscape. There, far below them, like an immense stain on the landscape, stretching as far to the east and south as the eye could see, was the darkness that was the Madwood.

Even from here, high above its vastness, Vaddi and Nyam could feel the power of the place. Waves of it lapped at them, as though the primal jungle emitted thick clouds of invisible energy, a dense miasma that was both chilling and poisonous. Instinctively Vaddi clutched at Erethindel, feeling its glow, a counterspell against the dreadful forces at play below. Nyam shivered, the steed beneath him also shuddering and shying away from the sight of the Madwood. Ardal was beside them, his face pale, his grim expression one of doubt.

He shook his head. "I have heard so much of this frightful domain, but seeing it for the first time, it fills me with an overwhelming dread. It is alive, watching us. What kind of twisted powers could have created such a realm?"

Fallarond grunted. "What else but war? But this was a war that took place long before the Last War that recently ended. The Madwood was born out of a long lost clash of dark energies, sorcery run amok. Dragons warred with demons in ages beyond our memory. The creatures that twisted the very laws of nature itself are no more than whispered myths today. The Madwood may once have been a clean forest, a healthy place, but no more. It is a corpse, an *undead* corpse, riddled with necromantic powers, and its denizens have become perversions of nature, mutated by the supernatural discharges that saturate its very soil."

Nyam grimaced. "Are we certain that the Murughel have taken Zemella there?"

"We are."

Vaddi shook his head. "I can feel it . . . *breathing*. I can feel its hate."

"Oh, yes," said Fallarond, "but we will enter it. Elves have done so before and lived."

Nyam turned to Ardal. "Back in Shae Thoridor, you said we would *ask* for permission to enter."

Ardal looked even more disturbed. "Yes. There is a way. The jungle is inhabited by many types of creature, some of which are prisoners. Once there were dryads and other tree spirits there, but over time they have become vampiric, slaves to the powers of the Madwood. They are torn between their dependence on the energy of the jungle and their craving to be set free. Their dilemma enables us to bargain with them."

"If we can find one," Fallarond said, "lure it to us, we can offer it freedom in exchange for aid. It will guide us in, but we must go down without further delay. The best time to lay a trap is at twilight."

The company began the descent, dropping down into one of the many narrow gorges that ended at the borders of the Madwood. Their steeds followed the course of a winding brook, splashing along its contours. It plunged over a few small falls and on into the jungle itself. Vaddi could see across the black canopy, but there were no birds circling and no sound disturbed the air. Time had become frozen, the air utterly motionless, a chill enveloping all the company.

"How far are we from Valen Bay?" Vaddi asked Fallarond.

"Half a day on foot. As close as we dare go to it, for the Murughel will have scouts watching for us. They know we will be coming. Just as our hawks have been watching, so will theirs. And something else has crossed the skies this day—some huge, winged thing. Did you not sense it?"

"The undead warrior on its soarwing, yes, that must have been it," said Vaddi.

"Once we are within the Madwood, we will be seen only by the jungle itself—and what festers there."

At the foot of the gorge, there was a narrow pool, the last healthy area of landscape before the first trees rose up, gnarled and interwoven, unnaturally fused into a solid wall. The stream bubbled silently along its course and under the lowest of their branches, which formed an archway to the pitch darkness within. Fallarond gave a signal to the Deathguard and they all dismounted and lead their horses to the water. None of the stallions would drink, turning their heads away, their eyes wild.

"We must let the horses go back to the highlands," said Fallarond. "The Madwood is no place for them."

Reluctantly Nyam and Vaddi dismounted. They said their

quiet goodbyes to the steeds, but it was evident that they were all eager to leaver this haunted place. A last word from Fallarond released them, and as one the horses cantered back along the stream and were soon climbing back up into the hills. Fallarond drew his sword and everyone else in the company did the same.

Tallamorn, the Deathguard necromancer who had interrogated Muhallah's corpse, led them around the pool to the very edge of the jungle. He took from his robes a slender rod forged from pure silver, its length cut with symbols. The company stood back while Tallamorn murmured a spell under his breath.

Vaddi tensed beside Nyam, and even Ardal looked deeply uneasy.

Tallamorn bent down and dipped the tip of his silver rod into the pool, which was deep, shadow-filled in the coming twilight. Light rippled out from the rod and spread. In its glow at the heart of the pool, something swam below the surface, circling. Tallamorn stood, raising the rod above him as a fisherman plays his catch and at once the waters of the pool burst up in a bright fountain, but it was no fish that erupted with the waters. It was man-like, though not a man. Vaddi and Nyam jumped back in shock, but the Deathguard had been prepared for this.

Tallamorn called out sharp commands to the figure, which writhed this way and that, flinging water from itself like a dog shaking itself dry. Scaled like a fish, with long talons and a sharp spine running down its back, the being glared at its tormenter. The face may once have been human, but now its eyes were huge, its nose a gash and its mouth a thin line that opened to reveal twin rows of sharply pointed teeth. The thing clawed at the air, hissing at Tallamorn, wriggling across the surface slowly but unable to get close to him.

"Who dares summon Ezrekuul?" snarled the twisted mouth.

"You see how this accursed jungle treats those it traps," whispered Ardal to Vaddi. "How perverse is its magic."

Tallamorn pointed his silver rod at the creature, which

writhed even more, cowed by its power. "We are the Deathguard," the necromancer told it, his voice low but filled with chilling power. "Your time has come."

"I serve Madwood. I *am* Madwood. Everything is Madwood."

"No, Ezrekuul. You are no more than a part of it. We have come to free you."

A long silence followed, then the creature writhed anew, as though fires licked at it, or some other power gripped it and twisted it, tormenting it. "You cannot. Only Wood commands!"

"No. It crushes you, grinds you under its roots, wraps you in its coils. It sucks the blood from you, as you suck the blood of the unwary. It chains your soul, your essence. It saps your will."

"Deceiver!"

"No," said Tallamorn, his words like a litany, a part of his working. Vaddi felt the aura about the necromancer, the weaving of magic, centered on the silver rod. "Your desires are twisted away from you. You are not permitted choice. You are damned. The Madwood has cursed you. You long for true freedom."

"It is you who are cursed," sneered the creature, but it had shrunk down, its voice dropping. "I am . . . not to be fooled."

"Your time has come. I offer you release from this nightmare. I will rip your false guise from you and show you. The spirit of the Holy Ancestors will purge you, if you so desire."

Tallamorn pointed again with the rod. As he did so, the creature began to blur, to shapechange.

Vaddi gasped at what it was becoming. At first it seemed to become no more than a pillar of shapeless clay, but then, encouraged by Tallamorn's working, it sculpted itself into a human form, an androgynous being, young and slender. Its beauty was marred by the intense sorrow in its face, which intensified as it looked down at itself and its new form.

"This is as you were, as you should be," said Tallamorn, "before you were corrupted by the evil of the Madwood. You were a dryad, Ezrekuul, and you shared the life of the great trees before they, too, succumbed to the horrors of this place."

"Yes, I remember. It was . . . before the darkness."

"Your time has come. I can release you from that darkness."

There were tears now in the eyes of the dryad. "But my trees
. . . they are dead. Worse, they are undead, twisted. I cannot go
back to them. I can only dwell in the stream."

"Would you be free of this life, this living death?"

The creature gazed at the last rays of the sinking sun beyond
the hill, fingers reaching out in sudden longing, as if to catch
the disappearing light. It shuddered, breathing a soft affirma-
tive.

"Very well, but first you must serve us. A small price for
your freedom."

"What must I do?"

"Guide us into the Madwood."

"Where do you go?"

"Where does this stream lead?"

"Into the heart of the jungle, then it divides. To the south-
west it flows into the Naalbarak. The other way it flows east,
entering the sea beyond the jungle's edge."

"South of Valen Bay," said Fallarond softly beside Vaddi.

"It is this second way that we would go," Tallamorn told the
dryad. "To the ruins, which are near it, are they not?"

"Khamaz Durrafal?" said the dryad with genuine fear in its
voice. "But I cannot enter them! The river runs near to them.
The city is overgrown, choked with the death-weeds of the
jungle. It is tempting oblivion to set foot near it."

"Take us along the river as far as you can. When it is no
longer safe for you, I will free you."

"You promise this?" said the dryad, eyes full of pleading.

"In the name of the true Undying and my revered ancestors,
I so swear."

"Very well."

"You must be again what you have become until I free you.
In the Madwood, you must don the guise of its slave, though you
are mine now."

Tallamorn worked yet another series of spells and the
others watched more in pity than in horror as the dryad was

transformed back into its original, twisted shape, flinching away from the same rays that it had groped for.

Vaddi spoke quietly to Ardal. "What is this place that Tallamorn named?"

"Khamaz Durrafal. There were cities in the Madwood once. We suspect it is there that the Murughel have taken Zemella. Its ruins are the nearest to Valen Bay. They are as far as the Murughel would dare venture into the Madwood."

"Are they safe?" said Nyam.

Ardal grunted. "Safe? Nowhere in there is safe, but in the past, there have been attempts to make pacts with the jungle. Such unhealthy alliances have usually centered on former Aereni cities. Khamaz Durrafal may offer a brief respite from the worst excesses of the Madwood—that or it will be a focus for them."

Nyam groaned. "You would risk that?"

"We have no choice, but this dryad will guide us."

"Yes, well that fills me with confidence," muttered the peddler, taking an even firmer grip on his sword.

Shortly thereafter, the dryad Ezrekuul led the way under the arch of boughs and into the gloom of the Madwood. Tallamorn and Fallarond were close behind the creature, the healer keeping his silver rod to hand. Vaddi, Nyam, and Ardal followed behind them, with the remainder of the Deathguard bringing up the rear. It was like entering a cave, hundreds of feet below the earth, so intense was the silence. For long minutes they were unable to see anything, but gradually light began to diffuse their surroundings, a corpse-light glow, eerie and unwavering, as if the very trees and weeds that choked everywhere were imbued with it.

Vaddi imagined he could hear the deep breathing of a huge animal far below the surface of the earth. The first real sounds that any of the company heard were the shufflings and slitherings from the matted undergrowth, as unseen denizens of this place, large and small, drew back from the hated intruders. It was as though a monstrous, amorphous entity tensed its coils.

As the company grew accustomed to the bizarre light, they could see above them the trunks of the trees, most of which were immense, like the columns of temples, bending and twisting upward, solid as stone, to a vaulted ceiling that allowed in not a single chink of natural light. In the convoluted branches that ran like beams far overhead, there were more scuttlings, more half-glimpsed movements of creatures best left unseen.

The company went along the matted bank of the stream, which had already widened into a small river, its black surface choked with rank weeds, broken only by the sharp fang of a rock. Ezrekuul swam slowly along, eyes fixed on the endless corridors ahead. On the shore, Tallamorn and a number of the other Deathguard were murmuring to themselves, spells to ward off the intense scrutiny of the Madwood.

Nyam felt a sudden stab of pain in his wounded shoulder, as though the jungle was testing him, looking for every weakness. He bent down and massaged his calf, unaware that Vaddi was watching him, but the youth said nothing. He himself had grown sullen. He tried to draw on the anger and bitterness that burned within him, but here in this ultimate domain of despair even the embers of that fire burned low.

PART
TO THE SHATTERED LAND
THREE

CHAPTER 15

Fallarond called a halt. Outside this enclosed world, the clean darkness of night had settled on the land, but within the oppressive gloom of the endless corridors of the Madwood, witch-lights flickered, obscuring vision, blurring all but the nearest of the titanic trees. The company fed on the rich elven loaves and the clear water the Deathguard had brought with them.

Ardal warned Vaddi softly, "Don't sip at the streams here. To drink in the Madwood is to invite a painful death—or worse, hideous transformation."

Ezrekuul swam around and around slowly in a wide pool of the river, uneasy and unsettled, like a caged beast. All the while the Madwood hung back on the edge of shadows, as though at any given moment it would launch itself at the small band.

"Are we still in Eberron?" breathed Nyam beside Vaddi.

"What do you mean?"

"All the distasteful tales I have heard of this jungle come back to me now. It is said that it is more closely linked than any other realm to Mabar, the Realm of Eternal Night, an alternate plane where all is darkness, shunned by light. Mabar can fuse itself to the Madwood, pouring its necromantic energies into it.

When this happens, it is possible to enter Mabar itself. Reckless traders have done it, in search of Mabar crystals."

"Mabar crystals?"

"Items of black power. They would be treasured by the Claw, ideal for its black workings and control of the undead."

"You think we have crossed into this realm?" said Vaddi, gazing about him at the walls of supernatural darkness that surrounded them.

"No. But the two planes must be very close to a conjunction. Elf magic could open a gate to it. Or close it."

"The Murughel?"

Nyam shrugged. "They are reckless, I think. Mabar crystals would serve their evil designs well."

"If they have taken Zemella to this Mabar realm, we will follow them," Vaddi said. "I would follow her to Khyber itself if I had to."

He had not noticed Ardal near at hand. The Valenar spoke quietly. "Your loyalty to her is deep, is it not?"

Vaddi stiffened. He nodded slowly. "No more so than your own, I imagine."

Ardal's expression was unreadable. "Yes. My life for hers."

Nyam could see the growing emotional turmoil in Vaddi. This was neither the time nor place for an argument to break out. "Ardal, how close are we to Mabar? It could hardly be darker than this pit."

Ardal rose, preparing to leave. "Not too close, but in the Madwood, it is never far from reach. It will snare you if it can. Like the jungle, it is alive."

Nyam groaned as he got up. "Well, not even I could sleep in this place. Trudging onward would seem our only course."

Led by the creature in the river, the company moved off again. Underfoot the weeds grew more and more matted and tangled, like emaciated fingers, clawing and rending, exerting every effort to wind around the feet of the company. Elf swords hacked at them and they writhed back, repulsed by the glowing wooden blades. Vaddi felt his own weapon, the gift he had been given, slicing through these horrors, but its light was clouded as he used it, as if poison worked upon it. The river dropped lower, and as it did so, the trees crowded in, smaller ones replacing the titans of the jungle edge, although above them other thick branches spread out like the gnarled arms of demons, poised to fall.

Vaddi could see forms and faces in the knotted trunks, baleful eyes, scarlet and hate-filled. Roots shifted, moving weed-smeared rocks. Undergrowth rustled, briars swung, unfurling, but the swords cut and chopped in a ceaseless, uniform movement as the company defied the malevolence of the jungle. From the river, Ezrekuul pointed ahead. Again the waters dropped, splashing over a wide fall to tumble a dozen feet or more into another pool. Beyond this the river divided, one tributary branching to the right, the other to the left. Each looked oily black and foreboding.

The company picked its way down the slippery left bank of the waterfall, taking great pains not to brush up against the undergrowth that tried to force them over the lip and into the gray cauldron of the pool. Nyam's feet betrayed him and he felt himself nudged outward by a branch that had lifted itself out of the moss, but a firm hand gripped his arm and swung him back on to the ledge before he could plummet. It was Tallamorn, the necromancer.

"Your wounds were not mended so that you could enter the service of the Madwood," he said.

"My thanks," said Nyam, though uneasy at the touch of the strange Aereni.

At the bottom of the climb, Ezrekuul swam to them. "That way," he said, indicating the right hand tributary, "is Naalbarak. Leads away from ruins."

Vaddi gazed in distaste at the river. It seemed to flow no more steadily than mud or pitch, wisps of eerie mist seeping up from its slick surface. As he studied it, he heard its voice, a sibilant whispering, like some blasphemous chant, redolent with evil and terror.

"The River of Whispering Evil," he said, recalling the Naalbarak's name.

"We'll not go that way," said Fallarond.

"I fancy we'd have to stuff our ears with mud if we did," muttered Nyam.

They all turned their attention to the other river. This flowed immediately under a tangled mass of branches and undergrowth that had wound itself into a tunnel within the darkness of the jungle. The turgid waters, no less thick and sluggish than the left branch, surged into this tunnel, which was like a wide drain. Around its mouth, weed and mold flourished. As the company edged toward it, they saw the gaping orifice as if it were a mouth, above it two deep black slits in the branches like eyes.

"We are to enter *there?*" said Nyam.

Fallarond pointed with his blade to the undergrowth and branches that had packed up around the tunnel, creating a solid wall, utterly impenetrable and fathomless. "It would take a lifetime to cut through that. The only way is in."

"Leads to the outer stones of ruins," Ezrekuul said. He splashed to the pool's side. "Beyond to east. Safer in tunnel than outside." He hesitated a moment, only his wide eyes above the water, then stood and said, "Hark!"

Vaddi swung round. He could hear distinct sounds in the coiling darkness—vague howls, partially smothered by the trees. The groaning of wood, the shriek of spirits, perhaps.

At the rear of the company, a Deathguard cried out, and as one they all turned. One warrior was clawing at his neck, where a serpent-like root had wrapped itself around it, choking the life from him. His companions hacked at the writhing monstrosity, but the warrior was dragged into the thick undergrowth. A mass of roots and branches swung out like a many-fingered claw, and two others were snared in the barbed tangle. Swords rose and fell, chunks of root and branch flying in all directions as the Deathguard smote the attacking horror. All around them, other branches swung down, and the very earth came alive as if with immense maggots as the roots closed in. It was too late to save the three warriors who had become trapped, and their helpless bodies were pulled away into the enfolding darkness, their awful cries smothered. The company was forced to back off, ever nearer the tunnel beyond.

In the face over the tunnel Vaddi saw the black eyes open, the balefires within them glowing with a malefic power. There could be no greater deterrent than entering the mock mouth below those eyes, but with three dead behind them, there was no alternative. Vaddi cursed and ran forward. He smote at the sides of the tunnel with his elf blade and fire blazed from it at once. The eyes above squinted in pain and for a brief moment the mouth of the tunnel *twisted*, as if in pain. Roots and fronds fell from the sides of the tunnel as Vaddi hacked violently at them, the anger inside him welling up.

Fallarond took his lead from Vaddi and joined him, also cutting into the overhanging vegetation. Between them they had cut enough away to widen the mouth so that they could pass through and along the bank of the river rather than drop down into it. Their blades glowed, and around them in the womblike curve, roots and filaments withdrew from them. Nyam and the remainder of the company entered the tunnel, and without another word, they moved on. A tiny wake in the center of the river showed where Ezrekuul still swam.

"How far?" called Fallarond.

"Little now," said the creature.

Behind them, silhouetted in the grayness of the tunnel entrance, a number of shapes squirmed and flapped, distorted and hunched. Whether they were trees or humanoid, it was impossible to tell. Their numbers grew, but something in the tunnel held them back so they did not follow. Instead they emitted furious shrieks, their voices ghastly, their cries murderous.

"Ignore them!" Ardal snapped. "Move on."

As the company did so, they felt the shuddering of the wooden walls around them, as though something huge was pressing against them from both above and the sides. The tunnel may have formed a temporary haven from the horrors that the Madwood had unleashed, but around it, the nightmare inhabitants of the jungle were swarming, and they were not content to remain outside. They were attempting to rip their way in.

*   *   *   *   *   *   *

Zemella opened her eyes on darkness so crushing that it weighed her down like several tons of earth. She was in a solitary stone cell, far below the ground where her captors had brought her, but it may as well have been sunk into the depths of Khyber itself. These cursed Murughel had done their treacherous work well. Her hands were bound, and the leather strips that held her were steeped in sorcery. Whoever controlled this band of Murughel was powerful, a mage of some kind.

They had taken her at sea, locking her away with chain and spell until their craft had broken the waters of the eastern seaboard of Aerenal, so they were not to go to Shae Thoridor after all. The knowledge had come as a blow to her. When the Murughel had taken her ashore, she knew by instinct that they had reached the very edge of the Madwood. In Valen Bay, they were met by more of their kind. No one had spoken to her, not even to taunt her. Their leader was cunning, well familiar with elf powers, and the cleric was by now far away.

She was no longer sure why she was here. She was so far from Vaddi that the cleric would be able to deceive him and turn him back upon the course he had originally set for him.

They must intend to kill me, she told herself, unable to avoid the thought. They dare not set me free. They know that the Finnarra would hunt them down, but why here, the Madwood?

Once ashore, she had been hooded, dragged along for a day or more, but she knew by the sounds and the smells that she was being taken deeper and deeper into the Madwood. Then it must be to a sacrifice! Her blood would be used to invoke dark powers in the Madwood.

I will not allow them to spill my blood, she thought. I will die first! By my ancestors, I swear it.

She sagged down in the darkness, head buried on her chest in despair. How? How could she achieve this? They would be watching her. Even here, in the total night of the cell, they would be watching.

❀ ❀ ❀ ❀ ❀ ❀ ❀ ❀

Far above her, in another room lit faintly by cold fire, two shapes sat at a stone table, looking out across a vista of thick treetops, above which gray fog curdled. The hooded leader of the Murughel was like a statue, his lidded eyes fixed on the pale figure before him.

Caerzaal smiled grimly, his white face vivid, even in this poor light. "So the flies have entered the jungle. Whichever way they turn now, they must stumble into its web."

"A score of them, no more."

Caerzaal leaned forward, face hardening. "Is the peddler with them?"

"He is."

Caerzaal's sharp teeth gleamed in the moonlight. "A minor issue, but it will please me to deal with that one. How long before they find us?"

"The Madwood has swallowed them. We may not know until they reach these ruins, but the Murughel are ready. I have mustered two hundred of them. Fifty will be given to the Wood after we have what we want."

Caerzaal scowled. "A high price in warriors. To become one with the Wood, its slaves."

"Your prize, Caerzaal, is greater."

"Yes, that is so."

"And the serpent god, Sethis? You still intend to invoke him?" The hooded one looked across from their high vantage point to a stepped pyramid beyond. Fires burned in braziers on its flat top, and a score of Murughel warriors kept guard there.

Caerzaal laughed coldly. "Of course. The Valenar bitch will be the bait that draws the Orien youth. With what he carries, he will be powerful. It will take the power of Sethis, my servants, and your Murughel to best him. But at the end, when the boy is exhausted, I will have him bound, and what he carries will be mine. And you," he added, a long finger stabbing at the Murughel's chest, "will know what power really is. The Emerald Claw will praise your part in this. You will know new joys and pleasures that you have not yet dreamed of."

The hooded one did not smile. He turned, scouring the misty roof of the jungle and the skies above it. "Did you sense something pass?"

Caerzaal studied the night like a hound scenting its prey. "In the skies? Who knows what flies above the Madwood? Its servants are many. Some are better not seen."

The hooded one nodded, but he remained uneasy. Whatever it had been, it was no small thing.

* * * * * * *

Several hours into the journey, Fallarond called a halt. Ahead of him, daubed in the wavering glow of their swords' light, a number of flat stones formed a crude bridge across the river. Ezrekuul came to the bank and gazed up at the Deathguard.

"How far to the ruins?" said Fallarond.

"Not far, not far," said the creature.

Above and outside, the sounds of pursuit had faded, although none of the company believed for a moment that the servants of the Madwood were not tracking them there. Everything had gone silent. Even the river moved without sound, slow as treacle, black as tar.

Fallarond turned to the company and indicated the way they had been travelling. "If any of you wishes to go back, now is the time. Once we cross the river, we are set on our course."

The Deathguard remained motionless, their silence a polite dismissal of his suggestion.

"What about you, peddler?" said Fallarond. In the poor light his skull face looked even more horrifying.

It is suicide, Nyam thought, and they know it, but they are prepared to die for Zemella and Vaddi. Some will die. I don't have their powers, but I won't desert him now.

"Let's get going," he said.

Fallarond stepped onto the stones. They were slick and treacherous, but the company passed over them to the other side of the narrow river, its southern bank. Once they were all assembled, Fallarond called Ezrekuul to him again.

"What lies outside these tunnel walls? Can we cut through?"

"Cut through? Why? The river take you to the first ruins."

"They will be waiting for us. If we go to the city through the jungle, we will improve our chances of surprise."

"But we would be fully exposed to the Madwood," said Ardal. "We'd be fortunate to get a hundred yards."

Fallarond shook his head. "Not if Ezrekuul helps us."

The creature shrank back into the river. "What you want of me?"

"When we cut through, summon others like you, those who were dryads. If they give us their aid, we will do all we can to release you from bondage. We are not without power. It will be difficult and some may die in the attempt, but you and those who aid us will at least have a chance for freedom."

Ezrekuul seemed reluctant, but he heaved himself out of the water and onto the bank—a bedraggled, diminutive figure of despair, waiting.

Fallarond used his sword to begin the arduous task of cutting into the wall of the tunnel, and helped by his fellow Deathguard, sliced through root and branch until a long gash had been made. It took a while to lengthen, but eventually they cut through to the jungle beyond. Fallarond sent the complaining creature through, then waited.

When Ezrekuul came back, he was pointing excitedly into the cloying darkness beyond. "A handful come," he whispered, "but worse things beyond ring of light. Madwood hungers."

"Nevertheless, go ahead," said Fallarond, easing out into the jungle.

Moments later the entire company emerged, swords held before them like torches. Their glow spread but encountered a wall of darkness more intense than any natural nightfall. They could hear vague whisperings within it, sibilant sounds, redolent with evil and suggestive of torment. Overhead the trees were like frozen giants, breathing but unmoving, needing only a word to set them in motion against the company, but their resolve held.

Vaddi and Nyam stood close to each other, and only by a determined effort did Vaddi not clutch at Erethindel. He sensed that here it might turn against him, its power overwhelmed by the monstrous will of this dire place. As he studied the shadows, he made out a number of blurred figures crouched down on all fours, their bodies scaled, their heads batrachian. They had bulbous eyes that barely reflected the light and long, spatulate fingers, incongruously clawed. Nature had been warped in them, contorted by the powers of the Madwood and its lunatic sorcery, but they had not come to attack the company.

Ezrekuul spoke for them. "These"—he hissed—"clay of Madwood. But will guide you."

"They must shield us from the jungle and whatever it sends against us until we get to the ruins."

"Other creatures like you in Madwood," Ezrekuul went on. "These have seen them, smelled their blood. Already corrupt. Elves drawn to dark powers. Secreted in ruins of city of serpent god, Sethis. If you had come to them from river, trap would have sprung around you."

"Why does the Madwood not attack them?" said Nyam.

"Who knows what black pacts have been sealed in this place?" said Ardal. "The Murughel may well serve the Madwood."

Fallarond turned his gaze upon the huddled creatures in the shadows. "You have a chance to win freedom and a return to true light, or will you taste the scorching of our swords?"

The gruesome company shrank back further, croaking and muttering, but the thought of some kind of salvation from their symbiosis with the Madwood stirred a last vestige of hope within them. Ezrekuul pushed through them and led the trudge through yet more dismal realms.

Nyam leaned close to Vaddi and Ardal and said, "I know nothing of this city and this serpent god. What is he?"

Ardal's voice was barely above a whisper. "Old tales say that Sethis is another aberration, partly of dragon blood. Whatever dragon spawned him was somehow trapped and then died here in the Madwood, a victim of its evils. It crawled into Mabar to escape being absorbed by the Madwood, but from out of that realm, Sethis, the great worm, writhed forth in the agonies of his birth. The city of Khamaz Durrafal, once ruled by elves, fell victim to the Madwood, its people horribly changed, just as the naiads and dryads of the jungle were changed. But the Madwood had them build a temple to Sethis, the blind worm, and when it was done, they were sacrificed to it. None survived."

"And Sethis?" said Nyam.

"He is said to have returned to Mabar, but there are tales among the Aerenal that at certain times, the worm god is still summoned and sacrifices are made to it."

Nyam and Vaddi exchanged glances, but mercifully the darkness masked their horror at this revelation. They concentrated on the way ahead, trying not to let the oppressiveness of the jungle crush their will to go on, but they felt it being leeched from them.

Ezrekuul's strange company fanned out ahead of them, and there were sounds of conflict and muted argument, interspersed with distant howls and groans. They came to a rise in the jungle floor, and Fallarond sensed a falling away of the land, a shallow valley. Ezrekuul pointed to it.

"Southern wall of city lies there. Battlements empty. Murughel farther north."

Tallamorn spoke. "We are followed! There is a great disturbance in the aura of the jungle. It may be one huge mass or many creatures. They creep like tendrils towards us. Not allies, but the worst of the Madwood's denizens."

The company tried to see back into the pulsing darkness, but it was as though a thick curtain had been thrown across the jungle. Behind it, they sensed what was drawing upon them, a force of awesome dimensions, as though the entire jungle itself heaved and bellied forward, impatient to smother them.

"Must go!" said Ezrekuul. "Must go!"

"If we can get on the battlements without being discovered," said Fallarond, "We will have an edge."

Without another word, he led them into the valley, everyone keeping close, aware that on both flanks the shapes of Ezrekuul's creatures shadowed them. It was not long before the ruined walls of Khamaz Durrafal loomed out of the darkness, their stones broken, choked with creepers and the clawing talons of dense undergrowth. As they clambered up the walls and onto their flattened top, they heard again the surge of pursuit, like an invisible black wave rushing toward them.

"City keeps it back—for a while," said Ezrekuul. "Avert eyes from what comes. Elves go mad at sight before. Black sorceries crackle like lightning fires."

The company said nothing, winding its way over the wreckage of stone and column, through collapsed archways and tumbled buildings that had not seen habitation for untold centuries. There were glyphs and scrawls, bizarre sculptures and statues, but none that anyone recognised. All belonged to an age beyond time, falling now into dust and dissolution. Even the Madwood appeared to have left this rotting domain to itself—at least in this crumbling section of the city.

"Heart of the city," said Ezrekuul. "Huge, flat-topped pyramid. Hollow. In its bowels . . . way to Sethis."

"Where are the Murughel?" said Fallarond.

"Send brothers. They look."

"Aye. Bring word."

Ezrekuul hopped off, lost to sight almost at once. While he was gone, the company ate the last of its food and drank the last of the water, knowing that it could be the final meal that any of them enjoyed.

"What is our strategy to be?" whispered Nyam.

"We need to know where Zemella is," said Vaddi. "If we can get to her and free her, we'll need to go back before the Murughel can overpower us. A lot depends on the help we get from these creatures. Do you trust them, Ardal?"

"I think so. If they had wanted to betray us, they would simply have let the Madwood take us. Ezrekuul must have persuaded enough of them to rebel."

"What about *that?*" said Nyam, jerking a thumb back at the oncoming horror from the jungle, though it had fallen silent, as if the city walls had withstood its flow.

"The ancient powers of the city contain it, but I suspect that will not last. We must free Zemella and be gone from here before the dam bursts. If not, it will simply swallow everything here like a tidal wave. The Madwood is not to be reasoned with, any more than you would reason with an ocean storm. Even the dragons could never control it."

They said little more, trying to rest and gather their strength for what lay ahead. All the time they felt that, at the edge of the poor light, something crouched, eager to pounce on their first movements. When something did at length slip from out of the darkness, they were alert, as one, but it was Ezrekuul.

"The Murughel leaders are close to the pyramid of Sethis. They have their own guards, but most of their forces are watching the place in the Madwood where they think you will emerge. We have not seen the Valenar girl, but there are chambers under the place where the leaders wait. Perhaps she is there."

Fallarond nodded. He turned to Vaddi and Ardal. "It is the most likely place for them to have imprisoned her."

"Then let's begin there," said Ardal. "If we take their leaders, everything else will follow."

❋ ❋ ❋ ❋ ❋ ❋ ❋

Like phantoms, the company moved out. Fallarond followed Ezrekuul, who squeezed his way through and over the ruins, taking the small band deeper and deeper into the city, down in its weed-choked canyons, through its broken walkways, across courtyards where flagstones leaned upward and where the ever-probing roots had taken their remorseless hold on everything. In the surrounding ruins, on either side, the other creatures moved forward, silent as clouds.

"Ahead," said Ezrekuul, ducking under an overhanging lintel. "Up stairs another parapet. Beyond it, place where Murughel leaders wait. Guards at foot of stairs."

Fallarond persuaded him to create a diversion with his unseen companions, a distraction that would buy precious minutes upon the parapets. When Ezrekuul had gone to carry out these instructions, Fallarond called his company on, slowly rounding the last of the columns. Beyond, they saw the stairs and the two Murughel who guarded them. One of the Deathguard took two arrows from his quiver, the points of which were tipped with light, the same energy that imbued the elf blades.

Stepping out from cover, the elf warrior released the two arrows in succession, the speed of his movement defying the eye. The two Murughel were knocked off their feet by the impact of the arrows, each of which had found an eye and driven straight through the skull. Fallarond was first to the fallen, and with rapid strokes of his blade he removed their heads. Almost at the same moment, some distance to their left, they heard a commotion, a dismal wailing, like the sound of souls in torment. The creatures had begun their diversion. In response to it, there came sounds from up on the parapets.

Motioning for the company to follow, Fallarond led them up the stairs, silent as a cat. As they climbed, a bank of cloud shifted aside to reveal three bright moons, and they realized that once they were on the flat top of the building, they would be exposed by their brilliance. They could no longer rely on the cover of the Madwood and its enclosing embrace.

On the battlements, hunched down, they spread out. As they looked up over the wall, they could see a level area, in the center of which a few columns supported the last of what had once been a massive roof. Whole sections of this had fallen in, but in the protected remains of the building, a group of figures had gathered. There were a number of Murughel, one of whom was hooded. Beside him stood another, taller figure. Even in this light, Vaddi was able to recognize his white face, his scarlet eyes.

"Caerzaal," he breathed.

CHAPTER 16

The Deathguard moved as a unit, each of them unleashing a dozen arrows in a blur of movement. Vaddi and Nyam were staggered at the speed at which they drew and fired. In a matter of seconds, scores of the energy-tipped missiles had fallen in a steady stream on the Murughel that lined the parapets of the building. Many were pierced fatally and toppled into the darkness. Others fell back inside, wounded, while some were spared death only to turn and face a second wave. Vaddi, Nyam, and Ardal leaped from cover and ran at the enemy, the Deathguard close behind them, unleashing a final hail of arrows before they, too, drew their swords.

Caerzaal and the hooded Murughel leader raced from the flat roof, crossing a narrow bridge that led up on to the higher top of the pyramid beyond it. There were other Murughel lining it, and they closed in to protect their masters. Vaddi's sword ripped into the first of the Murughel, cleaving him from skull to breastbone as he used all the ferocity his anger could muster. Beside him, Nyam used his own blade to deadly effect, sweeping two of the Murughel off the span and down into the hungry darkness far below. The creatures fell in silence, like rag dolls torn apart by the fury of the offensive, but something unseen in the depths fed noisily on the fallen.

The Deathguard followed their initial assault so swiftly that they closed off the span to the pyramid and cut down almost all of the Murughel upon the building. They formed a semi-circle and waited for the next wave to follow. As they did, Vaddi, Nyam, and Ardal raced up to the pyramid's vast, flat top. In its center was a gaping, circular hole, like the maw of a monstrous beast, a shaft that plumbed the deeps of the world. Beyond this huge orifice, waiting like priests caught in some act of worship, Caerzaal and the hooded Murughel stood, framed by the glow of moons that now flooded the whole area. On all sides of the pyramid, the Madwood seemed once again to close in, the vague shape of its bizarre skyline shifting, edging forward, forming a shadow audience that overhung events below.

A few last Murughel stood on either side of the abyss, barring the way around it.

"Vaddi d'Orien!" called Caerzaal. "I had no idea you were so reckless. Look around you. You cannot win. You are outnumbered ten to one."

"I think not," said Vaddi, gritting his teeth in an evil grin.

Beside him, Nyam was surprised by the sheer power that was almost dripping from the youth. He had become possessed by it. Nyam saw a terrible danger in this, but there was no time for deliberation.

On the steps below, the Deathguard unleashed another flight of arrows, cutting down a fresh wave of Murughel who had come up from the lower city to defend their masters. Although they killed and maimed scores of them, the Deathguard were hard pressed to hold the steps and were being forced back up them in fierce sword fighting, but they did hold, refusing to give an inch once they had reached the top of the stair. Below, the Murughel crammed together, trying to use their massed ranks as a battering ram to force their way up, but the Deathguard's blades ripped and tore into them, scattering each successive line.

"Such a sacrifice," Caerzaal taunted. "You should be with me, Vaddi."

"Where is the girl?" said Ardal, his eyes blazing.

"She is not for you," said Caerzaal.

Nyam had been looking around the pyramid's top, beyond the huge orifice. He pointed to a small, square opening. "That must lead below."

"She may be there. I'll see," said Ardal, and before anyone could stop him, he dashed across the slabs, cutting aside a Murughel who attempted to bar his way.

"I'll go with him," said Vaddi.

"Wait!" said Fallarond, gripping his arm. "It may be a trap. We must deal with these."

He nodded to Caerzaal and his grim companions. Behind him, the Deathguard still held the stair, though the heaving mass of Murughel forces threatened to break through the small company at any moment.

Vaddi, desperate to find Zemella, would have ignored Fallarond, but the Murughel around the pit also moved forward, determined to overcome Fallarond and his remaining force. Swords clashed anew as the battle was joined, and this time Vaddi, Nyam, and the others found themselves fighting a more resolute enemy. These Murughel seemed empowered with demonic energy, fuelled by the sorcery of Caerzaal and his hooded companion. The night air sizzled with light, fire from the swords caught and held on the shields and blades of the Murughel. Vaddi tried to see the opening down which Ardal had disappeared but dared not let his attention waver. He needed all his power to stave off the flashing blades that sought to hamstring him. He knew that Caerzaal's design was still to capture and not kill him, and that alone gave him an edge.

❁ ❁ ❁ ◉ ❁ ❁ ❁

While the conflict on the pyramid raged, filling the night sky with crackling light and fire, Ardal went deep down into the bowels of the building, his glowing blade lighting the gloom. He came to a corridor, and a Murughel warrior stepped out of the darkness, partially surprised by the Valenar's silent appearance. A second's advantage was all Ardal needed. He sliced the Murughel's head from his shoulders.

Along the corridor, two more guards met him, and again he had the advantage of surprise. He ripped open the first of them, but the other turned, meaning to flee. Ardal flung a long dirk, and the sheer force of the throw took the blade clean through the neck of the Murughel, snapping the spinal cord. The warrior stumbled into the wall, falling to his knees. Ardal was on him in seconds, cleaving his head open with merciless fury.

A few yards farther on was a door, slightly ajar. Ardal heard soft voices and saw a dull glow beyond. Pausing only for a moment, he pushed his way in. Two Murughel garbed in long robes flung up their hands in a shower of scarlet sparks. Their hasty spells exploded impotently against Ardal's blade, and in a blur he rammed it into the guts of the first, elbowing him aside before exercising a swift backward slash of his blade that severed the head of the second Murughel.

Zemella was tied to the heavy chair on which she sat, wrists behind her.

"Ardal!" she gasped.

In spite of their situation he grinned as he went to her and began carefully severing her bonds. "Can you fight?"

Nodding fiercely, she stood up, massaging her wrists. She winced as the pain of the returning circulation hit her. "Murughel sorcery! Their spells restrained me." She paused, like a hound scenting the air. "Is Vaddi d'Orien with you?"

Ardal's face betrayed no sign of emotion. "Yes, he's above, destroying Murughel with the best of them." But even in this poor light, he saw her catch her breath.

"Does he carry the talisman?"

Ardal nodded.

"He should never have come here! The enemy seeks him *and* the talisman. If they claim both—"

On the pyramid above, the Deathguard had at last been forced back from the stair head. Sheer weight of numbers had shoved them on to the flat top of the pyramid as the Murughel, spurred on by their grim masters and utterly careless of their own destruction, pressed forward. Fallarond and his Deathguard formed a solid knot of defense, close to the very lip of the pit. To Vaddi their position seemed helpless.

Mad with frustration, he watched as Ardal and Zemella emerged from the opening and onto the pyramid. Ardal unslung his bow and released half a dozen arrows as he and the sorceress ran to their companions. His arrows had a deadly effect, but the Murughel swarmed like flies in spite of the huge losses they had suffered. Zemella unleashed a bolt of white light that blasted several assailants asunder. Half blinded by the glare, Vaddi redoubled his own efforts, recklessly carving a path through the Murughel. Then he was closer to Zemella, whose teeth were barred in a feral grin.

She was but a few yards away when Vaddi saw Ardal stumble behind her, his own look of horror mirrored in Zemella's eyes as she turned to see what had happened. Ardal had dropped to one knee, but he staggered up. A length of steel, a barbed javelin, protruded from his side. His fingers, already bloody, groped at it with ebbing strength.

"No!" cried Vaddi, leaping forward.

He pushed past Zemella and stood over the fallen Valenar, lifting him to his feet, hardly conscious of the blazing white bolt of light that Zemella had flung about them to drive back their attackers. He watched despairingly as waves of agony broke over Ardal's face.

"It's no use, Vaddi," he gasped. "The steel is in deep. If it stays in me, I die. Remove it and it will be the same. Protect Zemella." He stumbled again.

"You'll not die here!"

"Save Zemella. My life for hers, as I told you."

Vaddi could see the light in Ardal's eyes fading. The Valenar's life was trickling away like water. Vaddi swung round. Zemella was behind him, eyes filled with tears.

"We must help him!" Vaddi cried, but beyond her, Fallarond was frantically urging them both back to the group. It was the only place they could hope to defy the Murughel now.

Zemella reached out and gripped Vaddi's hand, tugging him reluctantly away from the fallen Valenar. Ardal had slumped forward, head on the stone as if in prayer. They both knew he was already dead.

They rejoined the company and prepared for a final, desperate defense, but the assault eased and the Murughel drew back, their own numbers severely depleted. They formed a wide semi-circle around the Deathguard, surrounding them. From across the huge pit, Caerzaal's voice pierced the sudden lull in an incantation, but it was not to the jewelled skies that the vampire prayed.

"Sethis!" said Fallarond. "Caerzaal is summoning the serpent god."

"Then they mean to sacrifice us all," said Nyam. "Vaddi included."

Zemella's fist flared, a white glow of defiance. "They've killed Ardal. Let him be the last."

Vaddi's attention switched to the darkness of the pit and the stones around it. To his amazement, the Murughel who were wounded, several dozen of them, some critically, dropped their weapons and shields from suddenly nerveless fingers. They staggered, stumbled, and crawled to the very lip of the pit. Expressionlessly, like zombies raised from their graves, they gathered around the pit, and then at a command from their hooded leader, they simply fell forward into the darkness.

"Sethis!" said Tallamorn. "It is below us. I feel it *writhing*."

"Ardal!" cried Vaddi. "We must not let him be used."

Fallarond reached to restrain him, but Vaddi broke the circle and made for the body of the fallen Valenar. Nyam rushed after him, and a wedge of Deathguard, led by Zemella, followed. In moments they had ringed Ardal's form, lifted him up, and bore him back to the main body of the Deathguard. None of the

Murughel had moved. Their own ranks were motionless, the warriors lined up like statues, all their attention on the pit.

Vaddi felt Fallarond's withering gaze. "You put all our lives at risk!"

Before he could retort, a voice cut through the night air. "Vaddi d'Orien!" came the taunting cry of Caerzaal. "Give yourself and what you carry to me now, and all your companions will walk free. We will make you a god! You will know power beyond imagining."

Vaddi cursed under his breath. "I have to use the horn," he said, fingers reaching inside his shirt for it. "I have no other choice."

"*Wait!*" said Zemella, pushing his arm away. "That is what he wants! If you use the horn now, the power will be warped. It will flow into his designs! *He* will control *you*, and you will be damned. Vaddi, you must trust me in this."

Vaddi stared at her in frustration. "Then what can we do?"

"It rises!" said Nyam.

In the pit they heard a tremendous rushing sound, as though all the air from the subterranean depths was being forced upward. It presaged something far more terrible, for the shuddering of the stone around the company warned them that Sethis was responding to the invocation.

Vaddi turned and glared across the vast mouth of the pit to where Caerzaal and his hooded companion waited. Vaddi could see the scarlet eyes of the vampire, lit with triumph and eager for blood. Within him, Vaddi felt a fresh surge of fury, and more of the supernatural chains that Cellester had set about him snapped like dry twigs.

I am an Orien, with Orien powers freed.

With a howl that would have challenged the cry of a demon, Vaddi released this welling power.

"*Vaddi!*" screamed Zemella, for the youth had disappeared.

"What in Khyber—" gasped Fallarond, looking about him in fear.

"There!" said Nyam. "Beside the vampire!"

Vaddi had transported, made the brief leap across the void, and appeared beside the hooded Murughel. The latter reacted swiftly, blocking Vaddi's sword thrust that would have run Caerzaal through. The Murughel brought the haft of his own sword down, intending to knock Vaddi senseless with a blow to the temple, but the youth ducked away, using his new power to accelerate his movements. He beat away the Murughel's sword and rammed the point of his own blade into the hood, the blade grinding on neck bone and cutting it in two, but the Murughel still moved, flinging a ball of light from his free hand.

Vaddi dodged as the light fizzed past his ear and splattered apart on the stones behind him. Again Vaddi drove his blade forward and this time the head of the hooded Murughel swung forward on the creature's chest. Caerzaal kicked the crippled Murughel aside and stood before Vaddi with his own sword raised. It glowed faintly red, as though the blood of its many victims had been trapped inside it, giving it greater power. The blade wove a dazzling pattern, blurring in a cloud that made it seem as though a dozen such blades cut the air.

Behind him, Vaddi heard a shrill scream and knew that Sethis had emerged from the pit. He dared not look back. From beyond Caerzaal, a score of his own warriors came forward out of the darkness, more silent and death-like than the Murughel.

"You have no advantage, Vaddi," said Caerzaal as his blade clashed with the elf blade in a cloud of hissing sparks. "Hand me the horn. I will send Sethis back and set your friends free."

Vaddi was only too aware of the immense bulk of Sethis as it boiled up from the depths, its massive head blocking out the moonlight, weaving this way and that, now several scores of feet above the rim of the pit. Beyond Sethis, the remaining rows of the Murughel still waited in statuesque silence, as if mesmerised. Behind them, creeping forth from the darkness of the jungle, the Madwood's own regiments of creatures slid, hopped, and crawled up the stairway to the pyramid, eager to pay homage to the horrific god of the depths.

Vaddi pulled open his shirt and took out the horn. He held it up, and in the gleaming light of moons and stars, Caerzaal's face lit up with crimson fire, a look of intense lust in his eyes.

"Shall I defy us all and give it to Sethis himself?" said Vaddi.

"No!" screamed Caerzaal.

Vaddi realized he had struck a nerve. Perhaps there was a way to defy the Emerald Claw. He drew back his hand, Erethindel held high, and made as if to toss the horn into the pit.

"Vaddi, don't release it!" came another cry.

It was Zemella. Vaddi turned for an instant, his glance taking her in at the edge of vision, shaking her head frantically. In that second, Caerzaal struck, his sword swinging across and striking a glancing blow that rang against the horn itself.

Vaddi felt a tremendous charge of energy, his fingers, hand and upper arm rendered numb. The horn was torn from his grip and flew back toward the pit. Caerzaal staggered forward, eyes riveted on the sacred object as it hit the paving slabs and rolled onward. Vaddi did not turn to see what had happened. Instead he ran his blade up under the rib cage of the vampire with such force that he lifted him from the ground. As Caerzaal's body fell backward, the elf blade firmly held in place by the sheer power of the strike, he pulled Vaddi over with him, and they crashed down to the stone. Vaddi's face was inches from that of the vampire. His eyes still gleamed with malice, as though the dreadful strike had merely scratched him.

Erethindel rolled to within inches of the lip of the pit. As he struggled, Vaddi saw Nyam and Zemella standing rigidly, not daring to move while the questing head of Sethis hovered. He saw it like a titanic cloud above them, swinging this way and that, eyeless but with an open mouth the size of a cave, triple-ringed with needle-like teeth. It exhaled a foetid breath worse than any sewer, a gust that swept the company further back. Somewhere behind them, Vaddi heard the voice of Tallamorn lifted in a chant.

Vaddi realized that Caerzaal could not control Sethis

while locked with him. The beast must be confused, for the huge serpent head still swung this way and that, momentarily indecisive. For all its size, Vaddi guessed, it must lack a real brain, relying on the power of its callers to guide it in this alien light!

He heard the Deathguard adding their voices to that of the necromancer, and as their combined chant swelled, Sethis swung round, now facing the Murughel and the swarming denizens of the Madwood beyond.

Fallarond raced across the stones to where Vaddi was being drawn closer and closer into the embrace of the vampire. Caerzaal, drenched in blood from the wound inflicted upon him, laughed as he locked his arms about Vaddi and tried to drag the youth's neck down to where he could sink his fangs into it. Vaddi could hardly move. He strained to call upon his powers to snap free, but Caerzaal, too, had access to immense supernatural power.

Something dragged at his shoulder, and Vaddi was hauled partially aside. There was a blur of light descending in an arc of stars. Caerzaal screamed, the sound almost deafening Vaddi.

Fallarond had pulled him aside sufficiently enough to use his sword, and with the blade had cut clean through the neck of the vampire. Caerzaal's scream ceased as the head sprang away in a bloody fountain and skittered across the stones before coming to rest in a pool of its own gore. For a while Vaddi still felt the vile grip of the vampire's arms, but Fallarond hacked them ruthlessly aside, freeing the youth.

"The horn!" cried Vaddi as he lurched to his feet.

Both turned. They saw where the horn had come to a stop, so precariously close to the lip of the pit. A few feet from it, the scaly body of Sethis still wove from side to side, but the beast, now directed by Tallamorn's sorcery, had focused its attention and its appetite on the forces below. The massed ranks of the enemy, fronted by the remaining Murughel, waited in apprehensive silence. Instead of coming to witness a sacrifice, they were to be that very sacrifice. Sethis opened its immense mouth and dipped down, sucking up a score of hapless victims, the rows of teeth closing over its writhing feast.

Vaddi realized that Fallarond was reluctant to go to where the horn had fallen. The Deathguard commander nodded to him, but as the youth sheathed his weapon and prepared to fetch the horn, another vast shadow fell across this nightmare arena. Instinctively Vaddi and Fallarond ducked down as that shadow lowered over them. They heard members of the Deathguard letting loose arrows up into the night sky at whatever new horror the Madwood had unleashed.

Vaddi saw then what had come. It was not of the Madwood's making. It was a soarwing.

Perched upon its shoulders, hunched forward, directing the aerial monster, was its rider, only partially glimpsed, but surely Aarnamor. In spite of its huge bulk, the soarwing glided gracefully overhead, swooping down with deliberate intent. Its claws were huge and could have lifted a man with ease, but it was focused on one thing only—Erethindel. Too late Vaddi realized its purpose and ran forward. The underbelly of the soarwing struck him a glancing blow, enough to bowl him from his feet. As he struck the stones, he saw the claw tip curl around the horn.

Then it was lifted, gone from sight. The soarwing swerved to avoid the massive bulk of Sethis and rose up into the darkness of the night.

"Two riders!" cried Fallarond, helping Vaddi to his feet.

Vaddi gazed upwards in fury. "Two? Then the second was Cellester. He has part of his prize."

Zemella and the Deathguard were beside him as he watched the soarwing swallowed up by the darkness.

"Are you hurt?" said Zemella.

Vaddi shook his head. "Erethindel has been taken."

She stared coldly into the night, a look that would have put terror into hearts of many an enemy. "Then we will retrieve it," she said, "but for the moment we must get away."

Vaddi looked around and saw Nyam, who was staring in

confusion across the stones to where the decapitated body of
Caerzaal had fallen. But the body was not still. It spasmed then
began to *crawl*, fingers dragging it through leaking blood, inch
by inch toward the severed head. Vaddi watched as Nyam walked
calmly toward the animated horror and stood over it. His face
grim but set with determination, he cut up the body. Beyond
him, the undead warriors that Caerzaal had brought drew back
and dispersed, shrinking from the power of the elves' fiery
blades. When Nyam completed his grisly task, he went to the
severed head, lifted it by its long strands of hair, and hurled the
thing into the pit.

"We must leave this place quickly," said Fallarond.

Vaddi saw the body of Ardal and several other Deathguard,
all of whom were being carried by survivors.

Tears welled in Zemella's eyes as she looked upon the fallen
warrior. As the company made its cautious way to the far side
of the pyramid, away from the mayhem that Sethis still created
among the enemy host, he walked with her, not knowing quite
what to say to her.

"He gave his life to save me. Others of the Deathguard have
fallen, too. You all risked everything, and we have lost the horn,
too. You should have left me!"

Staggered, he shook his head. "No, never. We would not
have done that. Was Ardal your betrothed?" He blurted the
question before he had time to check himself.

She looked as if the words stabbed her heart, but she shook
her head. "No. Nor was he my lover. But he wooed my sister,
Herrenwen. She loved him. She teased him, but in time, they
would have wed." A tear fell from her cheek as she spoke.

"We must bear him back to Valenar," said Vaddi.

She nodded. "Herrenwen will be devastated. Their marriage was foreseen many years since. The future is tainted."

Their attention was snared by events behind them and they
closed ranks, shielding themselves from any potential pursuit.
Sethis had at last emerged fully from the pit. Well over a hundred
feet long, the colossal worm crashed down on the flat pyramid

and undulated with frightening speed toward the massed creatures from the jungle. What few Murughel that had survived
fled. They trampled their own company and toppled from the
heights of the buildings.

Tallamorn stood with arms raised, continuing the powerful
working that sent commands to the monster, using every vestige
of necromantic energy to divert it away from his companions.

A Deathguard scout, who had gone beyond this far edge of
the pyramid, reported back to Fallarond. "The Madwood has
been stirred into a frenzy. It has withdrawn from the city but
not gone away. We dare not enter the jungle here."

"Then we wait," said Fallarond. "Find cover."

"What of the worm?" said Vaddi.

"There is feast enough for that monster without turning
upon us. Even one such as that can be sated. Tallamorn's power
will return it to its lair."

"And Ezrekuul?" said Nyam. "Surely he and his kind will
have fled deep into the heart of the Madwood. We'll not be able
to rely on them, I fear."

"Perhaps," said Fallarond, "though I hope you are wrong.
Without them, our testing has barely begun. The Madwood has
been stirred like a hornet's nest. Its entire expanse will be awake
to us by now."

THE MADWOOD'S ANGER

CHAPTER 17

Exhausted, Vaddi and Nyam fell into a fitful sleep in a sheltered overhang below the apex of the pyramid. The elves took turns at watch as they themselves rested. During the deep reaches of the night, Tallamorn heard the return of the immense worm. He drew again upon the necromantic energies in this place to control the beast, which had evidently sated its vile appetite in the Madwood. He directed the monster to the pit and let it slide silently and swiftly back into its gaping lair, heedless of anything around it. Satisfied that it had indeed returned to whatever hellish dimension had spawned it, the necromancer did not disturb his companions.

Later Fallarond stirred, with dawn yet an hour or more away. He studied the jungle beyond the pyramid and central citadel. By the uninterrupted light of the moons he could see the havoc wrought by Sethis as the monster had surged out into the city, smashing a path through the ruins, leaving a distinct trail in which the corpses of numerous inhabitants of the Madwood had been pulverized and heaped to either side. The Deathguard commander gasped as he realised how vast an array of these creatures had been out there.

"Sethis has retuned to its lair," said Tallamorn. "It is sated for now."

"Then we must leave with all haste."

Fallarond had the company readied. They prepared to go back into the ruins, carrying Ardal and their dead with them.

"Which way?" said Nyam.

Fallarond stood at the top of the steps that led down from the pyramid. "We will try to head northwest to the border of the Madwood where we entered it. Sethis has caused so much destruction that the jungle's denizens must have withdrawn well away from here. We may be able to slip past them before they regroup."

No one objected. They were all drained by the events of the night, their brief rest only partially renewing their energy. Vaddi walked beside Zemella, wanting to talk to her, but the entire company felt hushed by the oppressive atmosphere of the Madwood. Instead, they made their cautious way down into the ruins, for the moment following the havoc that Sethis's passage had caused. In the darker shadows of the smashed buildings, shapes shifted and writhed, but nothing emerged to harass them.

The wide swath that Sethis had cut through the city led north, and only now could the company see the true nature of some of the horrors that would have beset them. Many were abominations that shunned the light, as warped and twisted as the worst spawn of Voorkesh, while others were beyond even those levels of corrupted living matter. There were a few dead Murughel among the fallen and scores of creatures not unlike Ezrekuul. In the early morning, steam rose from their carcasses.

At the wall of the city, itself reduced to a low heap of rubble for a hundred yards or more, the company paused, listening to the Madwood beyond and its unnatural silence. To their right, the first hint of dawn light edged the treetops like a bloodstain. The Madwood seemed to crouch, waiting for some signal.

"There!" said Tallamorn, pointing to the cloaking darkness ahead. "The jungle is yet alive. It does not mean us to pass."

The Deathguard readied their bows.

"Wait!" said Vaddi. "It's Ezrekuul."

He was proven right, for in a moment the hunched figure of the creature slipped from the shadows and came forward, face screwed up in a grimace. He bowed low before Tallamorn. "We wait." He pointed back with his root-like arm to the murmuring darkness at the jungle's edge. As the company studied it, they could see others there, reluctant to come out into the growing light. Some were similar to Ezrekuul, others were far more misshapen, but all had the distinct taint of the Madwood.

"You will guide us out of here?" said Tallamorn.

"You promised. Return us to light. Free us from Madwood curse."

"I did," said the necromancer. "None who wishes to leave shall be neglected."

"Many died this night," said Ezrekuul. "Sethis fed. Madwood forced back. Now ablaze with anger. Wants revenge! Must go quickly, while jungle licks wounds. Now jungle fears you, but won't last. Soon . . . aftermath comes."

"Then lead us," said Fallarond.

Ezrekuul needed no second bidding, skipping away to the jungle's edge. Shadows parted and as the company took its first precarious steps into the twisted trees. Beyond, still cloaked in darkness, the Madwood and its horrors yet brooded. Fallarond led the way, elf blade held high. The company took their lead from him. The green glow of the blades was a clear deterrent to whatever stalked them.

As they climbed out of the deep valley where Khamaz Durrafal had been built, with the early sun's rays trying in vain to pierce the thickening tree cover, there was further evidence of the mayhem unleashed by the giant creature. Huge trees had been ripped open and smashed flat, tangled in roots, vines, and creepers—some of which were still twitching, groping like claws for the darkness, as though eager to snare any prey that came within reach. The Deathguard had to use their swords to hack their way through the worst of it, splitting tendril and bough alike, drawing back from the treacherous ooze that gushed from the wounds. There were dead and maimed jungle dwellers here, large and small alike, but no one looked upon them for long.

Ezrekuul did not lead the company along any of the river courses, saying that in their energies would be too much of the Madwood's strength. Better, he said, to keep to the jungle itself, where the company could use fire and light to best advantage should an attack come. Thus they made their way steadily through the rest of that day away from the city and the wreckage left by Sethis.

During the darkest part of the night they paused once so that the company could eat what little food was left. As they rested, massaging their aching limbs and fighting back the strange lethargy that this place cast over them like a cloak, Ezrekuul grew more and more agitated.

"Some of companions fled," he told Fallarond.

"Do they not trust us?"

"Trust, yes, but we are followed. Madwood wakes. Behind us the dark wave."

"Dark wave?"

"All that moves, crawls, or writhes . . . gathers. Comes like tide. Will surge around us, swamp us, choking, rending."

"How far to the edge of the jungle?" said Tallamorn.

"Not far. You must be swift." There was a look of intense sorrow in the eyes of the strange creature. "We hold it."

Vaddi knew what the creature was saying meant suicide for his kind, but Ezrekuul was gone before anyone could protest. Moments later the silent beings of the jungle had eased back from the company and reformed behind them. Somewhere beyond, welling up from the heart of the Madwood like poison from a running wound, came the dark wave. Ezrekuul and his companions would surely not contain it for long.

Fallarond led the company forward, urging them to ignore the sounds that were growing like the gathering of a storm. Onward through the jungle they sped, conscious now that the very roots and undergrowth about them were springing to renewed life, eager to delay them or ensnare them if they could. The company was hampered by carrying their dead, but they forged on to the boundary of the jungle, the Deathguard taking turns to carry their burdens.

At last they came to a dip beyond which they could see the edge, but time was slipping away from them. The dark wave was rustling and rushing toward them on three sides, the very trees bending forward like eager giants, branches outspread like arms to gather in their living fare. Ezrekuul and his fellows had done their best to stem this tide, but there was no sign of them now.

For a moment everything fell silent. The company froze, chests heaving with effort. Salvation was but a hundred yards away, but the fist that was the Madwood's revenge waited only for them to move before it fell.

"Vaddi, Zemella, Nyam!" said Fallarond. "Run! We will cover you."

"We're not leaving you!" snapped Vaddi.

Zemella stood so close to Vaddi that their arms were almost interlocked. If I am to die now, he thought, linked thus to her, then I am content.

"Then we fought for no reason. We gain nothing!" snarled Fallarond. "You must go. You must get out and search for the horn!"

There was no time to deliberate. The jungle rose up now, a filthy, black curtain in which countless horrific faces leered at them—ghastly, twisted faces, teeth gleaming, eyes ablaze with madness, claws forming from the very substance of the dark.

The company fled, racing across the last of the undergrowth. To their horror they found the way ahead was not clear. More shapes rose up from the very last of the jungle, a solid wall of bodies. Fallarond would have rushed upon them, elf sword blazing, but a voice checked him.

"Drop down, brother of Shae Thoridor!"

"Bowmen!" shouted Nyam.

It was so, for a hundred or more elves were just past the farthest trees. They unleashed a withering hail of arrows above the heads of the company into the heart of the dark wave. Light fizzed and cracked as energies clashed. There were shrieks and screams, but not one of the company dared look back. Again and again the bowmen released their spell-tipped arrows.

Fallarond led the charge through the last trees. As the Deathguard broke through into daylight, the bowmen withdrew swiftly. Across a shallow stream they all fled, out on to the grassy hillside beyond and into the fresh morning light. They turned their eyes back to the Madwood. The entire jungle writhed and twisted, as though it floated on an undulating sea, wracked by tides and waves, pulling itself this way and that, but it could not advance beyond the stream, though the ground heaved and burst as root after root groped for the victims that had evaded it.

The sounds from the forest were awful beyond imagining, like the death throes of a leviathan. Vaddi hugged Zemella as though shielding her with his very life. He turned to find his eyes inches from hers. Hugely embarrassed, he released her.

She smiled then leaned forward to kiss him in the blink of an eye, but in that fleeting kiss he felt a supercharge of power.

"Are we free?" cried Nyam beside them, again wheezing as if his chest would burst. "I cannot go another step."

"Yes, Nyam," said Fallarond. "Thanks to these Tairnadal."

"Tairnadal?" Vaddi asked.

"Elves from Aerenal's northern steppes," said Zemella, "though how they came here mystifies me."

Satisfied that the Madwood had done its worst and could not pursue them out on to the clean sward of the hillside, the company, led by the Tairnadal, climbed higher into the fresh wind.

The leader of the newcomers came to greet them. "I am Aramil of the Valaes Tairn."

"We owe you our lives," said Fallarond. "How did you find us?"

"The horses," said the armor-clad northerner. "You were kind not to force them to bear you into that foul place. When you set them free, they came back to us, who bred them. You chose well when you bought them. They told us what you had done and where you had gone."

Fallarond held out his hand, and the two elf commanders clasped arms in a rare display of friendship. "It is not often that the Tairnadal and those of Shae Thoridor put aside their differences," said Fallarond, "but we are in your debt."

"All Aereni should be united against that foulness," said Aramil, looking down upon the darkness of the jungle.

"Elf pride," muttered Nyam, nudging Vaddi.

The latter grinned but decided on a discreet silence.

Aramil pointed to the crest of the hill where more of his warriors waited. These were mounted, and they had with them the steeds that had originally brought Fallarond and the company to the Madwood.

"We must return to our city," said Fallarond, "and in haste, for we have other enemies to pursue."

"We will not detain you," said Aramil, "but know this. It was foolish for you to come near this jungle. It will dream of you and of ways to find you and repay you. It has strange allies in many places. Even beyond Aerenal, I suspect."

Fallarond nodded. "I promise you, our business with the Madwood is done."

"Then may the Undying bless you and your endeavours," said Aramil.

With little more than a cursory wave, he turned his warriors aside and soon they were racing across the hills, back to their high steppes.

Soon afterward, Fallarond's company spurred back to Shae Thoridor.

❂ ❂ ❂ ◉ ❂ ❂ ❂

Sfarrag put aside the empty goblet, wiped his greasy beard on the back of his hand, and rose. Here, in the shadowed confines of the backroom behind the main bar of the drinking hall, secreted by friends who had been seduced by his gold, the dwarf had remained at bay, knowing that the Deathguard of Shae

Thoridor were hunting him. Since the debacle above the city when he had been party to the cleric's abduction plan, the dwarf had kept a very low profile, waiting for the opportunity to rejoin Vortermars. Until then, Sfarrag was spending his nights in an old, abandoned courtyard, tucked away like a fox in its den, away from the long reach of the hunters. He possessed enough magic and skill to trick the eyes of many and had survived in this foreign land for longer than most.

Cautiously he slipped out of the building and into a narrow side alley, blending with the darkness. The moons were partly hidden by cloud, and the dwarf picked his moments to scuttle for cover. Only the most observant of watchers would have seen him. He reached the leaning gates of the old courtyard, paused for a final look about, then went inside. Around him the partly ruined storehouse rose up, obscured by creepers and ivy, ignored by the busier folks of the city. He yawned, eager to curl up in his makeshift bed of straw, and made for the rotting door to the cellar where he was holing up.

As he came to its overgrown portal, something soft dropped over his head and shoulders, light as a spider's webbing. He swung round at once, reaching for his axe, but the more he moved, the more the webbing clung to him. Seconds later he was jerked from his feet, netted like a fish. He squirmed and writhed, but the net tightened, squeezing him into a tighter ball, like a moth wrapped up in a giant spider's cocoon. He knew it was no giant spider, for he had checked this place scrupulously before using it.

He was swung up off the ground, dangled like a pendulum, washed now by moonlight as three golden orbs slipped from cloud cover and mocked him. By their glow he could see the sparkling shards of the Rings of Siberys high overhead. It was the last thing he saw for a while. A sudden darkness smothered him as the net fell to the ground and he was dragged off. Somewhere along that unpleasant journey he lost consciousness.

When he regained it, he was again hanging upside down, though no longer in the net. Both his ankles were tied tight with a wire-like cord and he was suspended from a beam high overhead. Below him he could feel the heat rising from a brazier. He kept very still. The elves had him.

"You are Sfarrag," said a voice somewhere nearby. In the gloom of the chamber he could see nothing. By its tone, it was an elf and one used to giving commands.

"What if I am?" he said. "I've the protection of the city. I'm a legitimate trader."

"I know what you are, dwarf. Don't waste my time. Do as I ask and you'll be spared. Otherwise I'll have you lowered into the fire."

The dwarf grunted but knew his situation was impossible. "What you want?"

"Who is your master?"

"I'm my own master."

"I said, don't waste my time," came the voice, and the dwarf felt himself being lowered another foot or two. The heat threatened to singe his thick mop of hair. "You were part of the abduction attempt."

"Yes, yes. But I only had a small part in it. The cleric paid well."

"Cellester?"

"Aye, that was his name."

"You also serve Vortermars."

"When it suits me."

"You await his return?"

"Aye."

"When?"

"Sometime before dawn, though he'll not dock in Shae Thoridor."

"Will you earn your freedom?"

Sfarrag fell silent for a moment. This must be a trap. They had him and knew him for an enemy. They could kill him at a stroke, but they must want something.

"I'll not betray Vortermars. You may spare me for it, but he wouldn't. Better that you kill me now."

"There is no need for betrayals. All I want from you is for you to arrange a meeting with Vortermars. We wish to secure his services ourselves."

"He wouldn't trust you."

"Perhaps not. But you will arrange a meeting."

"If that's the price of freedom."

"If you fail us in this or seek to betray us, we will find you again, and it will not be a simple death by fire."

The dwarf was lowered again, but firm hands gripped him and swung him away from the brazier. He was upended and released from his bonds. He massaged his ankles, aware that he was missing his axe. Two elf blades hovered inches from his hide. A number of Deathguards observed him, their skull-like faces made more garish by the scarlet glow of the fire.

From out of the shadows, another figure emerged. The dwarf knew him at once. He shrank back, knowing now that his cause was indeed hopeless.

"Greetings, wily dwarf," said Nyam Hordath.

Sfarrag said nothing.

"I have been abroad in Aerenal since our recent meeting," said the peddler. "You would not believe the things I have seen. Have you visited the Madwood?"

The dwarf scowled. "Only fools go there."

"Then count me a fool." Nyam grinned. "Let me show you something."

He lifted from a table a small earthenware jar, out of which a solitary plant grew. Even in this hot light it had a sickly pallor, like a thick, bloated tongue, drained of blood. As the dwarf stared at it, the thing wriggled this way and that, like a finger seeking a grip.

"What is it?" whispered Sfarrag.

Nyam held it up close to Sfarrag's face. The writhing plant swung toward the wide eyes of the dwarf.

"I brought back some seeds from the Madwood. This is what they produce. The plant grows very rapidly—the more so when it has affixed itself to a victim, taking it over, digesting it and transforming it. We don't know for sure. We haven't tried it out yet. Revolting, isn't it?"

Sfarrag shrank back, but two swords pricked his back. "Keep it away from me!"

"Of course," said Nyam, casually tossing the plant out of the pot and on to the brazier. To Sfarrag's horror, the thing *shrieked* and tried to writhe from the coals, but their intense heat enveloped it and it exploded in a green cloud. The stench that it exuded was vile, and the dwarf put his hand to his mouth, gagging.

Nyam held out his palm to reveal a number of spiky seeds. "I brought quite a few more of them. Once planted, you'd be amazed how soon they grow."

"Yes, yes!" Sfarrag snarled. "I take your point. There's no need for this. I'm always prepared to bargain. You know that."

"Indeed. Then we can rely on you now." Nyam slipped the offending seeds away in a pocket.

"You want to meet Vortermars?"

"I do," said Nyam. "I am sure he wouldn't dream of coming ashore to speak to me—especially after recent events. I propose that you take me to his ship, the *Sea Harlot*. Just me."

"Why?"

"I want to commission him. He will no doubt laugh and suspect foul play. He has known me for a long time. We have done business before. He has earned the displeasure of the Deathguard by aiding the cleric, and I believe he may have had dealings with the Emerald Claw."

"Don't know about that."

"Don't be coy, Sfarrag. The Deathguard have long ears, and there is little that transpires on Aerenal they don't know about. Vortermars has forfeited his right to trade in these waters. Fallarond here will alert the authorities, unless Vortermars deals with us."

"What you want from him?"

"His ship. Her cover. In exchange for turning a blind eye to recent events. The abduction attempt."

"You put a high price on your importance."

Nyam smiled. "Not at all. I am merely a spokesman, but that is the deal. You arrange a meeting, and Vortermars has asylum for as long as he wants. And you, most fortunate of underlings, get to remain a dwarf, though you may find the climate in Khorvaire healthier than Aerenal hereafter."

Sfarrag glared at the brazier, where the last vestiges of the ghastly plant fizzed to nothing. He nodded.

"Sometime before dawn I think you said?" Nyam smiled.

* * * ◉ * * *

"Give me one good reason why I shouldn't have you keel-hauled and your bloody remnants fed to the sharks!" snarled Vortermars.

Nyam Hordath sat back and grimaced. He was aboard the *Sea Harlot* in the cabin, the ship riding easily at anchor several miles offshore from Shae Thoridor. Sfarrag had been as good as his word for once and arranged the meeting. Nyam had come alone, though Vaddi had argued fiercely with him that it was far too risky, but Nyam's stubborn insistence had won out. In the first wash of dawn light, his grin was pale and not a little sickly.

"Come, Vortermars, you and I have been freebooters for a long time. Since when did we start slitting each other's throats?"

Across the table, the pirate returned his stare, seemingly burning with anger. But suddenly his weather-beaten features split in a grin. "Curse it, I have to admire your nerve, Daal, Bereth, or whatever your name is."

"Nyam Hordath."

"Aye, well, you never lacked for gall. And I'm supposed to be swayed by your arguments, eh? You think I'll believe you're in with the Deathguard? You say they want to commission *my* ship, eh?"

"Vortermars, you and I are always pawns in the greater games, but we look after our own interests first. Isn't that so?"

The pirate laughed. "Go on."

"We are opportunists. You were given an opportunity back in Pylas Maradal—abduct the Valenar sorceress and transport her for the cleric. You carried out your part of the bargain. The Valenar are not pleased, but the real villain of the piece is the cleric. I assume you owe him no further allegiance?"

"Why should I, eh? He's not been back."

"Nor will he, I think. He has flown to his master. You have been paid for your part in the deal?"

Vortermars said nothing.

"I assume you are a free agent once more. The Deathguard have not put a price on your head. Not yet."

"They want this cleric, eh?"

"Yes. They have retrieved the girl."

Vortermars shrugged. "She's of no interest to me. Seems to me the cleric was more anxious to snare the boy, eh? The girl was no more than bait. What's so special about him, eh? What's he got?"

Nyam chuckled. "Nothing that concerns you, but the cleric and his master have stirred up a hornet's nest. Vaddi d'Orien and the girl are together in Shae Thoridor. They make a formidable team, given their powers."

"Yeah, it took a lot to control her."

"She has powerful allies—not the least of which are the Deathguard."

"Word is they saved you from the Stillborn."

"They did. And have done more. This business of ours will conclude matters."

"You say I'll have immunity, eh?"

"It will be part of the deal."

"So what d'you want?"

Nyam leaned forward. "We think the cleric has fled to Xen'drik. He cannot be allowed to go free. The Valenar and their families demand satisfaction. They want the cleric and whoever commissioned the abduction brought before them. The Undying Court would probably not sanction action—not openly anyway. You know how they are, and we have no idea how great a force is mustered in Xen'drik."

"Force?" said Vortermars.

"We assume the cleric is working for a powerful master. If we are to go to Xen'drik, we need to be shielded. What better way than to go as pirates? Who sails the seas as freely?"

Vortermars leaned back thoughtfully. "I see. You want to send a small force into Xen'drik, and you want to use my ship to cover you, eh?"

"The rewards will be significant."

"Journey like that, I'd want a big payoff."

"Of course. Quite apart from total absolution from your part in the abduction, you will be rich, Vortermars. I mean *rich*, the sort of rich that freebooters such as you and I have dreamed about since we were knee high."

Vortermars's eyes narrowed, but Nyam could see the gleam of lust in their gaze. "Go on."

"You have only to land us on Xen'drik's shores. There will be no need for you to involve yourself in any conflict, and once we have dealt with the cleric—"

"Presuming you're successful."

"Yes, yes. Then we will need returning here."

"When do I get paid?"

"There will be a substantial advance, of course."

Vortermars guffawed. "There'd have to be! What if your expedition to Xen'drik falls flat on its face? You're likely to be squashed like flies, once you land. I've contacts with the barbarians there, but *in*land? I'd rather visit the Mournland!"

"Arrangements will be made to pay you, whatever happens to our expedition."

Vortermars stood and paced the narrow cabin, his head bent to avoid the low beams above him. "I'm an old hand at this, Hordath. You and me both, eh? I smell a trap. Wouldn't you?"

"Probably. But you and I are small fish. I assure you, the elves are concerned with bigger game. Trust me."

"Honor among thieves, eh?"

"Quite so."

"So what's to stop me from dumping you overboard now and running with the next tide?"

"Probably the blockade awaiting you at the mouth of the inlet. It's not only the Deathguard who have a stake in this. One of the Valenar, Ardal Barragond, came here in pursuit of the girl. He died."

"Ardal Barragond? From Pylas Maradal? From the Finnarra warclan, eh?"

"Yes."

"Then there'll be a reckoning. Blood will have blood, eh?"

"Oh, yes. My guess is you'd rather it was the cleric's than yours?"

Vortermars sat down and pondered for a while. "You always did drive a hard bargain."

"I'd disappoint you if it were otherwise, eh?"

CHAPTER 18

An hour before dawn they laid Ardal Barragond and the Deathguard warriors who had died in the Madwood in their final resting place in Shae Thoridor. Vaddi and Zemella stood to one side, watching as the Aereni warriors murmured their last prayers, heads bowed in the soft morning light. They were gathered in a small grove at the rear of Fallarond's retreat, under the dissipating shadows of the trees, which themselves seemed bent in recognition of the passing heroes.

Vaddi and Zemella slipped away back into the cool corridors of the building.

"I still think it was headstrong of you to enter the Madwood," she told him, a mild look of rebuke on her face.

He groped for the words to explain himself, even more daunted by the thought that elves had died on that quest.

"You are the custodian of Erethindel, Vaddi. You should have put its safety before anything else."

"I could not leave you to the Emerald Claw. The thought of you—"

"I am flattered," she said, though she did not smile, "but we are now in a worse predicament."

"You are safe."

"I am not important!"

There is nothing more important to me, he wanted to tell her.

"What do you plan to do now?" she went on, arms folded across her chest, as if setting a barrier between them.

"I have to recover the horn. Nyam's plan is a risky one. . . ."

"True enough, but what if he does not return? What if the pirate sends back his head?"

Vaddi grimaced. "Somehow I don't think even Vortermars would do that. Nyam is a curious character."

"He has sacrificed much to help the Keepers. Since his family died, he has served us as loyally as any elf."

"I never really did believe he would betray me, though part of Cellester's deceit was to have me think so."

"Vortermars *would* betray you. His allegiance is to himself alone. You need to understand that, Vaddi."

"Yes, Nyam said the same thing."

"We'll need to sleep with one eye open on this crossing to Xen'drik—assuming Nyam's negotiations are successful."

His jaw dropped. "You don't mean you'll be with us?"

It was her turn to scowl. "Why not? If it was not for me, Ardal would be alive and Erethindel would still be in your keeping. You don't expect me to sit here while you sail off to Xen'drik. What do you think I am?"

"But there's no need—"

Quick as a striking snake, she slipped her sword from its sheath and wove a blurred pattern in the air. "No *need!* You think you're better equipped for this expedition than me? Draw your own blade. Show me that you are better qualified than I am!"

"Don't be ridiculous!"

"Ridiculous! I'll carve you to pieces!"

"Zemella!" The voice cut through the air every bit as effectively as her sword had done.

She swung round, face still clouded with outrage, to face Fallarond. He stared at her now with an expression of deep sadness.

"This is no time for childish quarrels! We still grieve for Ardal Barragond."

Humbled, she lowered her sword.

"Nyam will be here soon," said the Deathguard.

"If he's still alive," she muttered.

"He is," said Fallarond, a smile almost lightening his usually stern features. "Word has come from the quayside."

He left them, closing the door behind him.

Zemella sheathed her sword. "I am sorry," she said, looking away.

"You don't have to prove your worthiness with a sword to me. I've seen you at work with it."

"It's not something I enjoy," she replied, suddenly studying him. "No one should enjoy killing, Vaddi."

"No, of course not."

"I saw you fight, too. I saw a different Vaddi, not this shy young man stumbling over his words."

He grinned and managed to hold her gaze.

"You are very fast, Vaddi. Very dangerous. What do you feel when you kill?"

It seemed a strange question. "I don't know. As you say, it happens very swiftly. I feel anger, but I know anger must be controlled. It diminishes skill."

"Do you feel pleasure at striking down evil?" She came closer to him, her eyes fixing his. "Knowing that the powers that threaten you are being torn, shredded?"

He backed a pace, confused.

"And when it is me you fight for, cutting down those who would harm me, what do you feel? Joy? Satisfaction?"

Still he did not answer.

"Well?" she snapped, her face inches from his.

"Yes. I am glad to destroy those who would harm you."

She drew back. "I have seen it in you, Vaddi. The killing lust."

He opened his mouth to protest, but she raised a hand, cutting him off.

"It is another way the darkness uses us. You must be on your guard even more than the rest of us. There is power in you. You bear a dragonmark, your veins pump dragon blood through you, and you are the bearer of Erethindel. Such a combination in the wrong hands could be catastrophic. It is what our enemies crave. It is what Caerzaal sought, and it will be what Cellester's master wants."

"Then I will be cautious."

"You may not know when these powers are flowing in you— or how to control them. If you allow your anger to have its head, succumbing to the seduction of a berserker fury—"

"I'm on my guard." He stepped closer to her. "But if you are in danger, then I am more likely to fall into such a trap. Any threat to you, the very thought of your being harmed, draws that madness from me."

It was her turn to step back.

"Perhaps you should stay here," he said again.

She would have rejoined the argument, but the door swung open, flooding in light and the windswept shape of Nyam.

"Well, it is done!" he beamed. "Our ship is commissioned." He strode toward them, waving his feathered hat this way and that. "Vortermars saw sense. Rather than offend the Aereni, he's agreed to take us to Xen'drik."

"For a price?" said Vaddi.

"Oh, yes. A pirate to the end." Nyam's face dropped. "You would not believe how much it's costing me."

"Tell us anyway," said Zemella.

He waved this away, but she pressed him. "Tell us, Nyam. What have you offered him?"

"If you must know . . ."

"We must know," Zemella said.

"Well, during the long course of my own . . . experiences, I have amassed a not inconsiderable sum—and valuable items that Vortermars could hardly not wish for his own."

"You are emptying your own pockets to finance this expedition?" said Zemella. "How noble of you! Why is that? What do you expect to gain?"

"My dear girl, what do you take me for?"

She stared almost mischievously at him. "In Pylas, we say a pirate may shave his beard, but he remains a pirate."

"Surely you're not saying you don't trust me?"

Vaddi was laughing softly. "She doesn't trust any of us, Nyam. She thinks I'm going to lose my head and become possessed. One sniff of blood and I'll become a demon."

Zemella turned on him. "Be wary of such scorn."

"No, of course. You are right."

"If you have doubts about me, Vaddi," said Nyam, "I understand. All I can say is that I have done my best to serve you. But you know little about me and my past. It is not a glowing one. I have spent most of my life picking through the ruins of war and the conflicts of war's aftermath. We are said to be in a new age of peace and restoration, but how many victims of the War are benefiting from it? We have become jackals, many of us, survivors using our wits to glean even a meagre living. You, Zemella, have lost a great friend in Ardal, but to lose a wife, your children, this is something that teaches you the true nature of sorrow. Had my sons lived, they would be Vaddi's age. Not such fine warriors as he, perhaps, but sons to be proud of. Their loss has diminished me and not a day goes by that I am not reminded of it. They cannot be replaced, not fully, but neither the War nor their passing has robbed me of loyalty and compassion. Nor love, for that matter."

When he stopped speaking, a strange silence clung to the chamber.

"We'd better prepare to sail," Nyam said, abruptly turning on his heel and quitting the room.

Vaddi could hardly move, but he knew he had crossed over another bridge in his curious relationship with the peddler.

Zemella had also been moved by Nyam's words, knowing that it could not have been easy for him to express them so openly. "You heard him." She grinned. "So we sail. *Together.*"

* * * * * * *

Zemella found it difficult to contain her frustration at the lengthy haggling over the arrangements for the *Sea Harlot's* sailing. It was almost midday before the craft slipped out of the harbor of Shae Thoridor bound for Xen'drik. Vaddi and Zemella had to leave the captain's cabin while Nyam, Fallarond, and Vortermars thrashed out an agreement. The main bone of contention now was the crew. As far as the pirates were concerned, they wanted the security of having a large contingent on board, but if the Deathguard were to sail in force, there would be precious few places for Vortermars's freebooters. It was the promise of loot that won the day, and Vortermars at last settled for a skeleton crew, barely enough to be able to sail away from Xen'drik after the landing and to return to take the Deathguard off once the quest was done.

"The waters off Xen'drik are choked with dangers," Vortermars insisted. "You're putting my ship and all my men at risk."

"Then you'll have to hug the shoreline," said Nyam, "until we're ready to leave. There are enough coves to shelter in."

"You ever *been* to Xen'drik?"

Nyam shook his head. "I confess I have not."

"Well, it may not be as foul a place as the Mournland, but it's as bad as the Madwood, eh? Barbarians pick over its bones. Strange energies seep up from every rock and stone. Even stranger things roam its lands. I've visited its shores and a few of its small ports. Wouldn't repeat half the tales I've heard of the interior. I don't hold out much hope of seeing you return."

"But you'll wait."

"Aye. A month, as agreed. Not an hour more, eh?"

"My agents in Pylas Maradal will lead you to your reward," said Nyam, "even if you have to leave without us."

Thus it was agreed and the *Sea Harlot* sailed. Her decks were filled with Fallarond's disguised Deathguard, fifty of his finest warriors, many of whom were also excellent sailors, used to the trim lines of the Aereni warships. At the bow of the craft they set a seer named Gonardal, whose understanding of the sea and control over its mysteries were revered. Using his powers, he shrouded the craft in mists that kept it from the prying eyes, both undersea and aerial, for they were heading into waters where sinister forces were known to gather. The *Sea Harlot* cleared the waters of Aerenal and picked up speed, as though borne away by a supernatural current.

"This is a dangerous game," Zemella said as she watched Vortermars go below. She still found it hard to suppress her anger each time she set eyes on the pirate.

"He will be the first to die if there is treachery," Vaddi said.

She saw the earnestness in his look and softened for a moment. Before she could say any more she heard Nyam approach. "What, exactly, have you paid the pirate?"

He wore a pained expression. "A small fortune," he said. "Stashed away in Pylas Maradal over the years. No matter! What would I do with it?"

"What do you know about the cleric's master?"

"I suspect we are dealing with someone who is attempting to bind Xen'drik's dubious powers. If it's an army he is forging, it would be volatile, needing enormous control, hence his desire for the horn."

"When we reach the coast," said Vaddi, "what will be our next move?"

"Wherever this sorcerer is," said Nyam, "will be known to the people in Xen'drik. There are barbarians who roam there, renegade elves, other strange races. Word of this power will surely have reached them. We will find his seat of power."

"We're basing our mission on the hopes of possible rumour?" Zemella scowled.

"You have a better idea?"

Zemella said nothing.

"Will he use the talisman?" said Vaddi. "Even without me?"

"He may try."

"If he does," said Zemella, "it will be disastrous. He'll unleash something over which he has no control."

Fallarond came to them, his eyes fixed on the heaving swells of the ocean. "One of the lookouts reports something out there."

They saw Vortermars standing at the starboard rail, face clouded with uneasiness, and went to him.

"Strange currents on all sides," he said. "Weird way these waves rise and fall, eh? Don't like it."

"The Thunder Sea is aptly named," said Fallarond. "There'll be many such storms on this crossing."

"What's coming isn't from the skies," Vortermars growled. "It's from *below* the waves. If it's what I think, you're going to need all your elf powers to fight it."

Fallarond went swiftly to the prow, where Gonardal was studying the mists and the surging waters. The waves parted around the sharp prow in twin lines of boiling foam as the *Sea Harlot* raced westward.

"We have company," said the seer, "and they grow restless at our intrusion in their waters."

"Sea creatures?"

"Sahuagin. Many of them."

Vaddi turned to Zemella, having heard the exchange at the prow. "What are sahuagin?"

"Sea devils—humanoid, but with fins and claws. Usually they remain in coastal waters, but they have no love of elves. If they have our scent, they may well attack."

"Do you think Cellester's master has sent them?"

"Doubtful. They are a threat to all shipping on the seas to Xen'drik."

Nyam stood beside them, looking even more uncomfortable than usual. "I think what is relevant is the sheer weight of numbers. We seem to be surrounded."

The entire crew, Aereni and freebooters alike, were at the rails now, arrows nocked to bows and swords drawn in preparation to repel a powerful assault. Out in the mists on all sides, just as Nyam had foreseen, dark shapes lifted from the tossing seas and light gleamed on the scales of reptilian heads.

The sahuagin were indeed gathered in numbers, their mouths opening and closing slowly, revealing their razor teeth. Scores of large packs seemed to be circling the ship, rising and falling, supremely confident in their superiority.

The sahuagin wasted little time in studying the ship. As one, their host closed in, the sea thick with them. The crew, Aereni and pirates alike, loosed arrows into them, but for every arrow that took out one of the sea creatures, two others seemed to replace it. Dozens evaded the rain of arrows and swarmed up the sides of the *Sea Harlot*, wielding long, spiked weapons in their vicious claws. In no time at all, the defenders found themselves caught up in a ferocious battle for their lives.

Vaddi and Nyam fought side by side, their swords a blur as they cut at these demon-like spawn of the sea. The sahuagin, taller than Vaddi and the Aereni, had green and black striped skins, scaled and armored like lizards, with a sharp-ridged spine and a wide mouth filled with needle-like teeth. They ripped and tore with their talons, using their terrible clawed feet to devastating effect. Beside Vaddi, Zemella wove a spell and cast it like a vivid net of light around them. The huge eyes of the sahuagin screwed up tightly against the light, blinded by it. Vaddi and Nyam were quick to take advantage of this, cutting ruthlessly into their dazzled foes, who swung about wildly but ineffectively.

Gonardal also flung bolts of white light about the crew, protecting them, the beams cutting into the sahuagin masses like molten flame. Such deadly destruction did not halt the invaders, however, and they continued to swarm upon the ship. In the seas below, their numbers were vast, as though they had sent an entire army to attack the ship.

Vaddi's eyes were streaming as the spell held, but he watched as Vortermars and Fallarond fought shoulder to shoulder, common allies in the heat of this encounter. Vaddi gasped as the pirate's cutlass slashed and hacked with extraordinary dexterity, here severing a sahuagin head, there an arm or leg, the pirate shouting out his cries of defiance as he fought. Vaddi could see that Fallarond was equally as formidable in his use of his glowing blade, though he fought in silence, his skull-face hiding his emotions.

The sahuagin themselves shrieked maniacally as they fought, and where they pulled down an Aereni or a pirate, snared in their nets, they ripped their victims to bloody shreds, mocking their remaining foes with their victories. Their hatred of the elves was a living thing, and their will to overrun the ship was absolute.

Vaddi was glad of the power of his elven blade, for its light gave him an edge. He felt the fury in him growing as he fought, and he took renewed strength from it, carving a bloody path to the ship's rail, dispatching sahuagin to either side in a frenzy of slaughter. Zemella was never far from his side, using both the light and her own blade to murderous effect.

"Keep together!" she shouted to Vaddi. "If they surround you, I'll not be able to protect your back!"

Vaddi did as bidden, for only the quick action of the Aereni bowmen spared him a wounding as three sahuagin loomed on him. He lost track of time in that crimson mayhem, whirling and spinning, carving a path along the rail in a frenzy until he felt Nyam's touch.

"Hold, Vaddi! You've killed them!" said the peddler, indicating the three closest of the dead sahuagin at Vaddi's feet. "No need to carve them into strips!"

Vaddi shook the rivulets of sweat from his eyes and paused, chest heaving. He saw then that the sea devils had drawn off—at least for the moment. Like a wave they had come and so had they poured back into the sea. However, the waters were still thick with them, their huge eyes still fixed on the *Sea Harlot*, but as they waited, Gonardal sent his spells at them, blasting them where they swam. Many sank underwater for cover.

Zemella came to Vaddi, about to speak, but they both swung round when they heard a hideous shriek near the stern of the craft. Arriving there with Nyam, they saw that Vortermars had snared one of the sahuagin in a noose and had roped the creature tightly by the neck, dragging it onto the deck. It was the sahuagin that had shrieked, cursing its captors in a vile torrent of abuse, using a distorted but recognizable form of the Common tongue.

Vaddi watched as Vortermars approached the sahuagin with great care, for those claws, at both arm and leg, still swung about in dangerous arcs, capable of eviscerating a man in one sweep. Other nooses snaked out from the pirates and soon the sahuagin was trussed up tightly like a fowl about to be cooked. Vortermars placed his cutlass edge against the throat of the creature. Its eyes blazed as if they would burst from the sheer power of its hatred.

"Do I give your head and entrails to the tritons, you filthy scum, eh? Eh? Or should I allow you a quick death and toss your corpse back over the side to your mates?"

The sahuagin spat something in its own bubbling tongue.

"Tell me what I want to know and you'll go back to them with your throat cut, no more than that, eh?"

Vaddi watched as Fallarond stood close by, content to let Vortermars deal with the captive.

"Who sent you?" said Vortermars, never for an instant taking his blade from the sahuagin's neck. "Who paid you to attack us, eh?"

"We are sahuagin!" snarled the creature, squirming as if it could free itself. "These seas are ours!"

"*Who sent you?*" Vortermars repeated, drawing blood with his blade.

"We are our own masters! Our community fights for itself! You're in our seas, elf-loving pirate trash!"

Vortermars stood over his victim for a long moment, gazing at him. Then, to Vaddi's surprise, the pirate leaned hard on his cutlass, killing the sahuagin in one swift move.

Before Vaddi or anyone else could speak, Vortermars turned to them. "No point him lying about it. The sea devils weren't sent by whoever you're hunting. We're in their seas, that's all."

Fallarond nodded. "Their hatred of elves would be enough for them to attack." He turned to the rail. "This may not be over yet."

Vaddi and his companions all returned to the rail, each of them studying the still heaving waters. Vortermars had his dead captive flung out into the waves, where swift claws took it below. Countless scores of the sahuagin still followed the ship, but no second attack was yet forthcoming.

Vortermars leaned far out, cupping his hands around his mouth. "You've felt the blast of our spells!" he shouted. "Count your dead! Ten times more will die every time you try and climb aboard this ship! Go your way and let us pass!"

For answer, a steel lance came driving up from the sea, but Zemella had been watching and she deflected it with a ball of light. The lance dropped harmlessly into the water, melting as it fell. Vaddi sensed that this had the desired effect on the sahuagin, as if they understood that the *Sea Harlot* housed no ordinary foe. They did not press an attack, but as the craft ploughed on westward, the sea creatures were never far from her sides.

"The sea devil wasn't lying, eh?" Vortermars grunted to Nyam and Vaddi. "If they were in this for someone else, they'd have been at us again, thick as fleas. But they'll need watching, eh? Night and day."

❀ ❀ ❀ ❀ ❀ ❀ ❀ ❀

The enormous chamber was thick with shadows, gloomy and sepulchral. Far below the surface of Xen'drik, hidden away in the innermost heart of this fallen city, the dusty vault echoed to the rare sound of footsteps. A lone figure, draped in a cloak that merged it with the darkness, moved uneasily through this region, pausing at a huge door that had long since been bent back on its hinges. Beyond the cracked threshold in another even larger chamber, only the tombs waited. Them and one other. This creature rose up from its bed of dust and shuffled forward to meet the cloaked one. They were like two graveyard phantoms greeting each other across a haunted landscape, the air sterile and dead, the stone around them like the long rotted bones of a titanic corpse.

"Cellester," came the soft voice of the gargoyle-like figure. "You have come back to us at last."

The cleric stared at the homunculus in distaste. "Where is your master?"

"Zuharrin has much work to do. He has little time to spare. He has sent me to greet you."

Cellester grimaced, barely masking his loathing of this creature. "I must see him."

"Have you fulfilled your role? You seem to be alone." The little figure's eyes widened. "I do not see the Orien youth."

"Zuharrin will have him soon enough."

"Words will not be sufficient," said the homunculus.

Cellester pulled from his robe an object wrapped in leather. "I have baited the hook, and the fish has taken the bait."

The homunculus shuffled back, eyeing the leather-bound object with deep suspicion. "What is it you hold? I feel its hot power."

"The Crimson Talisman," said Cellester. "Shall I reveal it to you?"

"No!" cried the homunculus, shaking with fear. "Put it away!"

"Take me to Zuharrin. He will have no reason to doubt my success."

"Where is the youth?"

Cellester slipped the leather back inside his cloak. "Coming. He cannot bear to be apart from the Talisman. He will come to claim it. He has no choice."

CHAPTER 19

As the sun sank into the western clouds, its last rays completely smothered, the *Sea Harlot* eased into the offshore currents close to the coast of Xen'drik. There was a deep uneasiness aboard, as crew and passengers looked across the turgid waters at the shadowed coastline. Above them the clouds piled in, pack-like, eager for the night, fuelled by the vapors and smokes of the massive land mass.

Vortermars pointed to the blackness ahead. "Coast here's carved up by rivers and creeks. Biggest of them goes right into the heart of the continent, but it's a risky way to enter Xen'drik."

He looked out at the dark waters around them. Although the sahuagin had followed them for a long way across the Thunder Sea, they had not attacked again. They were no longer to be seen, but the company felt there was always a danger that they would return.

Beside him, Fallarond and the others studied the coast. "You told us earlier that you have contacts here," said the Deathguard commander.

"Aye. Barbarians. They fear nothing. They've small settlements. I trade with them, but I'll not sail the *Sea Harlot* into their port, eh? They'd swarm over her like rats! I know an islet or two offshore where we can lay up. You can go ashore in our light craft."

Fallarond turned to Vaddi. "You have a strategy?"

Vaddi glanced at Zemella. "Once we're ashore, we have to try and locate the horn. I'm not sure—"

Vortermars laughed. "I have a suggestion."

Zemella scowled at him.

"What is it?" Fallarond asked the pirate.

"Like I said, there's a lot of creeks. I'll take you to one. Hide yourself in its upper reaches, eh? Disguise yourselves good and proper. I'll have some of my crew visit the barbarians in Thargang—a little village a ways into the jungle. Maybe someone will have got word of this sorcerer, eh? Xen'drik's a big place, but they've got long ears in Thargang. Need to have. Survival, eh? Or profits, comes to the same thing, eh? They've contacts with Stormreach in the north. You elves aren't the only ones with spy networks. If there's word, I'll have it sent on."

"If you send anything but help . . ." said Zemella.

Vortermars laughed softly. "Don't worry. I'd be a fool to risk getting my hands on the rest of Nyam Hordath's fortune, wouldn't I? Xen'drik can keep what it has. Anything that comes out of that black hell bears a curse, eh? You'd all do well to remember that. No, I'll wait up at the islet. One month. No more. After that, I sail."

❂ ❂ ❂ ❂ ❂ ❂ ❂

Soon the company was climbing down into three long, narrow craft, filling them with their number. Each craft was manned by two of the freebooters, but they said little, morosely carrying out their instructions from Vortermars. Without further ado, the *Sea Harlot* swung away along the coast, heading for a rash of small islands a few miles from shore. The three longboats, oared by the Deathguard, slid across the water, blending into the darkness.

Once close to shore, they headed slowly along it, until the

pirate at the prow of the leading craft indicated a deeper darkness, a gash in the coastline that was the promised creek. Its banks were choked with thick vegetation, but in this moonless night they were as pitch, gently tossing their branches in a mimic of the sea's undulations. No sooner had the three craft turned up into the creek than those fronds seemed to close in, shutting out even more light. The shores on either side fell silent, the waters equally still.

Vaddi turned to Zemella, wanting to reach for her hand, but she seemed to be steeling herself against the subtle waves of evil that lapped at their craft. She held her sword before her like a torch, though it was cold, its power dormant. No one spoke, not even whispered.

They rowed their way through overhanging boughs, ducking to avoid their clammy touch, and beyond to a narrow tributary of the creek. It brought them to a mud flat, black as tar, and the pirates had them beach the craft. They hauled the boats ashore, sliding all of them save one smaller one under the trees where they would not be seen.

"We go back to Vortermars," said one of the pirates to Fallarond. "Wait here until word comes from Thargang."

"How long?"

"By dawn."

The pirates wasted no more time in getting back into the smaller craft and were soon rowing steadily back down the creek.

Vaddi looked around, though he could see little in the gloom. "This place has a strange feel to it. It's so silent, as if all life has left."

Nyam grunted. "Don't count on it. Not all the giants are dead, and the drow live here."

Fallarond nodded. "That is so, although these jungles are very thinly populated. Xen'drik is vast, but our enterprise depends on absolute stealth. We would do best to avoid the eyes of all who dwell here."

"How?" said Vaddi.

"You won't like it," said Zemella.

"What is it?"

She bent down and scooped up a handful of the black mud. "This. We cover our exposed skin in it. Blend with the scenery."

Nyam groaned, sniffing at the strong stench of the mud. "Is it absolutely necessary?"

"It will make it difficult to see us. You'd be surprised how easily one can see bit of pale skin even from far away."

"She is right," said Fallarond.

Nyam watched in horror as the others began the odious task of smearing the black mud over their hands and faces and even parts of their clothing. His long hair and thick beard masked most of his own features, but reluctantly he smeared on the mud and stood beside them, looking more beast than man, only the white of his eyes showing. Vaddi laughed at his predicament.

"You don't look so good yourself." Nyam snorted. "Nor do you smell too pretty."

After that the company could do little but settle among the trees, blending with the bizarre terrain as they waited out the night. Vaddi and Nyam dozed, getting what little sleep they could before the coming journey. Around them the silence seemed to thicken, almost as if the entire company had fallen deaf. No bird or bat flapped above the treetops. Nothing stirred the murk of the creek.

When dawn found them it was so pale that the light hardly changed. Oppressive gray clouds sat heavily over the coast. In a half sleep, Vaddi became aware that vague sounds were coming from the creek. He gazed through the straggling fronds to see the prow of a small craft, two men hunched over in it. One of them steadied the craft, while the other came ashore, bent over, apparently sniffing at the mud flat like a hound. It was one of Vortermars's pirates and he looked up at the forest, straining for a sign of the Deathguard.

Fallarond showed himself, though for a moment the pirate jumped back in horror, for the elf made a gruesome figure, smeared as he was in mud, as if shaped from nothing else. But the man recovered himself, grinned, and came forward.

"You have word from the town?"

"I do. I spent the night there among the barbarians."

Vaddi, Zemella, and Nyam joined the group.

"You'd fool the worst of them, that's no lie," said the pirate approvingly.

"What have you learned?" said Fallarond.

"No word of the cleric, but there's rumors of a dark power haunting the southern jungle. They know about it in Stormreach, and word's come down the grapevine to Thargang. Said to be powerful. Seems to be centered in a ruined city called Azzahareb. Used to be some place. Built by giants. Men found it and rebuilt some of it."

"Where is this city?"

"This here creek will take you to the foothills of the mountain range where you'll find it. Go south for a day. Then you got to climb the passes up to it. It spans a whole lot of peaks and valleys. Word is, in days gone by its towers looked out across the Thunder Sea toward Argonnessen. Always watching its enemies."

"What of this 'dark power?'"

"Locals whisper the name Zuharrin. The barbarians fear him. They reckon he walks freely in the darkness below. They say he consorts with all manner of horrors, makes pacts with demons, sacrifices his own servants . . ."

Fallarond turned to Nyam and those of his warriors who were nearest. "I have not heard this name."

Nyam was concentrating on something. "Zuharrin? No, it means nothing to me. Not that I recall."

"Like I said, he's said to haunt Azzahareb. With a big following. Xen'drik's a good place for secrets."

"Nothing of the cleric?" said Vaddi.

"The barbarians don't know of him, but servants of the sorcerer are said to use soarwings to go about their business. In the north, they are said to flock. If your cleric is here, he is likely in Azzahareb."

"These barbarians you trade with," said Fallarond, "were they suspicious of you and your questions?"

"Why should they be? They offered the information freely enough. They're happy to trade with Vortermars. In their interests to protect him and his trade."

"Do they know we are here in Xen'drik?"

The pirate shook his head and smiled grimly. "Nah. Vortermars won't betray you, if that's what you're worried about. He told me and the rest of the crew to treat you like gold. No one knows you're here, and covered in that muck, no one will! The barbarians wouldn't expect anyone to be mad enough to seek out Azzahareb. They keep well clear of it."

"What of Zuharrin's forces?"

"Who knows? Whoever haunts Azzahareb keeps well to himself, but no one who's come near the place has come back. Some treasure hunters outta Stormreach went in lookin' for some locals and whatever they could bring out. No one's seen them in months."

"Very well," said Fallarond. "Go back to your captain. We will be with you again in one month. Here, in this same place."

The pirate nodded, turned, and rejoined his companion. Moments later they were rowing swiftly out into the creek and through the fronds seawards.

"This Zuharrin will assume no one would dare steal upon him," said Fallarond. "He must feel doubly secure in his stronghold."

"Let's not waste any time," said Zemella. "I've had more than enough of skulking. Time to take the fight to them."

❀ ❀ ❀ ❀ ❀ ❀ ❀

Fallarond sent out runners to study the terrain as the company moved on. The land rose gradually, the jungle unbroken, the light no less dismal. After several days' travel through the jungle, they reached a place where the creek was nothing more than a spring, dribbling almost soundlessly from a narrow crack in a low wall of stone, the edge of the foothills. The jungle thinned out, but the company kept to its edge under cover.

Higher up the slope above the company, two figures were watching. They were armed men, their heads encased in leather helmets, their keen eyes looking out for the slightest movement below. One of them muttered something under his breath. Down in the narrow valley, at the first of the stunted trees, he had seen something move. Then another.

"Something approaches!" he hissed to his companion, pointing with his short sword. There was no response from the other, who had flattened himself up against the bole of a tree, though his eyes seemed to be fixed on that same spot below.

"D'you see, Karg? How many?"

"Too many to count. What are they? We must report this." He turned, gripping the arm of his companion, but it was stiff and unresisting. "Hurry! We must—"

The other's eyes were wide, but they wore a shocked, frozen look of horror. He was dead, pinned through the neck by an arrow to the tree.

With a curse, the warrior sprang back and turned, intending to flee, but as he did so, the ground rose up before him, leaves and earth tossed aside by the frightful apparition. Before he could respond, a sword plunged deep into his vitals. A single gasp escaped his lips as he sank to his knees. The last thing his eyes saw before they closed in death was the skull face of the Deathguard scout. The latter pulled his blade free of the corpse and spent a few minutes searching the surrounding trees.

Behind him another of the scouts waited. "Any more of them?"

"No." They left together, circling the edge of the jungle, listening for further signs of enemies.

Down in the valley, emerging from the trees, Fallarond and the company moved up and along the declivity of a narrow incline that led into the foothills. The commander had drawn his blade and his warriors had all nocked arrows to their bows as if they knew an attack was imminent. Vaddi, Zemella, and Nyam were kept at the heart of the company, though Zemella complained softly, eager to use her blade on anything that dared show itself.

"And you warned *me* against unleashing my battle lust," Vaddi teased her.

She glared at him. "Better a fight than this accursed waiting."

"Be silent," said Fallarond.

As he turned back to the trail ahead, the two ridges on either side of them seemed to erupt. Dozens of warriors leaped forward, wielding swords, axes, and spears, a mixed band of men wearing armor that seemed purloined from a dozen battlefields. Their intent was obvious as they bore down upon the Deathguard.

Fallarond's men were too well trained to panic. They formed ranks in a rough diamond shape and seconds later unleashed a hail of arrows. Vaddi was once again staggered by the speed at which they drew and loosed, drew and loosed, again and again. Each Aereni archer sent half a dozen arrows into the oncoming horde, and with terrifying precision, each arrow found its mark.

The oncoming warriors fell, those who were not pinned by an arrow tumbling into their stricken comrades. What had begun as a tide on two sides turned into instant chaos. There was worse to follow for the attackers. Behind them, on the two ridges that they had quitted, the Aereni scouts appeared, some dozen of them. With no less speed or accuracy than their fellows in the valley, they began picking off any of the assault force that still stood.

Vaddi drew in his breath, sword swinging idly. "Dragon's teeth! Not one of them left alive. There must be close on a hundred dead. In . . . how long?"

Zemella grunted, evidently unmoved. "They were poorly organized."

Nyam grinned through the muck of his disguise. "I'm sure you'll get a chance to use your sword before too long."

Fallarond's eyes flashed within mud-black face. "None must get away from here and report back to Azzahareb."

One of the scouts came down from the hill while his companions ensured that there were no survivors. "There were a few sentries up in the hills," he reported to Fallarond.

"You have dealt with them?"

The scout bowed.

"Well done," said Fallarond. "Retrieve what arrows you can, then rotate the scouts."

His orders were carried out at once.

"We must hug the landscape as best we can. There will be few trees to hide us from now on."

The others fell into place as the company resumed its quick march up into the foothills. Vaddi looked back at the valley below. The sprawled corpses attested to the fact that there had indeed been a battle—or rather a slaughter—yet even as he looked, the corpses seemed to melt before his eyes, becoming part of the terrain, indistinguishable from it. He turned to remark on this to Zemella, but she was murmuring under her breath.

Nyam winked at him. *A spell*, he mouthed. *To cover our tracks*.

Vaddi nodded, wondering what else was to emerge on this nightmare journey.

In the more open terrain, they made quicker progress. Through the cloud and vapors that clung to the terrain, they could now see the lower slopes of a mountain range. Its crags and scarps were uniquely shaped, as were the lands spread out below it. Strange structures poked up from the rocks and soil, remnants of the bygone ages. Steel and tangled metal leaned skyward like the bones of huge mechanical beasts, their purpose long forgotten. Black-winged birds flapped around them, squabbling with each other, but none came close to the company. Pools of oil and scummy water dotted the land for mile after mile, and wisps of greenish mist webbed everything.

Overhead, through an occasional break in the clouds, shapes swooped and dipped, some huge and saurian, others smaller, none clearly visible. But the magic that cloaked the company seemed to do its work well.

Ahead of and around them, the scouts remained watchful. They were moving south now, parallel to the mountains, as the pirate guide had told them. Throughout the day, mile upon monotonous mile, they kept up the pace, until the weak sun began its dip to the western skyline. Beyond the company, the low gorge became recognizable as a road, smashed and ruinous, apparently a one-time route to the fallen piles of an ancient settlement.

"Is this Azzahareb?" said Zemella.

"An outpost, I think," said Nyam. "The pirate told us we have to climb up through the passes to the city itself."

Fallarond joined them. "The scouts report that the way is clear. We can rest at the edge of these ruins. There is a pass near at hand, steep and treacherous, but it will take us to the city. Once we have eaten, night will be upon us."

"A good time to go up," said Vaddi.

"I agree," said Fallarond.

Moving on, they soon found themselves surrounded by what seemed to have been a city built by giants. It had been totally wrecked by some ancient and dreadful conflict that must have pre-dated the Last War by centuries. It was as though giant engines had mashed their way through it, heaping up whole rows of buildings, burning and melting the structures, fusing their steel into fantastic shapes, their mutated spars poking up at the night sky. Among that colossal debris, pallid light flickered, sizzling with magical currents, though purposeless, lashing out mindlessly at anything that moved. It would be far too dangerous to enter such streets. The city was not alive, but there were warped powers within it, energized like the mind of a madman.

Vaddi made to speak to Zemella, but something in her expression checked him. It was not difficult to read the stress there, the sure knowledge that they were going forward on a hopeless quest. Despondency would be as dangerous an enemy as the denizens of this bleak terrain.

∞ ∞ ∞ ◉ ∞ ∞ ∞

Deep down in the heart of the crumbling city of Azzahareb, in a citadel erected by giants eons before men spread like ants across Khorvaire, the acolytes of Zuharrin gathered in one of many restored throne rooms. Once it had been magnificent, its lofty columns bright with sculptures of the highest order, its tall glass windows brilliant with color. Now lush carpets again stretched across its immense floors, matched in glory only by the vivid inlays of the polished tiles. Tapestries and finely woven curtains hung from the beams in celebration of the majesty of those who ruled here. The immense domed room was no longer the pride of an empire, although there were signs of its former glory. The fallen debris of years had been removed, the columns polished, and the furnishings redecorated. Huge candles, thick as the columns, burned atop golden braziers, while marble statues and wooden carvings from across all of Xen'drik had been assembled.

The focal point of this new expression of power was a gigantic throne, carved from a single immense tree trunk, set with demons and demigods from ages long gone. Wooden serpents and winged beings gazed out from jewelled eyes at the grand room almost as though alive. Indeed, the spells that clung to the wood and the smoldering censers around it writhed in the air, humming with powerful magic. Most potent of all was the figure that sat in the throne, dwarfed by it yet resplendent in dark robes, his face serene but deeply majestic, ageless but vital.

Zuharrin surveyed the gathering before him. His servants lined the rim of the hall, pike shafts and shields flashing in the light from the braziers. They represented an army that had been a long time in the building, an army that waited in the city, sworn to serve Zuharrin and to die at his command, controlled by magics he had unearthed from this ancient city and set upon them all like chains. Beyond the dais where he sat, a score of dignitaries had come before the sorcerer, each of them in a warrior's uniform, a token of their own great power.

He stood, a smile passing over his thin lips, his green eyes sweeping them with a glance like steel. "The time draws near," he said, his voice cracking like a whip in the motionless air. "You are almost all gathered. From all realms of Eberron you have come, and again I do homage to your alliance."

Zuharrin bowed to his guests. He was the focus of power here in ancient Xen'drik, the one who had delved deepest into its dubious energies, the one who would bind them into a weapon surpassing anything seen for millennia, but it served his purpose to let his underlings think themselves near his equal. For now.

"It will soon be time to release T'saagash Mal. Our crusade will begin."

One of the armed warlords stepped forward with a curt bow. "My Lord Zuharrin, you spoke to us once before of a powerful weapon, a talisman that would aid us in this great crusade."

"Erethindel, the horn of dragon blood. Yes."

"You have this artefact?"

Zuharrin smiled and turned to his right. A block of obsidian marble stood at the foot of the throne dais. Across it had been draped a rich velvet hanging. The sorcerer went to this and lifted back the folds of the velvet to reveal the object beneath. Green light crackled with a sound like the burning of logs. Strange, alien sigils had been cut into the surface of the marble, protective charms against the latent power in the object they surrounded. There, motionless yet redolent with its own power, the Crimson Talisman rested.

"It is said that the elves carved this, but that is only part of its history," Zuharrin told the lords as they eased forward to get a better view of the revered object. "Dragons had a part in its birth."

"Yet," came a voice from beyond the warriors, "it is of no use to any of us, yourself included, Zuharrin, without its wielder."

Zuharrin scowled for a moment, the air around him curdling like a thundercloud, but as he saw the tall figure of the latecomer, his frown turned to a knowing smile. "Welcome," he said. He drew the velvet drape back over the horn.

"My apologies for my lateness. It has been a prolonged and arduous journey."

"We are glad to have you with us," said Zuharrin, and the other lords bowed politely.

"You have secured the Orien youth?" said the latecomer.

Every eye was fixed on the sorcerer. Zuharrin smiled again, and in that smile was more than a hint of dreadful resolve. "He is drawn to the Crimson Talisman as a moth is drawn to fire." He nodded at one of the tapering flames of a huge candle beyond them, where a cloud of moths fluttered perilously close to its light. "Soon he will be here."

"He will serve us?" said one of the lords.

"He will resist, but not for long. He has no concept of true power. Xen'drik has given me its deepest secrets. I will bend the Orien youth to my will until the only release he has will be to direct the powers within him and Erethindel into T'saagash Mal. Once the youth is snared, he can never break the chains. He will be no more than a vessel, doomed to remain so."

"Where is he now?" said another of the lords.

"He sailed with an escort of Aereni Deathguard bound for these shores, but his ship was attacked by the sahuagin. There was a fierce conflict, which alerted my servants. The unwitting boy sails directly into our hands."

There was a brief murmur, then a lord spoke. "To what end? Surely if he sought to oppose us, he would require an army."

"The youth and those who aid him are naïve," said Zuharrin. "They have no concept of our powers. Indeed, they know nothing of us. I have been served by a cleric, who until recently travelled with the Orien youth. Vaddi d'Orien comes to Xen'drik seeking him, thinking it is the cleric who holds the talisman. A strong company of the Deathguard is, Vaddi d'Orien assumes, all he needs to pry the talisman back from the cleric."

The warrior lord who had been the last to join them stepped forward, drawing his sword and putting its point to the marbled floor. He leaned on its crosspiece. "The boy's family has been a blight on my success for a long time. He is the last of them. If this youth needs bringing to heel, it will give me much pleasure to ride out and drag him here."

Zuharrin shook his head. "Let him find his own way. Azzahareb will be open to him. It will be a simple task to snare him, and once we have done so, we can begin the last chapter of the working. T'saagash Mal will rise, and all your armies will benefit from his powers. Across every continent, to the far reaches of Khorvaire itself, even beyond your own Karrnath." He looked to the tall warrior.

The latter grunted and put away his sword.

"You will have an altogether new understanding of power. Believe me, Kazzerand."

CHAPTER 20

The company moved up the steep-sided gully and into the foothills above the broken city of giants. Below them, spread out in a wide black stain, the outpost of the city pulsed faintly with its warped powers like a wounded beast. They could see far down into its fathomless, canyon-like streets, some choked with debris, weird lights glowing within them as if strange denizens loitered there, ever waiting to draw into their webs whatever morsel of life should chance upon them. This once proud metropolis, mountainous and immense, had been home to thousands, but now it had been reduced to a nightmare realm, refuge of supernatural powers.

They turned back up the gully and went farther into its shadowed confines. No moons lit the way and no light penetrated the deepening gash into the mountainside. If there had been a stream here, it had dried up or been diverted down into the black heart of stone below. A damning silence pervaded all once more and only a few of the elves' swords lit the way. On either side the stone walls were pocked with caves like windows so that it seemed to the company that it was passing through not a natural canyon but another deep street in a city beyond known time, yet nothing stirred in its walls. It was like passing through a mammoth graveyard of forgotten gods, where tomb after tomb crumbled reluctantly.

Zemella leaned close to Vaddi, clutching his arm. "You know what it will mean if we are trapped?"

He nodded, bemused by the scale of the walls.

"We must die before we let Zuharrin triumph. On its own, Erethindel will not be enough for him. He needs you alive. If there is any danger of his succeeding, you must perish and us with you."

"I told you," he said, attempting a grin, "that I would not let you die."

"You may have to. You may have to strike the killing blow. And I you."

His eyes widened in horror at the suggestion. "Don't speak of such things," he said. "We—"

"We have to agree now. A pact, Vaddi. You and I will strike each other down, if we fail. We *must*. If we fall into Zuharrin's hands, a new age of terror will begin. We cannot let it happen."

She is right, he told himself, but I could never do it.

As though reading his mind, she touched his face lightly with her fingers. "We must do this, Vaddi. We have a duty that goes far beyond our own longings. The dragon blood within us calls us to this."

He felt his heart racing. Briefly his lips brushed her fingers. She smiled and he nodded. "So be it."

● ● ● ◉ ● ● ●

"They are coming."

Zuharrin sat back, eyeing the man before him with little trace of emotion on his chiselled features.

Cellester, hollow-eyed and exhausted, stood before his master, though he knew that it was no more than a projected image that he looked upon. "It is as I promised. The Orien boy is bound to the talisman."

"I will allow them to believe that they have come upon me un-awares, and I will open the citadel to them. Already my servants have begun the Great Working. The Horn of Erethindel has been prepared in the Chamber of the Demon Gate. For all your failings, Cellester, you have done well."

The cleric kept his head bowed, eyes on the stone floor.

"When this is over, I will no longer hold you to my will. You will be free of me, if you choose, but think carefully. Would you rather risk your fate in a world that will change when the new powers arise or be a willing part of the changes? You have served me until now because I have forced you to do so. I would rather have you as a willing servant. You could achieve greatness in what is coming. Think on it. For now, just do as I have bidden at the Working. Betray the Orien youth a final time. Cripple him as you did for so long in Khorvaire."

Cellester looked up a few moments later but the sorcerer's image was gone. He knew it was pointless to disobey him. Zuharrin had long gained a terrible hold over him. He sagged down, exhausted, seeing again in his mind that night when he had first been subjected to Zuharrin's power.

Deep in the northern fortress of Marazanath, in an area where the troops gathered to drink and unwind after the day's labors, Cellester had revelled with them, easing the strains of another hard session of exercises and mock battles. Anzar d'Orien's soldiers were kept permanently readied for battle. Indreen, wife of the lord, had died no more than a week since, and Cellester had felt her death like a knife blow to his own vitals. He had sought to submerge his misery in a frenzy of exercise and revelry with the toughest of the soldiers. They welcomed his company, for there was no fitter, more accomplished warrior than he. They trained hard that day and drank harder that night. It was long gone midnight when the cleric lurched into the narrow street, head spinning, mind almost unhinged. Somewhere along the way, he collapsed, unable to drag himself home, but he was found and taken indoors.

Those who took him were, he was later to discover, servants of Zuharrin. They brought him round and filled the room with strange incense, drugs that softened his mind even further, until he became like a child, pliable and pathetic. They used his misery against him, bringing its full force to bear.

"She is dead," they whispered, like ghouls at a graveside. "Indreen is dead."

He repeated the words over and over, tears streaking his face.

"Lost to you forever."

He repeated this, too, his body wracked with sobs.

"What if this is not so? Death can be no more than the leaving of one room and the entering of another. Death is a transient thing. The Deathless know this. The Undying Elves know this. The Emerald Claw knows this. You, too, know this."

Cellester looked up, mind whirling, confused but trying to make sense out of what they were saying to him.

"She could be yours," said a seductive voice in the miasma of the room. "Death has freed her from her marriage vows. Raised again, she would be free. Indreen could be yours."

"For a price," said another. "Will you pay it?"

It was done in moments. He hardly knew what they were about. They drew his blood in a pact that swore him to the service of Zuharrin. They took it and through their vile workings bent him to their master's will in exchange for that grim prize. They would, they vowed, raise the fallen Indreen.

In the morning, waking in the street, Cellester realized what he had done, but it could not be undone. His arm bore the long scar where they had opened him. In his rooms, he washed it carefully, but it throbbed. In time to that painful flow, he heard a voice from the night. *We will raise her for you, cleric, but if you fail to obey, we will raise her and give her to the Claw. She will become a handmaiden to our queen.*

The threat of those words had hung over him for the years that followed. Now, in this dismal chamber in Azzahareb, he heard them again, and he knew, beyond doubting, that Zuharrin had the power to do the dreadful thing he promised. There was nothing else but to obey.

"Either the sorcerer feels very secure in his retreat," said Fallarond, eyeing the crags that loomed high on either side of them, "or it is a trap, but the scouts discern no movement."

"How far to the city?" said Nyam. "Have they seen its walls?"

"Aye. It hangs from the cliff like a gigantic bee's nest, but it is silent, shut in. There are no doors, and the nearest windows are far up. No doubt it is hung with spells."

"I have seen creatures of the air," said Nyam. "Soarwings and the like."

Fallarond nodded.

"Have they seen us?" asked Vaddi.

"Our own cloaking spells deceive their eyes."

They moved on, dawn yet hours away, climbing the last slopes of the gorge to the very roots of the mountainside from which the city of Azzahareb had been carved. When they came to it, they stood in momentary stupefaction at its scale, for it was truly gargantuan. Gazing up at its shadowed form, the company could see that it was the work of long-dead artisans, giants or demons or some beings long-gone from a time stretching back millennia. If there was a door at the base of those towering cliffs, it fitted so perfectly with the stone that its lines were hidden from the eye. But there was deep sorcery here. Like the humming of the city far below, with its pulsing supernatural energies, this place reeked of power, dark and deadly.

"How do we get in?" whispered Vaddi. "We could traverse this range for a score of miles."

Fallarond pointed upward. "The windows. Untold centuries ago, the giants of this city must have used them to look out toward the coast. Surely that was the purpose of Azzahareb."

"You mean to go up there?" said Nyam. "I suspect we will need to elicit the aid of the soarwings."

Fallarond shook his head. Instead he turned to a group of his bowmen. They stepped well away from the base of the cliff and, as one, released arrows that had web-thin cord tied to them. High up into the shadows those arrows rose, with enough force to bury their steel points into the rock. Like ghosts the bowmen moved up the wall. They reached a precarious ledge and gained enough purchase on it to be able to fire a second wave of arrows upward. When they had finished their work, a ladder woven from the thinnest of cord dangled from the near-invisible heights above.

Nyam grimaced at it. "Even a spider would blanch at the thought of climbing up this."

Vaddi grinned. "Would you rather we beat upon the door and woke all Zuharrin's guardians?"

"No, no, I'll climb. But you'd better be close behind me. If I should slip, it'll be up to you to hang on to me."

"You won't slip."

Fallarond led the way, with several of his warriors, then Nyam, Vaddi, and Zemella. The remaining Deathguard were behind them, the last of them pulling in the makeshift ladder as he climbed. High up over the hidden terrain they climbed, the night breeze buffeting them, its coldness suggestive of dark magic. They focused on the climb, shutting out the hostile air and the occasional sounds from the skies where unseen shapes flitted and swooped.

Dwarfed by the scale of the fortress, ant-like, they reached a high window in the vast wall. It would have been a tall but narrow slit in the rock to a giant, with a cramped balcony, but to the company it loomed over them like a high cave. The night air swirled about them as they clambered over the crumbling balustrade, the sound of the wind dolorous and mournful overhead, but they ignored it and slipped into the mass of the edifice. Their blades' soft glow lit the interior, casting blurred shadows among the vaults of a long, winding passageway that seemed more weathered than constructed. Their footfalls echoed softly in its huge dimensions.

There were signs of habitation, for on the high walls, in-scriptions had been carved, though in a language unknown to even the Aereni. The floor was as smooth as polished glass, with no hint of dust, as if kept pristine. Deeper within, there was no hint of sound, light, or movement, but the company eased along the sweeping corridor, which fed them downward in a gradual spiral toward the guts of the mountain citadel, countless hundreds of feet below them. Carved faces the size of houses leered at them from the stone walls—the glaring visages of giants, demons, and other grotesque beings, mocking and intimidating in their silence, as though a single word would spring them into life.

● ● ● ◉ ● ● ●

At the very core of Azzahareb, in the heart of the mountain range from which it had been carved, was an immense chamber, hollowed out of the bedrock by the giants in ages past. Its curved walls were riddled with veins of minerals that gleamed with inner fires, standing out like vibrant arteries, as if this chamber were a living entity, throbbing with its own supernatural life, the heart of a titanic demigod. Curved walls soared upward, lost in stone buttresses and vaults where the light could not reach. Statues hundreds of feet high lined the walls in a semi-circle, and on one side of them a circle of stone, itself even higher than the statues, dominated the entire scene. Blocks the size of small buildings framed this perfect circle, a masterpiece of masonry, their surfaces riddled with embossed sigils and carvings, a flowing tapestry of divinities and spirits from the history of this most ancient of places.

The circle contained within the frame of stone blockwork was a solid wall, its surface perfectly flat and unblemished, as if cut by a god. It had been in shadow for timeless centuries, but the huge braziers now lit in the chamber threw it into strong relief. Those who gazed upon the wall saw hints and intimations of movement within it that deceived the eye and threatened to jar the brain. A dreadful power was locked up there, stirring, edging to the light.

Opposite the huge circle, between two of the tallest statues, a balcony overlooked the chamber, its former balustrade swept away, revealing its floor to the host. Upon this, a dozen armor-clad warriors stood on either side of a great doorway, huge broadswords clutched in their mailed fists. Some distance below, spread in an arc along the curved wall under the balcony, was a long dais, its steps running down into the chamber. On this dais were assembled the warlords that Zuharrin had summoned from across the world. They gazed at the bizarre splendor about them, drinking in the mysteries of the ages, aware of the potential power locked within this place.

Above them, appearing on the balcony like a wraith, the figure of Zuharrin appeared. Although dwarfed by his surroundings, unquestionable power flowed from him, and when he spoke, his voice carried effortlessly down to the warlords and to the massed ranks of his own warriors, now visible at the feet of the array of statues across the chamber.

"Behold, the Chamber of the Demon Gate!" he called, directing a golden staff at the huge circle of stone on the towering wall opposite. "Created millennia ago by the powers who chained the demon forces, locking them deep down in the uttermost regions of the world. Soon the greatest of them, T'saagash Mal, awakens!"

The warlords watched him, stirred by his words. Even Kazzerand, most powerful of them, was impressed by the magnitude of this chamber, its suggestion of power. He heard a slight sound behind him and twisted round. At the center of the chamber, rising from its paved floor, a small column of stone was rising up from below to stand at waist height. Vivid green light cloaked the top of it, a force that crackled and flickered with the ancient powers of this forbidding place. As the green haze cleared a little, the watchers could see a single object resting on the surface of the column. It was the Crimson Talisman, Erethindel.

"Here is the key!" called Zuharrin, his voice sharp and clear. "It will unlock the Demon Gate. The dragon blood from the talisman will open the way for T'saagash Mal and the new dawn."

The Orien boy, mused Kazzerand. Where is he? Has he been taken? All this comes to nothing without him.

❋ ❋ ❋ ❋ ❋ ❋ ❋

Vaddi was worming his way with his companions down into the bowels of the citadel. Fallarond urged them forward with great caution.

"This silence disturbs me," Nyam whispered.

"There are many beings below us," said Fallarond, his senses attuned to the elements of this place. "I feel them, gathered in great numbers. There seems no other life elsewhere in the city. Attention is focused below. If there is an opportune moment to breach the heart of the city, it has come."

"There are many, you say?" said Vaddi.

"Many hundreds."

"And the talisman?" said Zemella.

Vaddi answered softly. "It is there. I can feel it from here."

"How easily can you locate it?" said Fallarond.

"Easily enough."

"They *want* you to be joined with it," warned Zemella. "It is the whole purpose of this. This Zuharrin must believe he can match your power, even when you take up the horn."

"Can he?" Vaddi asked her.

"There is a terrible energy in this place," she said. "Something stirs here that has been asleep for untold centuries. Zuharrin will use it, but we have something he has underestimated."

"Which is?" said Nyam.

Zemella grinned. "*Me*, peddler. Vaddi and me and Erethindel."

"As we draw closer, shield your minds," warned Fallarond.

"Win our way to Erethindel," said Vaddi. "Whatever powers it has will be unleashed to bring this place down. Whatever the cost."

He looked into Zemella's eyes as he said it, recalling her words of earlier. She nodded.

"Whatever the cost," agreed Fallarond. Beside him Nyam scowled, but he, too, nodded.

They moved onward and downward and still there was no guard, no hidden spell to challenge them. The darkness closed in, the walls of the mountains enfolding them as if they had wandered into the shadows of another world, a domain of perpetual night. It was difficult to suppress the feeling that the rock around them was *alive*, tuned in to their movements, listening to them. Time seemed to stretch out endlessly. Ahead the passage widened even further, becoming a stairway, curving ever downward in a spiral to the core of the city.

Vaddi motioned the company to a halt. "Erethindel," he whispered, and the word hovered in the air like a spell. "Below us."

"There is a huge chamber, carved from the rock," said Fallarond.

"The horn is there," said Vaddi, hand tightly gripping the haft of his elf blade. He felt Zemella's fingers take his left hand. He held them tightly, praying that she could not feel his fear, his dread of this place.

"Stay together," said Fallarond. "As a unit."

The Deathguard lifted their bows, arrows nocked. Slowly, inch by inch, the company lowered themselves down the wide stairs, each one as tall as a wall, yet cloaked in shadow. Below them they saw an open doorway, some thirty feet tall with thick columns on either side, wreathed in demonic art, gargoyle faces that leered, their eyes gleaming in the torchlight from the massive chamber beyond. At these columns the company halted, studying the bizarre scene below them.

In the chamber, lit by scores of tall braziers, the statues of a distant age reared up into the hidden distance of the dome. It was so vast as to seem like the open night sky, shrouded in cloud and darkness. Opposite the company, a huge circular wall, framed by stone blocks, rose up between two of the statues, whose stone arms and claws seemed to cling to it. Though cut from naked bedrock, they were disturbingly life-like, as if no more than a whispered spell would shake them into frightful life. The stone face of the circular wall shimmered in the ethereal glow, more like the surface of a deep pool than rock.

Vaddi drew back a step, sensing the animate nature of that wall. It was no more than a curtain, draped over some primeval pit, but his attention was snared by what stood in the centre of the chamber a hundred paces away. It was a single column, no higher than his waist, bathed in the protective green glow of sorcery. On the flat top of the column was the Crimson Talisman.

Is it to be this easy? Do we just cross the chamber and snatch it? He looked at his companions and could sense that they were asking themselves the same questions. *This must be a trap, yet—*

Fallarond nodded toward the horn. Time froze for a moment and then Vaddi nodded. Still gripping Zemella's hand, he led the rush into the chamber. The company remained banded together, those on its wings aiming their bows at shadows in preparation. They had crossed a third of the distance to the column when the shadows surrounding them came to life.

From all around the chamber, out of the cover of the huge statues, warriors erupted, hundreds of them. Whether they were men or demons, no one could say, for their armor completely shielded them and their helmets covered their heads, only their eyes visible. They carried broadswords and pikes, maces and axes, and they bore down upon the company in a circle that they meant to close like a fist.

Fallarond's Deathguard had been trained to fight such opponents and had been ready since the moment they entered Azzahareb. They loosed the first wave of arrows and without exception they tore through the armor of the attackers. As quickly as the first wave died, a second followed, and within the space of a few moments the Deathguard had unleashed a dozen arrows each, hardly one failing to bring down a target, but vast numbers of the enemy were massed here. They closed the circle.

Fallarond shouted a command and his warriors slung their bows over their shoulders and drew their blades. The air hummed with spells as they flashed, their light mingling with and crackling against the powers in the glow from the braziers. The company met the onslaught with a unified roar, and for the first few moments of the battle they repulsed the attackers, their weapons slicing through sword, metal and bone with sickening ease. A mound of dead cluttered the chamber, impeding the progress of the assailants.

In the resulting chaos, the company was able to move closer to the column and the horn. Vaddi cut again and again with his weapon, seeing in the faces of the enemy a kind of dementia, wild eyes that blazed like the feral eyes of the inhuman, as alien as any of the horrors he had encountered on his journey from his native land. He felt the upsurge of his own bloodlust, needing to loose it, but wary of Zemella's warning. Whether these creatures were undead or otherwise cursed by necromantic power, he could not say, but it was as though he fought against slavering wolves, more beast than man. They were careless of pain or death, cutting and thrusting like automatons.

It is not my death they want, though. Not one has tried to kill me.

Vaddi relaxed his defense, allowing the warrior facing him to swing an axe at him. Vaddi was right. The blow passed by him and the axe bit into the floor, sparks showering his feet, but he knew that the others were not protected, and he could see the ferocity with which the enemy attacked them. Already some of the Deathguard had fallen.

The carnage was dreadful, for countless scores of warriors, heedless of death, choked the floor of the chamber, their blood pooling, slippery and dangerous underfoot. Vaddi was trying to get a view of the talisman when he felt a tremendous blow strike him across the lower forearm. His sword fell from his hand, which felt suddenly very cold, as if it had been dipped into the ice water of a glacier. He bent to retrieve the weapon at once, but something crashed into the side of his head, knocking him sideways. He felt Zemella's fingers torn from his grasp. He heaved himself to his feet, other blades spinning a defensive web around him.

He saw through dazed eyes a huge warrior, the man who had struck him, beating back the blades of the Deathguard. But in those eyes, Vaddi saw a grim hint of amusement. This was no undead, no vampire. He was human. His broadsword, which had numbed his arm and almost knocked him senseless, was of a familiar cast. It was a northern blade. *Karrnath!* How could that be?

Zemella! his mind cried. He twisted and turned amid the growing press of bodies, for the conflict had become ever more constricted. He could not see her, but he felt her. She was somewhere behind the huge warrior, who was himself easing back into the mass of his warriors, broadsword cleaving the air before him, warding off the Deathguard who tried vainly to break through his powerful defense. Vaddi saw Nyam make it to his side.

"Who is that?" Vaddi asked.

Nyam, parrying the onslaught of another attack, cursed under his breath. "He's Karrn." He warded off another cutting blow. "Warriors from . . . all . . . over."

"Where's Zemella?"

Nyam had no time to reply as a huge wedge of the enemy drove in between Vaddi and the warrior from Karrnath. Almost at once the attack halted.

The Deathguard, whose numbers had been cut in half, formed a defensive wall around Vaddi and Nyam, their chests heaving, their arms dropping with exhaustion. In spite of the immense damage they had done to the warriors, countless scores still surrounded them, ready to close in, for the kill. Instead they eased back, stepping over the mangled corpses of the numerous slain.

"Vaddi d'Orien," said a voice. From out of the press, the huge warrior from Karrnath stepped forward, bloody sword pointed toward the youth. "You are a credit to your father. You fight as well as any man who ever wore the Orien unicorn." He removed his war helm.

Nyam gasped. "Kazzerand."

"Indeed." The warrior grinned. "And you, peddler, have fought nobly. But we have no need of you or these Aereni."

"Where is Zemella?" said Vaddi.

"Alive and unharmed," said Kazzerand. "She is in safe keeping."

He pointed with his blade, indicating the balcony opposite the circular wall, high up and overlooking the carnage below. Vaddi saw at once that Zemella was a captive there. Two black-armored warriors gripped her arms, preventing her from casting a spell, but it was the tall figure beside them that drew his attention. This must be Zuharrin. He was dressed in a flowing robe the color of night, which shimmered and rippled, uncomfortable to look at. His head, elongated, seemed almost insect-like, the eyes even from here like the orbs of a demon. Whatever powers this being trafficked in had long since drawn him into their influences. Whatever Zuharrin had once been, he was no longer human.

When he spoke, his voice rang out clearly over the chamber, sharp and as cruel as a predator's claw. "Welcome, Vaddi d'Orien. Now that we finally meet, the work can begin in earnest. See the talisman that you crave. It is before you. Take it. It has always been yours."

Zuharrin's warriors had been slowly pulling back from the center of the chamber. As they did, the single column with its glowing prize again came into view, but Vaddi stared at it as though it were a serpent.

"Be careful," whispered Nyam. "His influence over it will be great, and he has Zemella."

Fallarond, his breastplate slick with the blood of those he had slain, eyed Vaddi. "We will protect you to the last. Take the horn."

Vaddi moved forward until he stood beside the column. He could feel the intensity of the horn's power, as if it called to him.

"Don't touch it!" The voice of Zemella struck him like an arrow, and he drew back. Looking up at her, he saw another movement on the balcony beside her, and his heart truly knew despair. For he recognized the figure there.

It was Cellester.

DRAGON BLOOD, DEMON BLOOD
CHAPTER 21

Vaddi's instincts drove him to attempt the abrupt transportation that would send him in the blink of an eye to Zemella's side, just as he had transported himself in the Madwood, but his dragonmark was cold. He focused his energy on it, closing his eyes and exerting as much power as he could, but his skin might as well have been devoid of the mark. Something made him look up and he stared into the eyes of the cleric. Realization came to him then.

Cellester was suppressing his dragonmarked powers, as he had done for so many years in Marazanath and then on the journey south. Vaddi's efforts to use them were impotent. Here, where they were needed most, they were useless.

Zuharrin stood at the very edge of the broken balcony, his eyes blazing in triumph. "Take your birthright. Claim it!"

Zemella tried to struggle in the grip of the two huge demonic warriors, but they held her fast.

"Obey me," said Zuharrin. "If you do not, I will have your Valenar sorceress carved into a dozen pieces before your eyes!"

Vaddi felt another power intervening as his hand, still numb from the blow of Kazzerand's sword. His hand stretched for the talisman. He was unable to prevent it, as if Erethindel were dragging him to it. He knew that Zemella would curse him for his weakness, but he could not see her harmed. Zuharrin had him at his mercy. But the talisman itself was working on him, in spite of his resistance.

His fingers were through the green mist and closed around the horn. Vaddi lifted it, holding it at arm's length and gazing at it like one drugged. He could feel its powers, stronger than ever before, coursing into him, filling his veins. His anger was like fire, his nerves raw to its heat. Across the hall, the circular wall rippled like a mighty curtain, as if cut from fabric, not from stone.

Twice more the huge wall shook and then dissipated as though its presence had been no more than an illusion. Revealed beyond was a perfect circle of darkness, as if it gaped on the outer limits of the space beyond all worlds, but no stars glinted in that darkness, no Rings of Siberys, and no sound emerged from its infinite depths. Every eye in the chamber was locked on this vision.

Vaddi felt the horn working, drawing blood from him into itself. He was powerless to prevent it. Unlike the other times that he had used it, he knew that something else was controlling it, focusing its energy. He tore his eyes from the circle of blackness and stared up at Zuharrin. The sorcerer's demonic face wore a victorious gaze, for in this place he was at last realizing his dream of power. It was he who mastered Erethindel's secrets here.

In the circle of utter night, light coalesced, spinning to reveal what seemed to be a monstrous tunnel dug into the infinity of whatever dimension had been opened. The walls of the tunnel were like the curved workings of a titanic worm or serpent, as if they burrowed down into, not space now, but the heart of a world. Khyber! Vaddi knew it instinctively. Far, far down in that abyss, something stirred. He could discern a vague figure thrashing in pain or fury, wrenching at the bonds that secured it.

"T'saagash Mal!" said Zuharrin, and the name carried across the vast chamber to every ear.

As one, Zuharrin's warriors fell to their knees and then bent to touch their faces to the stone floor, remaining in this position of genuflection. The garish light from the pit bathed them, and in its vile glow they *transformed*, shifting into fat, reptilian figures, fanged mouths agape, croaking and belching out a nightmare litany to their master. The Deathguard held their swords before these horrors, as if their glow could ward off the vision in the pit. Kazzerand and the other lords drew back, but they were eager to watch the developments.

From Erethindel, blood dripped over its lip and splashed on the stone below. The flow became a trickle, snaking its way across the floor toward the circular opening in the wall. Zuharrin was murmuring a soft incantation. As the blood crossed the brink of the dark opening, the figure in the depths shook itself and a roar came up from the distance. Something flashed down there, like molten fire. The demon T'saagash Mal was free of his chains. As the watchers gazed at the beast, it began to grow in size, coming up the long tunnel like a swimmer underwater rising to the surface. As it came, its huge size became apparent. A dozen writhing arms, claws shining hotly in the fire-glow, reached for the chamber.

The Deathguard looked away. Appalled at what had happened, Vaddi tried to cast aside the horn, but he could not. He felt it draining more and more of his blood, his vital energies, power from beyond him. T'saagash Mal would burst into the world and he would draw into himself the powers of old. They would not stop him. They would *feed* him! Zuharrin's sorcery had unlocked the key to this perversion. Power crackled and sizzled like an electrical storm, colossal in its scope, mocking the paltry efforts of those who would hold it back.

Vaddi tore his eyes from the scene and looked in despair at Zemella. She, too, was aghast at what was transpiring, forcing her own eyes away from the monstrous form of the demon as he rose, gigantic and implacable.

Beside her, no more than a shadow in the proceedings, an afterthought, the cleric stood immobile, no trace of emotion on his own face, but his eyes looked into Vaddi's now.

Vaddi met that gaze. *Yes, he uses his power against me, just as he did on our journey. How? How can he have such power over me?*

Even as the thought hit him, Vaddi felt something within him snap then shift aside, as if he were sloughing off a dirty garment. Cellester's powers, as suddenly as they had snapped into place, had been withdrawn.

I have freed you, came a voice inside Vaddi's mind. *Act quickly.*

Vaddi read something in Cellester's eyes and understood. The cleric had rejected his master's work. There was no time to ponder why. Up on the balcony, standing in shadow, a minor piece in the sorcerer's moves, Cellester reached forward with both hands and gripped Zuharrin behind his arms, locking them.

"Go to Vaddi!" he shouted to Zemella.

The two warriors holding her were completely unprepared for the cleric's action, and stunned by it, their own grip on the Valenar girl weakened. She kicked and elbowed her way free of them, pulling a sword from the scabbard of the first and ramming its point up into his vitals. The creature hissed in agony and was flung back over the edge of the balcony to fall on the floor below. In the confusion, the other made to draw his blade, but Zemella had sliced into his thigh too quickly for him, and he toppled forward to meet the returning swing of her blade, which opened his face in a bloody line from crown to chin.

Zuharrin screeched in fury, but Cellester held him firm.

Down below, Fallarond had seen what had occurred on the balcony. In one flowing movement he unslung his bow, fitted an arrow, and sent it into the stone of the wall inches below the balcony where it lodged. Dangling from it was a length of the thin cord that the Deathguard had used to scale the walls of the citadel. Zemella needed no second bidding. Lithe as a cat, she leaped, bent down, and gripped the cord. In one flowing movement she swung outward and began her descent.

Kazzerand, also watching, swore and stepped forward, sword swinging. He would meet the Valenar girl at the foot of the dangling cord.

Vaddi, partly freed of the sorcerer's powers, called to the fallen sword he had dropped. Like a live thing, it rose up from the floor, green light vibrant about it. In a blur it shot through the air like a hurled javelin. Its point caught Kazzerand under the breastplate, just below his heart, and his armor was powerless to stop the plunge of the blade as it tore into him, splitting his heart in two, tearing completely *through* him and beyond, finally clattering to the stone in a steaming pool of blood and flesh.

Kazzerand's mouth opened, as if he would shout out his defiance of this act, but no sound emerged. He collapsed onto his face.

Zemella climbed down the cord and joined Vaddi. Not giving him a moment to protest, she gripped the talisman, her hand closing over it and his hand. She swung them round to face T'saagash Mal together. The demon had risen to stand at the very threshold of the chamber, his many arms weaving a grotesque pattern in the air, black powers cracking like whips.

❂ ❂ ❂ ◉ ❂ ❂ ❂

On the balcony, Zuharrin shrieked in fury and smashed aside the hands of the cleric in a blast of scarlet light. Cellester was flung back like a rag into the shadows behind him. Zuharrin turned to him, face ablaze with anger.

"Do your worst," said Cellester through waves of pain. His robes smouldered, his arms burned and blistered to his elbows, his hands a bloody ruin. He could not rise. He was utterly spent.

"Oh, *I will*," said Zuharrin. "You have no idea." He turned back to the scene below.

Zemella felt her own blood being drawn into Erethindel now, combining with Vaddi's. It seemed impossible that there was so much of it, but she realized that both she and Vaddi were no more than vessels for something else. This was not their body fluid but dragon blood, drawn through them by the horn from some other source, its flow governed by ancient magics.

The blood that flowed down from them stopped at the lip of the vast opening and ran around the rim, highlighting the bizarre statues there in a blaze of crimson light. The opening shivered like the hide of a great beast. Behind it, the shape of the demon halted its progress. Then it *screamed*.

It was like the fall of a world. Not pain, not the rigors of a mortal wound, but the howl of infinite frustration. The dragon blood that ringed the opening had sealed it anew. T'saagash Mal could not pass.

The demon rammed his fists at the invisible fabric that stood between him and freedom. The air shimmered like glass. Vaddi and Zemella could feel it vibrating, twisting to the intense pressures the demon was bringing to bear. They felt waves of power emanating from behind and above them as Zuharrin threw his own energies into the conflict. Bolts of white light struck the surface of the opening, but they exploded against it, dissipating in steaming gobbets of fire.

Vaddi was bathed in sweat, his whole body weakening with each blow struck. He saw the enemy warriors, changed now into obscene, hopping monsters, rise up from their obeisance and prepare to attack. Fallarond responded at once, drawing the last of the Deathguard in a protective circle around Vaddi and Zemella. Once again, a bloody conflict raged. In wild desperation, the demon warriors pressed forward, heedless of their own destruction, and one by one, Fallarond's indefatigable Deathguard were hewn or pulled down by the webbed claws of the massed creatures.

"Hold fast!" cried Zemella.

Vaddi felt his fury growing. He focused that madness,

forged it into a blazing light, and was about to hurl it along the course of the bloodstream toward the demon, but he checked himself, hearing again, like a faint echo, the voice of Cellester. He focused on the cleric and flung the light bolt up at the place where he had fallen.

He watched as Zuharrin snarled in contempt, the bolt passing him. Vaddi could see the sorcerer redoubling his own efforts to break T'saagash Mal's seals. It was only a matter of time before he triumphed. Vaddi felt himself weakening, succumbing to the intense pressure.

Vaddi saw his bolt strike Cellester, whose face writhed in agony at the searing pain. To his amazement, the cleric did not collapse, instead using the power of the bolt to reanimate his own flagging strength. Struggling to his feet, calling upon one last surge, he propelled himself forward, slamming into the back of the sorcerer. There was an explosion of brilliant light and Cellester was tossed like a straw doll over the lip of the balcony and down on to the flagstones below. He landed with a sickening thud, but Zuharrin had also been flung aside, and Vaddi could see that his powers had been deflected by the detonation. A wayward bolt struck the column beside the huge opening. It rebounded, tearing into the balcony and blowing it to fragments.

Zuharrin was catapulted out into the chamber. Vaddi watched as he landed across the very dais on which Erethindel had rested, his back smashed to ruin. Something in the dais, a residue of the horn's energy, perhaps, seeped into him and held him. He lay there, arms twisted and broken. Blood seeped from his mouth, eyes, and ears. A figure stood above him, the green glow of an elf blade in its fist.

Vaddi and the company watched as Fallarond drove his sword down, pinning the sorcerer through the heart, the blade going deep down into the stone beyond. The body of the sorcerer shuddered and convulsed, and its sides ripped apart. Black fluid gushed out, encircling the corpse. It rose up and coalesced into a dozen bizarre shapes, like statues carved from thick oil. These slithered on incomplete limbs to the circle of the pit, coming together and merging into one mutated shape. It flapped brokenly at the stone surface.

T'saagash Mal screamed anew. The demon beat for a last time at the curtain that held him, then one of the clutching talons reached through, closing on the malformed thing that had boiled out of Zuharrin's broken body, squeezing it. Thick black droplets dripped through the claws, then T'saagash Mal fell back, tumbling once more into the deeps that had kept him for so long.

All around the hall, the last of the demon warriors became like headless things, their control lost. Their armor melted from them, and their swords turned to dust. The last of the Deathguard stood back, no longer needing to defend themselves.

Vaddi and Zemella felt something within Erethindel ease back like the slow withdrawal of a wave on a shore. Together they set the horn down upon the column, then they were in each other's arms, holding themselves up, almost spent by their efforts. Beyond them, the dark circle on the wall closed once more, becoming cold stone.

The multitudes of transformed demon shapes in the hall, deprived of a focal point, swarmed like an infestation of rats out through the openings beyond the huge statues, like sewage floating away on a current, down into the furthest regions of Azzahareb, far from the light. For a long time the frightful sound of their passing came up from below.

Afterward Vaddi felt an arm on his shoulder and looked up through a haze of pain. Fallarond gazed down at him. "It is done," he said softly.

Vaddi looked around at the piled dead, the smouldering ruins of the demon warriors. Among them, not one of the lords from Khorvaire had survived. To his horror Vaddi saw that all but a handful of the Deathguard had perished.

"Nyam!" he gasped, breaking free of Zemella. "Where is he?"

Both Fallarond and Zemella looked about them, but at first they could not see the peddler. He was not standing.

Vaddi stumbled across the chamber, searching the fallen bodies, calling out the name of his friend. At last he found him, almost buried under one of the many-heaped mounds of the dead.

"Nyam!"

There was a groan of response then movement. Nyam slowly eased himself up on to an elbow. "Sovereigns, Vaddi, have I given up all my wealth to Vortermars for *this*? I can't go on—"

Vaddi laughed, tears of relief springing from his eyes as he hauled on the peddler's hand, dragging him out from the carnage.

"No need, old friend. It is over." Vaddi helped him to his feet, but it was clear that Nyam had been only slightly wounded, both in the arm, the thigh, and across the side of his face.

"I'll sleep for a month," the peddler grunted.

"If that is what you desire, you shall," said Vaddi.

Fallarond and Zemella joined them.

"We must quit this place soon," said Fallarond. "We must rendezvous with the pirate and leave Xen'drik. Zuharrin has been destroyed, but who knows what other horrors lurk here? But before that, we must honor our fallen." He indicted the Deathguard who had given their lives in the venture.

"Can we make a tomb of this citadel?" Vaddi asked. "Would it be a fitting place of rest for them?"

Fallarond looked sadly at the fallen bodies of his fellow Deathguard. "I think it would. What has occurred here today will be long remembered. Let us use this very chamber. Seal it up as we leave and wall our fallen safely in. Their presence will purge the last of the evil from this place."

While Vaddi and Fallarond spoke, Nyam limped across the chamber, himself looking with sorrow at the bodies of the fallen Deathguard. How they had fought! He came to the remains of Zuharrin's body, but it was like a broken statue, cracked open to reveal a hollowness within. It had been no more than a vessel, a convenient housing for the essence of the sorcerer. What had been snatched away by T'saagash Mal might have been that essence. Zuharrin had found his place in Khyber.

Nyam moved away, seeing another smashed figure under the shadow of the wrecked balcony. It was the cleric. This was no shell. His corpse was all too clearly flesh and blood, subjected to a grim ending when he had fallen from the heights. The eyes were open, but whatever vision they gazed on in death had given them the look of madness. An arm had been out flung from the blood-spattered robe, the fingers of its hand clutched around something. Nyam bent down and prized those fingers open. Discreetly he removed the object they had been clutching and slipped it out of sight in his own robe.

As he turned to go, the broken hand clawed at his arm. Nyam stared down in horror as something, a faint light, glowed in the cleric's dead eyes. Bloody lips pulled back and whispered words through a crimson froth.

"Never . . . meant harm . . . to the boy." Intense pain pulled at the cleric's face as the distant light receded. "Deceived . . . him. And you. But also . . . Zuharrin. To . . . thwart him."

Nyam nodded. "Be at peace, cleric."

"Loved . . . her. Always. Indreen. Indreen, I . . . saved your son . . ."

Nyam knelt, one hand on the object he had taken from the cleric, and saw the final darkness close over him.

None of the others in the hall were aware of this exchange. Nyam rose, saying nothing of it as he returned to his companions. He saw that Zemella had taken Vaddi's hand. Both were slick with blood, though little of it seemed to be their own. In Zemella's other hand she bore Erethindel. It was cold now, lifeless as stone.

"What of the Crimson Talisman?" Nyam asked.

"Vaddi must bear it." Zemella gave it to him.

"I will never call upon its power again," Vaddi said. "I see now why the elves wanted it sent far from their lands. It is dangerous beyond understanding. Too dangerous for one to carry." He slipped it into the folds of his shirt.

She cocked her head on one side and grinned at him. "You think so?"

"I think so. It will need at least two of us to watch over it. Always."

"That sounds like a major commitment," said Nyam, his smile full of familiar mischief.

"Yes, but I cannot command you," Vaddi told Zemella, a sudden uncertainty rising within him.

She laughed. "Perhaps. But I agree with you. It will take two. Always."

EPILOGUE

Moonlight washed the ruins on a night devoid of clouds, daubing the broken towers and overgrown walls in unusually brilliant light. A few figures armed with pikes spread along the ancient battlements, and a solitary flag fluttered in a breeze from the northern sea, far below the cliffs. Waves sighed as they broke upon the distant shore. On the tallest of the ruins a group of figures studied the citadel, a brazier burning beside them, smoke from its hot coals drifting up into the crystal skies.

"Marazanath," said Vaddi, looking down at the former stronghold of his father.

The forces that had brought about its decline had left it as feasting jackals quit a corpse whose bones have been picked clean. Since the fall of Kazzerand, the warlord's knights had largely withdrawn from it, leaving a few to garrison it. They were more relieved than alarmed at Vaddi's return, recognizing his birthright to stewardship of the hold.

Beside Vaddi, Zemella and Nyam Hordath took in the scene in silence. Since Vaddi had fled, the site had succumbed to the encroaching ivy and other weeds. In another few years the citadel would be so overgrown as to be no more than a relic of past times, a cemetery. Above the group, on its pole, the recently struck unicorn flag snapped open in a sudden gust, revealing its resplendent colors and motif. The three watchers looked up at it.

"There's an omen for you," said Nyam with a grin.

Vaddi also smiled, his fingers twining with those of Zemella, his new bride. "Yes. A favorable wind."

Their journey home had been without incident. They had gone back down past the immense ruins of the crumbling city of giants, along the river to the coast, where they had met Vortermars within the agreed deadline. It was evident the captain had never expected to see any of them alive. Fallarond's valiant Deathguard had been reduced in the battle at Azzahareb to a handful of no more than a dozen warriors. They sealed up the citadel, making of it a mausoleum for the fallen. They carried a weapon of each fallen back to Aerenal, and they murmured their prayers for those they had entombed.

In Shae Thoridor the company visited again the ancient grove in the forest above the city and had undertaken a last ritual of remembrance with the families of the dead and had blessed and buried the weapons. A few days later, Zemella and Vaddi were wed, and no one wore a broader, more beaming smile than Nyam. As he told the gathered Aereni, no father could have been more proud of a son nor have wished for a worthier daughter.

Not long afterward, they sailed to Pylas Maradal but decided against visiting Kalfar, in view of Nyam's previous turbulent relationship with him. There was a surprise awaiting the peddler at the docks, however. Vortermars took receipt of the promised treasury of his old rival with evident delight, for it was indeed a fabulous trove, but to Nyam's amazement, he was taken by several of the freebooters' ruffians to an isolated quayside. There, fully rigged and equipped, was a sleek vessel, not so large as the *Sea Harlot*, but nevertheless a redoubtable craft.

"It's yours," said one of the pirates.

Nyam stared at the craft suspiciously. "What's wrong with it?"

"Wrong?" snapped the other. "It's yer eyes that are wrong, peddler! That's as handsome a ship as you'll ever see. Vortermars must be mad letting you have it."

Zemella had laughed at the peddler's face. "By the time my family have checked it over for you, Nyam, it will be no less seaworthy than any elven craft."

"Does it have a name?" Nyam asked the pirates, unable to see what had been carved under the prow.

"She's the—"

"*Zemella*," said Vaddi.

"Yes, that was my very thought, Vaddi. From today, she is the *Zemella*. No prouder vessel will sail the seas of Eberron."

They had elected not to sail the long sea journey to Khorvaire from Pylas Maradal but had gone instead by airship, this time without incident. When they had at last reached Marazanath, Vaddi had sent word to the authorities in Thrane, which he had learned was itself in some upheaval following the disappearance of Kazzerand. Vaddi's rights at Marazanath had been recognized.

As Vaddi looked down at the hold below him now, he recalled the last night he had spoken with his father, which seemed a lifetime ago. He recalled the wild flight from here, with Menneath and his friend's subsequent tragic death.

His reverie was cut short by Nyam, who drew from his voluminous cloak a small casket. "I thought you should have this," he said. "This seems a propitious moment to give it to you."

Vaddi frowned. He did not recognize the delicate inlaid patterns of gold on the ebony lid of the casket, though they hinted at the strange arts of Xen'drik.

"I helped myself to the casket," said Nyam, by way of explanation.

Vaddi grinned. Yes, no doubt Nyam had found other items of value in those ruins, items that would go a long way to compensate for the huge fortune he had bestowed upon Vortermars.

"Ignore the casket. It is the contents you should look at."
So saying, Nyam flipped up the lid.

Vaddi glanced down at the velvet lining within. A single green teardrop jewel glistened in the moonlight.

Zemella gasped. "The family Dendris!" she whispered.

"My mother's family."

"It was Indreen's own jewel," said Nyam.

"Where did you find this?" asked Vaddi, lifting the teardrop and marvelling at its beauty.

"In Azzahareb, but it did not seem appropriate to give it to you then, with so much fury surging about us all. I took it from the dying hand of Cellester. He had carried it next to his heart these many years."

"Cellester?"

"Aye. He spoke as he breathed his last. His love for your mother had never dimmed. We must be thankful for it. Zuharrin tried to use it against him. In the end, it was what gave the cleric the power to resist his tormenter. It is how the cleric suppressed your powers, Vaddi—until he chose to rebel against the sorcerer. Your victory was his gift to you."

Vaddi gazed out across the distance, as though seeing again the chamber in Azzahareb where the sorcerer had been brought down. "I had wondered at his actions—why he defied Zuharrin at the very moment when his powers were about to be realized. In all that turmoil, it was Cellester who tipped the balance. You mean he planned it?"

"Yes," said Nyam, "but he could never have said so. He had to play his part to the hilt. His perfect deceit undid Zuharrin. The sorcerer's arrogance did not allow for Cellester's loyalty to another."

"Then we will honor the cleric," Vaddi said. "We will set this jewel in the new foundations of Marazanath."

They reflected in silence, while overhead the unicorn banner remained taut in the freshening wind. Vaddi's fingers closed around the Crimson Talisman that he had hung around his neck. It was cool to the touch, its powers dormant. He had no regrets. He would rather not have to recall them. He slid his arm around Zemella's waist. She, unlike Erethindel, filled him with warmth and energy, a sorcery older than time, and he had come to realize with a surge of elation, as enduring.